DANCE HALL ROAD

Also by the author

The Doubtful Guests
Bending at the Bow
Magic Eight Ball

DANCE HALL ROAD
MARION DOUGLAS

INSOMNIAC PRESS

Edited by Catherine Lake

Library and Archives Canada Cataloguing in Publication

Douglas, Marion K. (Marion Kay), 1952-
    Dance Hall Road / Marion Douglas.

ISBN 978-1-897178-55-3

    I. Title.

PS8557.O812D35 2008   C813'.54   C2008-901027-2

The publisher gratefully acknowledges the support of the Canada
Council, the Ontario Arts Council and the Department of Canadian Heritage through the Book Publishing Industry Development Program.

Printed and bound in Canada

Insomniac Press
192 Spadina Avenue, Suite 403
Toronto, Ontario, Canada, M5T 2C2

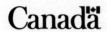

For my parents, Anna and Stuart Douglas.

I would like to thank Catherine Lake and
Gillian Rodgerson for their editorial suggstions
and helpfulness.

This morning, in history class, a photograph of an electric chair had fallen out of Adrian's textbook. He'd briefly lent the book to Jimmy Drake Junior and that, of course, explained everything. Jimmy hadn't needed it, he had his own textbook, but, as he said, or alleged, pages ninety-seven and ninety-eight had been torn out so could he quickly take a look at Adrian's to make sure he wasn't missing anything too important? Because of tomorrow's test?

"Sure," said Adrian, the same way he said okay or fine if asked to roll up his sleeve for a vaccination, which made him think, too bad there was no immunity from James Drake Junior. Not that Adrian was so childish as to think in terms of infectious cooties or any of the other maggoty insects capable of settling in nests of unwashed hair, but this was Ontario and there were rabid dogs and foxes and bats and therefore why might there not be the occasional rabid high school student? There had been some visible flecks of froth on Jimmy Drake's lips the day he gave his expository speech and it was common knowledge he was afraid of the water and couldn't swim an inch. Not one inch.

Hydrophobia, Adrian said in a whisper to the back of Jimmy's greasy head, just to see if he'd flinch but Jimmy turned around with such speed and malevolence, Adrian, to his own amusement, became the flincher. And ha ha, he thought, *The Ruffled Flax High Flincher*, a new type of bird species discovered right here in the pointless town of Flax.

"Thanks, then, here you go," said Jimmy, his face a bad actor's imitation of gratitude as he passed Adrian the book in a not-entirely-shut condition calculated to allow the picture to fall out and flop, image side up, on the brown, unwaxed and, in Adrian's opinion, probably haunted history classroom floor. Adrian had no doubt the photograph was for him, the message being, if my dad, Jimmy Drake Senior, has to be in the slammer, at the very least, Adrian Drury, you should go to the electric chair.

Jimmy and his dad had electric chairs and capital punishment as a hobby. Last summer they'd gone to look at a chair in Florida and taken pictures of it the way other people photograph monuments or rock formations. They thought Canada should bring back the chair, which showed you how misinformed they were, Canada never having had the chair, only the noose. Then, in February, when it was time for expository speeches in English class, despite his own dad being in jail for assault with a deadly weapon, Jimmy chose to do a talk on capital punishment as a deterrent. If only they could just bring back the chair for everyone who even thought about killing somebody—for no good reason, that is, Jimmy said, slowly and with emphasis—or at least force them to look at pictures of people being fried, make them look up close so they could see the sparks melting their eyes and so on, until Mr. Rigg interrupted to tell Jimmy to please get back to his main thesis point because there were still two more speeches to go that day. And Jimmy did return to his point, which appeared to be—no, was explicitly stated as—some people (obviously not his own proven-guilty dad) deserved to be dead. They think *they're innocent but they're not. They start a chain of events and before you know it, somebody's dead and somebody's in jail and usually it's the wrong person, Jimmy concluded, looking, for his finale, somewhat dimly at the three- to four-desk area surrounding Adrian.*

Adrian would call his sister Rose tonight, long distance to Toronto, and tell her about the picture, and she would say, Adrian, it's Jimmy Drake for god's sake, he's a complete jerk. By uttering the words "for god's sake," Rose could reduce the importance of any person or person's behaviour by many factors of ten. She had the worry capacity of a duck and could simply shake her feathers and propel worries on many trajectories from her head, like droplets of water. Even other people's worries could be sent sailing into the surrounding air, grass, and tree limbs. And along with her duck emotions, Rose had the genius capacity of a migratory bird, always having the very much larger, continent-sized picture of any situation stored inside a very small portion of her relatively bulky brain. Like a goose or a trumpeter swan, Rose was the world's leading expert on when and where to go. Not only that, as she made her decision to fly the coop, she was admired by others, most likely watching with binoculars, holding their breath: Oh, look, there she goes. And thus, Rose was in Toronto enjoying early entrance to university while Adrian languished in Flax, walking home from school with a colour photograph of an electric chair in his hand.

Now he holds it close for another look, queasy with Drake-o-phobia as Randy Farrell, Adrian's former best friend would have called it. Drake-o-phobia: a general disgust with all the belongings or interests of Jimmy Drake Junior. Here was this picture, a belonging, which represented an interest, and Adrian stopped right there to give himself an all-over shudder, a shudder so violent he could have detached his own ghost from himself if he happened to tear a couple of the wrong ligaments. Not so much because of the picture or its belonging to Jimmy but because Adrian was starting to think maybe now Jimmy voiced the majority opinion, and maybe that opinion was justified, many if not all of the people of Flax being more intelligent than Adrian. Maybe he should go to the electric chair for the events he may have caused; maybe he should save the judicial system the trouble and build his own chair in the basement from parts of his old electric train set: line a metal chair with pieces of track, plug it in, put on some wet clothes from the washing machine, stick his feet into a bucket of water, sit down and throw the switch. His father, George Drury, the dentist and also Canada's dullest man, would find him charred and smoking and soon the entire town of Flax would know and there would be further talk of reeling from another adolescent tragedy. That's what Flax had been doing, reeling, which if looked up in a dictionary meant to sway or rock under a blow, or, to sway about in standing or walking.

Don't kid yourself, Adrian, they wouldn't reel. That's that, they would probably say, and good riddance; now we can finally return to normal. As long as Laura Van Epp came to his funeral, Adrian thinks and seconds later concludes that if he is not going to the chair at least that thought and any subsequent thoughts about Laura Van Epp should go to a type of frying pan for unacceptable wants and wishes. An electric frying pan. You'd think he'd learn.

Adrian puts the picture in his pocket and carries on to Flax's main street, Huron Drive, which is precisely and ex-

actly the same as it always is: cars making two or three stabs
at parallel parking in front of the Royal Bank, people walking expectantly toward a two-for-one cereal sale at Pond's IGA
or standing outside the drug store holding a bag of fresh pills.
The only difference is: most are wearing jackets because even
though it's May, it's the kind of May you think has put on
the brakes and is reversing into April or even March. So the
cold breeze has them a little more awake than usual and moving a little faster than the habitual Flaxseed shuffle, as Rose's
best friend, Anastasia Van Epp—Laura's sister (there he was
thinking about Laura again)—would call it. Flaxseed as in
hayseed. Anastasia can always come up with the best ideas
because, as she once told Adrian, of her AB blood type, the
bloodiest of all blood types and therefore able to carry more
oxygen more quickly to the brain. Adrian believed this for
many years, which was an example of Anastasia's ability to
use her ideas to oppress others. She was like a regime you
might study in history.

   Adrian stands like he often does now on the street, experiencing the adriftness of having no clear-cut friends. He
assumes a post in front of Lalonde's one-star restaurant as if
he might be waiting for someone and then sees Maddy Farrell hobbling toward him and worries that people, including
Maddy, will think he's waiting for her. Adrian could very easily avoid Maddy but some part of him, a cross-section of his
feet showing a vacuole or two of courage, decides to stand
right there in front of Lalonde's and wait. Maddy's likely
going to the bank to deposit some fish eggs or whatever they
use for currency in East Flax and that is fine, that is nothing
to worry about. Adrian has no legitimate reason to dislike or
fear her. All she ever did was report to Randy, who reported

to Adrian via a handwritten note, what that old asshole Alfred Beel said which would one day be engraved on Adrian's
tombstone when he died, which mercifully would be soon.
And that epitaph would be: I really lay the blame at the feet
of that Drury boy. A gentleman would never have treated a
lady like that.

That's what Beel, the old goat who lived at an impasse,
at the end of a road way out in the country not even the snow-
plows could bother with, said to Maddy who told her brother
who passed it on to Adrian a few days before Randy's unusual brain advised him to stop talking and switch desks with
Jimmy Drake Junior. And this had certainly led to many ram-
ifications, as Mr. Rigg the history teacher liked to say, over the
past five months, including today's gift of the photograph.

Maddy's getting closer, hobble, hobble, hobble on her shattered leg—also now directly or indirectly the fault of Adrian
Drury who wants to know why she hasn't gotten rid of the
crutches yet, do the Farrells not take her for her treatments?
She's supposed to be getting treatments, everybody says, because of her shattered leg: shattered is the word everyone uses,
as if they all looked up broken or shot-at in the thesaurus and
found there in bold letters the only possible synonym. Her leg
is shattered and as a result people feel sorry for her; they think
she has suffered enough and probably never had anything do
with what happened to Cheryl Decker. Another town-of-Flax
phrase: what happened to Cheryl Decker. So Maddy's still
hobbling but Adrian will not accept any blame for that:
Maddy is hobbling because the Farrells are not the type to go
for treatments although Adrian wonders, if that family were
to undertake treatment, where would they begin? Each and
every one required treatment: Randy for his brain problem

and Angel for her sluttish inclinations and Frog for having the name of an amphibian. Yes, the whole entire family needed treatment so taking Maddy for her calisthenics or whatever might open up a whole can of treatment worms.

And ha ha. Adrian laughs to himself and enjoys his own thinking even if no one else does in this humourless town of Flax and that is why he is lonely and willing to talk even to Maddy Farrell on her incriminating crutch. No one except his ex-friend Randy Farrell enjoys Adrian's thinking, which he describes to himself as neither highbrow nor lowbrow but simply brow. Randy appreciates Adrian but—apart from passing him the note with the Beel quotation about laying the blame— has not spoken to him since November 8, 1970 for reasons Randy could no doubt explain with his crazy, unfathomable logic as having to do with the Tamarack Township dump and licorice pipes and manta rays hiding out in Minnow Lake. And Adrian realizes maybe he misses Randy's untreated thinking more than the other way around and this is a brain jolt, like getting the drift after the English exam, after listening to one or two smart girls talk, that you missed the entire point of the main essay question and can already visualize the mark, 1/15, in the foolscap margin, sarcastic red question marks above "What is your point?"

Adrian grins at Maddy, an unnatural grin but it will have to do and she says hi. Adrian asks how's it going and Maddy says it's going okay and her leg is getting better even though it doesn't look like it much. She leans the crutches against the brick wall of Lalonde's and shifts her weight to the unshattered leg.

That's good, Adrian says and thinks of asking about basketball and going to the States but concludes that would be tactless and says so to himself. That's the l.d. in him, the learning disabled portion requiring a cop of thinking and talking in there, some Jerome Limb-type constable saying or more likely yelling, don't say that you dumbass Drury, don't even think about saying that.

"How's Rose liking university?" Maddy asks and Adrian tells her she says most of the early entrance people are super-serious so it's not much fun but she's glad she went.

"She's got a phone number if you want to..."

"Nah, that's okay. My mom's not that keen on long distance."

"Yeah, my dad too. After five minutes of talking to Rose he's yelling, this is long distance you know, as if long distance is a very rare kind of precious metal with only five or ten ounces left in the solar system."

Maddy laughs a puff-of-air type laugh Adrian recognizes from conversations he has had with teachers and he gets more courage and asks, "What's up with Randy?" then, as a second question, "Anyway?"

"I don't know," says Maddy, looking away to indicate she does know something, she knows at the very least about the desk-switching with Jimmy Drake Junior. "He's always been a bit funny in the social skills department. I mean, he can be mad for three solid months, then start talking again. He did that to me once, actually set an amount of time. It's kind of like his arrangements."

"Yeah, Randy and his arrangements. Remember how last year he arranged all those yellow and black gumballs in rows to make the Bruins win the cup? And then he sent a letter to Bobby Orr telling him about the gumballs and Bobby Orr sent him a picture of himself."

"He's trying to get Montreal to win this year but he's not using the gumballs. Some other mysterious system in his room, maybe with red licorice."

"I wonder what," Adrian says.

Maddy shrugs and looks ready to leave.

"But, this has been more than three months now, though." He doesn't want her to leave, would even consider having a Coke with her in Lalonde's restaurant but what would that look like?

"Maybe it's a six-month plan," Maddy says.

Adrian is uncomforted by this thought. Despite Randy's appreciation of Adrian's brow-level thinking, this much is clear: he blames Adrian not for what happened to Cheryl, but for Maddy's leg. Hence the note. Because, just like Alfred Beel, Randy laid the blame at the feet—the healthy, fully functioning feet—of that Drury boy.

He watches Maddy as she reaches for her crutches and organizes herself for the trip to the bank. "Yes, that's likely what he's thinking," Adrian says. "That's how he operates, for sure."

"Yes, it most definitely is," agrees Maddy's head atop her six-foot self. She resumes hobbling and heads off without saying good-bye.

"See you," says Adrian. He might as well go home. He's feeling a little woozy, to use George Drury the dentist's term. He'll go home where there's a bit more oxygen than here on Huron Drive with all the cars and other lungs. Some days he thinks there might be a general shortage of oxygen in this town. Sometimes, like now, he thinks of Flax as a very large plastic bag fastened around his neck, containing a finite number of breaths.

Adrian called this the beginning, the last day life was normal. He and Randy were floating, at a thirty-five degree tilt, on the warm, bald plywood of the ski jump, Minnow Lake rippling beneath them as if a big fish heart on the lake bottom kept pushing the water along in little beats. Nothing appeared to be different. On the east edge of the lake sat rickety East Flax made up of the Farrells' dusty store, the closed-down mill where kids broke in sometimes to have parties, and a few little houses like Russell Hansen's that seemed made for short people, the way they sat too close to the damp earth. East Flax houses didn't have basements. Even the public dock had a forlorn look since somebody in the Ministry of Natural Resources decided to outlaw motorboats on Minnow Lake, causing everyone with enough money to own a boat to go to Blue Lake instead or further up the road to Lake Huron. Nobody understood the government's decision so Adrian had suggested to Randy that maybe they used a formula of not much depth times not much width divided by old exposed stumps plus mercury poisoning equals no motorboats.

Very funny, Randy had said, except there's no mercury, how would there possibly be mercury? Randy thought it might be that this proved there really was a giant manta ray living somewhere amongst the reeds, and the motorboats disturbed its habitat. Whatever the reason, East Flax was now a tourist ghost town with only the dance hall up on the so-called escarpment exuding what you might call architectural confidence.

The only thing that made this day different was it was the day after the day Jimmy Drake Junior and his dad got back from their trip to Florida to see the electric chair. No one in Flax or Mesmer or even crazy East Flax would have climbed into a car the summer of 1970 and driven two thousand miles in the overcooked American heat to see an electric chair except for the Jimmy Drakes, Junior and Senior. Senior Drake had a sister living in Gainesville and her husband knew somebody who knew somebody who could get them inside.

Now they were back with pictures, and already Jimmy Junior was over at Beel's property shooting cans. Beel told him he could—I have standing permission, Jimmy Junior says. The pop of the gun carried across the water but less sinister than usual. Maybe the humidity slowed the sound and mushroomed it, as if it were coming out the other side of their eardrums.

Randy said, "He came into the store around noon and he was all puffed up with his big news. How he sat in the actual chair with a sponge on his head because that's what they put on you to conduct the electricity. His head was almost glowing like a light bulb with his important new opinion. 'I wish we had the death penalty in Canada' he says to the assembled crowd of my mom and me. If Flax was a person he'd cause it to have a seizure."

Randy had epilepsy and had been educated by his nerve doctor on the uses of electricity in the human mind, the role of lesions, the chaos of too many plugs and not enough outlets. Adrian had seen the effects with his own eyes: Randy's body out of control on the gymnasium floor, trying to throw its own self to another location as if it were an Olympic sport, the human body shot put.

"I'd have to agree with that," Adrian said. Randy's seizure talk was the one topic he never argued, not wanting to antagonize him and trigger a high-voltage event in what was probably a low-voltage brain.

"Jimmy Junior's got way too much charge in him," Randy went on. "If he stood in the lake we'd probably get electrocuted on this ski jump, even despite its being made of plywood. And the boat's metal. Keep your feet away from it," he said, suddenly agitated and mock serious.

"It does kind of seem to be trying to get us," Adrian said. Powered by ripples and wind, Russell Hansen's leaky rowboat had managed to climb the jump a few inches, thinking it might like to join them, thinking nobody ever asked it if it wanted to be a boat. Two rusted coffee cans washed around in the stern clattering against one another illustrating some law of physics pertaining to listlessness in objects.

Randy sat up now and asked, "Have you ever noticed on the map of southern Ontario how we're completely surrounded by water, how the Great Lakes are like a monster chain around us? If somebody got the idea to put thirty or forty high powered electrical cables into one of them, who knows what would happen? They're all hooked together and underneath us there's the water table, which is more or less like a circulatory system, and in some places there's got to be one or two veins a little too close to the surface. So I imagine with all that electricity in the lakes and the water table, every once in a while some innocent bystander could get zapped by a random conduction through wet mud, especially if you happened not to be wearing shoes."

"I don't think Jimmy Drake Junior's got the capacity for that much charge."

"I didn't say Jimmy Junior; I said a bunch of high powered electrical cables."

"Well, that's what you meant." Then, sitting up with a start, "Hey, hey, grab the boat," Adrian said. "That was almost a wave there. Wonder where it came from? Maybe one of those springs over in Turtle Bay farted it out. Hey, I've got an idea. Tie the boat to your foot. Why did we never think of that before?"

"Maybe it's the special ed. in us," Randy offered.

"Speak for yourself, Farrell."

There went the gun again. "Funny how we never hear the sound of a tin can falling. Maybe he always misses."

"Or maybe like Mr. Felske said in English, if a tin can falls in the forest and there's nobody there to hear it, did it really fall?"

"Yeah, but we're here to hear it, which is not far from the forest."

"We're not *in* the forest, however," Randy said, wrapping the soggy rope around his ankle. Mission accomplished, he lay down, hands behind his head, armpits exposed. Adrian glanced, shimmied closer to

his side of the jump, and asked: "Have you ever noticed how Jimmy Junior's so-called goatee actually
looks like it's made of armpit hair, not beard hair? Like
there was some kind of horse-up there?"

Randy laughed. "Yeah." Then said, "Hey, listen."

Adrian heard nothing, a red-winged blackbird, a
dog from so far away it sounded trapped under
ground. Nothing.

"Don't you hear that thump, thump, thump? Listen."

Adrian listened. "You can't make your ears hear
things they can't hear, you know. You can't open and
shut them like eyes."

"Oh, I did not know that Professor Drury. Just listen from up in the dance hall."

Adrian turned his mind to the dance hall, the cliff
they called an escarpment, the way the earth hung
open, as if it were a big cut of meat. Then he heard it.
Thump, thump, thump. "Okay. I hear it."

"That's Maddy practicing up in the dance hall. Basketball."

"That was the object of the hearing test? To listen
to Maddy practicing basketball?"

"Well, she's good."

"It's hard to tell that from a ski jump. Anyway, I already knew that."

"Fine," Randy said, shrugging his pink shoulders.
He didn't tan, went directly to burn, a symptom of his
problems Adrian thought, his multitude of East Flax
problems. Adrian could overlook most of them in exchange for passing the time on this ski jump. He loved

floating, loved the sound of the oars creaking in their oarlocks and nothing to look at but sky, which today was reminding him of his own paintings from elementary school, entirely blue because you were too lazy to add clouds.

"Do you ever wonder why your sisters are so different?" Adrian asked. "Cora's so perfect and Maddy's so not?"

"Mmmm. Yes and no."

"I guess Cora comes from the Angel side and Maddy's from the Frog side," Adrian said.

Silence from Randy, interrupted by one last crack from the gun. Then Beel's roaring voice, "Okay, you can take it home now."

"I think he just lets Jimmy shoot on his property so he can yell at him to go home," Randy said.

"But you know what I mean," Adrian said, "about the Frog side. Not that Maddy looks much like your dad but there are ways she looks more like a guy than you do."

"So what's your point?" Randy asked, annoyed.

Adrian gave no reply. This was not a day for fast talk. This was the kind of summer day so summery bulrushes got tired of holding themselves together and silently exploded into white, seedy fluff.

"I guess my point is it's interesting how different two sisters can look."

"Well, that's not much of a point," Randy said, waving a black fly away. "Anyone with even a kindergarten level of genetics can tell you there's billions of ways the genes can come together. Look at you and your sister Rose. She's got black hair and pale skin and you've got pale hair and dark skin. How do you explain that?"

"But I look like a guy and Rose looks like a girl."

"Well, congratulations."

"Fine, fine, I'll drop it. But only if you tell me about your dad again."

"That's such an old story."

"Pleeease." Adrian knew Randy liked telling it.

"All right," Randy sighed in fake exasperation, "but this is it for the summer. No more times this summer."

"Agreed," said Adrian. "I won't ask again until September twenty-first."

Three, four, five little ripples and then Randy began. "Long ago," he said, "and far away, they used to call my dad the frog-swallower."

Adrian rolled onto his stomach. "And why was that?"

"Because," Randy caught a deer fly hovering above his chest, smashed it into the plywood beneath his flattened palm, "because he swallowed a SINGLE frog once on a dare. Then he got a reputation for swallowing frogs all over the place. So he had to swallow a second one at the Blue Lake dance hall once. Then people started saying that frog went through him and came out the other end live, which did not happen. Then people made up a story about some new line of brown frogs related to the one that supposedly came out my dad's rear end. It was all made up. Anyway, it was because of my dad's reputation as a frog-swallower

MARION DOUGLAS — 25

that my mom, the former Angel Cobb, married my dad and as a result, I am here today."

"That's a good story. I never get tired of it. It makes me feel at peace with the universe."

"I know. You've told me that," said Randy, scraping fly guts from his hand.

A jet trail formed straight overhead, one end just now becoming a little ragged. No sound though, which Adrian loved; jet trails with no sound, so far away they couldn't be bothered. He liked to imagine people five miles high in a silver capsule of quiet, and sky brighter than down here, blue like you would dye the sky if you could, give it a bit more jazz.

"I think Jimmy Junior has gone home," Randy said.

"Yeah, I noticed the air was a little fresher," Adrian said, leaning his head over the edge of the jump so as to stare into the water and the weedy lake bottom. "I guess I should be heading home soon myself." For some reason the bottom of Minnow Lake made him shudder; no matter how many times he saw it, he got goosebumps.

"You know what, Randolph? I saw on a *National Geographic* show how goosebumps are from a long, long time ago when we were covered with fur. The pores would get all tightened up and the fur would stand on end and make people look bigger, just like cats when they're scared. It's called piloerection. How do you like that word?"

"It's better than some," Randy said, "better than frog-swallower."

"That's probably two words. Anyway, I get goose-bumps each and every time I look at the bottom of Minnow Lake. I get like a furry animal trying to defend itself."

"Well, that's a waste of energy," Randy said. "It's just mud. What's so scary about mud when it's under water?"

"That," Adrian said, pointing to the water and its contents, "is not just mud. What about all those roots and logs and things?"

"Well? Same argument. What's so scary about roots and logs under water?"

"I don't know," Adrian had to confess. "The fact they're rotting, I guess, and you can't get a very good look at them so you imagine the worst. Stuff bloated with slime, and eye sockets, and skin floating around with nothing inside it. I'm surprised people actually come out here to swim."

"Not many do. Not many people come out here period."

"That explains why I like it," Adrian said, watching the lake sparkle, "even though it gives me piloerections. Someone could pull the plug on this place and in less than a day you'd have acres of muck and a few misshapen fish flapping in the sun with googly white eyes and maybe ears, like people from too much DDT."

"What people do you know who've had too much DDT?" Randy asked.

"I don't know. Maybe Morley Nickle with his water head."

No response from Randy. He never liked to make

fun of people's problems, having so many himself. "So I have a question for you, Randolph," Adrian said. "What was the busiest shopping day ever at your parents' store?"

"I don't know. It used to be busy all the time in the summer, before they outlawed motorboats. Up until the summer of nineteen sixty-four there were lots of busy days, especially weekends. People would be lined up at the till."

Adrian squinted, merged the sparkles into one wavering light. "Maybe it would be easier to identify the least busy day."

"There's only been one day when nobody bought anything. It was last November. My mom has it circled on last year's calendar. People came to the store but nobody bought anything. The regulars, that is. The three old regulars who come every day, Alfred Beel and Russell Hansen and the Maestro, but for some reason that day in November even they didn't buy a single thing."

"Wow. That's something for *Ripley's Believe it or Not*. You could send it in."

"How 'bout let's not and say we did."

Randy crabwalked down the incline to the boat, threw a coffee can to Adrian, and started bailing with the other. "I should get going," he said.

"Yeah, me too."

Once Russell's boat was empty of water it would get them back to land, taking on an inch or two during the trip. Neither was a good swimmer but submersion posed no real threat since, between the ski jump and shore, Minnow Lake was four feet at its deepest. And Adrian always brought shoes along because it was his fervent hope never to have to touch the mushy bottom of Minnow Lake with bare feet. Randy could say all he wanted about only mud and old branches from the time of the flooding but with only one leaky boat for support, Adrian's fur wouldn't relax until they reached the shore.

Reg Decker, Cheryl's father, was counting his words, cutting back on talk. He called this the Word Conservation Plan and he liked it. Allocating a half-page quota of words for each new day was one method of punishing the human race for the death of his son, Richard. His wife, Loretta, Cheryl's mother, was sick and tired of the whole business. She had told him more than once she was going to call the town meter reader, tell him to stop by Reg's Ford dealership, separate the thinning hairs on her husband's steaming old scalp, and see if he could find a row of slowly climbing numbers embedded there. At least Cheryl found this funny. Then Loretta would get the town of Flax to charge Reg a monthly fee and see if that would smarten him up. Counting words wasn't going to change a bloody thing. What's dead is dead and what's gone is gone, she said, and by that time Richard had been dead and gone for one year plus forty-one, forty-two, maybe forty-three days. Loretta kept track on the calendar Cheryl tried not to look at but did every day anyway, the way people glance at a broken bone that's come right out through the skin.

One year plus forty-two days since Richard took that Mustang from his dad's car lot, late on the night of July 2, 1969, which made the date in fact July 3, after days or more likely months, who would ever know, of calculations based on formulas cooked up in physics class. His plan? His plan was to race the CN freight train and miss it by a heartbeat. And you'd think he could have done it, winning all those prizes in science fairs the way he had, getting a perfect 100 per cent on one of the June finals. The problem, Reg said, was not Richard; the problem was the velocity of the freight train. How could anyone, no matter how smart, ever predict that? It was an unknown and thus something to let X be equal to and as long as there was an unknown, that proved it wasn't suicide, that's for sure, anyone could see, with the plans he left behind, his diagrams, his conversations with Nathan Thom, it wasn't suicide. IT WAS NOT SUICIDE.

Richard left some rubber, though, a car-dealer point of pride for Reg, visible to this day where Concession 21 meets the highway. That's where Richard took off from. He knew what he was doing, knew he needed a car, a Mustang, that would accelerate accordingly. Exactly 2.5 miles to the level crossing. Reg could see it, saw it every day, the brilliant white eye of the train closing in on Richard's peripheral vision like a near-death experience but yet not. There would be the thrill. He'd have believed in his flawless timing until the final millisecond, believed in himself, because that's what Reg had taught him.

Nathan Thom said Richard had had six beers, or maybe more like eight most other people said, and this allegation fuelled Reg's word-cutting rage and blame because Loretta was a drinker. Not serious but regular, daily, and on display. In summer she drank gin and tonic on the front porch, and in the spring, vodka, also usually on the porch, weather permitting. In the fall she liked to have red wine at the Legion, and in the cold of winter, rye and ginger, inside her own house in the La-Z-Boy. Maximum three per day. But the maximum wasn't the issue, Reg told her; it was the dailiness.

Why?

Because it's the example, Reg said, combined with the chromosomes. Look at Loretta's mother, she died of cirrhosis. On the Booth side, Reg thought maybe the genes were shaped like microscopic bottles or corks or maybe they tinkled together like ice. Maybe *that's* what he was really hearing when Loretta walked around with her drinks.

"Well, on the subject of family history, let's take a look at the Deckers," Loretta had said more than once. "They don't need alcohol because they're hopped up on testosterone and that's the opinion of many, not just me. Ask anybody in Flax about the Deckers and they will use those very four words: hopped up on testosterone." Take, for example, Reg's brother, Clive: he couldn't keep his pecker in his pants. And their old man, Martin, got his nose broken so many times it looked like a bag of chopped walnuts by the time he died. And, most incriminating evidence of the super-naturality of inheritance, Richard's great-granddad Decker had been famous for racing trains on horse-back, until he got thrown under one. According to Loretta, the women's side had no effect, got skipped over like checkers. Decker's checkers, she called this phenomenon of suicidal sperm and she said to Cheryl, prepare yourself for it. Your children will be all, pure, unadulterated Decker.

Be that as it may, Reg was too tired to fight and he didn't have the words for it, literally. He wanted nothing more than to sit in the showroom, especially that day and time, late afternoon when sunlight poured into the place as if it were a customer and this was the one place on earth it wanted to be shopping. Reg wanted to sit there alone and swivel in his chair without that sullen girl of his, Cheryl, his angry wife, Loretta, and most definitely, without the aggravating Jimmy Drake Senior who was on his way over to the dealership to show off his vacation.

Jimmy Senior had pictures; he always had pictures because of his darkroom, and plenty of talk, and his talk on hot days was like white lard he'd layer onto his pictures until listening was similar to being force-fed a soggy white sandwich. Reg could tell by the sound of Jimmy on the phone that since Ohio, no Florida, he'd been planning what to say and how, interviewing and rejecting certain vocabulary, even gestures. No doubt he'd have a new theory. Jimmy Senior liked his theories, liked to extract *larger* meanings from *small* events because, and Reg quoted, *this was the noblest work of the human mind.* He could not shut up because he laboured under the illusion, as George Drury would say, that he was a public speaker. Even the administration at Flax Composite High, where Jimmy Senior was custodian, had been shanghaied into allowing him to make comments on the public address system. The kids had told Reg and they'd had some good laughs over it. Richard could do a mean impersonation. "Let's say one day you kick your locker door in frustration and break a hinge," Richard once said, in the spooky, dirty, confidential voice of Jimmy Drake. "Your locker is no longer secure. Someone plants something in it, you get blamed and really, who do you have to blame but yourself? Who do you have to blame but yourself?" Always said the last thing twice and this became the best part of the joke for Richard, repeating himself for emphasis, to the amusement of all, back in the days when Cheryl used to laugh.

Who do you have to blame but yourself? This was invariably the Drake Senior message, with intermittent encouragement to blame the provincial government or the federal government and once, when he went too far, the Pope, after which Jimmy fell silent for a couple months. But then he was back, same as ever: "Good morning ladies and gentlemen of the jury." In the halls, Richard said and he was right, no one even stopped moving, everybody just talked louder. More to be pitied than despised, Reg supposed, and it was pitiful, the way Jimmy relied on Reg to be impressed but who else was there besides that whore Angel Farrell.

Reg tapped the eraser end of a pencil against the

courts put a stop to it.' Larry pulls it out, says 'Here' and slaps it onto my bald spot. Says, 'We wouldn't have to go to the trouble of shaving you.' That's when I got the heebie-jeebies. Took me til Ohio to get rid of them. The guy was an ass. But Jimmy Junior wanted to see that chair."

Deciding to crowbar a single word from his aggravated mouth, Reg said "Kids."

Loretta blew a smoke ring, the sign she was a little impressed, and her idea of sexy sarcasm. Everybody but Cheryl watched it travel decisively to the wall, collide with the Valvoline calendar, disintegrate like a quiet atom bomb.

Jimmy looked into the showroom. "I heard Bill Laine's thinking of getting himself one of those Mavericks. That right?"

"He's been in a couple of times," Reg said, swivelling, steady as a pendulum; swivelling felt good between the legs.

Jimmy had a few words of wisdom about Mavericks, something he'd read in the States. Then he was back onto the chair again.

"Anyways, the thing I realized after I left that place is that there are certain things you remember forever and that chair was one of them."

"Oh, oh. I smell a theory close by," said Reg. Fine. He'd throw in a couple of words for now.

"You don't know that, Jimmy," Loretta said, putting out her smoke. "You have no idea what you'll remember when you're eighty-five. You might be like my grandpa was and remember nothing but some poems you learned when you were six."

"Oh yes I do, Loretta Decker," said Jimmy pointing a wienerish finger at her. "I know what I remember and what I forget and that chair has gone right into my memory bank with all the unforgettable things and do you know why?" He was worked up now, had failed to calm himself as Loretta suggested. "I'll tell you why. Because it's a thing that looks exactly *not* like what it's supposed to be. It's a chair, see? Designed for comfort and rest, right? Like that swivel chair. Only this chair wants to kill you. So you can't ever forget it. It's like when that tornado rolled in last August. The sky was really blue, then kind of too blue and everything was perfectly still. It was a peaceful day and yet it wanted to kill us. So I never forgot it. Also, another example: the men on the moon. Suddenly there's the moon, this yellow circle we see in the sky, and now it has people walking on it. That's not supposed to happen. Since then you look at it and it's not the same, because it did something it wasn't meant to do. It *looked* one way but it *was* another. Once that happens to a thing, you can't forget about it. Not only that, you can't *stop* thinking about it. So there you go. Chairs, the sky, men on the moon, they're all capable of raising the hair on the back of your neck. That's my theory."

Reg shook his head as at a recurring problem, a dog shitting on the porch or a Kotex clogging the women's room john at the dealership. "Here we go again, Jimmy. That's not a theory; that's an opinion. You're not Charles Darwin and you're not Albert Einstein."

"Well, I've thought about it quite a bit. It's a long drive from Florida to here and Jimmy Junior's not much of a conversationalist. Ask yourself, do you remember a noose in the same way? Does it make you feel a little crazy? No. A noose might make you not want to break the law but it won't make you feel queasy to your stomach. And why is that? Because a noose is what it appears to be. It's a noose. It doesn't have some other clandestine purpose."

"Clandestine, huh?" Reg rolled his eyes. He condemned the blowhard trait in others. "Anyway, I still say it's an opinion. Not a theory."

"Same difference."

"Fine with me," Reg said.

Loretta leaned her head back, stretched her arms the way she did before any important announcement, took a couple of steps toward Reg, and said, "You know what, dear? I just thought of something. I don't want to do the books anymore."

Reg locked his eyes on her, stopped short in midswivel. This was news. Even Cheryl looked up. "What do you mean?"

"I mean I'm tired of doing the accounts. Rocket can do them. I'll show him how. All it takes is a bit of time and the adding machine."

"Suit yourself," Reg said, shrugging. If Loretta wanted a reaction, she'd have to get it elsewhere.

"I'm going to take on some more hours with George Drury. He asked if I would. He wants his girl to take the rest of the summer off, says he'd rather have someone a little more professional in the front office."

"Suit yourself," Reg said again. Words repeated only counted once.

Just take the bike and go. A flat and lifeless Wednesday afternoon, mid-August, sky the colour of white weather that wasn't about to change. And Rose, Adrian's sister, redundant as they sometimes said in the newspaper, fired from the dentist's office by her own old man. So why not go out of town on the bike? Go someplace new? She had her licence, could take the little Vega whenever she wanted but cars were no good for stealth. You still had to ask, or at least make an announcement, explain yourself. And even with the windows down, sixty miles an hour, departure roaring past your ears, that car was contaminated. Owned by one Flaxian after another, passed down from Limb to Limb to Drury; the thing was full of Flax. Caked, Rose had told Adrian more than once: the car was caked with the town of Flax. Emerge from the blue interior and behold the crumbs as they fall from your lap. Could be in Mesmer with Adrian, could be in Kitchener-Waterloo with Anastasia—didn't matter. Flax was stuffed between your ears like old cake.

Away she went. Even at this age, seventeen, and on a fat-tired girl's bike, taking off without telling Dad was as good as truancy. Not that Rose was often, or even ever, truant and if she were to be, excuses would most certainly be made, her history clattering like a museum printing press behind her back, publishing counterfeit notes of permission. If you looked you could almost see the grey ink of explanation on everyone's fingers. Yes, Rose Drury, such a lovely girl despite everything, her mother and all, so long ago now, ten years, eleven is it, but no doubt she remembers and a girl needs a mother, such a help to her father and that *brother*.

Downhill was the only realistic direction, entering humidity like the school locker room, and insects wanting up your nose, thicker than the smell of sweaty girls. Rose had never taken this or any gravel road out of town, her best friend Anastasia living on the Mesmer Highway, the Number 4. Though this was hardly gravel, all of the loose stones having been nudged to the edges by country tires, leaving a smooth surface, more or less the colour of a Band-Aid. Rose sped up, faster than the bugs and the time of day. Nobody else in sight, the quiet of summer heat in her ears, and growing toward her from both ditches, those dusty, dusty grasses. They were like little towns of roadside ghosts, thousands of them, stooped, greying, maybe looking for some company. Why don't you stop, girly? they seemed to be muttering. Why don't you stop?

No reason. Except for she was probably scared.

Here now the road became flatter with curves, grass giving up to evergreen trees and swamp. Rose kept an eye out for the mud-loving forms of life, hopping things that took on water and popped like grapes if you drove over them. She didn't want to spoil her record. For more than two months now, since Skokie'd gone to sleep, she hadn't killed a single creature, not an insect or, she said, even a blade of grass. Mos-

quitoes, she shooed away. Houseflies were encouraged
to use the door. Yeah, well what about single-celled or-
ganisms, Anastasia had asked, finding her friend's new
Jesus-type, seeing-the-little-sparrow-fall worry a little far-
fetched; what about, for example, a tiny bit of mould
you might wipe up and swoosh down the drain? "It's
not anaerobic, you know," Anastasia said. "It can't survive without oxygen."

"I can't control everything," Rose said, "much as
I'd like to."

"That's right," said Anastasia.

Anastasia liked to undermine the good intentions
of others. No big deal; Rose was used to it. She ped-
alled faster, then braked, coming to a complete stop
beneath the overhanging trees. Look at this: bulrushes.
She walked her bike closer to the ditch. Might there
be a baby Moses abandoned in the reeds? She wasn't
kidding. One secret she had never told Anastasia: Rose
was often on the lookout for abandoned babies. She'd
look in cardboard boxes outside grocery stores or behind exhibits at the fall fair. It was a kind of hobby.
But if Anastasia ever found out she would turn it into
an art-scene with her Barbies and invite everyone over
for a laugh.

No babies today, no crying to be heard and still no
traffic, nothing. Even the frogs shushed as she approached and so she stood perfectly still, wanting to
experiment, waiting for them to think she was gone or
an unusual species of tree.

Ha! They fell for it, one or two choirmasters clearing their throats and the others joining, freakishly in

unison as if someone were conducting.

"Ahem," said Rose and they stopped again, all at once, apparently under the influence of one collective frog worry. Maybe they couldn't see her but the inhabitants of these ditches were listening with their tiny flap-ears. She'd seen them in biology, during the dissections she'd never do again. The school allowed for conscientious objection and, unlike the baby-hunting, on this issue Rose was prepared for the scoffing of Anastasia, could even predict her response. *You know, nature's not all sweetness and light. Remember that plant somebody brought into biology class last year? That pitcher plant? Doesn't that prove to you that nature isn't as nice as you might think? Nature is made up of carnivorous little throats with spiny slanting hairs that drag flies or spiders to their doom. Slowly and with malice aforethought, Rose Drury.*

Rose would admit this road was a little like the mouth of the pitcher plant. She couldn't seem to turn around, there was no going back, and the smell was amphibian, like breath held under water for long periods of time. And here she was with nothing but a bike, no money, not even any identification, nothing but too much Anastasia on the brain. Rose looked over her shoulder. If a farmer were to drive by, would he shoot her? Such malfeasance occurred in the country, there being such a chronic lack of witnesses. Any outsider might be shot for target practice, left to fall into the ditch, spouting a tie-dyed bloodstain into the lonely murk. Eye-to-dying-eye with bullfrogs as big as softballs. A banquet for mosquitoes although you had to wonder: did they like dead people? Perhaps the freshly dead. Just ask Adrian, he would probably know. He'd be pretty sure they would not like blood blended with swamp water. That they would not go for. His guess: you would lie there forever, Rose, decomposing until you were just a few bones, unrecognizable even as a skeleton. More like pick-up sticks. What are you doing, going out there on your bike anyway?

Rose pushed off and rode further to a break in the trees, up a steep little hill, past a barren field of yellow grain and a green road sign. East Flax. Oh yes. Rose's knowledge of East Flax was a View-Master reel of images, the dentist's daughter's three-dimensional impressions of rotten teeth and disregard for higher education. But that wasn't all there was to East Flax. Don't forget the lake. Rose had been to Minnow Lake twice, for the eighth grade picnic and once on an outing with Mom, long ago, before Rose was even in school. By then Mom would have had the cancer but not known, or known and not told anyone so that the day's events stood back and watched the way they did when you were keeping a secret.

They were supposed to have a good time, just the two of them. Adrian stayed home with Dad, but some man talked Mom into waterskiing, tried to convince her to go over the jump, and he wouldn't take no for an answer, he said. Don't be crazy, Mom said, laughing. It was all in fun but seemed a little dangerous. Dragged by a boat over a piece of wood in the middle of a lake? Rose remembered how the ski jump angled out of the water like her one loose tooth and she had made a deal: pull out the tooth, the ski jump will sink, and Mom will be safe. But she couldn't; those rags of skin anchoring it to her gum were tough as old meat. And Mom didn't go anyway which was a big relief. From the point of view of kids, Rose realized now, adults' ideas of fun often seemed to overlap with sinister.

Rose cycled past Dance Hall Road. She decided to go and take a look at the ski jump; it was still there, Adrian made frequent reference to both it and Randy Farrell. Still no traffic. Where were all the people? Even on the sleepiest Sunday in Flax you would hear lawn mowers, screen doors or one of the Limb kids practicing the piano. Apparently, on a business day in the outskirts of East Flax, people were told to keep it down. Dogs were muzzled. Shhh. As if Minnow Lake were some big sleeping baby that might be wakened.

Now Rose could see the lake and smell it. Not a bad smell but also not the good smell of Lake Huron with its ocean-sized capacity for washing and dissolving and rubbing things smooth. Minnow Lake was so shallow and warm, it smelled more like something cooking, the water table rising up and offering you a mud casserole. And some people said not all residents of East Flax had septic systems, so who knew where their toilets flushed. Rose did remember at the eighth grade picnic, the feel of the lake bottom curled up between your toes like wet diapers or worse. *Nobody* had wanted to come to Minnow Lake but there were already three schools booked at Blue Lake, so that was that. Since they'd built the pavilion and boat ramp and restaurant at Blue Lake, everybody went there. And you could see why. Rose let her bike clatter into the tall weeds at the edge of the gravelly beach. Beach? Hardly. The owner of Blue Lake resort had hauled in loads of sand and strung buoys in the water to define the swimmers' area. If you went past them and drowned, it would be your own fault.

East Flax had definitely seen better times and so had Minnow Lake. One slanted dock and Russell Hansen's old rowboat under three inches of water. And there stood the ski jump floating on its unsinkable oil drums, a hollow-brained tribute to the laws of physics. And up there, the dance hall, clearly visible on its cliff, watching the lake from its row of windows. Rose knew there was a store, the Farrells' shaky enterprise, but would it be open or even still in business? Probably, this *was* East Flax, birthplace of unlikelihood and home of the beautiful and intelligent Cora Farrell. No one for a minute thought *she* would be chosen school queen. Anastasia said, simply by entering the competition Cora had taken the Farrell chromosomes as far as they had ever been selected to go, that Cora was born to be a runner-up, but she beat Lillian Gee and Connie Laine. You could almost see the town of Flax's eyes bulging in communal disbelief.

Rose knew the entire Farrell clan was weird, what with Randy and his habits, his need to have the inside of his locker just so with little plastic horses glued to the shelf and that time he asked Adrian not to go *in* the shop wing door because he hadn't gone *out* the shop wing door. Their father, Frog Farrell, had swallowed a frog and their mother, Angel, had a reputation. And Cora's sister, Maddy, was a girl-boy, or a boy-girl and the hero of the basketball team, so had done some chromosome-hauling herself.

But most quizzical of all was the Farrells' store. Who exactly on earth would shop there? It would seem the road was closed, for example, to cars. Maybe in these parts people walked, in which case, would they ever arrive or would they fall asleep en route? Fall asleep in a dusty ditch, sprout little roots from the soles of their feet and, upon awakening, find they had grown leaves. No need for the Farrells' store now, honey, we've got photosynthesis. Cancel our account.

Rose was thirsty and a drink would be nice. She didn't have a cent but maybe she could finagle one with her Flaxified charms. Worth a try. Rose rode back along the weed-rimmed lake access, turned right past a tipsy mailbox, a long laneway ending at a metal-clad house by the lake, a former garage with its single out-of-order gas pump. More weeds, foxtail and milkweed and goldenrod crowding up to everything, green and wavery bodies intent on pushing past and under and into the civilization of the humans. Finally! A car, driver waving in slow motion, driving in slow motion, lifting a spectacular cloud of dust, a billow of billows. Rose licked the grit off her teeth. No wonder frogs jumped to the nearest bog. Skin-breathers could be asphyxiated with each passing vehicle.

There was the store, plate glass windows dark as night beneath the overhanging balcony. Looked like someplace out of *Gunsmoke*, Miss Kitty's sister's place perhaps. Empty, no doubt, closed for the afternoon.

Everybody out hunting varmints or settling feuds. But to Rose's surprise the Drink Pepsi door opened into an unlit habitat, the nocturnals' exhibit at the zoo. Her eyes adjusted to the gloom. Where she anticipated wombats and opossums were three old men in chairs, hillbillies she presumed, and at the till, the beautiful Cora Farrell.

"Hi, Cora," Rose said, six night-vision eyes of old men fixing on her, Geiger counting her history, DNA, purpose in this store, and on this earth.

Cora was not bothered by the unexpected, living as she did in the municipality of Oddness, so Rose Drury shopping at her parents' store probably made as much sense as she herself working there, as much sense as her Flax Composite High crown probably being used, by now, to repair a broken leghold trap.

"If you're looking for Maddy," Cora said, "she's up at the dance hall."

Of course. She should be looking for Maddy. Maddy was her age, also heading into grade thirteen whereas Cora was finished, a graduate and a queen. Rose wouldn't be here to inquire about Cora's plans. And she couldn't very well claim to be visiting for sociological reasons, or would they be anthropological? "Yes, I'm conducting some research for the University of Mesmer and I've been wanting to interview Maddy Farrell for quite some time now. It's about that ridiculous orange hat she wears in the winter. She's so tall, and well, what both I and Anastasia Van Epp would like to know, as well as the public in general, I'm sure: Does she think she's a character in a Dr. Seuss book?

Does she think she's living on Mulberry Street?"

"Well, in fact, I was just out for a bicycle ride, finding myself unemployed because my father, the dentist, George Drury—maybe you know him, maybe you wish you didn't know him—anyway, he decided he doesn't really need me working in his office and so I thought why not go to East Flax? Maddy might be around." Rose saw her voice landing on the shelves of dry goods and from there, watching the action wonderingly. "I'd buy a drink but I didn't bring any money. Not a single dime."

"Dentist's daughter should have a dime," said one of the men from his old and mud-coloured armchair. Alfred Beel, Rose now saw, an occasional patient and known to be a grouch, known to be the type of person who looks at young people who are laughing as if they are waving their private parts in the air and therefore should be hidden behind a portable divider. The other two, opposite him, sat on wooden chairs, mute and slouchy, soft spined in appearance, creatures who had just yesterday made the switch from water to land and weren't quite sure what to make of the move.

"Yes, she should. That is true enough."

"Well, have a drink," Cora offered. "My treat. What do you want? Orange? Root beer? Cream soda?"

Rose had wondered if the place was even wired for electricity. No lights appeared to be on. But behind Alfred, the glass-fronted cooler emitted fluorescence. Designed for cuts of meat, most likely salvaged from an old butcher shop, here in East Flax it contained single bottles of soda pop arranged in rows and off to one side, packages of wieners and Velveeta cheese stacked in, Rose had to admit, rather decorative pyramids. That would be the renowned work of Randy Farrell.

"So what'll it be?" Cora was behind the cooler, sliding the door open.

"Cream soda."

"Good choice." And Cora, moving her arm like a mechanical device to the head of the cream soda row, withdrew the lead bottle, edged the others forward a spot, and said "Here. You likely know Randy likes to organize. If we don't keep the pop in rows and the other stuff in stacks, he gets a little fidgety or something. Anyway, the opener's on the counter. See that string? If we don't tie it down, it grows legs." She was busy finding a replacement cream soda from a carton behind the cooler. Rose figured that, according to what she knew about Randy's brain, the bottles on display were required to line up and take turns.

Having engineered the free drink, Rose was ready to spend some time with Maddy. Maybe. Could be educational and she didn't want these four mouths speaking unkindly of her when she left, in particular the two mushy-looking men on the wooden chairs. She didn't want them hissing and bubbling judgments through their East Flax gills.

"I guess I'll go find Maddy now."

"Sure. You know where the dance hall is?"

"Yes. Oh yes. Everybody knows where the dance hall is," and she left, the door slamming shut behind her, its rusty spring unloosened by many years of use.

Hard to believe that out there, even in East Flax, arrangements had been made. Rose had not thought the vast trellises of Flax, able to support the monster-vine of familiarity would have made their way to the inhospitable climate of East Flax, but they had. Now she would *have* to see Maddy Farrell because later today Cora would ask, "Did that Drury girl come to see you at the dance hall? She dropped by the store looking for you." Maddy shrugging, saying no. But weeks later at school, still wondering, watching Rose from her position below the trellis, not far from where the stalk met the mud, yet never daring to ask: Why were you in East Flax? Did you come to laugh at my orange hat?

Tall, weird Maddy would have to be seen.

Dance Hall Road. Here it was already, complete with the steepest hill for miles and such a case of wash-board bumps, Rose had to push the bike. You'd think the place would be quiet but yahoos were forever driving out there to spin their tires to the top of the hill, stretch their white arms out the windows, and hurl empties over the roof and at the trees. A type of sport, Rose had heard, called bottle darts. And in the winter, cars made a habit of sliding into the snowy ditch, trees looking a little ashamed in the headlights, possibly embarrassed for the drivers. Nothing happening today, though, unless you were to count the breathing of Rose and the occasional bleached-out grasshopper.

At the crest of the hill, Rose stopped to look around. Funny that the dance hall still felt like the dance hall, even in broad daylight. She guessed the place had memories, as did this very parking lot, home to seventy years, at least, of dance-hall anticipation. Even Rose had enough experience to know it wasn't so much the event or even the hall as the stepping out of the car or roadster or buggy and into the plans, the thinking: maybe I'll see someone, or better, maybe I'll be seen. The shadows of the leaves could in reality be what remained of the secret criss-crossings of a thousand brains attached to hearts. You never knew. Rose gave a little shudder. Six or seven weeks until the September dance, always the best of the year, everybody said.

All right. She had come this far, too late to turn back now. What was the protocol? Did you knock at a dance hall? Better do. To walk in might give Maddy a scare. But how would she hear above all that thumping? To open the door and call *Maddy* would be a ridiculous intimacy, like opening the door to Dr. Graham Rochon's mental health office and calling, Graham? Graham? Are you in? I have some new confessions for you.

She knocked again. Knock, knock, knock. And again, louder. KNOCK, KNOCK, KNOCK. An ominous silence and then the door swung open.

"You have a guest," said Rose.

Maddy Farrell was taller than most boys at Flax Composite High. She was six feet, one inch. Everything about her was long and narrow, including her face, which she lengthened and narrowed by tying back her frizzy, paper bag coloured hair with a paper bag coloured elastic. She looked puzzled right now but that was normal. Even at predictable events such as the lunch bell or assemblies, Maddy conveyed puzzlement, as if each event had somehow been snipped from its short little history and its inconsequential little future and was free-floating, without context. Rose thought that's how Maddy saw the world.

"Do you know who I am?" asked Rose, inflecting her voice into the nearly arrogant range, even though that was not her plan.

"Yeah," a little defensive. "You're Rose Drury, the dentist's daughter and Adrian's sister. My brother knows Adrian."

"Yes, they're friends. Or at least they seem to spend time on the ski jump. Anywho, I was riding my bike and wound up in East Flax and went to the store and your sister said you were up here so I thought I'd come and see you."

"Oh." The puzzled look, appropriate in this case since there was no context. "Well, come in. It's not exactly my house as you can see, it's not really set up for hospitality, it's a dance hall. But it's not really set up for basketball either and yet, here I am shooting baskets. Quelle surprise" she said, her voice flat and unsurprised. "We could play some one-on-one if you want."

"No thanks. I'm no good at basketball. Half-good at volleyball except last time I played my wrist turned purple," said Rose, extending a tanned and healthy wrist for emphasis, showing off, the first sign she was already liking Maddy Farrell.

"Oh."

Now what? "Can I look around the dance hall?"

"Sure." And Maddy lead her through the place as if she were a realtor and Rose a prospective buyer. "Here's the kitchen. And the cupboards. As you can see, dishes for two hundred. Ever seen that many identical cups and saucers?"

"Nope."

"It's almost like art, maybe, or something really symmetrical or in a giant pattern. Or it could be Randy's been out here putting things in place. I don't really know what I'm talking about."

Art? Anastasia would have something to say about that.

"So the Women's Institute holds meetings here and sometimes they all come together in a passel, my dad says. A passel of women. It's kind of funny," Maddy said, watching Rose's smiling, unlaughing face, "or maybe not. I mean, like a herd of cows or a pride of lions. It's actually my dad's sense of humour, not mine. And these are the eight mysterious roasting pans. Only two ovens, that's the mystery. Want to see the men's washroom? It's really the best part."

"Definitely."

They walked to the wrong side of the darkened basement, pushed open the scraping men's door, and observed the three wondrous urinals. "Welcome to the stand up world of men," Maddy said.

"My friend Anastasia would love this tour."

"Oh. Her." Two conflicting opinions of Anastasia Van Epp clattering against each other in the pause. "Do you want to see the stage? There's a microphone."

Rose would be honest. This was not the type of girl she had expected. Where were the grammatical errors, possibly gap-toothed for emphasis? The basketball prodigy with no knowledge of sound equipment? But seconds later, squeal, "Testing, one, two, three." Maddy's voice important as the mayor, preparing to tell a joke or two.

"Well, without further ado," Rose said, grabbing the mike, determined to extemporize more and better than Maddy Farrell. "I've brought you here today to ask you the following. Okay. How many of you, given the chance, would move away from Flax?" More squeal of feedback.

"I'm from *East* Flax," said Maddy, seated now on the edge of the stage, long white-as-a-urinal legs bare and crossed.

"Oh right, right. Let me re-phrase this. How many of you, given the chance, would move away from Flax *proper* tomorrow?" And Rose returned the microphone to its cradle, "Don't touch that," jumped to the dance floor, faced Maddy, raised her hand, "I would" then leapt, not as nimbly as she had hoped, back onto the stage.

"Now, how many of you," taking a deep breath, "given the same opportunity, would move away from *East* Flax?"

Craning herself around to look at Rose, Maddy said, "Realistically? I'd probably stay."

Adrian wakes up mad. Monday morning means one more bottomless week of Randy Farrell's obstinate back. Randy's back at his vocation floor locker with its extra shelves made in shop, covered in wood-look MACtac. Randy's back in the locker room after gym class, his baggy-assed, half-grey underwear hanging like a threadbare and pouty face, asking to be kicked. Randy's back in history, as of last November, one row over, three desks up. His idea, Randy's, to distance himself by switching desks and a stroke of vengeful genius to trade places with Jimmy Drake Junior. Now a different and worse back occupied the seat directly in front of Adrian, closer it seemed than Randy had ever been, close enough for Adrian to stare fixedly at loose threads trying desperately to unravel themselves and make a getaway. They'd crawl like inchworms if they could to get away from Jimmy and so would Adrian if there were someplace to go. But there isn't, so Adrian usually goes to bed mad too. He lies awake, visualizing the red-brown quills of Jimmy's greased hair, imagining the day when, porcupine-like and with rear-view precision, he expels them into Adrian's soft neck, killing him. A reason for Randy to turn around and applaud.

Adrian shudders in his bed. Hard as he tries, he cannot stop this memory. It's on a circuit, he's decided, with himself as the switch. Soon as he wakes up, there it comes, like electricity or some other matterless yet zapping substance, thought waves, he supposes, thought waves you have been commanded to think. It was winter or at least wintery, a week or two after the desk trade, a time when the dusty fallout of Cheryl and Maddy was heavy as nuclear attack, every morning the first peek out of an air raid shelter. In history, Mr. Rigg was handing back their essays when Jimmy Junior turned to

Adrian and said, "I guess we're both in this together, Drury."

"In what?" Adrian asked, knowing exactly what.

"This," Jimmy Junior said, gesturing toward the window, the wide world, "this dance hall mess."

Outside was overflowing with crowded, haphazard flakes of snow, the first of the year. Inside, everyone sat mesmerized, as if by looking, by being perfectly still, they might just for once sail supernaturally through glass and away from school without being cut.

"Really?" wondered Adrian. "This dance hall mess? We're in it together?"

"Yeah," said the profile of Jimmy Junior, hopeful. He was in something together.

Days like that Adrian thought if anger were a natural resource like zinc or nickel, he would be a mine, a rich vein. He would be pictured in geography books and, around the world, children would be asked to draw his face on maps; Ontario, they'd memorize, famous for its anger. He'd even have his own symbol on the periodic table. Ad or Dr, he wasn't sure which. He kept meaning to pop into the chemistry class to see if one was taken.

Adrian shook his head and heaved the cumbersome, vinyl zip-up binder from the book rack beneath his seat, thumping it onto his desk top with enough noise to startle the class in its snow globe daze.

"Adrian, must you?" asked Mr. Rigg, always a little tired and ironic.

"No, I mustn't," said Adrian, eliciting a few titters.

"Har har," said Mr. Rigg and turned his back. With satisfying gusto, Adrian zipped open the binder and found his geometry set. "Psst, Drake," he said, "turn around."

Jimmy Junior swivelled to the left, crossing his legs in the aisle; they were too long to cross beneath the desk, Jimmy having a kind of flamingo physique, nine parts leg, one part round, puffy abdomen, even puffier now that he was living with his mother.

"What's the name of this company here," Adrian whispered, "that makes these geometry sets? What's it say?"

"That's an easy one. It says Westab," said Jimmy Junior. "I can read, remember? I'm not spas-lexic like you are, Drury."

"Did you ever notice it's a compound word, Einstein?"

"What do you mean compound?"

"I mean," said Adrian, using the compass to scratch a line in the aluminum case between the e and the s, "I mean it doesn't say Westab, it says We stab. We stab, Drake, do you get it?"

"Get what Drury? That there's more than one of you? That it takes three or four Adrian Drurys to stab somebody with a geometry set? Ooooh, I'm scared, I'm going to tell Mr. Rigg." And Jimmy raised his bone-sized arm as if he might actually squeal.

"Okay, okay, man," said Adrian, "put your damn arm down."

"Do I hear an apology?" asked the sideways face of the ghoul called Jimmy.

"Fine, yes," hissed Adrian. "I apologize for wanting to stab you. Just don't say we're in anything together again, not now or in the foreseeable future. Understand?"

"Calm down, Drury. Take a Valium," Jimmy said, answering a question for Mr. Rigg in the very next breath, something to do with supply and demand.

Take a Valium, Adrian says to his alarm clock, tired and ironic as Mr. Rigg. If anybody should take a Valium, it's Randy Farrell. Randy Farrell should take a Valium like Leo Laine had to take for his vertigo, a medication that would stop his dizzy thinking, his blaming of Adrian.

Time to get up. For this, Adrian has a nine-step system. First, forcefully throw off sheets and blankets, as if they were, because they are, woven up with all of the dust mites and skin flakes from 1970. Then, scissor legs to bedside and over the dangling cliff beneath which hangs the day. Next and most challenging, sit up, feet on floor, skin to skin with the present. Await paranormal event. Accept that there has been some delay. Give up; move on. Fling top half of self backwards and with the equal and opposite energy generated, bounce forward and out of bed. Give the paranormal one more chance.

Six paces and Adrian is across the hall and in the shower, one of the few reliably good moments he can expect from his day. With yesterday's microbes and bacteria washing down the drain, Adrian is sufficiently at peace to daydream about the past, days when his most pressing worry was proximity to a rabid fox or, might he be pecked by a bird if he happened to fall asleep after he and Cheryl had done what they used to do. Nowadays he would gladly lie naked in a field of seagulls or crows, let them pierce his chest or feet with their yellow beaks, have a rabid fox draw near, breathe its hydrophobia into his own two nostrils, trade any torment for another chance. Then the first good moment is over.

Adrian cranks off the hot, then the cold, wraps himself in one of the blue towels he likes and crosses the hallway back to his room. His dad is up. There is the smell of toast, which, since Rose left for university, Adrian dislikes, signifying as it did now wordless, lonely chewing with the dentist. Chewing had lost much of its appeal, as had family life, if you could call this a family, one dentist-father and his community-outcast son. Adrian has been thinking of a liquid diet, three or four Joe Weider milkshakes per day, no wasted material, all nutrients rushing directly to the muscles. Get outta the way! Me first to the spindle muscles, the sheath types. Every once in a while, biology had some application.

"How are you this morning, Son?"

"Just fine, Dad."

"I made you a couple boiled eggs."

"Thanks."

There they were, two eggs in a bowl, shelled, unformed, unborn. Now eggs make him wonder if Cheryl might have been pregnant, and as much as Adrian doesn't like birds, he feels a crazy sadness for these and other eggs that didn't get a chance. Still, they are soft and require little chewing.

"I'm getting started early this morning, so I'll see you after school. Don't forget your lunch."

"Yeah, Dad."

Adrian slices into one egg with the side of his spoon and reaches for the salt. Salt. He cannot to this day believe that Randy Farrell has not uttered a single word to him since the completion of the salt project, since the conversation in the store, he knew the date, everyone did, November 8, 1970, about Rose's car, the Vega, and of course, salt. Even Randy's last words as he gave Adrian and Rose some licorice pipes just before they left: Smoke these on the way back to Flax. That was it. Smoke these on the way back to Flax.

Other people were starting to forget. The Deckers' car lot

was under new ownership, Rocket Lalonde, and everyone was happy about that. The Flax pool was opening on the May long weekend, no matter what, no matter how cold. Anastasia Van Epp was heading up the prom committee and no one seemed to object but then, what did they know? They knew nothing. Not like Adrian, standing in the middle of events like a lightning rod in bare feet, as Randy Farrell would say, on the muddy shores of Minnow Lake.

Adrian takes a bit of egg white, dips his toast into the soft, warm yolk. What were the Farrells eating at this moment? Were they eating wild animals, trapped game? No idea. Adrian misses the Farrells and East Flax, Minnow Lake and, he would say this out loud if it would make a difference, Randy. One entire East Flax winter had now come and gone and Adrian has missed every moment of it, every rabbit, every grey wolf, every chance to walk on the frozen lake, slide as close to the channel as you could without sinking. Randy's channel.

Winter before last when they were both in grade nine, Randy talked Adrian into coming out to East Flax to see something. It was the middle of a cold snap and Randy wanted to show Adrian how the lake didn't freeze in one section. He said it was called the channel. There was a current of warm water underneath and you could walk up close and look through the ice and see everything, fish and turtles, he said. He said it was like a TV channel. Only Randy would make that kind of connection.

So Adrian rode his bike out, it was freezing but he welcomed the chance to wear a balaclava, the gangster's disguise. They met at the edge of the lake and walked out past the ski jump. Everything was frozen solid with occasional big, blue cracks until they came to a place where the ice was thinner and this was The Famous Channel. Adrian had to admit it was something to look at, like a black vein in the lake. And Randy was a tour guide, inventing what you could see, saying there were tropical fish, the giant manta ray, it was better than Sea World, and crawling on his stomach to where the see-through part was. Follow me, he said, follow my lead. Step right up; no, I mean, don't step right up. Crawl right up.

Adrian thought he was joking, dragging himself along like a water snake on ice so he walked right by and up to the edge of the channel to have a look. Part of him believed there might be dolphins or neon fish like the Limbs had in their aquarium only fifty times the size, as big as chainsaws. No, no, no, Randy was saying but too late, the ice was giving as if it were cardboard and Adrian sank. He experienced the sinking feeling, its literal version, as Mr. Felske, the English teacher would say, a very strange feeling, as if every part of him were arguing with his eyes and skin: this can't be true. Oh yes it is.

Then he was eye-to-snake-eye with Randy who had memorized proper techniques for ice rescuing. Stay on your stomach, throw some kind of line (his jacket), and pull the sinker back to thick ice. They'd had to walk to the Farrells' nutty store so Adrian could change into Randy's formerly-worn-by Maddy clothes and get driven home by Frog Farrell and his huge dashboard of mess. That was Adrian's first adventure to the channel with Randy Farrell and the only time he sank but just as well to be a little prepared for this new sinking feeling, this business of being blamed, like each day grabbing for snapping-off bits of ice and having your clothes seem too heavy for your back. Perhaps that was as paranormal as it got.

Adrian puts his dishes in the sink, brushes his teeth, gets the brown bag lunch from the fridge. Outside, the air is cold, snow along the hedges and the northern exposures frozen stiff. Spring is never going to come this year. What the hell is wrong with 1971? Even the weather is distorted.

He waves to Cassie Limb as she steps outside in her track suit, running to school as part of her training. Hi, Cassie. How many teams are you on, anyway? She doesn't hear. Well, never mind. Bye. Adrian has another reliable pleasure-of-the-day to consider. Less than three blocks to the pay phone where he has stopped off daily since mid-February, sometimes after school, sometimes before, to make a friendly call to Alfred Beel. Mornings now Alfred knows for sure not to answer but Adrian lets it ring, knowing the old asshole's there, staring at the phone as if it were swarming with earwigs or their larvae. When Alfred does pick up, Adrian pretends to be Loretta Decker, using his one all-purpose female impersonation, the whispery voice of Marilyn Monroe. It's good enough for Alfred Beel. What's Adrian supposed to do, anyway, go to a special school for phone impersonators just to convince Alfred Beel? Not likely. Adrian hates the old fart and wants him to suffer. If he had a heart, Adrian would slice a spoon through it right now like a soft-boiled egg. Gag. Sometimes Adrian gives himself the creeps.

The phone booth. Adrian loves the phone booth, the way the door is hinged in the middle, pushes inward and flattens out. Adrian would like to know who came up with that idea for a door. It's on the main drag, Huron Drive, but a little removed from the downtown, if you could call Flax a town with a down. He's pretty sure no one sees him, because it's in front of the veterinarian's office where Skokie met her maker and they keep their dusty blinds down out of respect for the crowds of dog and cat ghosts trapped inside. Plus, they don't open the front office until nine.

There's his favourite message carved in the wood: "Louise is a four-letter word." And beneath that, someone has written, "whore." Adrian doesn't know a single Louise. Maybe she lives in Mesmer or Telluride and her boyfriend used to call from here; this is where she told him to take a hike, so in a moment of rage, he tried to write an insult but liked Louise too much. Then somebody who doesn't know Louise but can't count added in the whore word. This is a short story Adrian likes because no one can really blame Louise.

He has one dime but never uses it without first checking the coin return. Twice he's found a dime which saved him twenty cents he'd rather not spend on Alfred Beel but spend he must. No dime today. He picks up the receiver—does a Bell employee ever, ever drop by and clean it?—drops his coin and dials. Being Loretta makes him laugh harder than anything else.

The sun breaks above the rooftops, warming the back of Adrian's neck and Adrian hopes, hopes, hopes his neck does not in any way resemble that of Jimmy Junior, always one or two red zits against skin pink as an eraser. Alfred picks up on the first ring, taking Adrian by surprise but he's ready, has a dozen scripts at hand.

Alfred says nothing, his usual morning response.

"Hello, Alfred," says Adrian in his whispery voice. "I guess you've been missing me."

Beel clears his throat. This is a bit out of the ordinary but only as unordinary as the remedial English substitute tearing up a slightly dirty short story about a woman named Louise and her boyfriend, Adrian. Adrian smiles, carries on. "I've certainly been missing you, Alf. You are, after all, the handsomest man in the tri-county area." Adrian is saving his laughter now, holding it for later. He can hear Beel breathing. "Have I ever told you I love the way your breath whistles through your nose hairs, Alfred."

"Keep talking, Drury. Just keep talking. You're hanging yourself, you know that? Hanging yourself."

"What do you mean, Alfred?" Adrian coos. "Has Loretta done something to make her lambikins angry?"

Adrian feels the door to the phone booth open, its spine against his, a rather cozy arrangement, and he turns around thinking Louise might be behind this unexpected sensation. No. Oh, for Christ's sake. It's Jerome Limb, the cop, and apparent confidante of Alfred Beel, who is laughing now and shouting, his voice like a large fly trapped inside a phone line, "Are you busted, Drury? How does it feel? How does it feel you little bastard?"

Constable Limb takes the receiver. "I'll take care of this, Alfred. Yeah. Yeah. Enjoy your day now."

Now there is a fly, buzzing angrily behind the collapsible door, and Adrian guides and shoos it out. Chances are it would lay eggs on the receiver and the mouthpiece, drop them inside those little holes thinking they'll be safe in there. Next thing you know, maggots are forming.

Limb is talking: "You might want to stay away from the pay phone. Otherwise I'm going to have to talk to your dad and I don't think he'd be impressed, would he?"

Adrian is unfazed by the authority of Constable Limb. They grew up next door to one another; his sister Rose, spying on the Limbs' backyard, once saw Jerome taking a syn-

*chronous shit with the family dog. It was a big joke, munici-
pal in size, all over town.*

"Did you hear what I just said?" Limb asked.

*"Yes I did, and yes you're right. He wouldn't be im-
pressed." There's no point arguing with the uniform.*

"Good. We see eye-to-eye on that."

"I guess so."

*Jerome lights a smoke. "You want a ride to school in the
cruiser?"*

"Sure. I'm kinda late now."

*"I'm not surprised. Well, it's down the block here," Limb
says, pointing toward the Lutheran church. "Say, did you hear
about the catfish out in Minnow Lake? Beel told me this.
The lake's still half frozen so it must have gone a little haywire from the delay in melting. I don't know what catfishes
think but anyway, it came up to the shore where the ice is out
and jumped right onto the land. Beel was standing there, having a smoke. He thinks it was after him, wanted to take a
bite out of him, misjudged his size, maybe thought he was a
rabbit or something. They'll do that you know, come right out
onto the shore and flop their way back. Beel just stands there,
lets it flop its way back to the lake. Ugliest thing he ever saw,
he says. Did you hear about it?"*

"No," Adrian says, "I haven't been out there for a while."

Alfred Beel had one worry that was beginning to
worry him, and this, while in the company of Mrs. Ila
Van Epp, mother of Anastasia and also Laura, gave
him a case of the jitters. They had a tricky relationship,

he and Ila. Since he'd seen her after the election, at her absolute worst, she'd made it her business to read his mind. She was pretty sure there was at least one story in there worth hearing, one tale of woe to settle the score. And maybe there was but what business was it of hers, especially when he, himself, wasn't certain what the worry was. Maybe he was just stewing. Who wouldn't in this weather? It was a summer designed for stewing in your own juices.

That morning Alfred was at the Van Epp farm, finishing off a deck he'd made for Ila. She wasn't single, naturally, she was married to Peter, a dairy farmer with no time for deck building and little appreciation for the effort and craftsmanship involved. Ila did, however, have time to appreciate, and she paid attention, too much attention. Today, she had set up her sewing machine in the kitchen, just beyond the open sliding glass door, so she could talk to Alfred while he worked, so she could see him and he, her. More of a bargain for her, Alfred would tell you, because, despite his melted chest, he's been told—once, by Loretta Decker when she was drunk—he looks a little like John Wayne, around the eyes. Whereas Ila, because she wears those round glasses and turbans almost every day of the year, Ila looks like an accountant from India, one that's too interested, one that presses for details.

"Well, Alfred, anything new with you?"

Alfred didn't always have the strength for Ila. Only ten in the morning and the humidity was like strained soup hanging in the air. The two big maples in the Van Epps' backyard would have dropped their leaves just to get a bit of breeze on their old limbs and King, the round and woolly dog people called Satan, lay motionless in the relative shade. Once again, as was usual that summer, there was nothing but white overhead, a white that seemed more worn oilcloth than cloud, hanging low, warm and wet with the effects of yesterday's steaming bowls of green beans and new mashed potatoes, corn on the cob no one wanted to eat, much less talk about. And here was Ila asking if anything was new. Yes, Ila, something was new: Cora Farrell, whom Alfred liked to imagine as his girlfriend, was leaving him.

"Not a whole lot," Alfred said, avoiding her gaze, trundling off to the shade to offer King a Milk-Bone he'd brought along for this very purpose. He'd known Ila for too long, for three years, since that summer day she'd come to his door. She was running for a seat in Parliament. He was lonely. They both liked Pierre Trudeau. Simple as that. She talked him into helping her canvas, convinced him she had a good shot at winning. Did it really matter that the Conservative incumbent for Grey-Bruce, Clive Decker, brother of Reg, was married to her cousin, Jean? Possibly, but not probably. That some thought Ila's bid for the seat a little symptomatic of her lack of judgment? Maybe. She had a problem with credit cards and continual redecorating, as if all upholstery and paint and bedroom suites had the life expectancy of a snowman in April. Not to mention decks. She had a mania for the look of things, but so did Alfred. In that respect, they were a good team.

Alfred crouched in the grass next to the sleeping King. "Here boy, here's a treat." King opened one eye as if to say, just set it on the counter, leave it by the phone. "You remember the election, don't you boy?" Alfred said under his breath. "I'm sure you do. That was a bad turn of events." People called it a landslide loss for Ila; she had seriously misread the electorate. "I guess Trudeaumania was no match for Deckermania," Ila said, again and again and again, hoping a reporter might show up to record this quip, followed by someone from Ottawa, a scout, a page, anyone at all. *You're needed in the shadow cabinet, Mrs. Van Epp. Come with me.* Long into the night Alfred watched her watch the entrance to Liberal HQ, that being her own front door, for a future that did not arrive. Alfred would have brought it if he could, he liked her that much then, possibly even loved her. But, he was usually if not always in love with somebody who did not love him back. "Oh the folly of relationships and associations. Right King? You have the right idea. Sleep. Grass. Rejection of Milk-Bones tendered."

The next morning, after the landslide loss, Ila was up at dawn gathering signs from ditches and boulevards. Alfred had just caught up with her when she found the first of several that had been defaced by Adrian Drury and Cassie Limb of all people. For a Just Society, the signs said, vote Swami Van Epp. They had joined the I and the L in Ila and added an S and an MI to spell swami, which never had seemed much of an insult to Alfred but caused Ila to burst into a series of hard, unstoppable sobs, wooden checkers coming up her throat. He couldn't bear it, he wanted to stop her by means of reverse resuscitation, put one hand on her chest, the other on her back and squeeze her into silence. "Stop," he'd said, "stop it right now. I command you."

That was one cold morning for October, the sun nothing but a nasty red hole in the eastern sky, illuminating a day it would have preferred to leave in the dark. "It's not that bad," Alfred went on. "It's just a prank because you like to wear those turbans. It's nothing. Look at the things people say about me."

At least this had got her mind off herself. "Why? What do they say about you? I've never heard anything."

"Well, for example," incredible he had been moved to confess this, unbelievable, to this day the blood drained from one quadrant to the other at the memory. "It has got back to me that I lost more than chest skin in the land mine."

"Meaning what?" Ila asked, round watery eyes behind salt-stained glasses.

Oh for heaven's sake. "You know. You've heard."

She shook her head, perplexed.

"Never mind then, never mind. Let's just say, my sanity. Maybe some people think I'm a little touched."

"They do not," Ila protested, "That's what they think of me. Why else wouldn't they have voted for me?"

"Tradition," he said. "They didn't not vote for you, they voted for Clive because that's what they did last time. Now listen. I'm driving you home. I'll come back for the signs. Go to bed. Stay there until you feel better."

Bad advice. Alfred stood up now, knees creaking. Ila had stayed in bed for two weeks, Alfred feeling increasingly responsible, everyone asking, "Have you heard how Ila is? Does anyone know how Ila is doing?" Why would *he* know how Ila was doing? He wasn't her husband. Open the door a crack and people crowded in with their questions. What did they expect to find out? Finally, *finally*, Peter made her an appointment with Doctor Graham Rochon, psychologist. "Go," he said. "You have to go. I won't have you sulking. Enough." Merciful relief. Ila managed to put the election and the swami insult into perspective. Calm prevailed. Clive Decker asked Ila to lunch, maybe she would consider doing some committee work for him, he liked to think of himself as a Red Tory. End of story, except for this. Ever since that crazy little intimacy, *Let's just say I lost more than chest skin, let's just say I lost my sanity,* Ila expected more. What was this insatiability of people? Could not each individual brain in each individual skull keep its distance?

"Ila," he said, back at the deck, hammer in hand, "I just remembered something interesting. I know that Rose Drury girl is a friend of your daughter's," Alfred said, "but *she's* had to go to Rochon, you know. She was out in East Flax yesterday nosing around for no good reason, so I made a mental note to tell you this. I'm not that fussy about her, truth be told. I see her sometimes at Dr. Drury's when I go. She works for her dad when Loretta can't or won't and, I don't know if you've ever noticed, but she spends an inordinate amount of time looking through the files. She'll let the phone ring off the hook while she's holding somebody's x-rays up to the light. Just checking for decay, checking for some sign of rot. Loretta doesn't do that; it's not part of the job, for heaven's sake. Plus, x-rays should be kept confidential. I don't like that Drury girl."

Ila heaved a sigh. "Alfred, you're very negative you know. It's a sign of age. Nothing good to say about the young people. Also, I suppose it's a symptom of childlessness. People without children are intolerant. I'll have to think of some way to curb this tendency in you." Tendency-curbing was Ila's business.

"Oh really?" Alfred said, brightening. "Does this mean you're offering to bear my child?" knowing immediately his idea of humour was all wrong, too abrupt, almost offensive, probably illegal in some countries. Part of the worry, a symptom of the problem.

"No," Ila said, patiently, as if to a child. "I'm offering to remind you that you were also that age once upon a time and probably, dare I say, less than perfect yourself, *and* that I am quite fond of Rose Drury."

"Then you don't want to hear the Rochon story?"

"That's not what I said. You know I can't resist even though I think it's very indiscreet of you."

"Indiscreet of me? What's indiscreet if the story stops with you? You're the gatekeeper of any indiscretions I commit around here, Ila Van Epp."

"The gatekeeper? Oh please. What's the likelihood of that if the story's already gone from Philip Rochon—

a Reverend, I might add—to you? These things are like chain letters."

"Then it's Philip's fault. He shouldn't be such a bigmouth at the Legion. I divest myself of fault." Alfred opened an aluminum lawn chair and sat down. Time for a break. "Maybe I'll grab myself a drink of water." And he was up again, shimmying past Ila and her sewing machine to the kitchen sink.

"Well, I think it's pretty obviously Graham's fault," Ila half-shouted over her left shoulder. "He should be keeping everything confidential. That's his job. I don't care if Philip is his father."

"Do you want to hear the story or no?" Alfred asked, drips of water falling from his chin. Finally, Ila had focused her attention on the blurred action of the needle, stabbing away in a well-oiled frenzy as if it hated this and all other cloth.

"Yes, yes, I do want to hear the story. You know that." Yes, he did.

Alfred returned and sat himself down, sighing and groaning with old-man pleasure. "Man oh man. This heat. Okay. I'm ready. Firing on all cylinders. So," and he took another sip of water, "as you have divined, the Reverend Rochon is my source. Anyway, it was Rose Drury's father, the dentist, who insisted she go because she was tormenting her younger brother. You know which one he is. Bit of a bad seed. She took it into her head to start calling him Adry-Anne. Instead of his real name which is Adrian. She told him Adry-Anne was what appeared on his birth certificate and it was time he knew the truth. Phone rang for him, she'd call

'Adry-Anne! Phone!' Time for dinner? 'Adry-Anne!' she'd yell out the back door. Finally, he smashed his fist through a pane of glass in the garage and that's when the head-shrink Rochon was called in. He gave her a talk about how they were both suffering some confusion because of the absence of the mother figure but that the brother was obviously suffering more confusion than she was so to leave him alone and worry about her own potential mix-ups.

"So what does she do in response?" Alfred asked, very happy with his story, gleeful, having practically what might be called a story-erection. "Looks right at his crotch. He's too *modern* to have a desk between himself and his patients. She looks at his crotch and then at his eyes and, can you believe this, licks her lips and asks, 'Is that everything?'

"Trouble brewing, the Reverend Rochon says. And he should know. Look at what went on with his girl."

"Oh dear," Ila said, worried now about her own daughter. Birds of a feather, after all.

"Some of the people in Flax," Alfred said, "really are very overdue for a comeuppance."

"Well, I would include the Reverend Rochon in that group of *some*."

"And Alfred Beel, I suppose, too."

"If I included you then I'd have to include myself for encouraging you," Ila said, lifting the sewing machine foot so as to re-position the suffering fabric. "Sometimes I think Anastasia should go to see Rochon. She's got her tendencies, I must say. Though I'm not sure what I'd call them. I guess that's Graham's job. Seems a pity not to make use of the service, now that we have it."

"Well, if you want all of metropolitan Flax and East Flax to know about these tendencies, by all means go ahead and send her. And as far as the service goes, I view it as nothing more than a high-priced landscaping operation. The government pays Graham Rochon to drive his Jaguar up here twice a month to rake up the mess, stuff all the psychological debris and dogshit into big, orange garbage bags, which he leaves in the alleyway behind the Reverend Philip Rochon's house, the easier for him to root through, eat dinner with his old man, then drive back home to London. That's what we're getting for our tax dollars: landscape maintenance for the collective mind. Fortunately there's enough accumulated trash in the heads around here to keep him more than busy. And, as with most beautification projects, there's no *real* benefit but things look good as a result."

"Oh, come on Alfred. There you go with your negativity again. First of all, you like beautification projects even though there is no real benefit and secondly, Graham's helped lots of people. We're lucky to have him. They don't have anyone like that in Mesmer, for example. I'm certainly glad he was here when I went off the rails after the election. Even the self-sufficient Alfred Beel must consider going once in a blue moon, just to mull things over with a third party."

Aha. There she was, fishing for mud. "I do my mulling with myself," Alfred said.

"That's not the same. You don't have any training

in the art of insight."

"You don't need training to have insight. That's a crock. Anyway, it's people like me who blab too much who are the reason Alfred Beel would never wind up in the office of the shrink. Not that there'd be much for him to work with, slim pickings for that doctor." Alfred kept his mind as tidy, as organized, shelved and categorized as his house and tool shed. Anyone, most of all any doctor of psychology, could stroll through at any time of the day or night and find peace, order, and sense. Lids nailed to shelves supporting a hanging taxonomy of bolts and screws, none of them loose.

"Oh, you must have something you'd like to discuss." Ila had left the sewing now, was watching again from behind her small engine. "You can't be entirely worry-free."

She certainly deserved high marks for perseverance. "Well, I am. I'm a psychological marvel, in fact."

"Oh come on. Nobody's that tranquil."

Alfred whistled. From the parched grass, King raised his head an inch or two, dog-hopes in the shape of meat or gravy charging through his central nervous system until the falseness of the alarm became evident. Back to sleep. Still had not condescended to eat the Milk-Bone. Alfred whistled more, a merry non-tune intended to signal important carpentry work ahead.

"I'm going to have to go into town and get some more deck screws."

"Naturally."

Ila's use of the word naturally got under his skin. He stood now at the foot of the new deck stairs and ex-

amined her, coolly he hoped, a little burst of inappro-
priate words taking shape in his marshalled and or-
derly mind. Was he going to speak them? Yes he was,
one spurt, like blood from a major artery. "What do
you think of that phrase, deck screw?"

Ila shook her head and smiled the way he reluc-
tantly knew he liked her to. "I don't think I'll dignify
that question with an answer, as they say. You know, if
you were half as risque as you think you are, you'd be
a danger to society."

"Well, I'm off then. Might as well go to Mesmer.
They're always out of everything in Flax. They can special order it, of course. It'll only be two weeks."

"What did I tell you about negative?"

"I'm off."

He left wearing his carpenter's apron, around to
the front of the house where his white pickup truck
awaited, windows open to allow the invasion of dozens
of houseflies and the sodden air they seemed to find
festive. Onto the pale highway, a little damp like skin,
the colour not much different from his own if he did-
n't start getting out a little more, stop staying in most
evenings hoping Cora Farrell might make an appearance. Which was wacky, he knew, so as far as any
shrink might be concerned, and since they were on
that topic, Alfred could admit to harbouring one secret hope *tangential* to Graham Rochon. Quickly now,
the man would be charging by the minute. All right, all
right, yes, fine then. Alfred cleared his throat and sped
up his thoughts. He hoped that one day Cora Farrell
would seek Rochon's counsel, profess her love for Al-

fred, understand, *at last*, it was meant to be, drive in high heels and tight blue jeans to his house. Open car door. Walk—click, click, click—(despite driveway being gravel, the sound of heels on pavement) little ass sashaying with desire for a grumpy old man with a belly the size of a double-decker anthill. Embrace the waiting Alfred. This was both a recurring daytime fantasy and a nighttime dream. Not much insight required there.

Although, if a lull occurred in the conversation, and Dr. Rochon was in truth charging by the hour, and if he could be sworn to secrecy with a contract bound tighter than a World War Two tourniquet, Alfred might allude, with soldierly jocularity, to his one worry, his only worry. He'd pose it as a question in the third person. Do you think, he'd ask, Dr. Rochon, he'd add, that by spending so much time in the Farrells' East Flax store, Alfred Beel had been shelved within a living museum of evolutionary outcasts? The problem wasn't him so much, no not at all, it was the company he kept: two old men, one an effeminate and possibly homosexual, retired music teacher and the other a sexless simpleton. Though some said he, Russell Hansen, like Randy Farrell, possessed sparks of genius. Ha. Alfred Beel would like to notify the bylaw officers of this and every other jurisdiction that genius and stupidity were never close neighbours. Genius, like Alfred, lived at the dead end of a tree-lined concession road whereas stupidity, in the form of Russell Hansen, lived in a poorly insulated, badly constructed house on the main thoroughfare of East Flax. Place lost so much heat in the winter, icicles hung like javelins from the eaves to the ground.

The Maestro was undoubtedly a pansy but you had to give him credit: despite the community talk, he'd apparently hewn for himself a pleasurable, a dignified existence, whereas Russell Hansen had none whatsoever, neither pleasure nor dignity nor an existence. Did the man even own a penis? Alfred would admit to wanting to take a look, pull those elastic-waistbanded pants out from that Tweedledee stomach of his and see what might be there. A baby-sized appendage, unchanged since birth? A simple pelt of fur?

These were his peers. Chilling. What do you make of it, Graham, he might have the audacity to ask by the end of his hour, leaving insufficient time for an answer. Were it not for Cora Farrell, he would have long ago made other arrangements. He'd have to soon enough, Alfred would hasten to explain: Cora was leaving for nursing school at the end of August and certainly once she was gone there would be no good reason for spending every afternoon in that museum of obsolete reproductive parts.

Pathetic how he asked daily, "Cora, would you be a good girl and empty this ashtray?" watching her hover close by, bend to manipulate the bowl from the Farrells' old floor model support. Sometimes the proximity of Cora's zipped-up jeans, that cleft of girlness right there behind two layers of fabric, was all it took to make Alfred glad to be alive. Make his pecker glow like a flashlight with a fresh set of batteries. Make him feel a little like the bronze female atop the ashtray, arms extended and ready for flight, a hood ornament for any aircraft leaving Cape Canaveral.

Oh, he didn't really know what this new nervousness was. Even if he wanted to tell Ila or Rochon, he couldn't name it and neither could they. Whatever the cause, sooner or later, every day the same little tickle of fear coughed its way up his spine and into his brain where it blew a little bubble and popped. What on earth was he doing with his life? What if he had actually suffered some brain damage over there and was the only one not to know? That was how brain damage worked, the brain being unable to reflect upon itself with any objectivity. How could Alfred know whether twenty-six years ago some tired army surgeon working on two or three other busted heads at the same time hadn't shoved some tissue into the wrong space? This is going to have to do, he's lucky to be alive, tape this grey matter to that, hook the times tables up with bird calls, and that section, that's the love and marriage lobe, just leave it, this guy's not going to need that. Or was it that guy?

Fifteen minutes later, past fields of Holsteins and ripe barley, through pockets of animal and harvest aroma, here was Mesmer, population 5500. Won't You Stay A Spell? Alfred slowed to thirty and scanned the sidewalks for anyone he might know, someone to wave at and smile and scrutinize. Another small worry: he'd taken recently to watching the faces of others for a sign, that patronizing moment everybody knows, eyes clicking against one another's like guests at some banquet of the unbraindamaged. A toast. As yet, he hadn't collected much evidence, though he knew Cora rolled her eyes. That was to be expected. But what about Ila? She was a more reliable barometer. Was his talk of deck screws a gram or two heavier than Graham Rochon's scale of conversational weights and measures would allow? Was he out on some limb others would have broken years ago or avoided altogether?

Alfred honked twice and waved. There was Mrs. Belfour, owner of the dress shop. He'd built a rumpus room for her and the husband last fall and they loved his work. Sent him a card. Another quick beep and she looked around—who was that? But by then he was half a block gone.

Adrian is beginning to think Randy might have some good ideas. He wasn't necessarily bright—obviously, he was in Resource some of the time with Adrian—but his brain was full, and not just with facts but also with connections other people would never dream up. Like the channel being a television channel and Rose's rusty Vega having craters and the Great Lakes scheming an underground plan, not to mention his enthusiasm for salt and the Upper Paleolithic period, as if it were two months ago. In the mind of Randy Farrell, time was not a normal tick-tock kind of map. Ten thousand years ago could be right around the corner; maybe in East Flax it was. And apparently the future came crawling out of the Tamarack Township dump. That's what Randy said: hence, the arrangements.

At first, the arrangements had seemed a little comical to Adrian, then somewhat eerie—Randy's voodoo hands always fiddling around with stuff better left alone or in a jumble. His bottles of pop in the store—grape, orange, grape, orange, grape, orange—or the dozen licorice pipes in his room, side by symmetrical side in the hickory rack he'd made in wood-working. The animal figures glued in place on his locker shelves. But once you heard his explanation, the arranging made a little sense, maybe a microscopic amount.

Back in the days a year ago, when, except for Adrian's mother's dying, nothing too terrible had happened, Randy explained it to him. They were out on the ski jump, as usual, on a sunny day in July when Randy asked, in his classroom presentation voice, "Did you ever notice the future is more or less like the Tamarack Township dump? It's a big mess of bed-springs and tea bags and who knows what else hidden beneath. Jimmy Junior says he and his dad found a doll-sized skeleton there once in a burlap bag."

"Since when does a doll have a skeleton?" Adrian asked, one of the few stupider things he said in the last decade.

"Doll-sized. Don't you get it?"

"It was probably a cat. In a bag? That's what people do with cats. The cat's in the bag. Haven't you ever heard that saying?"

"Yeah, I've heard it but it doesn't make a whole lot of sense to me. You want a gumball?" Randy asked, carefully opening a foil-wrapped pattern of blue, green, blue, green balls. "Take a blue and then I'll have a green."

"What if I take a green?" Adrian asked.

"Then I'll take a blue."

"What if I take two greens?"

"Then I'll take two blues."

Adrian took a blue. It wasn't worth the energy.

"So at night," Randy said, biting into his gumball, "as you probably know, people visit the dump with their flashlights, shining these yellowy circles around looking for something to be scared of. Standing there, going what was that? What was that? Was that a bunch of dead pups or just some old socks? Then they dig a hole and dump in a secret box or two of mess themselves. Then these contents mix up with the others and the sun rises over this big, tangled up situation."

"It doesn't look like a tangled up situation. It looks like trees and houses and the sky," Adrian said. He was keeping his gumball for later. Already the blue was dissolving in his hand.

"But you can't see it. You can't see the future."

"I'll agree with you there, Randolph."

"So," Randy said, still in his school voice, "by way of conclusion, the morning is nothing more than a giant pair of hands trying to get a comb to go through the minutes, breaking off a lot of plastic teeth in the effort of all that. And my feeling is if you can help out the future in any way, organize a few moments for it, get them in place, your efforts aren't wasted. And things might go a little more smoothly for you."

"So what you're saying is that by lining up some gumballs in tinfoil you can control the future," Adrian said, deciding to chew the thing after all.

"Not control it, just smooth it out."

"Like a bunch of guys laying concrete."

"Kind of."

In one quick move, using the full force of his legs, Adrian pushed Randy off the side of the jump. "Did your gumballs see that coming?" he asked, laughing at the sputtering and enraged Randy.

"Go to hell, Drury," Randy shouted, dragging himself back onto the plywood.

"I was just trying to make a point."

"Well, that's not how to make a point," Randy said, almost in tears, Adrian could see, but too late now to be sorry.

"Oh really? Well, I don't actually have time to hear how a point works, except for maybe the one on your head. I have to get home, so let's just go." Why was it again he wasted his time with Randy Farrell? And away they went, silently rowing into one of their longest estrangements, the remainder of the summer.

Back at school last September, 1969, (which Adrian realizes now seemed like a very different decade) except for Richard Decker being dead, it was as if nothing had happened. They both went back to their normal abnormal selves without missing a beat, which spooked Adrian a little. What lining up and pasting and wrapping in foil had Randy done to bring that about? Did he know some special gumball spell for erasing memories and grudges? Adrian decided he would rather not know.

Today is different though, much, much different. First of all it's a cold, endless May and Adrian can hardly remember his or Randy's normal abnormal self. And second, this time it is Adrian who needs to make some arrangements and this means a phone call to Randy. Conditions are as good as they can be. The dentist is out; there's no one around to eavesdrop. Just dial the phone. It's only Randy. What can he say besides get lost? If his mother answers, that's a little worse, and with Frog, Adrian gets that feeling of memory poison Anastasia invented, shuddery, weak, even more worse.

But Randy will like being asked for advice, treated like

an oracle or a guidance counsellor and for sure he would have some ideas on how to shape the future. For absolute sure. Even a fraction of an idea or a tiny, geometric wedge because lately, Adrian certainly hadn't been doing very well. Now, along with everything else, he had goddam Limb onto him.

Best not to think too long. Go to the hallway, walk down the pale green, carpeted stairs to the phone and dial. It's not as if Jerome Limb has managed to have all his calls recorded or rerouted to the police station.

Adrian lifts the receiver and dials, holding the last digit for ten, fifteen, twenty seconds before releasing himself, freefalling into the burlap bags of the Tamarack township dump. Half a ring; that was it.

"Hello."

Oh no. It's Angel. "Hi. I was wondering if I could speak to Randy."

"Is this who I think it is?"

"Yeah. It's Adrian." Business like. No worries here.

"Well, Randy's indisposed right now."

This is what she said last time. "But it's about a school project."

Pause. Sigh. "Uh huh." Very sarcastic. "Well, I'll tell him it's you. Hold on."

The receiver clunks down hard. Adrian can see it on that shelf in the window in the wall where they hand the phone between the store and the house. A Frog Farrell innovation. Adrian hears nothing. Nobody in the store, nobody watching television. Frog's out cleaning probably, Randy's in his room, and Angel was likely interrupted by the call, interrupted in her routine of slamming pots and pans around.

"Hello."

It's actually Randy. "Hi. How are you doing?"

"I'm okay." *He's eating, taking a bite of something chewy. Sounds like red licorice, softer than the black kind.* "What do you want?"

Adrian has to talk fast in case Randy decides to hang up. "I need some advice from you. About the future. You know what you used to say about organizing things to help out the future? Well, I want to organize things so I can get Alfred Beel, in the near future."

"Too late. I don't believe in that stuff any more."

"What do you mean? What do you mean you don't believe in it?"

"Just what I said. Except for hockey outcomes, I don't believe in it."

Now there are pots and pans in the background. Water coming on.

"Well, if you did still believe in it, or if Beel was some kind of unusual hockey team, what would you put in place to make sure he lost?"

"I don't know. I really don't know." *His voice isn't normal now, it's rising like a kid who's frustrated and might cry.*

"C'mon Randy. We're talking about your sister here. He's the one who started all that talk about ladders and times of death. Even if he did change his tune later, he still started it."

"I know. I know that. Anyway, I gotta go." *Voice box quavering like weak elastic bands.* "See you at school." *And the line goes dead.*

There was a thunderstorm rolling in from Lake Huron. The western sky was dark as windows when you're outside, with sheet lightning flashing up and down the horizon, and Cheryl Decker thought, it's a little like a haunted house on the move, back and forth and closer and closer. And this was evidence she'd been spending too much time with Adrian Drury because that was exactly what he would have thought, not her. He would think a storm was a house full of haunted birds flocked against the rafters and floors covered in hard-as-teeth beetles but with electric backsides grafted on from lightning bugs. He'd think of ways to give the storm a brain, albeit blindfolded, or moving on a track. For Adrian, agents of terror were usually moving on tracks; they couldn't be stopped.

Cheryl was feeling unhappy and all she wanted to do was trace. Here she was on the roof of her parents' back porch tracing a picture of Charles De Gaulle from the cover of *Life*. Tracing was her hobby and had been since the age of seven. Now she was fifteen, meaning more than fifty per cent of her life had involved onion skin paper. Other girls stopped tracing when they were eight or nine, but not Cheryl; she liked tracing for the sake of copying. And besides, if you added a bit, coloured, and gave dimension with shading, tracing could become a cartoon. Someday she might like to draw cartoons for the newspaper, one image with several meanings, detailed cause for thought.

This summer, the gently sloping porch roof had become her cottage. She'd looked down upon it from her bedroom window for years but, unless you were a cat, the angle seemed impossible to jump. Then she'd found a piece of plywood in the garage, taller than she was and maybe eighteen inches wide, that her brother Richard had used as a bike ramp, one end supported by a pile of sawed-off two-by-fours. She wished she had a photograph of him flying over it on his three-speed, crashing down with his bum in the air, boys' knees absorbing the shock the way they do. If she had a picture she could trace it and add in something, *Life*, she thought, looking down at the cover of the magazine.

She'd had the idea to haul the plywood up to her room, past her mother, smoking and electively blind, at the kitchen counter, extend it like a sideways gangplank from her window and slide to this holiday destination. And it was not so different from a cottage on a beach; the multicoloured beads of asphalt embedded themselves like sand in the backs of her thighs and the smell of baking tar could be the flat roof of the french fry stand at Grand Bend. And there might not be as many people to watch, usually just the Coutts twins with their bundle buggies of groceries, alone or in a pair, and Martha Trimble, but there was nature, their two big maples and the Trimbles' chestnut tree and Cheryl's new friends, the birds living in them. There was even a body of water if you counted the Trimbles' round, plastic pool. Martha seemed to like to look at it as if it were a lake; she watched the reflection of the sun and the leaves of the horse chestnut tree that floated on its surface. But no one knew for sure what Martha thought because she had cerebral palsy and never said much more than yes or no and one or two

other words including Pellett, the name of what used
to be Richard's dog but was now, Cheryl guessed, her
dad's dog. Martha gave the impression of wanting to
say more but the effort was exhausting, as if each individual sound might have been an Olympic event. For
Martha to say what she thought of the plastic pool
would have been the decathlon of talking. And that,
too, was something Adrian would have said, not her.
Adrian had been going on about the Olympics since
1968, since before Cheryl really knew him.

Cheryl liked to think Martha Trimble was the best
friend she never had. They'd been in the hospital together, born one day apart, but Mrs. Trimble had trouble, a labour that went on and on while Loretta's had
been too fast. And so the potential best friend of
Cheryl suffered an injury at birth, altering what could
have been. Not that Cheryl didn't like Martha the way
she was, everyone did, even Anastasia Van Epp who
came and took her for walks (though that was for some
kind of credit at school) and Cheryl's own father, Reg.
He liked Martha because Pellett liked Martha and he
liked Pellett; the three of them could have been happy
stuck on a deserted island, a triangle of non-talkers because Reg had *had it* with talk. Talk was nothing but
hot air mixing with hotter air, he said every other day,
especially at this time of year; he was surprised there
weren't more explosions, talk-related explosions.

Martha got put places like a figurine and sometimes, because of Cheryl's sadness, she envied this.
Usually, like today, Martha's back was to Cheryl, positioned that way by her mother who could then look

out from the living room window and make sure
Martha was okay, meaning not choking. She was in her
wheelchair, her white legs knock-kneed out of her
Bermuda-length shorts. You couldn't tell from here,
but her legs weren't shaved and it was hard not to stare
when you were up close, again, much like at the beach
where every once in a while there'd be some woman,
usually speaking an unfamiliar language, who didn't
shave her legs. But if Cheryl was on the porch roof already, Mrs. Trimble would point the chair at her and
say to Martha, "There's Cheryl. Can you wave to
Cheryl?" and help lift her arm. And Cheryl would
wave back causing a jolt of happiness to travel through
Martha's body like a very bad scare. And she would
look up at Cheryl, then at her pool. Who knows?
Maybe Martha thought Cheryl was the best friend she
never had and wished Loretta's uterus had cut off her
oxygen supply and put her in a chair in the Deckers'
backyard. Maybe she thought of them rolling around
Flax together with their out-of-control muscles.

Now Cheryl had Adrian and he could be called a
friend, or a boyfriend, someone to copy or trace,
though much of what they did was furtive. Everyone
knew they were dating, but no one, as far as she could
tell, knew they were having sex. Hard to believe only a
few short months ago she was a virgin and now, since
February 14, she had done it thirty-one times. In
Adrian's garden shed, in Adrian's bed when his dad
was at the Rotary meetings and his sister doing homework with Anastasia, on a tarp at the back of the Van
Epp's property, in a sleeping bag in the middle of a

cornfield. Cheryl liked it, she had to admit. She liked the planning and the preparation and the removal of clothing in unlikely places, liked watching Adrian wrap on the safe and even liked the word: safe. Liked the act itself and derived an odd enjoyment from the ensuing guilt. The thinking: what if everyone knew? The imagining: possibly they all do. The aerial photograph she kept in her mind of the geography of her history, glowing red dots from five thousand feet—and that's where we did it by the creek and that's the garden shed—gave her body a chance to feel like it might occasionally, in the dark, with no one around, be capable of twinkling.

Although these days more likely she would be noticed for a different kind of body, remarkable for its faded, overcast quality and the fact it didn't talk much, which was another reason for liking Martha. If Martha were her friend she could maybe tell her, through telepathy, about Reg and Loretta. Living this close, she wouldn't have to throw the thought waves with very much force. Then Martha would know Reg and Loretta hadn't always been this way. Before Richard's accident, they'd been almost sexy, even Cheryl knew that. They were the type of couple who had the power to make other married, halfway middle-aged people believe they too could be sexy, the kind of people everybody liked. Back then, Reg was always talking. He said people say talk is cheap but it's not; he said talk could be mathematically exchanged for deals, three hours of talk was the equivalent of one Ford Torino, four hours might unload a Lincoln. Playing cards, at Lalonde's restaurant, at the Legion, Reg was always talking and

Loretta was always watching. She noticed everything, the way Reg looked at other women, the way Reg sent drinks to certain couples, the way Reg went on sprees of buying new ties as if needing to impress someone. She mentioned her observations over breakfast and Reg told her she had a suspicious mind. A couple times they had fights and Reg threatened to hit Loretta. Then Richard died and Reg stopped talking and buying ties and making fists and Loretta developed her elective blindness.

Cheryl had asked about it in biology class, this type of blindness, and yes, it was possible Mr. Busby said, it was a case of the nerves just throwing in the towel. No way, everybody said, no way could you just stop seeing with your eyes wide open but Cheryl had the proof at home. Not more than one week after Richard's death she had been coated in her mother's vanishing cream and was more or less invisible except for special occasions, her birthday or would you like white meat or brown, Cheryl? Once in a while, at her most melodramatic, Cheryl was positive her parents would like to kill her just for being alive. She envisioned them, one of them, usually her mother, pulling out the shotgun at dinner and BLAM. More potatoes, Reg? Cheryl enjoyed this image, a symptom of her cartoonist's temperament, she supposed, enjoyed her ability to unfurl scenes of chaos and blood behind her passive, nice face. Thoughts she'd never shared with Adrian, but with his interest in death, they might even be his, copied by her like some overdue homework.

Also like Adrian, Cheryl had been to see Graham

Rochon, twice, at the urging of the vice-principal. Her parents hated the whole business of counsellors and clergymen and people wanting to know your business but when it came to school authorities they were both spineless. "Yes, certainly," her mother had said, hanging up the phone after Mr. Greig's call. "What on earth's been going on at school?"

"Nothing."

"Mr. Greig says you haven't been yourself. Why didn't you say you'd fainted?" This was Loretta in a spring housedress, smoking a menthol cigarette, looking beautiful. Fainting was embarrassing, so was crying at school.

"I don't know. It didn't seem important."

"Well, they seem to think you should see Rochon." And Cheryl had thought that was the end of it until her mom said last March, "The appointment's after school."

"What appointment?"

"You know, with Rochon," her mom had said, looking out the window, ashamed, most likely, of a daughter needing to see a psychologist. Nothing more had been said since.

To her surprise, Cheryl enjoyed her visits to Rochon's office and thought of it as the land of opposites. No matter what she said, he told her the opposite; you feel guilty for being alive, you have a lot of unresolved grief. No, she didn't, not at all. Yes you do. No I don't. She made the mistake of telling him about being shot by her parents and this opened up a gaping moment of silence, longer than Remembrance

Day. Graham Rochon gave off a certain heat when he wanted to hear more, maybe he had some vents inside his ears like little radiators and at those moments Cheryl knew to go no farther. She was well aware of the boundaries of talk, beyond which lay that spongy sensation of betrayal, embarrassed chatter among the internal organs.

Rochon knew everything about her parents anyway—his dad, the Reverend, having had to speak to Reg and Loretta during their troubled times; he knew all about Richard too. Rochon had heard the suspicions of suicide, the opinion that Richard was a jackass just like his dad. A little too hopped up on testosterone. Normal people did not race trains. But the Deckers weren't entirely normal.

Cheryl cancelled her third appointment and that was that. Although to this day there were times she thought of what she could have said, or more likely should have said if she'd wanted to provide Dr. Rochon with some job satisfaction. She would have said that, just like this porch roof, she relied on Adrian Drury to get her out of the Decker household. She would have said that sex with Adrian Drury was her personal salvation because it was the only part of her life unaffected by the smashed Mustang and Richard.

The night of the accident, Nathan Thom had run to the service station and called right away, giving her parents time to beat the ambulance to the tracks and the train's light, still glowing its white tunnel around Richard and the car and the likelihood of death. Like a big flashbulb of a reporter at a crime scene.

"Just stay here, Cheryl," they'd said, when they arrived at the wreck. And she had, because she wasn't supposed to have come along, but they hadn't had the time to fight with her. With the windows rolled down, she heard it all: the ambulance she thought would save him, cars stopping, doors slamming, it's the Decker kid, the Decker kid. Rain for the third day and night in a row. And the sounds from her parents, voices calling Richard, Richard so loud and jagged Cheryl thought for sure they'd have the power to hook any life that was leaving, drag it backwards into crushed lungs and a smashed up heart but no such luck. As it turned out, while the worst thing you could ever imagine was happening to her brother, Cheryl had been sitting in the back seat of a car that still smelled a little like the pizza they'd picked up earlier that night, bits of which would still be in Richard's stomach. Cheryl couldn't remember if she'd thought that then or recently, after the fact, compliments of Adrian.

Something to do with that smell of pizza and rain from outside the car window that night had managed to get stuck inside her. Apparently, where there had once been kidneys and a stomach and bones, there was now a fresh supply of mud, maybe the earth left over from Richard's grave. Cheryl could still see it piled up there, full of rain and gloom and the bewildering fact it was above the grass. And with all that interior mud, even though Cheryl wasn't any bigger on the outside, on the inside she was much heavier. Some days her legs did not seem to have the power to support the dense, hard burden inside her and a new type of concentration was required just to stand and walk, a form of concentration mud might use, were it able to think, murky little half-thoughts with worms for syllables.

Maybe also the type of concentration needed for basketball because, months after the accident, when she'd gone back to school in the fall there'd been one strange paradox: Cheryl was suddenly half-good at basketball. Despite the reluctance of her legs, with the new weight beneath her skin, Cheryl could run faster; she got a place on the junior girls' team. She developed new muscles, pounded up and down the gym floor yelling; she was a team player, a real digger. Cheryl had no idea why. Part of her felt a little like Martha, placed here and there by invisible figures behind her.

Reg and Loretta didn't come to the games. After all the times they'd been to see Richard, they just weren't ready to go back. Cheryl didn't mind, didn't want them there in fact. At the games, she imagined herself the star of a gentle horror movie about a girl capable of vanishing into and rising up from the floorboards. Nobody knew *what* went on in the windowless gym when the lights were out. The horror movie would end, Cheryl liked to think, when the girl got pressed forever between the polished wax and floorboards, replacing the purple falcon at the very centre of the gym. For the credits, nothing but shining lights, cheering spectators.

Oh no. Here was the rain on onion skin paper, dime-sized plops on Charles De Gaulle's hat. And there was Mrs. Trimble running for Martha. "You're going to get wet," she called to Cheryl. And she inch-wormed her way along the plywood and into the worn-out air of her bedroom.

The fan hummed and rotated and circulated the heat and Loretta wondered if her feet might smell. She had her shoes off, reclining in George Drury's dentist's chair. She was having a drink while next to her, on the wheeled stool, sat George, listening and smiling and fiddling with the bottle of gin on his instrument tray. Wednesdays the office closed at noon and it was now after two on one of the hottest afternoons of the summer. Outside the open window, behind and beyond George's wavy, black, pomaded hair, was a day that was ready to call it quits. A day that wanted to get out of its own atmospheric pressure, lie down on a white sheet, and be put to sleep.

Loretta was talking about booze. She'd been drinking too much all last winter and even part of the spring, but she'd cut back now, way back. In fact, this was the first drink she'd had in four days, the sign she had a problem because only someone in love with alcohol would so carefully mark the time between dates. So she'd decided the thing to do was to drink only in certain circumstances, like, for example, the dentist's chair. Then there would be prescribed limits. Gin could still be a friend, but one who happened to live at a business address. "I mean, I'm not going to get up and walk to your office at two in the morning, break down the door, and crawl into this chair so I can pour myself a drink."

"I *could* give you a key, you know. I've been thinking about that lately, as a matter of fact, now that you're going to be here more."

"George, you're missing the point. Only you could miss that kind of point. I don't want a key. A key is precisely what I do not want. That's why your chair is the designated drinking spot." Loretta took a sip and asked, "You've never had a problem with self-control have you George?"

"I wouldn't go that far now. Every once in a while I dip into the gas, just to relax myself." He looked at her sideways. "Are you surprised?"

"To be honest, I think most people know that. Your children talk a little. Not that I don't think they're good kids. And I'm really glad Cheryl and Adrian are seeing each other. It's made a huge difference in Cheryl. She actually smiles once in a while." Then, checking the time, "God," Loretta said, "I should get going. The house is a mess. Just top mine up a little there, will you George?"

"You need a bit more tonic, too. I'll run and get some from the fridge." The office was actually a framed-in and insulated porch that ran the front of the house. George had to exit his office and pass through the waiting room, then enter the living quarters through what used to be the front door, into the vestibule and down the hallway to the kitchen. No trouble if it was for Loretta and Loretta knew that. He'd be back in one second, enough time for a luxurious and faintly sexual stretch in the chair.

She did like working here. Even if she couldn't work in George's office, she might volunteer for the simple pleasure of being surrounded by mirrors and chrome, sterile instruments, the smell of disinfectant and this: the peace that passeth all understanding. Maybe everyone should live in an office. Set up a cot and a hot plate next to the filing cabinet. Domesticity required far too much fuss and bother. Two sets of dishes, always the fear of chips. A freezer full of meat: what if the power goes out? Dish rags smelling of mould: throw them out or boil in bleach? Beds unmade and made only to be unmade again. Old dog with occasional poop wattles, impossible to keep off the sofa. Husband. *Daughter.*

Here was George: "Well, anytime you want a drink, my chair is available, providing the office is closed, of course. I couldn't ask someone like Muriel Cobb to take the suction and go stand by the sink while I pour you a drink."

"Take the suction. That's pretty funny," said Loretta. "Take the suction and get out of town. I'm not exactly sure when it would be appropriate but who cares?" Loretta admired the polished toenails at the end of her feet and laughed. "This is a good arrangement. This is a very good arrangement because this, George Drury, is my refuge. It seems far away from home here, even though it's only about eight blocks, so it's a little like a vacation. And I know you won't let me get carried away and I like that. You always put the gin away after three drinks and one little top up and I appreciate that. And do you know why I appreciate that?" This was it, time for some talk, she needed a smoke, where the hell was her lighter? "I appreciate that because there is nothing in this world more depressing than the sight of a falling down drunk. Being witness to the falling down drunk, George, is not a pleasure as I'm sure you know. And I'm not talking tipsy here, gregarious and friendly like we are. I'm talking, you know—oh *here's* the damn lighter—crazy hostile talk about some twenty-year-old grudge nobody on this planet cares about or, almost worse, *god, I love you. I really, really do love you. I mean it.* That's what I want to be spared...Just one more smoke and a splash of gin and I'm out of here. I have *got* to get home." Loretta shook the lighter and got it going with the third turn of the flint.

"I know exactly what you mean," said George, with uncharacteristic vim. "I was at a wedding reception a couple years ago, nobody you know, the son of a fellow I went to school with, and one of the guests threw up on the table and fell asleep with her head in the pool of vomit. Her husband just left her there, her hair with this congealed mess in it. At the time you can gloss over it but the next day it all seems a lot worse."

"That's because it is a lot worse. People at their worst. It makes you want to give the whole human race a bath, drop them into the middle of the Atlantic so they have nothing on them but nice, pure salt. So they're like the rims of a lovely margarita glass."

"Now there's a thought," said George. "We should have margaritas sometime. I could get Rose to make us up some mix. That would be just the ticket."

"I don't know George. Margaritas are almost too good. No, not almost, they are. But that's fine, that's fine because it leads me to this topic and a confession I would like to make. Oh, it's not really a confession. How can you confess to something everybody already knows? It's more a disclosure. "

Suddenly aware of her teeth and tongue, Loretta reached for one of George's tiny mirrors to study them. In the small, round surface, half an arm's length away, was the reflection of a mouth, one pair of very familiar lips. Well, she *was* in the dentist's office. Give the mouth its due. Put it in charge. Listen as it drags the rest of you along. But first, dab that bit of lipstick from your right incisor.

"Margaritas are what got me into a bit of trouble this past winter when I started going to the Legion a little too often. I thought it would be a nice quiet place to ponder my fate but it turned out to be the opposite. You *have* to drink there; the Legion makes you feel like it's your duty to the war dead to drink. And I thought all they had was draft beer and cheap red wine but as it turned out, they had every kind of mixed drink you could imagine. I'm sure you heard about my episode. The Incident."

"No, I can't say I did," George lied.

"Good answer, George. You can't *say* you did even though you did. Precisely. You can't say you heard about it even though you did hear about it because there isn't a person in Flax who didn't. I guess that's exactly why I want to tell you about it. So you can say you've heard about it." Loretta crossed her ankles. Her legs were tanned and so was the rest of her. George probably knew that about her, knew about her backyard tanning and her two-piece swimsuit.

"Well, simply put, I went too far. It was a very good example of that point between having a good time and falling down drunk, the moment when you should look at yourself, get some distance, as if you're in a movie and say 'that woman really needs to go home now.'

"Needless to say, it's a bit hazy but this much I know. I was at a table next to Alfred Beel but we might as well have been sitting together and we were talking about space exploration, was it necessary to put a man on the moon? Why did they bother? All very serious. Then, as can very often be the case for me, after three or four mixed drinks, I was struck by the heretofore unnoticed beauty of someone, in this case, Alfred Beel." Loretta tapped the end of George's nose with the dental mirror and returned it to the tray.

"So... I *had* to pay him a compliment, which he of course pooh-poohed. I told him he looked a little like John Wayne, around the eyes, maybe the mouth. He said piffle and I said, no, really, Alfred. I insisted. And this became the problem—my insistence. Suddenly, *he* was the handsomest man in the place. Which quite possibly he was, but he wouldn't stop with the modesty and the self-effacing talk and this was as a red flag to the insistent and drunken bull. I had to stand on my chair, George. Have you ever *had* to stand on your chair? I mean, since you were eight or nine?"

"Ummm, well, to reach things," George said, "although I don't think that's what you have in mind right now, is it?"

"You haven't stood on a chair to make a procla-
mation, in other words," Loretta said, taking a sip, con-
serving the final ounces, "haven't stood on a chair in
a public place so as to *proclaim* someone the handsomest man in the tri-county area. The tri-county area.
I made that up at the time. As you are I am sure aware,
nobody uses that expression around here, there is no
tri-county area. But I rambled on about Grey, Bruce
and Huron counties and their county towns like some
geography teacher who's gone missing from the home.

"Part of me was enjoying what I thought was the
Legionnaires' attention while another part of me was
realizing nobody wanted to step forward and put a stop
to me because of who I am: Mrs. Decker, the grieving
Mrs. Decker."

George interrupted; she knew he would. "You
can't blame people for feeling a little awkward."

"I'm not," Loretta said. "I'm just explaining how, I
guess, the process whereby the back of my mind took
over the front of my mind. Realizing no one was going
to stop me, I got the brainwave to introduce their dairy
princess to the Legionnaires, myself of course, Bonnie
Big Udders. I thought this was hilarious. And even
more hilarious, Bonnie Big Udders was going to crown
Alfred the handsomest man in the tri-county area. I
was making a little crown out of cigarette foil when
Keith the bartender, grabs my arm and says 'there's a
phone call.' Well, that got my attention," Loretta
snapped her fingers, "snap, just like that, I'm in a panic
because phone calls at night always remind me of
Richard."

George placed a hand on her shoulder. If she hadn't had the glass still in one hand and a burning cigarette in the other, she might have touched back.

"Mercifully, there was no phone call, just Keith trying to spare himself the agony of watching me. Then Alfred Beel got up and left, and from behind the bar the whole place started to look like through the looking glass or I guess it was actually down the rabbit hole, a bunch of guys with hats and faces like face cards. I got all the details the next day from Reverend Philip Rochon. He summoned me to the manse—a special dispensation. Said, 'I'm not going to spare you any embarrassment, Loretta'." She laughed and George withdrew his hand. "Up to that point, I had forgotten he was even there."

"That was last January, when I quit going to the Legion. Do you ever go there, George?"

"Once in a blue moon. I'd rather go to the Blue Lake Inn, play some golf, have a couple drinks in the bar there." George was stirring his drink with a pick.

"Didn't you just use that a couple of hours ago to poke around in Leo Laine's mouth?" Loretta asked.

Withdrawing the instrument from his drink, George studied it and said, "Now that I think about it, maybe gin should be prescribed for gingivitis, not that Leo Laine has now or ever had gingivitis."

"You're the expert," Loretta said. "But anyway, back to the story, the Legion. You've never made a *speech* there, have you?" Loretta wouldn't give up. "Oh never mind. You see? I'm going on and on about this. Anyway, since that day, I've been pretty good. Reg, by the way, said nothing. Nothing at all. I'm sure he must have heard all about it. How could he not? I think they managed to print the whole story in invisible ink in *The Reminder*. Well, whatever. Water under the bridge. But this," Loretta said, handing George her empty glass, "this Wednesday afternoon business I could grow to like. Maybe just one more tiny drink for the road, or the sidewalk, in this case."

"Not a good idea, I don't think. Especially if you're counting on me to stop you at three and a bit," said George, screwing the lid onto the bottle and rising from his stool.

"See? There you are. You're a good man; you put on the brakes. No. No. No, that's not accurate: You *are* the brakes. If George Drury were a car part, he would be brakes. Whereas Reg, if he were a car part, which he virtually is, he would be the gas pedal, permanently to the mat. He might not look like it but inside, eight thousand rpms of something, all the time, night and day. A very high idle. Vrroom, vrroom. See? And that, my good man, is the sign to leave; the minute I start with the sound effects. Along with the fact you're on your feet and obviously want me to head home. So, George" she said, standing up, working her feet into the white shoes she loved to wear, "perhaps a small whiff of gas next week?"

"I can't see that it would hurt but it would have to be in lieu of gin. Although that may not be in keeping with my reputation as a brake," and taking her arm he guided her through the waiting room, past the reception desk, his very white smock causing Loretta to want to say the single word raiment for some gin-induced reason. But she did not, mindful of the Legion and her inclination to flights of drunken fancy.

"We all have our fraying cables, don't we? Well, toodle-oo, George. See you tomorrow morning."

Outside the door, right away, there was Flax, hotter than the office and humid as a kitchen filled with bubbling canners and sterilized jars. Loretta didn't mind though; she liked the humidity. The resistance on her forehead and arms reminded her she had skin. And living with Reg, it was easy enough to forget. For now, Loretta felt a little happy, real happy not booze happy. Buoyant, even, with a spring in her step. Were it not for the humidity and barometric pressure, gravity might lose some of its grip on her ankles, allow the effortless bounding and hopping of the men on the moon. One problem being, she realized, half a block from home, with moon-sized steps she might overshoot the door, maybe even the entire house. *I meant to come home, Reg. I really did. I'm at the Trimbles now but I'll make another run for it later. If I miss again, I'll be sure to call.*

Since he was eight, Adrian has had an electric train set. Only recently, though, did he realize that what he likes so much about his model train is not the engine or the cars so much as the tracks. Tracks create an undeviating route, which is why, Adrian guesses, he finds them comforting and also a little menacing. All routes, all undeviating routes, not just train tracks. The reason he both envies and fears birds with

their small heads and massive flight plans.

Once, Randy Farrell tried to minimize the genius of birds by saying he'd read that during the Ice Age, the birds' trip south for food wasn't that far, a hop, skip and a jump over a kind of belt of ice in the middle of North America. Once the ice started to retreat, the birds maintained the tradition, each year having to go a little further south until they found themselves flying thousands of miles. By that time, the route was charted into their otherwise empty chromosomes.

Same with some eels he'd also read about that cross the entire Atlantic from Bermuda looking for freshwater food in the rivers and estuaries of Europe. Then when they're done eating, they swim all the way back to Bermuda and die. All because of continental drift. Gradually, inch by inch, the trip got longer and they kept swimming it. Over hundreds of thousands of years, the eels have never learned that by heading west, they might find freshwater food a little closer to home.

"I don't care about eels," Adrian said. "Just birds. And slowly increasing the distance over and past the damn Ice Age makes no difference. They've still got a lot of maps in a very small brain."

"Not much of a map," Randy snorted. "One direction. South. How hard is that?"

"They come back, you know."

Randy said nothing.

"You don't really appreciate birds, Randolph. Like, for example, did you ever stop to think that a bird's eye view is more than a view from the sky? Have you ever had a bird look at you? That is a bird's eye view."

"Well, what is it?" Randy asked.

"I don't know. I'd like to find out. I get the feeling they

can see you and everything behind you, miles and miles of scenery and roads and people doing dumb things, taking the wrong turn. I feel like they can see most of the way to Cape Horn."

Again, Randy had nothing to say.

Adrian had temporarily forgotten but now he remembers: Randy Farrell is one of the dumb people so why look to him for help where an undeviating route was all that was needed. That way, the future had no say in the matter or very little and he, Adrian, had all of the say when it came to a plan for Mr. Alfred Beel.

Adrian opens the fridge and serves himself a bowl of cherry Jell-O before disappearing into the basement. Smells like tree roots down here and laundry but not bad. He sets the bowl on the dryer and plugs in the track. Laundry is Adrian's job and usually, when he's down here waiting for the dryer, he plays with the train. It's a big setup, covering three side by side ping-pong tables, having grown Christmas after Christmas until he was twelve. He has the engine with the operating headlight and smoke, tank cars, grain cars, flat cars with plastic logs, two cabooses, and more. Several Tinkertoy people lie and stand on the green table inside the track, and underneath, Adrian keeps a metal bucket. For some time, the object of the train set has been to knock a Tinkertoy person from the track into the bucket. Easier said than done with only one stretch of track running the very edge of the table, and that section compromised by the papier mâché cliff stretching to the floor; he, Rose, and Anastasia made it one rainy weekend years ago. Once the Tinkertoy man has tumbled off the track, it must strike one of the cliff's several ledges and bounce from there into the bucket. Lucky if it happened one in twenty times.

Adrian decides to push the track to the other side of the table, creating a sheer drop for his victim. This job completed, he returns to the dryer for his Jell-O, hoovering each spoonful into his mouth. Early evening and his dad is in the backyard, pruning and clipping. No need for explanations. Adrian returns the bowl to the kitchen, rinses it, sets it on the draining board, and goes upstairs to Rose's room.

To be in this room without Rose is undeniably spooky. Adrian can see how places become haunted because even though Rose's body is more than a hundred miles away, she is in this room. All of her, her entire past, probably a thousand sleepovers with Anastasia, crying fits from losing figure skating competitions, and the place by the window she used to like to sit on a footstool and watch the Limbs. Rose always liked to watch the Limbs more than she liked television and this was one thing about her Adrian actually loved. This, along with her telling him Cheryl was already sad. Believe me, I know, Cheryl was already sad.

He knew where the dolls were, in the four shoeboxes in Rose's closet, three full of Barbies and shoes and accessories and one with a lonely Ken and a few suits and swim trunks. Ken is more than a little haunted himself, thanks to Anastasia and Jimmy Drake Junior, but Adrian commands himself to put that out of his mind, knowing already the command will be disobeyed. Adrian has learned thoughts cannot be put out of the mind and the more you try, the more they return. Thoughts are like cats or birds. Might as well accept that. Cheryl, Maddy, Anastasia's Ken doll, Alfred Beel and the other Farrells—all are permanently sharing his skull. It's made of bone, after all. Where are they going to escape *from?*

Here's Ken wearing some blue pants with frayed cuffs that are supposed to be jeans. Beel does not wear jeans, ever; he usually wears a beige kind of trousers or else black with a plain white shirt or maybe a pale blue shirt. That should be easy enough, you'd think, and it is. Ken has some black, shiny pants, from a suit no doubt, and a white shirt but it's a little frilly, more something Tom Jones would wear than Alfred Beel. But that's all right. Maybe no shirt would be better. Best, in fact.

They say Beel is all scarred up so Adrian carries Ken down the hall to his room, finds the jackknife in his desk drawer and carves some flesh wounds in the chest. Then turns him over and with a ballpoint pen, writes BEEL. Adrian knows the correct spelling from the phone book.

Back in the basement, Adrian places Beel perpendicular to the path of the train, legs stretched out above the abyss, head and shoulders on the ping-pong surface and whittled torso perilously asleep on the track. He positions the empty bucket about twelve inches past the point of impact between engine and doll, taking into account this, that, and the other thing, velocity, inertia, gravity—forces Rose and Anastasia would recognize as pertaining to physics but what Adrian considers to be the laws of doom.

The train is on the other side of the track, beyond the first curve, before the papier mâché cliff. He'll keep it slow at first, then accelerate for the collision. If Beel lands in the bucket, that means full speed ahead with a plan. If not, let it go. Pay attention in school. Wait for Randy to turn around and speak. Try to be normal.

The entire process takes less than thirty seconds. Round

*this end of the oval and into the straightaway, where engine
and Beel connect, Beel tipping off the track a little sluggishly,
very undramatically, and with insufficient hoist. In descent,
the back of Beel's neck strikes the metal lip of the bucket,
pitching him forward and onto the floor. An ambiguous message.*

*Adrian stops the train and admits this is an unintelli-
gent way to make a decision. Picking up the Ken doll, shoving the bucket beneath the table, Adrian concludes: just
because I'm in Resource doesn't mean I have to act like it.
What's to plan? He doesn't need a plan. He'll make a trip
to East Flax and deal with the old fart.*

Since Rose's session with Graham Rochon, she
had tried in her way to nurture Adrian's maleness, not
wishing to incite more window-smashings or any of the
dire outcomes predicted by the psychologist with his
unblinking eyes. No trouble at all to drive her brother
to Mesmer to buy condoms. Adrian wouldn't be sixteen until September and there was no way he was prepared to make intimate purchases at the Flax Pharmacy
from Bill Laine, the pharmacist, or his wife, Cornelia,
or worse, their son Leo, purveyor of diet pills, friend of
girls, stranger to confidentiality. Best to keep Flax's
nose out of your business. And the trip had preten-
sions of evil to it, unlike other benign drives to Mesmer. On these condom runs, Rose and the Vega passed
through a type of atmospheric membrane that
stretched and broke, much like a hymen would, alter-

ing everything. Especially on days like this, heavy with humidity and bloated as if the very sky itself might be about to have a menstrual period, all moisture contained about twenty feet from the earth's surface. No relief from the hovering womb.

They had just left the town limits when Rose asked, "Would you say that you're in love with Cheryl Decker?"

"For now," Adrian said, then leaned his head out the open window. His hair, almost shoulder-length, was still wet from the shower.

"Well, would you marry her?"

"What?" Adrian yanked his head inside, shook his hair back and said, "I'm not even sixteen. And Laura Van Epp is the only person in Flax I would ever consider marrying. By the time I'm in grade twelve, I'll be going out with her. It's my genetic destiny. But don't get me wrong. I like Cheryl Decker a lot. It's just that someday I'll take a kind of predestined turn. I'll be walking along in one direction when some invisible muddy hands will rise up from the earth and just twist my ankles in another direction."

"And you will have no say in it?"

"Well, do you honestly think you had any say in your two dates with Foster Limb? Or the fact that Anastasia is your best friend? Did you decide those events?"

"Yes, actually, I did."

"Well, no, actually you didn't. But I don't want to argue about it and antagonize my driver so let's just leave it. The way it works is I like Cheryl Decker right now almost as much as I'll like Laura Van Epp a couple of years from now, if you know what I mean."

"Not really, to be honest."

"I didn't expect you to."

"I'm not surprised, though, as you know." Rose worked hard at being unsurprised. Nothing Adrian or any other resident of the town of Flax might think or say or do would ever take her off guard. This was her pledge. Rose was a living watchtower, all-seeing, ever-prepared. Once in a while, a moment of vertigo might be brought on by Anastasia and her abrupt and sometimes cruel observations but then, simple enough to regain equilibrium. Look straight ahead. Contemplate the visual field of the giantess. Here we have treetops, over there, chimneys. Should Anastasia one day decide to focus her telescopic eyes more closely and menacingly on Rose, she would just find ladders with extensions and start climbing. Anastasia did possess the power to keep Rose a little anxious, but that too was not surprising. And with Anastasia's power in mind, Rose asked the question she'd been pondering since reversing out the driveway, since watching herself inch along Huron Drive behind Jerome's cruiser like someone in a cortege, since accelerating the minute he turned down a side street.

"Adrian," she shouted. His head was out the window again.

"Yeah?"

"What do you think of Maddy Farrell?" And, that's a warm question, she could hear Anastasia say, a very warm question, Anastasia's term for any inquiry left sitting a while inside the body, digesting itself with pleasure and mild terror.

"Nothing. I think nothing of Maddy Farrell," came Adrian's disappointing response, "other than she kinda looks like a guy."

Rose couldn't argue that. "Maybe a little," she said, "but so what? It's not as if there aren't guys who look like girls."

"I didn't say there weren't."

"But you implied it with your tone of voice. If you put a dress and a wig on Leo Laine, he'd look like a girl. Anastasia drew some hair around his picture in last year's yearbook. You should see how much he looks like Patty Duke."

"But that's dressing up and drawing in hair. Maddy Farrell is not dressing up and she has girl hair. When she's playing basketball with her hair tied back, she looks like a stretched out version of Prince Charles."

"Oh she does not. And anyway, what's so wrong about looking like a guy? Who decides what a guy looks like anyway, and what a girl looks like? The makeup industry, that's who. Backed up by the military-industrial complex."

"Oh, you and your military industrial complex. Guys look like guys because they look like guys. They're born that way. Even little kids with the same hair and clothes, you can tell the difference because girls are cuter. That's not any makeup industry."

"Ok, fine, end of discussion. I need to focus on the road."

Adrian hung his head out the window one more time while Rose pushed the radio buttons past weather, news, accordions, then off. She had another question. "Adrian!"

"How do you expect my hair to get dry at this rate?"

"Do you think it's true what they say about the Farrells having a trapline and eating trapped meat? Have you ever seen any signs of that when you're out in East Flax like skins or pelts or...?"

"I saw a fish head once in their yard but their yard hooks right onto Minnow Lake so it could have jumped up on the grass and died. Other than that, I can't say what wild animals they eat because they never invite me to stay for dinner. They give me ice cream sandwiches once in a while. Oh, Randy did bring a rabbit's foot once to school and also a rabbit sandwich in his lunch so I guess they eat rabbits just like that woman in Toronto who freaked you out into not eating for a whole weekend."

"That was just one twenty-four hour period and never mind."

Now Adrian turned on the radio: Johnny Cash, commodity prices, heat wave news.

"Why can't we get CKLW?" Rose wondered out loud.

"I don't know. Too many aphids and bugs and barometric pressure."

"Speaking of which, did you hear what the temperature was yesterday? Ninety-eight degrees Fahrenheit."

"Uh huh."

"Don't you get it? Ninety-eight degrees—probably actually ninety-eight point six. It was the same temperature outside as it was inside. I was so glad I didn't have to help dad while he was doing a filling for Muriel Cobb, so very, very glad it was Loretta Decker's job and not mine. Hearing that on the radio yesterday, I was so happy to be away from teeth and mouths for the rest of the summer, because if it stays at ninety-eight point six degrees for much longer it's going to be like not only are we living in Flax, *Flax* is living inside somebody's clamped shut mouth. Somebody like Muriel Cobb."

"Does it have to be Muriel Cobb's mouth we're in?"

"Not necessarily, but you know what I mean. We're trapped inside a Flax mouth with one or two cavities and no ventilation. That's this summer in a nutshell."

"Now, now, as Dad would say. It's not that bad in Flax. It could be worse; you could live in East Flax," Adrian said.

Rose hesitated, then said, "I've decided I kind of like East Flax. Maybe because it's at a different elevation. You know how they have elevation maps in different colours? I think if you got a detailed map of Ontario, East Flax would be a different colour. Mint green maybe. Cool and refreshing."

"Or feces brown perhaps."

"Will you stop saying feces? I hate that word. Say what you want but stop saying f-e-c-e-s. Anyway, it's cooler in East Flax and that's what I like about it. Heat rises so it's below the heat belt or whatever you want to call it. Haven't you noticed that when you're out there with Randy Farrell, lounging on the ski jump?"

MARION DOUGLAS — 115

"I don't pay attention to the temperature. Randy Farrell takes up all my spare energy. Talking to him is like talking to an alien. That's why I like him and that's why I don't like him. His brain is like a Frankenstein Certs project or something: two, two, two brains in one. Except one is smart and the other can only think of one thing at a time. Plus, he *always* has those licorice pipes, the ones he likes to bring to Resource. Last year, he'd bring those pipes to school and hand them out when Mr. Dreyfuss was out of the room so there we'd all be with a pipe in our hands or our mouths, smoking like intellectuals. Ha ha. Intellectuals in Resource. I had to hand it to Randy for that. Except for once you encourage him, then he has those pipes all the time. He'll give me five and look at me like I'm supposed to sign him on to the Maple Leafs. Plus having licorice pipes all the time means having licorice on your teeth all the time."

Rose wasn't listening. "They're related, you know," she said.

"Who?"

"Muriel Cobb and the Farrells. Muriel Cobb and Angel Farrell are sisters."

"They are?"

"Didn't you know that?"

"Wow. How different could two sisters be? Although, look at Maddy and Cora. But Muriel Cobb and Angel Farrell? One's almost a prostitute and the other one is a big spinster who probably never screws anyone, except maybe her customers."

"That's not true. Everybody says she's a good

lawyer; she doesn't rip people off."

"Yeah, I know," Adrian said. "I just said that to make a joke about screwing. It's almost compulsory to make a joke every time you use the word screw."

"Well, har har. Anyway, look at us. We're siblings and we're pretty different."

"So you think I'm almost a prostitute?" Adrian asked.

"Oh shut up, will you? And Angel Farrell is not almost a prostitute."

"Everybody says she whores around a lot."

"Everybody says. And everybody says you're a nitwit. Does that make it true?"

"Oh thanks a lot, Sis. Thanks for reminding me. Thanks for reminding me that the holidays are almost over and soon I'll be back in the special education stream with all the other l.d.'s and retards like Randy Farrell. Thanks. Maybe I'll go home and smash my hand through a window."

Whenever Rose wanted to scream at her brother, she pictured herself on an extension ladder, higher and higher, oak leaves, acorns, blue bottomless sky.

"Okay, okay. Sorry."

Entering Mesmer. "Hope you stay a spell," they said in unison.

"How many are you buying this time?"

"The usual. Three at Fehr's and three at Diamond Drugs." Adrian's face was as see-through as a windshield. Bad enough for him the pharmacists in Mesmer would know he was having sex, but for them to know how much—they could respect and forgive caution but not piggery. Hence the two stores, which regrettably doubled the number of cash register transactions, line ups, chance encounters with patients who had just that afternoon seen his old man. Smiling, nodding while the gears of time ground in Adrian's middle ear. Rose had offered to buy them for him but he said no, it built character.

"Why do you suddenly have East Flax on the brain anyway?" Adrian wanted to know.

"It's my new vacation destination."

"Oh yeah. East Flax. The Riviera of southwestern Ontario."

"Why not?" Rose found a parking spot in front of Diamond Drugs. "Here we are," she said, turning off the engine. "Are you mad at me about the nitwit comment?"

"No. You drive me around, don't you?"

"Yes I do."

"I'm not going to smash any windows, if that's what you're worried about."

"I know...well, go then. Go."

"All right already, I'm gone."

Thank god. Adrian made her want to cry and scream and laugh all at the same time, reduced her to a pathetic triangle of emotions drawn by Miss Clevitt in health class to make a point. Hoping not to be seen, Rose slumped down in the sticky, vinyl seat. Windows open, air resisting the trip to the lungs, *we're already too hot*, the molecules were thinking, bracing themselves against sweaty nose hairs. And speaking of sweat and nose hairs, why had Adrian forced her to think about

Foster Limb? Last June, she'd had a total of two and no more dates with him before he went off to BC to plant trees. The dates were enjoyable enough, more or less like going to a movie with an older and more polite version of Adrian. Which was the problem. She'd lived next door to the Limbs her entire life, which made Mrs. Limb a surrogate mother, and Foster, a ... foster brother. That's what she told him, trying to make a joke of it.

Then, as a kind of third date, she'd seen him masturbating. From her bedroom window, Rose could see into Foster's room and for reasons best known to himself, not long after the second date, he chose to lie down in the lamplight and masturbate. Shake his dick like a soda can when you're planning to send carbonated water sky high.

Foster wasn't coming back after the tree-planting; he was staying out west, maybe going to school, the reason her dad bought the Vega from him. "Something for Rose to tool around in." She knew she was being squeamish, Flaxian to the core as Anastasia would say, but from time to time she couldn't not wonder: how often did Foster wash his hands? Was the steering wheel coated in sperm?

To entertain herself now, Rose examined the hot plastic wheel. In these conditions you'd think spermatozoa would be melting off, falling like dead sea monkeys onto her bare knees.

Nothing visible. Up that close, everything blurred. Never mind. Better to be far-sighted and Rose sat back, closed her eyes and wondered: if she climbed the Mesmer water tower, would she be able to see East Flax? Would the Farrells' traplines catch the sunlight and be visible as extra long zippers on the surface of the earth?

A new day in the Drury house. Even though it was still the middle of the month, George was getting Rose and Adrian up earlier these days, resetting their biological clocks for school, and Adrian was complaining. "There's no real point to this, Dad. I'm going back to bed the minute you're busy with your first patient," he said. "The first week of school is for resetting your biological clock because you've got nothing better to do than stare at the real clock, the one that ticks..."

Rose, preoccupied, above all this, interrupted to ask, "Why is it we never go away? Why is it again we never go on vacation? We didn't even go to Expo. You can't use the excuse that you're a dad on your own because even Jimmy Drake and his dad went on vacation this year. And to Expo in sixty-seven."

"Great example, Rose," Adrian said. "He's hardly even a dad. In fact, if somebody from the Children's Aid Society showed up today to give Jimmy Drake Senior a pop quiz on fatherhood, I doubt very much he'd pass."

"Vacations take a lot of organization," George answered, setting down his toast, rubbing fingers and thumb against one another, the sign of an impending breakfast pronouncement. "You can't just wake up and take off. And you know it's very difficult to close the practice. There's always somebody with an abscess, not to mention the money angle. As you know, I'm trying to build up enough savings for both of you to go to university, and yes, Adrian, that includes you."

"No doubt. I'm sure they're already awaiting my application at the University of Slow Learners. They're used to waiting there."

"Oh, stop it, Adrian. By the way, I want you to put that stain on the deck today and this is the last time I'm asking." George was pointing a buttery knife for emphasis.

"Well, still," Rose had been waiting to say, "you have to give Jimmy Drake Senior some credit for actually having the wherewithal to..."

"Okay," George said, standing, rinsing his plate, beginning his defence now in earnest. "I have nothing against Jimmy Drake Senior, but if you want to throw money away, money you don't in fact have, if you want to buy now and pay later, and, worst of all, if you want to be wearing dentures by the time you're forty-five, then by all means jump into a car right now, on impulse, and drive thousands of miles to see an electric chair. That's my advice," he concluded, grabbing the very white dentist's smock from the back of his chair and buttoning it huffily. "You two really are quite spoiled; you expect too much," he said on his way out of the room, stomping in the manner of an angry dentist.

Adrian interpreted. "Rose, you still don't get it. For George Drury to take a vacation, for him to even consider closing the practice, he would need, first, a galaxy-wide stoppage of time, and second, access to a surplus

of days set aside in a vault, two spare weeks accumulated, like a bank account, for the exclusive use of the
Drurys. And on top of that, everyone else who might
get an abscess would need to be in a state of suspended
animation."

"I guess I forgot for a minute there; we Drury off-
spring must create our own vacations." Rose took one
last mouthful of cereal and said, "So therefore, I'm
going to East Flax again today; I'm taking the bike."

"You know, you don't really like vacations anyway,"
Adrian had to say. "Remember when you went to
Toronto with Cornelia Laine and you freaked out and
wouldn't eat."

"Adrian, you just mentioned that a couple days ago
and now you're saying it again. Enough already." Rose
didn't like to be reminded, many many times had
wished Leo Laine would get to work on that memory
tablet he kept talking about, the truffle-pig pill he
hoped to invent, chemically designed to root out your
worst memories and devour them. Just swallow and
wait to forget. Although, what she really wanted to forget was that nothing much had happened; she'd simply been away, gone for two days and one night with
Cornelia, the pharmacist's wife, and Muriel Cobb, bar-
rister-at-law and sister to Angel Farrell. A cultural getaway, Cornelia and Muriel called it. They planned one
every year and thought it would be good for her. Mu-
seums, theatre, and shopping.

Couldn't she bring along Anastasia?

No.

To this junket, George Drury had given his bless-

ing. "By all means, have a good time. I'll give you some
cash," he said, digging into his faded, fat wallet. He was
doing Rose's girlhood a favour.

At first, all was well, Muriel driving, Cornelia's big,
flat face offering up egg sandwiches from the front seat,
a thermos filled with iced tea, talk of who was and was
not still teaching at Flax Composite. All was well, if
somewhat strained and frankly phony. There *must* have
been signs she missed, some reference to growing older
and more female, but it wasn't until they reached the
lingerie floor of The Bay department store that Rose
understood: from the beginning of this trip, full-busted
womanhood had been the destination. *We thought you*
might like to buy some brassieres.

We? Who's we? Someone—her father? the Rotari-
ans' wives?—had plotted against her and this knowledge
made her head spin and then bulge to the size of a
horse's. Like Anastasia's pony Marmalade the time the
car backfired at the Mesmer parade, Rose got spooked.
She wanted to run. Nothing looked familiar, especially
human faces, especially those of Muriel and Cornelia.
They might have been poppable balloons or oversized
lollipops, the kind you win but never want, which was
why she couldn't eat, she had told Adrian, wanting
him to hear about the spooking part, the compulsory
brassieres, the way she'd grown a horse head.

And furthermore, Rose had not needed or wanted
new bras, she'd been doing just fine with Sharon
Limb's castoffs and, as for underwear, she was happy
with the worn out things she'd had for more than two
years, supplemented with the occasional pair Anastasia

threw her way. She'd rather have done without underwear, truth be told, she'd rather have lived with a naked ass than enter a change room with Muriel Cobb but, in the end, she left with six brassieres and ten pair of underpants, all paid for, inexplicably, by Cornelia Laine.

After that, she couldn't eat. A horse is a vegetarian, and marinating in the fridge of Muriel's lawyer friend were two spindly, skinned rabbits. Even in death and sprinkled with herbs, they looked terrified. Rose told her hostess she wanted oats, oatmeal would be fine, and she wasn't feeling well, maybe she would eat in her room. She was sorry and so were they. Being the pharmacist's wife, Cornelia delivered the oatmeal and touched the back of her hand to Rose's horse forehead. Too much excitement for our small town girl, was the diagnosis, after which Rose had lain awake all night and in the morning been packed and ready to leave by six. Got up and sat by herself, looking lovingly at the telephone, knowing it could connect her to her dad and Adrian, even Skokie if need be. Pulled on the cord when no one was looking to make sure it wasn't a prop, it was connected to the telephone exchange and had wanted to cry at the thought of that homey phrase: telephone exchange.

And the worst? Rose *had* actually cried when Muriel asked if she wanted to stay at the rabbit marinator's house while they went off to some brunch affair and matinee; she'd become hysterical, in truth, cried like a horse would, if it could, after centuries of being spurred on and whipped into cantering in parades. No, she needed to go now, she'd go on the bus, the bus went right through Flax, it would be no problem.

They wouldn't hear of it. They'd have to take her home. There was no way around it. She was a sensitive girl.

The hostess, the cooker of rabbits, her name was Astrid, hated Rose. This was obvious from the way she'd asked: "You wouldn't be content to lie down while we go out for a few hours?" *You wouldn't be content? You wouldn't be content because you are apparently a malcontent, a whining crybaby, and an ingrate. Look at all the free undergarments you have received. No, you would never be content.*

Yes, Astrid had openly detested Rose and she'd made no concessions and that was something worth remembering for the girl whom everyone liked and excused, a memory to be spared Leo Laine's pink amnesia pill. As for Muriel and Cornelia, they were understanding, forgiving and empathic. "We'd better take her home," Muriel said to Astrid. "She's had nothing to eat but oatmeal."

"I actually did eat while I was there," Rose corrected Adrian now. "I just didn't want to eat the marinated rabbit."

"I told you the Farrells eat rabbit. Randy brought a rabbit sandwich to school once."

"I *know*. That's different," Rose said, "and anyway, I'm leaving now."

"How's it different?" she heard Adrian ask as she went upstairs to brush her teeth. She'd wear what she was wearing, denim shorts and a white, sleeveless shirt, the flip-flop sandals, conscious of being a fashion example to Maddy.

Outside, Rose checked her watch. Nine forty-five. She didn't want to be too early so this was perfect. The store would have opened at nine. She'd take her time, the weather was better, today the air was chilly. Some uncorking to the east had apparently permitted the stockpiled weight of too much weather to slosh out to the ocean, allowing this new, thin temperature. Two weeks of holidays left, but the scent of fall was somewhere, a little beyond the scope of the human nose but other life forms were no doubt getting the drift. Horses and ponies, the unpleasant Marmalade, for example.

Maybe Adrian was right; she didn't like vacations. The trip to Toronto was more than two years ago and indeed, Rose had not been away overnight since, except to Anastasia's. Well, so what? Was a love of other places compulsory? Did not most people complain about other places: the food, the humidity, the customs? She was picking up speed now at the edge of town, pedalling fast down the first grade.

And what would she do on a real vacation at, say, Green Gables, anyway? It was nothing more than an empty house. Visiting the Limbs would be more exotic, even the Van Epps, most certainly the Farrells. Yes, this made more sense: the bicycle trip to East Flax had been the first day of her first *real* vacation and this was the logical time to return. East Flax was a resort after all, or an ex-resort, but so much the better. You didn't want the place crawling with day trippers.

Cooler now, she was already changing altitude. You

see? It *was* a different climatic zone. The trees for example, closer to East Flax there were more and they were tremblier. Poplars and aspens. And they seemed to be dropping their chlorophyll into the air, something like gum, resin, and sap and breath fresheners. Then up the little rise and past Dance Hall Road and into the zone of empty fields of yellow stubble and no trees on either side.

Rose wondered: did Maddy know the term deciduous as it applied to teeth? She would know the tree connection for sure but not likely the baby teeth business. Deciduous teeth fall out. They were nothing more than little white leaves in the mouth. Rose loved sharing information, but "Did you know?" could be insensitive, especially to someone like Maddy who came from a place like East Flax. Although it was always possible Maddy would lie and say, "Oh yes, I knew that, everybody knows that." Rose herself occasionally said things like that.

There was the lake. Rose rode down to the boat launch and gazed across at the ski jump. Today the water was all cold little ripples, mud puddle grey but that was how she liked it, she decided. This time she'd brought money for the store, one dollar, and would buy a ginger ale, maybe two she was so thirsty. Back on the road, Rose observed, not unkindly, that even on a cool and cloudy day, East Flax left a layer of dust on your palate and trachea. She knew all the parts, having studied so many posters in her father's office, everything red and blue and purple like pictures of Jesus from several centuries ago. And yet having to do with

room. Would it have boy wallpaper? "Maybe I'll use the bathroom," Rose said. "I'll be right back."

"Okay. That's okay. I have to get back to the store. Just promise me you won't go into Maddy's room. When she has her sign up that means she wet the bed last night so it'll smell like pee in there. She'd be embarrassed." Now Cora was a nurse in her underwear, objective and no nonsense where matters of the body are concerned.

"Oh, no, I wouldn't dream of it. I'll just use the bathroom and head home. Maybe I'll see Maddy next time. Or probably back at school. God, that's less than two weeks away."

"Well, whatever. Not for me. No more Flax Composite High School for Cora Farrell." And she was down the stairs, thump thump thump. And another set of thumps.

Rose stood at the top of the wooden stairs. *Maddy peed the bed?* This wasn't possible. Cora was obviously jealous, saying this to divert attention away from Maddy to its rightful object, the school queen. Maybe she'd just peek inside the room, no harm done, but the crumbly purple and green letters of Maddy's sign made her think better of this plan. Bad enough Rose went through her dad's x-rays but this would be worse, like going through Graham Rochon's files, paper nosebleeds of privacy. No, she'd have some respect, she'd walk right on to the bathroom and close the door. It was not that bad, on the surface, nothing worse than deep rust stains in the tub and sink and a melamine coffee cup ringed with dry toothpaste froth. Above the sink and toilet, exposed and rather nefarious looking pipes. Did they even work? What if indeed there was no septic system? Rose leaned over the tub and listened for the piped in sound of frogs, pictured her used toilet paper adrift on the washboard waves, clinging to the mossy side of the ski jump. She decided to hold her urine. No wonder Maddy peed the bed; it was the lesser of two evils.

Rose slipped downstairs, past the slumbering and enraged Mrs. Farrell. "I'll see you guys," she said. "Next time I'll phone," but she wasn't sure. Maybe Adrian was right, vacations really weren't her cup of tea.

It's almost ten at night and George Drury is in bed. Adrian looks into the bedroom, says, "Pssst, Dad," and waits. It's finally warmer. The window is open and from outside come the few remaining sounds of that day: the wind, which is picking up and whistling somewhere between the screen and George's window frame, and from next door, Cassie Limb practicing her piano lesson, which could be the soundtrack to a hopeful movie about dogs rescuing people. "Dad," Adrian says again but George Drury does not stir.

The keys to the car are in a dish on the kitchen counter and Adrian can picture them in his mind, glowing like the very small skeleton of an uncomplicated vertebrate, probably something out of Minnow Lake. Adrian will make up a story about homework or the science fair if he has to explain himself and his father will believe him because, unlike George, when Adrian lies his face and remaining body co-operate down to the level of the smallest and most gullible blood vessel.

Turning on the car is the worst moment, the engine having no capacity to be hushed and Adrian reverses cautiously, tiptoeing the Torino up the street where he turns right and is on his way, along the road allowance where Loretta was last seen. It will be good to return to the dance hall, he hasn't been there since that day with Anastasia. He has told himself he should perform at least one brave action for Cheryl but already at the backside of the Welcome to Flax sign he knows this is bullshit because he is not now on this evening afraid of the dance hall or the road or even the surrounding forest as long as he is not in close proximity to the Cheryl tree. All fears, all imagining of paranormal, accusing eyes and skinless, pointy fingers are eclipsed by his anger and his hatred of Alfred Beel. I lay the blame blah blah blah....A gentleman would never.... Already, one tenth of the way to East Flax and the experience of thinking about Beel while simultaneously drawing closer to his place of residence is an energizing combination, a piloerection of desires having to do with smashing fists through smashable compounds and smiling at the terror in those beady Beel eyes.

Everyone cannot blame Adrian Drury and Alfred Beel knows this because many people should blame him. Beel was the know-it-all who saw Maddy with the ladder, who blabbed to Jerome Limb and Jimmy Drake. And it was Beel who, indirectly, caused Adrian's own sister to have to perform an act of oral sex on the town psychologist, which most likely also indirectly resulted in more people excusing Maddy and blaming Adrian with renewed gusto and vim.

The entire situation was like a bird's nest made out of threads from Maddy's stupid orange hat and Anastasia's *freak-show Barbies, Jimmy Drake Senior's pornographic pictures, and Jimmy Drake Junior's x-rated drawings. And if a bird the size of a hornet but with the strength of ten owls came along and pulled at the outermost orange string, unravelling for six or seven months past all of the days, there would be at the centre, not Adrian Drury but Alfred Beel or at least people like Alfred Beel, humourless, grouchy, mouth-frothers, rabid with built-up resentments,*

The one paradox of hating Beel is Adrian loves the road allowance and has for years. He's been there half a dozen times with Randy who explained to Adrian that the road allowance was a place set aside for a road that never materialized. Randy's word: materialized. For once Randy didn't have any original thoughts on a concept—another of his words—and it was Adrian who embellished the idea of a place set aside, entertaining himself with thoughts of a brother allowance. For at least three years he kept his old clothes and toys, even his faded swimsuits for an imaginary brother, Oswald Drury. Adrian used to talk out loud to Oswald but only when Skokie was in his room, as a cover. Eventually the brother allowance became the allowance allowance, a run-way-width bit of mental geography where all potentially possible events were milling around waiting, a reverse purgatory kind of place from which at any moment someone might appear, Adrian's script in hand. And that was how he wound up with Laura Van Epp. She just suddenly and without warning stepped out of the allowance and more or less expected to be taken to the dance. It was like someone finally dropping off Oswald; of course you had to take him in.

Now Adrian is at the hall and he is refreshingly and dazzlingly clear and yet planless. There is the moon, almost full and more yellowy than in winter. Adrian gets out of the car to look at the lake below him, still half-frozen but melting, hoping you might take a walk on its vanishing ice just to see what could happen. And Adrian begins to feel like he always does in the company of Minnow Lake, gladdened and full of a crowded loneliness. The roof of the store is visible above the shrubby trees of East Flax and Adrian takes a deep breath and yells "Farrell" and again, this time in two distinct syllables, "Far-rell."

There is no response because it's too far and even if it weren't Randy is no doubt busy inside fumbling with his breaker box of fortune-tellers, dusting off his licorice rack, and adding extensions to a couple of gumball troughs. Adrian concentrates and tries to think like Randy and then remembers a time when he used pebbles to try to cast a spell on a dog. Randy was afraid of this Coco dog and his brainwave was to create four piles of pebbles representing the letters of Coco's name—three pebbles for C and fifteen for O, based on their positions in the alphabet. Then as he scooped up and threw each pile, he cast the so-called spell "Coco will no longer chase Randy Farrell." It didn't work, Randy explained later, because it turned out Coco's name was spelled with K's.

It was a technique worth trying though and Adrian decides to gather up some stones, the moonlight being so helpful, and soon he has two piles of five, a pair, and one group of twelve. And with each toss into the lake, Adrian says, Alfred Beel will be out in his yard; Alfred Beel will be unarmed; Alfred Beel will be terrorized by Adrian Drury; and Alfred Beel will run for cover like a scared rabbit.

Then he is back in the car, following the road allowance, tracing, to use Cheryl's word, the route Loretta took when

she left Flax, past the gaping Rocket Lalonde who'd been fishing lower down so that he was a witness, the only witness, the
man people couldn't ask enough times: how did Loretta look?
What was she wearing? What about the radio—was it on or
was she listening to an eight-track? Did she say anything? Did
she say I blame Adrian Drury? Did she? Or did she say everybody knew Cheryl was already sad and it didn't help to make
her the captain of the basketball team because she hated
those phony efforts to fix her? She hated having a guidance
file that said "at risk" and she hated everybody staring when
she asked Mr. Busby about the last living passenger pigeon.
What did you expect? Her dad wasn't getting haircuts and
wouldn't say more than fifty words in a day and her mother
was falling down drunk at the Legion and sucking on laughing gas at the dentist's office and the whole town was staring
at the remaining Deckers as if they were three electric chairs
plugged in and ready to go. You had to give Jimmy Drake
Senior credit for that observation.

Most of the underbrush is flattened down from curiosity-
seekers driving this route, looking for clues or wanting to take
a walk and check out Turtle Bay bog for white Mustangs formerly owned by Loretta Decker. Or get close to the Cheryl
tree. One good thing: there wouldn't be a lot of weeds stuck
to the undercarriage for George Drury to notice first thing in
the morning, probably before he even woke up, responding to
a paranormal message from the town's postmaster: Hey
George, take a look under the Torino. Where do you suppose
those weeds came from?

And another good thing: George Drury always bought
white cars. If only Adrian had thought to bring along a
blonde wig—maybe Rose had one somewhere in her old Hal-

loween stuff—or even to put on a scarf so he looked like Jackie Kennedy or somebody female so that Beel might think the Torino was Loretta's car risen from the bog and be scared so shitless they'd find him the next day standing in his yard but transformed into a mushy-textured substance such as day-old Cream of Wheat. Easy to smash.

Now the Torino is out of the woods and practically in Beel's front yard, where the road allowance hooks up to the actual road that did materialize. Beel's car is in his driveway but the place is in darkness. The old fart is probably in bed masturbating with his missing penis. Maybe he keeps it in a jar next to his bed and just gives it a shake. Ha ha. Adrian drives a little farther and stops. Both windows are down and the wind is blowing, treetops are whipping around but it's a warm wind. Spring is coming along with the birds and their small cranial plans. It is clear Randy Farrell's mumbo-jumbo doesn't work but if a bird can fly from Texas to East Flax, surely Adrian Drury can dream up his own map of plans. He doesn't have one yet though and the Torino seems to know this, accelerating as it does now, past Beel's creepy house and out his laneway to the road the snowplow can't be bothered with.

East Flax had changed now. Even as the colour of the sky hardened into September blue and stubble stood in the fields thinking its job was done, some improvement could be seen. The sun was considerate, wavering on the lake like a genie before it forms. Perhaps tonight, after school, while the swallows scooped up the evening's insects, Maddy might lay her palm on the kind and restless skin of Minnow Lake and make a wish. Say a name. Rose Drury.

Nothing was impossible. Until recently, Maddy had thought the circle of horizon surrounding East Flax to be secured, a blue cotton sky stitched to burlap earth. Visitors were allowed some access where seams had loosened but always went home, never making a destination of Maddy Farrell. Now here was Rose Drury, or there she was and had been, twice. She could re-appear at any moment and the effect on East Flax was a yellowing of the sunlight and a bluing of the lake. East Flax, once pointless and faded, was like a garment washed with a load of fluorescent lights. All because Rose Drury had visited twice.

Of course, Maddy did not trust her own happiness, so inclined as it was to betray her, sets of eyes behind a curtain awaiting comeuppance. Happiness came from hope and hope was, generally speaking, refereed by the likes of Anastasia Van Epp: the rules and strategy in a pamphlet somewhere, most likely her dresser drawer. The facts alone would tell you, this was nothing to write home about: the attention of a Flax girl with long, straight, near-black hair and the perfect teeth of a dentist's daughter. But, for now, Maddy knew nothing she could do would stop the artesian well of wishing, the captive geyser that swelled against her stomach and up to the fluid in her eyes. Made her feel like a fish that had come up to shallow water from deep. And Greta Leopold did not help. That square dumpling of a body sitting next to her on the orange school bus was a living message that wishing for Rose Drury was a stupid kind of wishing; only a dolt would kowtow to Rose Drury and her ilk. The world was filled with dolts and borderline dolts, Greta would tell you with very little prompting. So don't ever talk to Greta about Rose Drury or the possibility of something better.

Best to say nothing. So Maddy sat in silence while Greta said she was not sure she wanted to stay in Mr. Drainie's chemistry class; she might make an appointment with the counsellor, Mr. Kipling, to inquire about transferring to Miss Hart's class. Miss Hart had won an important teaching award some years ago. Did Maddy know that? It was a provincial award, meaning Miss Hart was the best in the province. Greta spoke always in the dialect of instruction. This was her obligation. She was and always would be superior to Maddy because her mother, Joyce Leopold, had once reported Angel Farrell to the Children's Aid Society. The Leopolds were plain, hard working and captains of the 4-H industry. Except for one infestation of head lice, which could have happened to anyone, they were beyond reproach.

Greta asked, "Did you bring your lunch or are you eating in the cafeteria today?"

"I brought my lunch," Maddy said, patting the bookbag on her lap, then deciding to open it and take out her history text. On the inside cover was a column of names. Marjorie Kerr, 1967; Gloria Harper, 1968; Laurence Czerniawski, 1969. To this worthy list, at the very next stop, Maddy added her name. No one on earth knew this about Maddy Farrell but she held onto the academic stream at Flax Composite High like a drowning person to a life raft, with one important difference: she gave no indication of need. Maddy was a hanger-on, a condition she understood from the magazines sold in her parents' store. According to all the laws of diminishing returns—every year her marks went down—she should have been in the vocational stream, carrying slim and functional texts filled with business practice, rather than mathematics books deepening into abstractions half understood by Maddy. Well, no, sixty per cent understood.

Toward the end of grade twelve, she'd been advised by Mr. Kipling to think about a switch to something secretarial: come back for grade thirteen but take some bookkeeping, improve your typing. You need to think about employment. He'd given her a form to complete, sign, and return to the school secretary, Mrs. Liebling, and this had been like receiving a traffic ticket, or worse, a summons. We've been watching you for some time and have at last concluded you are not the girl you think you are. Look at your brother: he'll be lucky to graduate in this lifetime. Your sister is a different story but now is not the time to delve into that. Please sign here to confirm you are a Farrell of the Frog clan.

"No sweat," Maddy had said. "Sure. Whatever you say, Mr. Kipling."

"Of course, you'd still be on the basketball team. None of that would change."

"Sure. I'll talk to my parents about it."

She signed the form and brought it to school every

day, carried it in her pocket, folded up like a little white window most likely everyone could see into. On the last day of school, during the awards assembly, she went into the main floor girls' bathroom, farthest cubicle, ripped the paper into tiny bits and flushed. Not the most satisfactory conclusion, because then she'd had to spend the summer worrying the school would call or Mr. Kipling would show up in his little MG, or Mrs. Liebling would simply purse up her lips one hot July afternoon and assign Maddy to a roster of classes she thought appropriate to an amphibian. So when Maddy Farrell first saw Rose Drury at the door of the dance hall her worried mind went immediately to course selection. Maybe Mr. Kipling had sent one of Maddy's peers to convey the news, urge her to make one more counselling appointment and come to grips with reality. She'd had that head-to-toe startle like a zipper going up her bare back, colder than her cold and breathing skin.

Just like hearing Rose Drury had been invited *upstairs* and even further up to Cora's stuffy attic with its nails instead of a closet. At least Maddy's room had a closet with a light bulb and a little chain. Cora had assured her, in her oddly unreassuring voice, that Rose had not peeked into her room. She was a snob and a school queen and not the world's best sister but at least Cora had been kind enough to tell Rose the room was a mess and the bed wasn't made so don't go looking in there. And Maddy believed her. She only wet the bed on rare occasions now but despite the scrubbing of the mattress, the rubbed-in baby powder and the vanilla car deodorizer hanging from her bureau mirror, she knew for sure the room smelled faintly of pee. That's why she had two paying jobs. Once Maddy had saved enough money for a new mattress, she would drag the old one to the dump herself, leaving a trail in the gravel road and telling people a giant snail must have scraped by in the night. Maybe the tabloids might be interested. East Flax was the kind of place the tabloids liked, their idea of a home for buttery fat babies born bigger than the giantest dance hall roasting pan, or prisoners of war who'd been missing since 1944.

Was there one good reason they did not sell reputable magazines in the store? The entire place was an embarrassment, really, with its sagging chairs and ashtrays and smell of old scalps. The novice customer might think the Farrells were retailers of geriatric men. No wonder they were in debt to everyone: Lowney's, Coca-Cola, Weston, Dominion Meat. Sooner or later those corporations would dispatch a white panel van to transport her family to debtors' prison and that might be a merciful release. Maddy had asked more than once, "Why don't you give up on this place, Mom?"

"It's my independence," she always said.

"But you'd be more independent if you worked in the TV dinner factory or even cleaning houses."

Her mom had shrugged her shoulders, offering no further information.

Maddy had her independence and there had been so little cost. For helping her dad with his custodial work, she got twenty dollars a month and her house-cleaning brought in another twenty. She cleaned both Alfred Beel's and Russell Hansen's houses. Alfred was the only one who could afford her really, but once he'd asked, Russell had to as well. The Maestro lived in Mesmer and had a *man* clean his house. In actual fact, Alfred hadn't asked Maddy, he'd asked Cora who'd said no. But since Maddy was right there, she volunteered, an offer she knew Alfred couldn't refuse, much as he'd wanted to. Cora was the one he wanted inside his house to look at and to bait from time to time with phrases such as *social intercourse* or *let me just ejaculate here*. He thought he was clever but he was not. Maddy never reacted and as a result, Alfred hated her. One thing Maddy had learned though was hate could be a solace in its own way, a little body that was yours to examine like a dead cat or squirrel without the smell.

As a result of her employment, Maddy had more money than Cora until she went off to nursing school. Her mother didn't pay Cora for working in the store and it didn't really matter. Cora managed by sewing her own clothes, mixing and matching and trusting in the government. "I'll get a fat student loan," she said, "because look at us. We're living in poverty. We're a documentary. I'm surprised someone from Ottawa doesn't come and take before and after pictures. The beautiful Cora before her loan and after. Now aren't you glad you voted Liberal?"

Not that she had looked any different after the money. Cora, with no bank account throughout high school, had always looked good, displaying evidence of future queenliness as early as grade nine. And Maddy, with a balance now of almost three hundred dollars, had always looked bad. She could forget this unpleasant reality during the summer because the one mirror in the Farrells' bathroom had lost so much of its silver you could fill in the blanks any way you wanted. Whereas the high school was filled with polished and full-length mirrors, that had been architecturally designed to invite examination and worse, comparison. Mirrors in the change room, the home economics room and, of course, every girls' washroom.

Last winter: "God, Maddy, you scared me. I thought you were a guy. You shouldn't tie your hair back like that. Come here." And Ella Littlejohn had done a sort of makeover on her right there in the washroom. "And you shouldn't use elastics. They break your hair. See, with your hair down, that's better. Softens your features."

Since that day Maddy had spent a great deal of time examining and admiring others in mirrors, as if she were forever conducting quick experiments, herself (the experimental group) compared to the control group. How much unlike a girl could you look before being denied entry to the girls' washroom? She thought she might be on an adolescent trajectory that would one day cross a line. Ella Littlejohn would be the one selected to tell her. "I don't know. Maybe you could use the staff washroom, Maddy. The girls just don't feel comfortable."

The reason for wearing the orange hat. Ella had told her: accessorize in a kooky way. Look at Marni Galbraith. Marni wore strange hats and army clothes and she was a little funny looking but when all was said and done, cute funny looking, girl funny looking. And her parents let her go to Toronto on the train and shop on Yonge Street so that in the end, everyone knew that Marni looked different because she was ahead of her time at Flax Composite High. To compare Maddy to Marni would be like comparing Olive Oyl to Twiggy. But once she'd worn the orange hat, she couldn't not wear it the next day, as if she had lost her mind or entered a clown dimension, as Anastasia Van Epp liked to say. So she continued to wear the hat, stuck some pins on it, then some fishing lures, then an enormous scarf, yellow, Carnaby Street, they'd all think. Spring finally came and released her from her prison of accessories.

Here they were, entering Flax, rounding the curve into the day's anatomy. Greta was rustling in her bookbag, looking for her schedule. Maddy didn't have to look; she had it memorized. Today was physics. Maddy was not allowed to think about physics until inside the Flax town limits because limits were what was needed with this situation, too lush, like a hybrid of giant and fast-growing wild orchids that might take over the entire county in a week unless something were done. The first day of class, Rose Drury had manufactured a reason for them to sit together, made up a lie, just like that. More unexpected than Minnow Lake draining in one hour like a tub, more inexplicable than the manta ray people said lives there.

"I'm tutoring Maddy this term. Why don't we just ask if you and Maddy can trade places?" Rose said to

Evelyn Jardine, her assigned lab mate. "Miss Eustace, would it be possible for Evelyn and Maddy to trade places since I'm tutoring her this term?" said Rose again.

Miss Eustace was not sure, did not want to set a precedent, but finally agreed to make an exception in this instance only, *for purposes of tuition.* "Maddy, move your things," she'd said. "Evelyn, go." It had all happened in less than two school-clock minutes, unnoticed by most but for Maddy they were moments x-rayed and found to be perfect, like her unbroken wrist the time she'd gone to the hospital in the social worker's car.

This was a miracle of science. Since then the physics room had been relocated, lifted through an architectural exchange program to a foundation of unpredictable soil, clay perhaps, a medium for tiles, flower pots, and skeets. That was to be expected from physics, the science of matter. Move things around in your hand long enough and they might become something else. Or, watch. Observe patiently. Every day the room looked a little more impending, the Bunsen burners, the silver plated gas taps, all the confident equipment of science ready to make a point. The scientific method required little more than watching and waiting. That's what you did. You looked out the window of the dirty, loud bus and saw Rose Drury on her way to school, walking along Josephine Street, and your heart ticked like the clock on the science room wall.

Sorry, we're closed. Be back at noon, no—one o'clock, Angel decided, adjusting the clock face sign and locking the store behind her. Thank God school was back in session. With Frog at work and the kids in school, her life was hers again.

Off to Flax. Jimmy P. Drake was expecting her. She'd been seeing Jimmy, off and on now, for most of the last decade. Some people settled for monogamy and that was fair enough but Angel was not some people and she required more and she'd be happy to explain this to anyone who asked. She'd give a speech; she'd be happy to give a speech to the Women's Institute of Flax, for example, introduced by Cornelia Laine or even her nemesis, Joyce Leopold...*Last week we heard from the District Home Economist, Lois Yates, who charmed us with her talk entitled "From Soup to Nuts—Fall Menus That Won't Break the Budget." This week, Angel Farrell will be speaking to us on the subject of Extramarital Affairs: What to Look for in a Dick. Consulting her notes, no, that can't be correct; I'm sure what Angel means is what to look for in a man.*

Ahem, Angel would say, ahem, setting aside her notes, speaking off the cuff, unembarrassed and you had to respect that quality in her. Sometimes Angel thought embarrassment was the plasma of life, a clear and colourless fluid holding people in place.

Ladies, Angel would say, let me suggest that you find yourselves someone like Jimmy Drake Senior— not Jimmy himself, he's spoken for—but someone like him, someone who never calls, never begs or threatens and, more importantly, whose flexible work schedule allows him to be available at your convenience. He should be comfortable talking dirty and well, being a little dirty. And along with these attributes, he must have size on his side and don't let anyone tell you ladies that it doesn't count. From the sample Angel had sampled, Jimmy had the most, literally speaking, to offer, and here Angel would pause for polite laughter.

The one recommendation she would strongly recommend, Angel would say, suddenly running out of vocabulary, was Don't let the guy take pictures. She might have to stress this point by writing on the board, plaintive gusts of chalk dust signalling her one regret. Do *not* let the guy take pictures. And, the problem now was, Angel would continue, deciding she might as well tell the entire story, she couldn't even blame him because she'd been the one to suggest it. Let's take some pictures, she had suggested, as if she were talking about cedar waxwings in the backyard. Pretend porn kinds of things. C'mon, Jimmy, thinking he would balk. But he wasted no time building a little darkroom, learned how to develop and print and now they had scores of photographs, mostly of Angel bending over dressers or lying on the kitchen table or bursting out of bras one size too small. What had she been thinking? What?

She'd admit she'd gone a little too far, having been the one to come up with the whopper series. And what exactly was the whopper series? Well, it was a parody of the fish photos *The Reminder* ran from time to time, usually of Rocket Lalonde hoisting a giant pickerel or perch he'd caught in one of the surrounding lakes. For these shots, Jimmy set the camera on a chair, pushed the red self-timer button, and they scrambled into position, Jimmy kneeling at a right angle to the shutter and Angel crouching, holding his pecker at the base and head. These pictures contained no faces or identifying features, and this, ironically, was an extra source of worry for Angel, because if he could get away with it, Jimmy was not above sending one of those pictures to the paper with a ridiculous and dirty caption penned in: This one didn't get away! or Mama's Dinner. Jimmy derived no end of pleasure from inventing stories with his own dick in the starring role. And here Angel might come to an abrupt halt, having failed to establish a conclusion or a moral for this story. But, if the ladies had any questions or even objections, she was more than happy to entertain them now. No? None to speak of?

Her sister Muriel was the only person on the planet who'd ever had the balls to confront Angel. One sunny morning last fall, she'd called her to her office and given her the keys to a brand new AMC Gremlin, identical to her own. "I want you to get rid of that old Chevy with the big fins. Everybody knows it's yours and everybody knows when you're in town doing whatever it is you're doing with Jimmy Drake. Maybe you don't have the decency to be humiliated by your own transparency but I do. So I'm giving you a car that's the same as mine and when you're in town you *will* park it outside my office. I don't drive to work; I leave mine in the garage ninety per cent of the time. People will think I'm at the office and at least they won't be able to follow your comings and goings with pinpoint accuracy, a situation I find deplorable." Muriel had walked to the venetian blinds on her office window and tightened them shut. Then she'd turned to Angel and asked, "Why him of all people? Just to be oppositional, am I right? Thumb your nose at some abstract enemy?"

"Maybe in part," Angel had said, searching for a rationale suited to a sibling lawyer. The stories Jimmy told certainly weren't going to impress Muriel, tales of what he and Jimmy Junior got up to in the school on weekends when no one was around, turning on the public address system and telling dirty jokes, impersonating Principal Hodgetts or Mrs. Liebling. *Miss Hart, Miss Hart,* one of them would say, *you're wanted in the nurse's room. Please report to the nurse's room for your hot meat injection.* Or going through the files and disciplinary notes, taking down combination numbers for Jimmy Junior's future reference.

"And you know, he *is* a direct descendant of Sir Francis Drake: he's had the Mormons do the genealogy. That's why he thinks nothing of driving hundreds of miles to see a point of interest like, for example, Wolfe's monument or the Plains of Abraham. He's got the blood of an explorer." That may seem ridiculous, but when was the last time Muriel had pulled over to look at a cairn, Angel wanted to know? Developed her own theory? Maybe he talked a lot of delusional crap but it was uttered with confidence and that was what Angel adored. She liked a man who blabbed opinion and insight and crackpot observation because she knew from experience this would be a man who also gushed compliments and wasn't afraid, she hesitated, then said out loud, to talk dirty in bed. Shocked the pants right off of Muriel Cobb, spinster and who knew what else. LL.B. Lesbian Lawyer at the Bar, gay bar that is. Not here of course, in Toronto, where no one knew her AMC Gremlin from a '59 Chevy.

By way of responding, Muriel had adjusted the cuffs of her very white shirt and snorted.

Never mind, Angel liked to advise the surrounding plasma. Never you mind. She rolled down the window and saw that this was one beautiful September day, then slowed to a crawl among the curves, pulled a little off the road and stopped. Less than five hundred feet beyond the trees lay Turtle Bay bog, the spring fed source of Minnow Lake. Only the locals knew about this bog, this pool on a foundation of moss. Walking to it she always felt lighter than human, or should she say lighter than a human slut; she felt like a new kind of animal with hollow bones and organs, specially adapted for leaving no trace.

Sphagnum, Randy said when they walked through the trees last fall to see the geese, sphagnum moss. The Drury boy came along. They'd heard the geese from the ski jump and she'd driven them here to take a look. Must have been hundreds of birds landing and jostling and honking out ideas or maybe theories, like Jimmy. What a racket. Ankle-deep in moss, ears happy to be alive, Angel decided that day that nature generally had just one word to say and the geese were saying it and it was "urge." Maybe with Muriel, if she'd simply opened her mouth and honked, not a regular honk but the autumn version, she'd have made a better case for herself.

Angel could see a car approaching now, someone heading home from Flax, having bought groceries at Pond's, no doubt, a local traitor. The car sank out of sight behind O'Dell's hill, then returned to view, billowing dust with no sound as if this were their useless television with no functioning volume knob. Angel wished she could hear some geese and turned off the engine in hope. Nothing. Here was the car now, close enough to identify and wasn't it Joyce Leopold, slowing to see what was the problem, stopping parallel to Angel, her trunk without a doubt filled to capacity with boxes of bread and cereal, flour and apples, bananas, head lettuce, luncheon meats, wieners the girth of Jimmy's fingers.

"Car trouble?" Joyce asked. She had a new look. Her bangs were straight all the way to her eyebrows while the rest of her hair was tucked behind her ears and permed in tight black curls.

"No. Just listening for geese back in Turtle Bay. Your hair looks good," Angel said.

"Why thank you. Stan's not so sure," Joyce said, rolling her eyes.

"Oh, he'll come around," Angel assured her, aware of a plume of discomfort between them, knowing this, knowing that.

"I guess Cora's off to London, is she?" Joyce asked, grabbing a tissue from the box on the dash, giving her nose a forceful blow. "This dust. Anyway, you'll be missing her."

"Yes, she was a big help around the store. Maddy's going to have to pinch hit."

"No doubt. No doubt. My Greta's thinking of veterinary science now. More girls are going into it. Small animals, of course. I don't think she'd be one for steer wrestling." Another blow of the nose followed by a rueful laugh.

My Greta! Who else's Greta would she be? "Good for her," Angel said. "Not sure what Maddy's planning. If she could just play basketball for a living...Oh, I see there's another car coming. Guess we better not tie up traffic."

"You're right. Looks like one of the Haugh boys," Joyce said, squinting into the rear-view mirror. "Nice talking to you, Angel."

"You too, Joyce."

The minute she was home, Angel knew Joyce would call one of her town friends: Iris, I want you to check and see if there's a Gremlin parked in front of Muriel Cobb's office. Right now. Go. Call me back.

Despite Angel's brave imagined speeches, one-on-one encounters were a little difficult. Up close to Joyce's new hair and Stan's reserved opinion, all the lovable woes of marriage, Angel was an irredeemable tramp. That was the truth. The very bald realization of which sent Angel's mind skittering for explanations, grasping at respectable excuses, as if there were any. Maybe she was lonely, she wanted to call after Joyce; maybe that was all there was to it. Frog *was* a virtual mute, unlike Stan, while Jimmy she could depend on to talk preposterous nonsense and make her feel alive even when he was goading, needling, and simply stupid.

And he was stupid, and a gossip and aggravatingly persistent with his filthy speculations. What would he want to discuss today? Or who? Last time, which had been, God, when had it been?—June, she supposed—he'd wanted to hear about Alfred Beel. What's with Alfred? Is he getting it on with Ila Van Epp? And if so, how? Maybe he gives good head. Do you think he gives good head, Jimmy had asked by way of inquiring if Angel might know from experience.

No, nothing's going on between Alfred and Ila, Angel had said. She knew what went on in Alfred's life and she wanted to make that clear, make Jimmy understand she enjoyed other intimacies. Because apparently a husband and a boyfriend were not enough for her. She needed more opportunities to provoke attention than the average woman and that wasn't so wrong; show-offs abounded the whole world over.

Angel told Jimmy, in order to understand Alfred you had to appreciate he was more like a teenaged girl than a middle-aged man. Maybe that was the result of his accident, Angel offered: some hormones were missing. Alfred would take one event and moon over it for years. Loretta was the case in point. They had a conversation last winter at the Legion. She told Alfred he was the handsomest man in the area and if she were free, she'd go after him. And that's not all. It always brightened her day when Alfred showed up in the dentist's waiting room. She'd had a few drinks but Alfred didn't know how to factor that into the equation. So he thinks, Loretta loves me. Do you see how he's like a teenaged girl? Only Cora would be more mature—she'd laugh it off.

"I wonder if she's been out to see him," Jimmy said. "Ila Van Epp goes out there. I'll bet she's getting head."

This was when Jimmy became tiresome. "No, believe me, Ila is not getting *head* as you so gallantly put it."

"How do you know?" Jimmy wanted to know.

"Alfred would tell me."

Jimmy gave her a look.

"It's true. We have an unusually frank friendship."

"Unusually frank. I guess that's one way of putting it. What about Loretta? She could be going out there? He must be getting it on with somebody."

"Not to my knowledge and my knowledge is exhaustive."

"Hmm. I'd like to have a picture of Loretta getting head."

He thought he could shock Angel with this sort of talk. "Well, I don't think you'll get it from Alfred Beel. He doesn't go in for homemade pornography and tales of the whopper. He actually has a bit of class."

Mention class and Jimmy looked at her with his round brown eyes, wet little points of entry to a head full of compost. What else did Angel discuss with Alfred? Heat rose between his ears and made him swallow. "Do you want me to go down on you?" he asked.

"Not particularly." But he did anyway. Angel hadn't resisted.

What would he be doing when she arrived? He was always ready in some way, maybe sitting naked at the kitchen table, a towel draped over the chair seat for reasons of sanitation, his big sausage on display. Or he might be on his back in bed, the camera watching from its tripod, a big leering stick insect.

Ladies of the Women's Institute, Angel had to say, tired now, by way of conclusion, you all know that truth be told, Jimmy P. Drake is faintly repulsive, and paradoxically Angel liked that about him too. Did anyone understand the paradox of Jimmy Drake? Show of hands, please? His house smelled a little like the interior of the store cooler, as if there might be old dried blood heating on a motor somewhere. She'd find it someday. Nothing was forever out of sight, out of mind. Look at her, dutifully parking the Gremlin in front of Muriel's office, two blocks away so as to sneak along the alley to Jimmy's back door. What was the use? People would see; they'd notice the car. Muriel never parks there so Angel must be in town. Joyce's friends would be on the blower but so what? It wasn't as if there was an Adults' Aid Society they could report her to. She hadn't broken any laws and if nothing else Angel knew the law. Her sister was a lawyer and her brother was a judge and she was an untrained interpreter of the rules and regulations meant to make our short lives miserable. If the Cobbs and rule-makers had their way, every possible ounce of available fun would be packaged and dried up like Lucky Elephant pink popcorn with no prize. Sorry, we missed that box.

Saturday, September 12. The first week of school had come and gone. When the clock said 2:00 p.m., Cheryl Decker would leave her parents' house, meet Adrian where the sign said Welcome to Flax, and ride with him to the dance hall. Adrian's idea and a good one. They'd never gone there, so by nightfall a new dot would shine on the topographical sex map. Cheryl liked the dance hall, not the hall itself but the trees behind, which would be yellowing and murmuring and resembling an endless and unexplored forest from some other time—King Arthur's perhaps—or place, Adrian would say, like the set for a horror movie. In the morning when he rode out with the sleeping bags, finding his way through the trees to a secluded flat spot, memorizing the route, Adrian would have been thinking: what about the birds? Maybe not all of them, but one or two of the bigger-beaked were already in the planning stages of a future attack. He would interpret their weekend chirping as strategy. Same with the insects: cicadas were known to be secret plotters.

Sometimes Cheryl admired Adrian's capacity to find fun in horror. At home, she tried to create a playful game of her parents' burrowing wish to kill her and themselves and burn the house and all its contents. Imagined, for example, calling the fire department and volunteering the Decker house for firefighting practice, like the Raines had done with their old barn on the edge of town. But the miraculous resilience of horror meant Reg and Loretta would emerge from the flames,

burned and singed to carry on, half-cooked yet still able
to live among the smouldering ruins, nothing more
than a few floorboards and of course, the furnace. As
if you would need heat. Loretta would make toast. Coffee, Reg? Have you seen Cheryl anywhere?

Unlike Adrian, she couldn't find the fun in this.

Other times, Cheryl tried the opposite, pictured
her parents in a Disney movie, happy and enjoying a
moment like they used to before time and fate and ac-
cidents had moved in permanently like an ever visible
piece of art that cost too much to get rid of. But she
failed at that game too. Her imagination had decided
to go its own way, grown hundreds of little see-through
fly wings, and got itself lost between the place it em-
barked and the landing pad of pleasure. Well, there
was no landing pad. Adrian would understand this if
she tried to explain. Cheryl could imagine her parents
prior to the current haywire, see them playing cards,
dancing in the kitchen like they used to. She could
hear the way they used to talk, but the comfort she
once felt was on the other side of town, maybe even at
the Telluride airport, a luggage handler wearing those
puffy, grey headphones, a long and muffled distance
from its own thoughts.

Cheryl would have left a few hours early if she
could have, but then what? A girl waits half a day by the
Welcome to Flax sign, not just any girl, Cheryl Decker
who is "at risk": she'd seen the verdict written on her
file at school when she was having a talk with Mr.
Kipling about credits for piano lessons. He'd had to
go to the office to get the pamphlet from the Royal

Conservatory and she'd flipped open her file for one heartbeat and shut it just as fast. "At risk" explained the way people looked at her so in the end it was better to know. Their expressions seemed to suggest she might decompose before their eyes, might be an alien in a zippered up skin, a kind of grape or soft, fruity textured being with seeds instead of a brain. They thought she might eat beetles and smile, exposing insect legs caught between her teeth, maybe she'd even show up like that for school pictures. Adrian would probably love to hear about "at risk" and its creepy accompanying fears but not today, Cheryl wasn't in the mood for talking.

She'd left only a couple minutes early, hoping to be able to wait, lean her bike against the sign post and watch Adrian's approach, watch him pretend he wasn't excited to see her. But Adrian was already there and this both pleased Cheryl and caused concern. Was he that anxious to have sex with her? And was that good or bad? If another grade eleven girl had been there instead, would Adrian have simply gone with her? What exactly was the difference between one vagina and the next, really, Cheryl wanted to know. Did it make much difference who was attached to it? A vagina was in actuality just an empty space with a body around it.

"Hi," they both said.

He was wearing jeans with a white T-shirt. Even if the earth moved fifty thousand miles closer to the sun, I would never wear shorts, was Adrian's first rule of fashion. Fine with me, Cheryl had told him more than once. If she had to say what she liked best about him, it would be that place on his upper arm where his tan faded to white. "It's the two colours of chicken eggs," she told him once at the pool. "The brown ones and the white ones."

They rode side by side on the empty country road, sun washed out and vague behind a sky the colour of salt. Everything humid and sticky and clotting once again, as if the landscape had forgotten it was supposed to be thinking of fall. They were quiet. Some temperatures and conditions were opposed to communication and besides, maybe it wasn't necessary. In this heavy weather, thoughts could hang there in the air next to you; sound might just make them sink.

On country roads, Adrian liked to shift into third gear, pull away, brake, skid in a circular spray of gravel, return. Cheryl knew he would and he did.

"Adrian, don't go ahead like that."

"Just one more. I'll be right back."

"No. Don't go ahead. I like riding side by side."

But he took off, veering into the gravel on the shoulder for maximum slide and danger, braking hard and throwing up a stooped little figure of dust, not even a breeze to give it a bit of ooomph, almost as if he'd skinned off a little bit of himself. Now he was back.

"Look. You made a ghost of yourself from the dust," said Cheryl. He would like this observation.

"Yeah. It kind of looks like those pictures people have, where they say they took a picture of a ghost. In a church or somewhere. Have you seen that on TV? It's completely bogus. Probably some guy hiding between the pews blowing out a few smoke rings. Have you seen that?"

"I saw something like that once. It was a documentary."

"Yeah. That's the show. Remember the part in the church with the kind of foggy shape? Just like the ghost I just made out of dust. So maybe it was the janitor had just turned the vacuum cleaner on reverse and made a little shape of dust. Maybe he sprayed out some dust and then sprayed some kind of lacquer onto it and it held it there. Who knows what they can do with different products, especially janitors? They're all pretty familiar with industrial-strength dust lacquers, I imagine. Anyway, to my mind that's not what a ghost would look like. A ghost would not look like a stooped over, shiny cloud of dust."

"Well, what do you think it would look like?"

"I don't know. But I plan to make it my business to find out in this lifetime," Adrian said, taking off for one last skid.

This section of the road was straight. Still no cars and the air was no fresher than the inside of the Decker house, as if her parents were just above the cloudy layer, breathing out their heavy hearts. Cheryl was frantically relieved to be with Adrian, she had to admit. She could have cried like someone on a game show.

Adrian circled back and pulled up next to Cheryl. "Do you know who I hate?" he asked.

"No. Who?"

"I hate Jimmy Drake Junior. One week into school

and that asshole already has my combination. He comes up to me after gym and gives me that sideways look he gives like he's a detective or something and says, *another year of surprises, Drury.* Meaning of course he's going to start putting shit into my locker like last year. Pictures of stuff like, I don't know, he makes drawings and says, Adrian and Greta Leopold, or Adrian and Maddy Farrell, you can probably imagine and he sticks them in my locker. Then the next time I see him he looks at me like he just wiped his ass on my shirt. I hate him and he hates me."

"What did you ever do to him?"

"Nothing. Oh, no, that's not true. I did do something. I bought condoms at the drugstores in Mesmer."

"So?"

"So if I *bought* condoms, I'm *using* condoms. Anyway, I wish Jimmy Drake Senior would get fired from that job. Randy Farrell might be kind of weird and Maddy Farrell might look like a guy, but at least Frog Farrell you can trust not to be letting his kids get everybody's combination."

"Do you have the safe, speaking of you-know-what, just by the way?"

"Needless to say."

"So... is it getting hard yet?" This was how Cheryl liked to talk to Adrian, practical and scientific without being dirty.

"Now that you mention it..."

"Does it hurt when it gets hard inside jeans like that?"

"Nope. Getting hard never hurts."

"I want to touch it now," Cheryl said. They were less than half a mile from Dance Hall Road. Still no cars and nothing but trees and swampy water in the ditch; twenty degrees further south and there might be crocodiles. They set the bikes on their kickstands and kissed. Cheryl always wore skirts for her dates with Adrian and he ran his hand up her behind, inside her underpants. She placed a hand on his crotch, tried to read it like a barometer, detect the subtle differences in calibration with each grope.

Car coming, so they rode some more, fast, out of the curves and trees and up the grade to Dance Hall Road, rode as far as they could up the hill then ran their bikes the final bit and there was the dance hall. They'd have to hide their bikes in the trees because Frog Farrell was always around with his brooms and mops. Seemed like he was everywhere Cheryl and Adrian wanted to be.

"They say he's got some traps back in here," Adrian said. "A whole trapline I've heard, so we'll have to watch our steps."

"Traps for what?"

"I don't know. Coons maybe. Maybe they eat them. Maybe the Farrells eat trapped meat. Wild lynxes and old foxes that run faster than Skokie ever could. Maybe that's why Maddy's so good at basketball. Who knows? Maybe if you ate some trapped meat..."

"I'd never be as good as Maddy. Even if they stretched my legs another ten inches on a rack."

They let their bikes crash to the forest floor and Adrian led the way. Cheryl considered offering an in-

nuendo on trapped meat but that seemed too trashy
and the way it usually went, the closer they were to the
sleeping bags the more inclined she was to silence. The
more inclined she was to find it all very foreign, as if
she had crossed the border into Lichtenstein or Hun-
gary, a country known to her only through black and
white photos in history texts. There was no great need
for colour back here behind the dance hall anyway.
With the pale and sagging sky just above the encircling
treetops, what was there to see? Dark old trunks spear-
ing at you with naked lower limbs, everything looking
half-dead from lack of light and smelling like rope or
basements. Reminded Cheryl of her grandpa in the
old folks' home for some reason.

"Here we are," Adrian said and set to the zipping
together of the bags while Cheryl took off her clothes.
This always made her think of the picture of that girl
in Vietnam, running from the napalm, and she wished
she had a more compelling reason to undress, worried
a little about photographers. Then Adrian removed his
clothes and also always, Cheryl did this: knelt down
and sucked on his penis for a minute or two. Which
transported her to another current event—buried in an
earthquake, scratching at the fallen timber and plaster.
Why an earthquake she wasn't sure except sucking and
scratching seemed similarly linked to desperation and
survival. Until she stopped, smiled up at Adrian, and
they slithered into the sleeping bags, he rolled the condom down his sturdy hardness and climbed on top of
her. She was always ready. The talk and the sucking
were enough. And later she felt like the girl who'd been

found five days after—there was always one in every earthquake, squinting into the sun and applause. Carried away on a stretcher.

"You can fall asleep," Adrian said. "I'll stay awake and make sure the birds don't get us."

In all his years, Alfred Beel could not recall such incredulity, such marvel. What on earth had he been thinking? To dress up in what he now knew was this unfashionable suit, climb aboard Ila's Mercury Meteor Rideau Victoria, and drive to London. Drive to London, listening to the radio, pushing buttons from channel to channel, whistling like any ordinary man with a reasonable destination, a nephew's wedding or perhaps a visit to the lawyer. Dear God: the humiliation drained the blood from his essential organs in one circling swish, flushing like a toilet.

This was the problem: the human mind. The body was easy enough, like a domesticated farm animal really, a cow, obedient and predictable. It was the mind that would wake up one morning, all dolled up in fantastic ideas and irrational encouragement. Yes! Why shouldn't you drive to London to see Cora Farrell? You have as much right as the next person and she'd be happy to see you. Sure she would. Remember the way she used to pick up that ashtray? Remember? That was her way of saying, I like you, Alfred. Trust me, the grey, corrugated voice inside Alfred's skull had said; without a doubt Cora will be missing you by now. She might even have realized, as nothing more than a vague unhappiness with nursing school, she wanted something else now, something more immediate and responsive and corporeal. Alfred. She wanted Alfred. If only he'd come to get her. The oatmeal mass in its darkened shell was indisputable.

He didn't go alone though, you really could not do that in Flax. People wanted to know where you'd been and why; they asked questions until they had answers. Alfred didn't like long drives unaccompanied and Ila had reason to be in Stratford with her sewing and her costumes, so why not travel together? Plus, Ila owned that old Mercury everyone loved to ride in with its elaborate and swooping chrome grill, like a bird in flight. That 1956 Mercury, manufactured in the same year as Alfred's Botany brand suit and tie. Yes, they were a matched set.

Oh dear, he thought, oh dear oh dear oh dear; there went another whoosh in the plumbing of humiliation. Why had he been so slow to get the gist? After all, when he arrived at the farm, Ila's first comment was, "Well, well. Since you're dressed for the car, you'd better drive it." At first he'd thought dressed for the car as in dressed up, gone to some effort; he'd also chosen to wear his hat. He wanted to look good, not just for Cora, but also for Ila. He liked to think he and Ila might impress other motorists as a handsome couple, a successful pair on their way to the theatre in their snappy, shiny, three-tone car.

"So clever of you to dress period for the car," she said again as they left the driveway.

Dress period, he thought, the two words lumbering around in his mind, looking for a place to organize themselves into sense or push up against some long-lost context. What *was* Ila on about now? She could start in on any number of topics and leave you floundering: the Liberals, Graham Rochon, the girls and their habits.

The business of the suit took several miles and more than an hour to register, a metaphor for his failure to perceive the changes in menswear over the past fifteen years. Another deficit with this brain of his: it took notice of the women's styles but not the men's. Was he a transvestite? Apparently the men's fashion section of his brain was unlit, cordoned off by the metal plates, a corner of a department store that had undergone flooding, then a ceiling disaster, then finally, quietly, been walled off. During that time, pant legs and lapels had apparently narrowed, ties also; hats had seemingly vanished. You're welcome to wear this baggy old suit if you want, sir, but really, we would caution you against it.

Into Perth County where the barns and Holsteins and corn grew larger and still Ila could not say enough about Alfred's *parodic* fashion sense. "Peter couldn't parody his way out of a paper bag. Unlike you, Alfred, he really is the original nineteen fifties man. So if he's simply representing himself, it can't be much of a parody, can it? But you, Alfred, you're a man of the present, really, a seventies male."

"You know," Alfred said, "I'm a little like Mark Twain. I can live for two months on a good compliment." He still didn't quite follow but found himself leaning closer to Ila, glancing at her profile, glancing again, considering the benefits of climbing right inside her mouth, sitting on her tongue, getting as close as possible to her words and their meaning, dissolving like the peppermint she was sucking. "You really think I'm a man of the seventies? You really think so?"

"Absolutely," said Ila. "How many men around here have friendships with women? I'll tell you how many. One. You. And the suit with the car, it's certainly not typical Flax behaviour, as remote from the mind of Peter Van Epp and his crowd, conceptually speaking, as the Arctic Circle."

"Really? You really do believe that?"

"Please. Peter Van Epp would think it was *vaguely fruity*, as he likes to say. If it doesn't concern corn hybridization, it's suspect you understand."

And here the peppermint melted into gritty bits of sugar between Ila's teeth because, finally, Alfred got the drift: his suit was old and unfashionable, a contemporary of the Mercury Meteor. Period costume. Of course, Ila and her theatre talk. The suit was as old, older in fact, than the car. Cora Farrell and all of London, Ontario, were, at this very moment, holding their breath as he approached, waiting to guffaw. Here comes the fashion clown, the man who can't tell the difference between a compliment and ridicule. Here he comes in a vintage car, like a float in a time-warp parade. Ha ha. Ha ha ha.

Well, hardy har har. People would have to forgive this old veteran if he hadn't had time for suit-shopping in the past fifteen years. There'd simply been no occasion, no weddings or funerals; he didn't attend church. And a suit, after all, was a suit, possessed of two legs, a waistband, a jacket with sleeves and buttons. It wasn't as if they'd been replaced by space-age garments made of metal alloys. God. Dear God. He wanted to whine and he wanted to pray, maybe cry and beg or buy himself five minutes of radio time to explain his situation, his war wounds and suffering, his failure to thrive as a baby; it all added up to much more than you might think at first glance.

In Stratford, Ila had him given a barrage of instructions—just stay on number seven and then go south on four, you know that, don't you, and then once you're in London—but he hadn't been paying attention, knee-deep as he was by then in second thoughts. He'd told Ila he'd be at least three hours, possibly four, said he was booked for his biannual head x-rays and a few other routine tests because he'd wanted enough time to take Cora for lunch. So now what? Soldier on, he supposed. He wasn't about to go suit shopping and he wasn't intending to spend half a day in the St. Joseph's Hospital cafeteria twiddling his thumbs. And now that he thought about it, what would Cora Farrell know on the subject of men's suits? Her old man probably didn't even own one and neither did Russell Hansen, he'd wager. But she'd just finished high school and gone to the graduation and been taught for years by fops like that Kipling who, Alfred remembered now, made occasional appearances at Lalonde's for lunch, always in a suit, usually black, probably from the late sixties, maybe even 1970. On his salary he could afford to buy one or two new ones every year. It was a known fact that teachers are overpaid.

Downtown London, and he was lost. Nothing looked familiar. He and the Meteor were circling in an eddy of disorientation when he decided to pull over on a busy four-lane boulevard. His face was red, his suit grey and old, and the painted silk horse on his too-wide tie, he couldn't help noticing, had a glue factory look of fear in its eyes, as if it might have guessed this was its last trip. What excuse could be offered for his appearance? None. Accept this fact. He had no choice but to ask the two approaching men for directions, insurance types in their narrow pant legs and very white shirts, everything about them lean and tailored. Fine. Let them look, size him up and clink their eyes together in a gleeful drink of we're not you and we never will be.

Alfred was not about to get out of the car. Nor was he going to remove his hat, or mention in passing he was dressed period for the car. "Excuse me," Alfred called, rolling down the passenger side window, pulling a muscle in the effort, "excuse me!" The two men stopped, heads turning to take in the car. "I'm trying to find St. Joe's."

"Nice car," said the shorter one. "A Meteor, right?"

"Yes, yes, it is." Grateful for this unexpected admiration, Alfred suddenly found himself close to tears. Oh no, dear God, don't let them see that. He played with the gearshift for a moment, as if some adjustment were needed.

"St. Joe's, huh?" the other man said. "Well, you're not too far off track. You gotta go east two lights then north on Waterloo, then go left on Grosvenor. You'll see it right away. You can't miss it."

"Yes, yes. Of course." How could he have got so mixed up?

"No problem. Hope it goes okay for you." As if he were going in for a triple bypass or some dementia medication. And he'd caught the look as they glanced back at him, knew immediately it was about the clothing, as if the horse tie might be a symptom of some deeper disorder. Their ties were unpatterned, he had observed, the uniform of serious work, mutual of this and that, Omaha and the like. Oh damn everybody to hell, Alfred said aloud, stomping on the accelerator. He'd find the visitor parking and the front desk, and he did, with very little difficulty. Anger seemed to activate his inner compass.

"Are you here to see a patient?" the receptionist asked, eyes busy watching someone behind him.

"No, I need to get to the nurses' residence."

Now she looked at him and asked, "Is your daughter studying here?" her enunciation suggesting Alfred might not understand English, was from the old country, had lived a life without benefit of immunizations and haberdasheries.

"Yes," he said, "of course." What did she think? That he was just a neighbour in a dated suit on an ill-conceived quest, a cliche really? I *need* to get to the nurses' residence. Don't all fifty-year-old men need to get to the nurses' residence? Was it possible hospital receptionists studied slide-projected images of suspiciously craven gentlemen just like Alfred in their introductory courses? Yet, she believed him. "Well then. You just go back outside here sir, and go left and keep walking until you come to a boulevard and you're going to go right and you'll see the nurses' residence. It's called Tupper Hall."

"Thank you, miss."

At least she appeared to have believed him. Was it perhaps a strategy of hers to intentionally give the wrong directions, sending him and others like him back to the insurance men, caught in an endless Möbius loop of the aghast and the appalled? No. Now he was becoming paranoid. He would command himself to enjoy the walk to Tupper Hall because it was finally a fresh autumn day and here was the boulevard, as promised. And it was lovely, unexpected, beneath an arch of American elms, a hardy tribe that had managed to survive the plague. Maybe proximity to the hospital had kept the Dutch elm beetles away. Maybe parades of nurses night and day had kept their spirits up. He knew they would certainly lift his.

Alfred drew close to a tree and examined the trunk. Hale and hearty, the bark deeply rutted and not a sign of disease. The last time Alfred could recall having shed a tear was the day he realized the one majestic elm at the end of his laneway had the bug, was on its irrevocable way out. Rather than let it die a slow death, he'd cut it down himself and burned it ceremoniously, throwing some of the ashes into Minnow Lake for crazy sentimental reasons. He reasoned that from the very top of that elm, Minnow Lake would have been visible and maybe a tree had the occasional yearning—maybe. Especially an elm. Maybe a yearning to take a hike or two before it died. Who could say?

This looked like the place. Alfred climbed the stairs, heaved open a churchly door and entered. Immediately to his left, another receptionist, at first glance more invulnerable than the last, much more, to the power of ten, he would estimate.

"Yes?" she asked, this single word managing to suggest she had seen hundreds of men like him, listened to their stories and, unhesitatingly, thrown them out. Parents came in twos, her nostrils clearly implied; mashers, perverts, pedophiles, and the delusional came in ones.

"A neighbour of mine's in nursing here and I thought I'd..."

"And she's expecting you?"

Was that irony or sarcasm? "No. I just happened to be at the hospital. I had to get some tests done and..."

"Oh. I'm afraid all our girls' guests must be announced," said the receptionist, sounding not in the least afraid. "If your neighbour had been expecting someone, I'm sure she would have apprised me and I would have your name here. You see?" she asked, holding aloft a listing of three sets of Misters and Missuses. "Who's the girl?"

"Cora Farrell."

"No. No." Satisfying little negations. People liked to say no. It was better than yes. If no were a floor it would be made of the best hardwood whereas yes, you could dig a thumbnail into it if you wanted, that's how soft it was. "There's nothing here for Cora. No one. She's not expecting anyone."

"Oh, I hadn't realized. Certainly next time I'll call and make arrangements."

"That would be advisable."

A group of three girls rounded a corner from the stairs then, one of them Cora, in jeans and a sweater and looking like she'd never return to East Flax for the obvious reason she'd never been from there in the first place. And the sight of Alfred Beel, even he couldn't lie to himself that convincingly, the sight of Alfred had worked through the muscles of her face like an effortful swallow, one last bite of a taste you'd rather forget.

"Alfred? Are you sick? What are you doing here?" Friends of Cora watching with mouths held in the balance, somewhere between mirth and calculation.

"Oh, just having some tests done and thought I'd look you up."

"Really? I talked to Mom last night. She didn't say anything."

He hadn't thought of that. "Well, you know. Hospital stuff. Better left unsaid."

"We're just going out for some lunch," Cora said. "Otherwise..."

"Oh that's fine. It was just an impulse." A lurid Norman Rockwell type of impulse: deranged man in old suit, head full of plates, hat in hand covering hardon in pants. Six soon-to-be-laughing female eyes. "No, no. No problem. I'll tell your mom and dad you're well. I should be going." Should be bowing and scraping. The muscles of his heart going hard now, giving him away. If only he could reach through his own melted chest and squeeze that ridiculous organ shut, squeeze the blood and humiliation right out of it, wring it like a dishcloth.

Well before the prearranged time, he was back in Stratford, waiting for Ila in the massive theatre parking lot. One car in a field of concrete, grey the colour of his suit. He would have loved to shed the thing right there, leave it lying chameleon-like on the concrete field. No one would notice it. And Ila would invent some conceptual motive for the underwear and socks outfit. Ninety minutes he sat there, thinking: what exactly did I think was going to happen? Wondering: how long will Cora talk about the three crazy geezers who spend every afternoon in her parents' store? The Maestro, the man with no genitals, and Alfred Beel, always trying to get her to empty the ashtray, checking the clothesline for her underpants. And would the receptionist throw in her two cents worth? "I've seen some doozies but he takes the cake. And that suit. It reminded me of Dick Tracy." Until Ila opened the passenger side door to say, "You know, I've got a tweed suit and Persian lamb coat one of my aunts used to own. Maybe one day I could wear that and we could go out for dinner."

Alfred didn't know what to say and no response was necessary. Ila was full of news; a few miles south of Mesmer, he assured her his head x-rays were normal as usual.

At home, Alfred took off the suit and laid it out on the kitchen table along with the horse tie and four others, all illustrated and no doubt twice as wide as the insurance men's. Oh well. In his own house with its shelves and drawers and shining floors, he began to recover. Maddy'd been in to clean and the place was immaculate and pine-scented. And frankly, he liked his ties and, frankly, he did not see what the problem was. What was style but a social plot to make the preoccupied feel bad? To make the aesthetically superior painted silk tie seem ridiculous when held next to the narrow and the synthetic? It was all relative and subjective and he would not be made to feel inferior. He would not. Clothing and style were not his problem. His problem was a male problem, a normal problem, which in any other normal community would be understood as such. Only here, in this colony of reproductive lepers, those with a fully functioning set of gonads, himself, for example, and Cora Farrell were the misfits. Bad enough that Cora was gone, and this was the other half of the problem, but in her stead was Maddy, a kind of athletic version of Russell Hansen. Half this, half that. The spectre of her underwear on the Farrell clothesline actually made him shudder, made him think of the flags and pennants waving in the wind outside the freak show at the CNE. Why he didn't find another cleaner was a mystery to him. Important reminder: very little in East Flax made sense. If you held onto that thought like an angry compass, you might make it safely back to your house by sundown.

Adrian is in his room, looking down upon the white yards of Flax. Incredibly, last night there was snow, the wet spring kind nobody likes, not even kids because by now, May, they are riding their bikes to the empty outdoor pool and looking in. Yesterday, Adrian himself made this trip. Now that he has his Lifesaver's, he hopes to be working at the pool this summer. This summer, when this winter is finally and forever over.

Yanking his head away from the window, Adrian falls back onto the pillow. This fresh layer of snow is a physically nauseating sight, he decides, like acres of uncoloured candy floss which, upon melting, would be wanting to rot the earth's teeth. Think about it. Dentists would need to be called up from other places, maybe the army. George Drury would be in charge of general excavations. Backhoes everywhere; Adrian, you're going to have to drive this one out to the cemetery. Wanting to and not. Better to look at the ceiling. Across the hall, George the dentist is in the bathroom shaving and singing and readying himself for church. "Guide me O,"–pause–"thou great Redeemer,"–pause, pause–"Pilgrim through this barren land,"–tap, tap, tap of razor against bowl of sink. He's in the choir and rarely misses a Sunday; unless he has a stroke, or is called to a dental emergency, this morning will be no exception and the universe will unfold as it should.

Since late Friday, Adrian has been developing his Plan for Alfred Beel and it is now complete, the events of Friday's history class having expedited the process. "Working in pairs,"

Mr. Rigg said, read, in fact, as if he were a substitute, "you are to prepare a class presentation on the history of a Canadian industry," anything from his list, which included salt. Thinking he and Randy could save valuable time and energy by recycling last year's geography project on the same topic, Adrian signed up. Thinking bygones might instantly become bygones, leaning and stretching to pass the list across two rows of grabbing students, Adrian said, "Salt! Look at this Randy. I got the salt topic for us."

Right away, with his worst hangdog face full of grievance, Randy said, "I think I'm gonna work with Weidman."

Adrian had to give Randy credit where response time was concerned. What everyone needs in a best friend, a quick-thinking jackass. In his most incredulous whisper, Adrian hissed, "What? But it's salt. Don't you get it?"

"Yeah, I get it. I'd just rather work with Weidman on dairy. His dad's got a big operation plus he's a local history buff. He'd more or less do the work for us." Randy was opening his binder, threading papers into place, snapping the rings shut, repeating the process.

"Local history buff," Adrian echoed, out loud, to convey his disdain. "Oh fine, Farrell. Be an ass because that's what you are. You have no choice in the matter. No, wait a minute. Do you know what you are?" Adrian asked, grinning. "You're an ass that's stuck in the mud. Your ass somehow got suctioned into the bottom of that bog you call a lake..."

"Hey, hey, hey. What's going on here?" asked Mr. Rigg, taking the list from Adrian and passing it to another set of hands.

"Nothing," Randy said. At least he wasn't a rat.

"Yeah, nothing," added Adrian, zipping up his over-

stuffed binder.

Later, at Randy's funhouse locker with its shelves and rows of plastic horses and soldiers and bags of licorice pipes, Adrian asked, "At least give me what's left of the original salt project. I can use it as a prop kind of thing. I'll drive out and get it this weekend. I can't start from scratch and you'll notice nobody signed up with me. Thanks again, Farrell."

"I'd actually rather keep it in my room," said Randy, knowing he was being weird and would have gladly handed over the remains of the project if he weren't, knew it was crazy not to, but *in my room* said it all.

"You mean now it's part of an arrangement that can't be unarranged. Am I right?"

Randy reached inside his locker and positioned the bag of licorice pipes between two symmetrical and opposing rearing plastic horses, as if this might explain his nuttiness. He knew enough to look as foolish as he was. "Yes, that's correct."

Adrian shook his head like a teacher at a loss for what to do, a teacher who would have gladly shaken Randy if it would have done any good but there was no shaking the arrangements out of that big head of his. They were attached like an extra set of teeth, protected behind the first and with roots longer than the average thumb. Since that moment, Adrian had not stopped thinking and this was the plan.

Adrian has a pen pal, an ex-pen pal named Harold Terwilliger. Last year, in geography, the entire class had pen pals from places all over Canada and his, Harold, lived in Vancouver. Luckily, that was where Loretta was rumoured to be; at least Beel would think she was there as much as the next person. All Adrian had to do was write a few letters postmarked Vancouver, leading Beel to believe Loretta wanted to meet with him somewhere, maybe in Winnipeg or better yet, right there on Beel's property so Adrian could watch the old fart waiting, maybe even leap out from behind a tree in a wig causing him to have a heart attack from the humiliation and disappointment. Or better yet, just deliver one good punch in the teeth, one satisfying right hook to the face of the man who'd felt the need to take a bad situation and make it worse than worse, transform it into a mess that went beyond the scope of any grammar book ever written.

There was George Drury in his bedroom now, dressing and whistling, whistling and dressing. Hurry it up, Pop. Hurry. It. Up.

Unfortunately, the personality of Harold Terwilliger was the direct cause of the two weaknesses in Adrian's plan. One, he was the most miserly pen pal assigned. After writing only two letters, he had asked Adrian if, in future, he wouldn't mind including an SASE—that's self-addressed, stamped envelope, he explained. Harold was saving up for his own television set and did not want to dip into his budget for stamps and envelopes; his parents were instilling independence, otherwise he'd use theirs. Compare this with Jimmy Drake's pen pal whose father worked for Air Canada and flew Jimmy to Calgary for a weekend. Adrian supposed the penny-pinching Terwilliger could easily be persuaded to assist in this project with one dollar compensation enclosed for each letter mailed.

Ah, the minstrel George draws closer. "On a hill far away, stood an old rugged cross." Two crisp knocks on the bedroom door. "I'm going now, Adrian."

"Okay, Dad. See you later."

"No shortage of eggs in the fridge if you want to make yourself an omelette," meaning, don't kill yourself while I'm out, Son; there are plenty of simple pleasures left in life.

"Yeah, okay. Thanks, Dad."

He was on his way. Praise the Lord.

The other problem with Terwilliger was his weird goody-goodiness. He was always wrestling on the "horns" of some moral dilemma having to do with ratting on people, like should he phone some guy's parents and tell them he had seen their son shoplifting a single Dubble Bubble gum? How important was that, he wanted to know in his colossally boring pen pal letters. So obviously, if Terwilliger happened to open one of Adrian's fake letters to Beel and deduce what he was up to, that would be the end of the game. Although maybe his advanced moral development, as Terwilliger himself liked to describe it, would not allow for invasion of privacy. To be on the safe side, Adrian would have to invent a motive, preferably scholastic, something like a game of Cross-Canada History Clue. People pretending to be someone famous, dropping clues in whatever method might be available to them. Letters from a woman in Vancouver would be ideal but who would he say he was? What famous woman living in Vancouver would be writing sexy letters to an old goat in East Flax? Adrian would think of something. If worse came to worst, he would tell Terwilliger he was too lazy to do the research and had just made up a fictional character.

Adrian listens for the front door then plans to wait another five minutes. Not uncommon for George Drury to forget something and return. A good opportunity to think about dogs, Skokie in particular. If Skokie were still alive she'd be on the bed with Adrian now, maybe hoping to lick his feet if they popped out from beneath the covers or just sleeping, and Adrian moves his hand to the place she would have been. She used to exhale sometimes, a larger than average breath, then forget to inhale, causing a sort of listening panic for Adrian until she breathed again and went back to normal. Although he never really thought she was dying, just holding her breath or needing to be prodded to inhale. She was definitely still always fully alive; you could tell from the ambience, as Anastasia would say. Amazing how different sleeping while alive was from sleeping while dead, how much difference lungs could make, mixing up oxygen and red blood cells. Which reminds Adrian of Anastasia's AB blood, the rarest, the reddest and the bloodiest.

Apparently his dad is going and almost gone. Adrian cranes his neck to the window once more and can see the exhaust, the snow swept from the windows of the car but not the roof. It'll blow off between here and the church parking lot. There he goes, backing out the driveway and Adrian feels a sad plop in his stomach, as if a miniature human figure had nosedived into it, from a ping-pong table or some other ledge. But there's no time to waste and Adrian must strictly follow his multi-step plan for getting up and pad directly down the stairs in bare feet and pyjamas. Past the kitchen and the plenitude of eggs, through the door into the office. Here are the metal chairs with the red vinyl upholstery, the desk—formerly for Loretta, more formerly for Rose—the telephone and the two filing cabinets, gunmetal grey. Everything brighter like the time they took the blinds down to paint but this time it's the snow.

Adrian has never got used to the smell of dentistry. You'd think the son of the dentist would have developed an indifference but to Adrian the room smells of smoky drilled bone and fear. Even dogs could smell it and knew not to get too close. When Skokie was alive she preferred to stay out of the waiting room but positively avoided the so-called surgery with its hydraulic too-reclining chair and restraining trays and mouth-proportioned instruments. Adrian shudders and gets to work.

Beel's file would be in the top drawer. A's. B's. Baldwin, Beaton, Beazley, Beel. Ha. Adrian pulls the file, body resonating instantly with wrongdoing, as if he has been wired to the telephone exchange, his chest a switchboard connected to each and every household in Flax, East Flax, and possibly Mesmer. Will they all know tomorrow? Awake with blame rekindled for that Drury boy? They say he can't leave well enough alone.

Here's the information he needs. Address: R.R. 1 Flax. That's it? He might have guessed as much. And here's his date of birth: September 22, 1920. Might come in handy. Returning Alfred to the drawer, Adrian thinks what about Loretta? Of course. He hadn't thought of this. In order to impersonate her, he needs to know something about Loretta. Same drawer. Decker, Decker, where are you? Cheryl's file is gone, of course; Richard's too. The entire D section has been gutted but Loretta's still here and with trembling fingers he manages to write her date of birth, May 31, 1932.

He's scared now, eavesdropping on past fears with his switchboard body. Cheryl was once in this room. Worrying. There's a germ of her fear somewhere close by, living the way germs and viruses survive, tucked inside the glue of an old magazine, or clinging to the oily tracks of a file cabinet drawer. Adrian slams the thing shut but can't leave yet. He needs Loretta's signature. Sitting at the desk he rummages through the top drawer. Thank you God, it wasn't locked.

The new receptionist, Janice Byrne, isn't that thorough. George has said so.

Adrian is shivering and blaming the snow. It's too cold in here and there's nothing in this drawer except for pens and paper clips, a few coins, a tube of lipstick, and a black receipt book. Receipt book? Yes. Back, back, back Adrian flips through the months to November, dirty carbon paper pages reminding him of seagulls' wings, filthy and dirty to the touch, and here it is. Here she is. Received from Rocket Lalonde the sum of forty dollars. One extraction, one filling. Signed by Loretta Decker. A perfect sample. Her handwriting is easy, almost like printing but joined and Adrian rips the carbon copy from the book, slams it shut, and the drawer and the door behind him. Runs upstairs to hide the evidence in the drawer of his side table and turns the shower on to scalding. Hot as the human skin can endure without burning, blistering, and turning to scab. Certain days the cold of Cheryl gets inside his blood. Memory poison, Anastasia would say. You have a near-fatal dose, Drury.

"I still don't get it," Anastasia said. She and Rose were in the students' parking lot surrounded by fumes, engines, burning oil, burning cigarettes, the best part of the day spilling its exhaust. "You're going to go *swimming* with Maddy Farrell. Maddy Farrell of the orange hat and fishing lures. The escapee from Dr. Seuss. In East Flax, no less."

"It's not just Maddy I want to see; it's partly the lake," Rose said. "It has sentimental value. I used to go there with my mom." Any reference to the deceased mother stopped Anastasia's questioning mind in the way of news of an approaching and disfiguring epidemic.

"Well, I'd better get going then, head home, forsake all plans involving my former best friend Rose Drury," said Anastasia, perplexed and yet amused by her own perplexity. "Let you get off to the soggy land of the bed wetters."

"I wish I hadn't told you that," said Rose, opening the door to the Vega. "I really wish I hadn't told you that."

Anastasia shrugged and smiled, her mind mixing up the ingredients for a series of warm, warm questions. "Til next time," she said. "Adieu, adieu."

Waving a glad farewell, Rose reversed, anxious to be free of Anastasia and her oversized opinions, her big radio transmitter self, generating thoughts with the amplitude of a full-grown maple tree, invisible to most but there they were now in the rear-view mirror. Slow frequency influence rising from the double crown of that very blonde head as it talked to Connie Laine. Good-bye, Anastasia, Rose mouthed the words. *I'm going to Minnow Lake.* She hadn't been for almost a month now and the longing to revisit was like something pinned inside her chest, a mixed-up brooch, those orange touch-me-not flowers that blow themselves up in the race to reproduce. All it takes is a breeze or someone walking by. When Rose saw Maddy in the hallway, out popped this question: "Are you going to be home after school? I thought I might come out for a swim."

"Yes, sure, come out before supper. It's been so hot this September, more like July. I'll meet you by the dock."

Rose would have given her a ride but walking with Maddy to the parking lot, driving home with her as if she were Anastasia, (wait here, I'll just change into my suit) all seemed too unlikely, even unnatural. As Adrian would say, like geese deciding to fly in another letter, a W or an S. Instead, as an alternative gesture of solidarity, Rose had gone home at lunch and changed into her bathing suit, knowing Anastasia would notice right away, and need to be told. But better, and regardless, knowing that the suit, beneath her clothes, would provoke constant, close reminding of swimming and lakes and the prospect of Maddy. If, at the final hour, she'd said no, don't come, I won't be there, I'll be vacuuming the Mesmer Hall, Rose would have gone anyway. Bathing suits had a certain stretchy determination. More than halfway there and Rose stopped, pulled off her shirt, threw it into the back and rolled both windows right down. Further on, in the marshy curves, she slowed down to listen to the biological noises now associated with Maddy, then sped up.

Maddy was waiting, of course; Maddy would never not be waiting. She was standing on the grassy, buggy bank in Cora's pink, too-small bathing suit, the back climbing up her ass. There was Russell Hansen's row-boat semi-submerged, tethered to the wildly angled dock. Could and should be the village flag, emblem of all things barely hanging on, tilting towards disaster.

And within seconds, the news was out. Maddy couldn't swim! Rose had never had a friend who could not swim. Not only that, up to her neck in water, Maddy confessed she'd never even put her head under. *Was it because of the septic systems?* But the water smelled clean and the sun was deep in the west, already a little red as were the tips of the tiny waves, as if all the red-winged blackbirds for miles had been organized into shimmers.

"Oh, come on," Rose said, a little more than happy to be there. "You have to at least put your head under. There's nothing to it." Although if there was nothing to it, why could she remember so clearly her own first dip beneath the surface of the Flax pool? Ears filled with chlorinated silence, Anastasia's legs separated from the rest of her like two skinny roots. So this was what the fish saw. "Do it, Maddy. It's just a little strange, that's all."

Maddy obeyed. She bent her knees and sank, not bothering to hold her nose, and stayed under for too long, hair breaking the surface like muddy smoke, like there'd been a small explosion in the lake bottom. What was she looking at down there? It was a bit like someone climbing beneath your skirt or under your desk. Or maybe she didn't know to come up for air. Look at Randy Farrell. Adrian said he could hold his breath until he fainted. The normal biological instincts were perhaps slightly off-kilter with the Farrells; the dials were all knocked sideways like the oven control on the Limbs' stove where 350 meant 200. Rose pulled on Maddy's hair and up she came, easy as pie.

"You have to come up for air, you know."

"I know that. You think I don't know to breathe?" Maddy asked, pushing the hair back from her face. "I was looking around, that's all. You said it's a little strange. That's what I was looking at, how strange it is. I know I have to breathe, for God's sake."

Oh brother. Now Maddy was angry, meaning Rose would have to show her something. "Okay, watch. I'm going to swim to the ski jump and back. Watch this. I'm going to show you how to dive."

What a relief to kick her feet like a motor and swim better than Maddy could ever play basketball. Rose would have to start this visit over again without any heads under water. That had been a mistake, proving Maddy wasn't as easy to get along with as she should be. And there *was* something funny about her looks. Rose hated to think Anastasia might be right, but when Maddy'd come up from the water, her hair pushed back and nothing but face, Rose could see what she was getting at, saying Maddy might have a chromosomal disorder, maybe two x's and one y.

"I'll bet that's what she has," Anastasia said once, sometime after the orange hat phase. "She's a creature struggling to be female. But her family would never have the wherewithal to get the test."

"What test?" Rose asked.

"The genetics test, dummy."

"What difference would getting a test make? You can't change your chromosomes."

"The difference is," said Anastasia with deliberate patience, "you could apologize. You could say 'Hi, I'm Maddy Farrell and I have some sort of syndrome which caused me to wear ridiculous clothing last winter. I'm sorry. Because of my condition I am exempt from any responsibility for my fashion sense.' Then all would be forgiven."

"Maybe you should get a test, Anastasia," said Rose. "Maybe they'd find out you have a condition where both your x's have little horns on them. Then *you'd* have an excuse."

"Very funny, Rosita," was all Anastasia had to say.

Close to the ski jump now and wanting Maddy to be watching, leaving a wake that would sooner or later, no matter how diminished, slap itself against the shores of this sad lake and whisper See? See? Maddy *had* to be watching. What else was there to do? Twisting her neck and shoulders Rose caught a glimpse of the blurry figure, seemingly following her progress from the shore, watching in the appropriate direction at any rate. Renewed energy. This is called the Australian crawl. Watch, Maddy, you might learn something. This is what Rose thinks when she's swimming; she thinks purl, purl, knit, purl. On knit, she takes a breath. Swimming has a rhythm just like knitting, which she learned from Mrs. Limb. Purl, purl, knit, purl. Are you watching, Maddy?

Here was the ski jump. Now she'd have to climb its furry slope. Gag. Why must all that murky water life forever want to crawl up the sides of anything half-wet? Like unbrushed gums attached to bone-dry, sun-baked plywood, warm to lie on but not now. Maybe one day with Adrian. Time to get on with the show, stand at the apex and wave to Maddy who was yelling something frantically. Oh dear. Rose did not like frantic or any of its associates, franticide or frantigelic. Frantifarious. Good one. Consult with Anastasia. Add to dictionary.

"What?" Rose shouted, listening closer for the rippled and refracted words.

"Don't dive. It's shallow."

"I can do a shallow dive," Rose called back, her words lost in a chilly gust of wind, teeth suddenly chattering like when she was little and on the edge of the pool listening to rules, fingertips wizened.

Dive right in, electrified with fear of paralysis and wheelchairs and the bottom of the lake, all gruesome with water-logged trunks and what resembled a knot of barbed wire and back to the surface. Unparalysed! And swimming hard, the sun hot on her shoulders and the final days of summer making a protest, wanting to stay right here in East Flax, pull themselves from the calendar's grid and swim. Swim back to Maddy on the bank in her threadbare towel, imperfect as always, two poofs of pubic hair escaping on either side of the front of her suit.

Rose stood and breathed, that's all she could do. Frantic, she thinks, frantelepathy. Wondered if Maddy could tell how near-to-collapse she felt. Remembered a time at the pool with Anastasia, staring and pointing, "Shave, gorilla girl," she'd said. "Your pubes are showing."

"You sure can swim fast," said Maddy, her voice blurry and separate from the rest of her, a tape recorder with the batteries low.

"Yeah," Rose agreed, exhaling hard. "Yeah. Let's

leave the car here and walk. That okay with you?"

"Sure. Do you want to bring your clothes and change or...?"

"No, I'll just wear the towel, leave my stuff in the car." And they walked to the store, saying nothing, Rose still a little winded, thinking like a fish, their flip flop sandals reminding her of gills, the way they separated from and met their feet. "If only people could breathe the oxygen out of water," she finally said. "That would be good."

"But it would be kind of going backwards, wouldn't it, evolution-wise? I mean if we came from the water in the first place."

"True," Rose said, feeling a little more herself. "I guess you can't have your oxygen and drink it too. Ha ha."

Maddy didn't laugh. Did she ever? Rose couldn't say, not having studied Maddy as closely as she hoped to be studied by her. At the few basketball games Rose had attended last year, she could recall not one outburst of Maddified jocularity. Not that even Rose would have laughed at her own oxygen joke because it was more a George than a Rose Drury type of rejoinder, threatening to break into a lesson plan: even in humour, a point must be made. And what exactly had Rose expected? Perfectly synchronous hee, hee, heeing, in the style of Wilma Flintstone and Betty Rubble? One thing Maddy was not was Wilma Flintstone or Betty Rubble. Because of the chromosomes, Anastasia would add. No, Rose would argue, because she lives in a *Gunsmoke* store.

Outside the Drink Pepsi door, Rose stopped Maddy. "Maybe you should tuck that hair in. Or wrap the towel around your waist. Those guys..."

"Oh yeah, right." Maddy blushed. "The towel's not really big enough."

"Just hold it in front of you then. Like a fig leaf."

At this, Maddy sniffed a half-laugh, which gave Rose courage. Had Adrian, she wondered, ever noticed the air was yellower in East Flax than other places? This time of day, at any rate. Maybe closer to evening the sun ricocheted itself up from the lake and painted East Flax twice.

Maddy had prepared for every possible contingency, especially this one: the unmistakable rustle of plastic as Rose sat on Cora's old bed. "Oh that's the mattress cover. It's new. They got it for me when I moved into Cora's room." When the truth was she'd stapled a plastic sheet over the old thing, obtained from her dad, no questions asked.

All over the surface of her mind, Maddy had conversations thumbtacked, as if it were corkboard in there, things she would never say to her family or Greta Leopold, ridiculous made-up sentences intended to sound spontaneous about how much she'd like to buy a telescope once she had enough money saved because she might go into astronomy one day. Or, what did Rose think of Karmann Ghias? Weren't they cool cars and someday she'd have one. But from someplace behind the corkboard, the first uncomfortable silence delivered this: "What do your friends say about you spending time with me?"

"They say nothing," Rose said.

"Oh. Then I guess they're nicer than Greta Leopold," said Maddy, pulling a balled up pair of shorts from her dirty laundry to put on.

"Who's Greta Leopold? Oh wait, wait. I know her." Rose Drury was waving her hands as if she had swallowed something hot. "Is she short and wears an old fur coat sometimes? And her bangs look like they just came out of a roller?"

"That's Greta. She lives about two miles that way," Maddy said, with a northward gesture, "and we were sort of best friends, last year, well, since elementary school in a way. We used to sit on the bus together until she saw me talking to you a couple weeks ago, and then on the bus she asked me if I would be, quote, converting to a snob, end of quote. Then just by pure coincidence she wanted to come out to the lake for a swim today and I said you were and she looked at me the way she always does when she's planning some revenge." Maddy stopped for a moment, happy to have quoted and ended quoting.

"Which is?" Rose asked, drying the ends of her long hair with the sun-coloured towel.

"Well, she looks a little like a cartoon with a balloon picture over her head of her tripping me or pushing me in front of a moving car."

"She wouldn't do that, would she?"

"No, of course not," Maddy said, tossing her own

saturated towel into the laundry basket, "of course not. You sure have a strange view of people out here, don't you? You think we don't know you can't breathe under water and we push our friends in front of cars if they make us mad."

Rose stood, scrubbing at her head, offering no explanation. Maybe with the sound of terrycloth against her ears and scalp, she hadn't heard.

"She just gets that dumb revenge look," Maddy said, pulling at a fraying quilt square. "Maybe your friends don't get that look, like you'll never guess what I have in store for you." The quilt square came free of its moorings, being old enough to crumble into ash between Maddy's fingers. "Do they?" she asked.

Rose's hair fell straight along the sides of her face, like a folk singer or a demonstrator. "With Anastasia it's more she gets mad when things don't go her way. She gets a look on her face then. It's like she's concentrating, like she's having a B.M. right behind her eyes. I told her that once and she didn't speak to me for a week. And since then she tries not to get that expression on her face but it's still happening. I recognize it; it's all about planning way, way ahead to get things back on track, her track. It's probably not all that different from Greta."

Now Maddy took a walk to her dresser. She was thinking B.M. The only other person she had known to use that term was Russell Hansen, and from him those two otherwise innocent letters sounded affected, like Maddy talking about art in the dance hall and she realized this was the problem with talking to Rose.

Each of Maddy's stabs at worldliness or belongingness was converted, as Greta would say, to a B.M. Rose could come right out and say anything, admit to wetting the bed, to having a jewellery box filled with fishing lures, and both practices would instantly become the envy of girls everywhere. Rose could make reference to the actual living business of taking a dump and from her, B.M. itself would take on new meaning. Maybe it already had. Maybe it was a perfume, invented by Revlon, with Twiggy as its ambassador and Maddy as its joke.

Opening the top drawer of her dresser, Maddy said, "Look at this."

Rose came close, opened her eyes wide. Sometimes Maddy just couldn't wait. She'd planned to save the drawer at least until Rose's next visit but here it was, open, a revelation, stacks of chocolate bars and potato chips, Smarties, Life Savers, and Cherry Blossoms, all organized and arranged as if by Randy. "Want a Jersey Milk?" Maddy asked.

"Mmm," Rose pursed up her lips, "better not. Too close to dinner."

Maddy nodded, "Yeah," gently pushing the drawer shut so as not to jostle its treasure. But this had obviously got Rose thinking.

"Do you think your mom would let me use the till?" she asked.

Maddy smiled. "Nope." That should close the discussion.

"Couldn't I ask anyway?"

Having pictured them talking in her room, foreheads close and laughing, for, she realized now, an infinitude, Maddy was reluctant. "Does that mean you want to go downstairs to the store?"

"Don't you?"

"Well, the men are down there. I try to steer clear as a rule." Maddy found a sleeveless blouse in the bottom drawer and put it on. Rose had worn a similar shirt to school that day.

"You shouldn't let them bother you. It's your store, not theirs. You shouldn't allow yourself to be controlled by a bunch of old coots." Rose tied the towel around her waist, giving her hair an authoritative toss.

"Plus," she went on, "your store is interesting to me. A store has got to have a lot more to offer in the human interest department than a dentist's office. For one thing, you most likely don't have to listen to people moaning."

"You have to listen to them talking, though, which is way worse. But, let's go" Maddy said, supposing there might be some prestige to be had in human interest. "Let's face the music."

Rose led the way, down one set of stairs, past the barricaded balcony and Frog Farrell's spelling mistakes and then the open door to Maddy's old room. Was that a faint whiff, or was it the lemon polish her mom used? Next, the second set of stairs with the peeling wallpaper, appliances where they shouldn't be, the hall with its extension cord snakes, the kitchen smelling of drains. Maddy took a deep breath. Welcome to the store and everything about it—its debts, its tabloids, its questionable owner with her inventory of fly swatters and mousetraps and dandruffy old men, cartons filled with bad ideas waiting to be unpacked.

"No ma'am, you may not use the till," said Maddy's mother, "unless that is you can verify in writing that you are a Farrell or a Cobb by birth. Family only with the rare exception being made for that man right there," gesturing to Alfred Beel. "There have to be firm policies on that kind of issue. That's how the bigger stores operate and smaller stores go under by failing to operate like the bigger stores."

If there were one incarnation of her mother Maddy disliked, this was it: the indisputable, no, worse, the imperious Angel Farrell, as if she were dispossessed royalty. What a joke. Did she not know the Van Epps were Flax's variation of the long lost Romanovs? And Maddy stopped herself short. Did her mother even *know* the Van Epps? Oh yes, of course she did. Some of Angel's sources said Ila had practically been in the mental hospital over that election business; others said she'd actually spent a night there. And Peter. Peter wrote disgraceful letters to the paper. Letters complaining about *living* people in the community. That, Angel said, was declasse and not the intention of a letter to the paper. Letters were supposed to provide an opinion on an issue. Ask Alfred, Angel said, ask Alfred. Ask Alfred, ask Alfred, ask Alfred. He could tell you what was what.

That's for sure. Maddy knew he'd be hatching up a topic right now, an issue sure to aggravate her. Usually, having a friend in the store caused an odd veering in his interests toward the intimate. Not that Maddy often had a friend but even Greta Leopold seemed to get to Alfred via her. Last time Greta was here, he'd wanted to discuss the value of physical education in schools, almost as if he were on Maddy's side, which he wasn't—that's how far he would go—against the tubby and clumsy Greta.

But Greta had risen above the bait, which is what Leopolds did. Without even a blush, she agreed with Alfred, said she thought PE was important but "qualified" her comments by observing that some, like Maddy, were born athletic, while others had to contend with hormonal problems that might cause an imbalance. "And those individuals," Greta concluded, "just have to make the best of it, make the best of what they have, which in my case is brains," and that's what Greta intended to do. She would invite them all to the first, of what would likely be three post-secondary graduations.

"Hear, hear," the Maestro had said. "And she's a crackerjack trumpet player." What could Alfred do but grimace and fumble for his smokes? What could Maddy do but crack her knuckles and head for the door?

Now Alfred said to Angel, "But the bigger stores don't have discussion groups, do they? That's a critical difference." Holding high one all-knowing pointer finger, he went on. "Try having a discussion group at Loblaws. They'll throw you out for loitering. By the way, Maddy, where are your manners? Get your friend a drink. She likes cream soda as I recall."

Already. Maddy'd thought he might be distracted

by grocery chains and Angel's rules of order but here he was, here he was turning his big, brown sights on her.

"I happen to know she prefers orange," Maddy said, happy, *very* happy, to share a knowing look with Rose. Her first, and it went straight to her head, like a report card filled not only with A's but hand-written compliments spilling beyond the allocated space. *Maddy is such a pleasure to have in class.* She grabbed a bottle from the cooler, handed it to her friend.

"A rose who likes orange. Doesn't seem right to me. A rose should like cream soda, don't you think, Maestro?" No reprieve. Here came the opinions, jockeying for position, getting themselves into a sweat.

"You didn't walk from Flax wearing those little plastic things on your feet, did you?" the Maestro asked Rose. "I don't know how the kids these days can wear those things on their feet. I wear a solid shoe winter and summer. Some future podiatrist is going to get rich from this plastic sandal trend."

"I have a car," said Rose, opening her drink. "We left it by the lake so the seats wouldn't get wet."

"So the seats wouldn't get wet," Alfred said, as if this were the punch line to an off-colour joke. "Well, I'm not surprised the dentist's daughter has a car. A lot of money in dentistry."

Maddy watched Rose shrug off this observation. Marvelling at Rose's indifference, Maddy gave herself a moment to look, to take in the big yellow beach towel, enough length to wrap any average sized person twice, the pale blue bathing suit, straps criss-crossing at the back because it was designed for serious swimmers, not people who'd never been under water. Maddy blinked to memorize this image, swallowed hard to store it near her breastbone. Take off her clothes tonight and maybe it just it might show up. You never knew. Cameras were designed after the human eye.

"Anyway," Alfred clapped his hands, "six people. Let's get down to business. We have a quorum. That means we need to have a discussion. Any topics? Angel?"

"You and your topics. I'll give you a topic. Empty the ashtray."

"Maestro, the ashtray."

"Russell," said the Maestro, pointing at the collection of butts.

"I'm afraid my job description made no mention of ashtrays," said Russell with a grin.

"Never mind, never mind. I'll get to it later," said Alfred. "Now then, since we have two young ladies in our midst, how about dating? When should the modern miss be allowed to date? A contentious subject. Rose Drury, why don't you begin?"

"That's easy," said Rose, making an adjustment to her towel skirt, "I think sixteen." She was at the counter, her back to the till. For better viewing, Maddy had stayed by the cooler. And everyone else was in position: to her right, the Maestro, and to his right, Russell. Directly across from the two of them in the biggest and saggiest chair sat Alfred.

"And you are...?"

"I turned seventeen in July."

"So you've been dating for the better part of a year."

"No," Rose laughed. "I had two dates when I was fifteen. Then I decided to take a break."

News to Maddy but how would she have known?

"So you haven't followed your own guidelines. Or is sixteen your father's idea?"

"My father hasn't really had much to say on the topic. He doesn't set a lot of rules. Something happens and then he might make one up after the fact." More hair tossing. "Like, after my brother brought some beer home, suddenly there was a no beer rule. And also, for him, homework before you go out. For me, not so many. When I got asked out on my first date I told Dad I was going out and he said I guess that's to be expected. There was no rule and as it turned out, I didn't need a rule because two dates were enough."

Maddy watched Rose take a long drink of orange pop. Her turn was coming and she was ready. Funnily enough, today she wasn't disliking Alfred so much, was not fearing him one bit. Today she would have said he was more like a team than himself, maybe he was the Mesmer Lady Mustangs, all six rushing toward her from their end of the gym but, through a series of pivots and fake-outs, more than likely she'd sneak past.

"Permissive I see. I assume he's read Benjamin Spock. And, it's none of my business but who was this first escort?"

"Correct," the Maestro interrupted. "Your assertion is correct. It is none of your business."

"Point taken, Maestro."

"Oh, I don't mind naming names," said Rose. "It was my next door neighbour, Foster Limb. I know him almost as well as I know my own brother. So I told him that was the problem, that he was like my Foster brother."

"Foster brother," Russell repeated, his belly laughing to itself.

"And Maddy," Alfred said, eyes connecting with hers at last. "What about you? What age for dating?"

"I agree with Rose. Sixteen." She knew where he was going.

"And you are what age now?"

"I'll be seventeen in November."

"And thus you have logged, let me see, ten months of dating experience?"

"No, Alfred, I have not," Maddy said, leaning an elbow on the cooler's white top.

"Meaning?" Alfred asked.

Now Maddy shrugged. "What do you mean" she wanted to know, "by meaning?"

"Meaning she's never been asked, Alfred," Angel interrupted. "Maddy's not Cora, as you know and Cora's not Maddy."

Meaning what? Maddy wondered.

"Yes, I'm well aware of that," said Alfred, shifting in his chair. "I was simply endeavouring to obtain Maddy's views on the subject because it is a subject that interests me. My meaning of meaning was that, nevertheless, despite an absence of personal experience, what are your views?"

Angel tapped a pencil against her lips. "You're just trying to get Maddy's goat," she said, "and you know that."

"Not at all," said Alfred in his own defence. "Not everyone dates but there can be some vicarious pleasure obtained in the discussion of courtship. I myself will admit I have not been on a date in decades, nor, I would venture to guess, has Russell here. The Maestro here is anybody's guess. As for Maddy, my only point would be that a suitable age for dating becomes moot if nobody's asking. A moot point. Use that in an essay Maddy and you'll get an extra mark." He crossed his legs, cupping both hands around a knee.

Maddy tapped her fingers on the cooler, thinking. Then, "I'll remember that Mr. Beel," she said. "Although, I suppose a corollary, as they say in math, of your moot point might be, at what age should an old man *stop* dating, if he's not anyway, that is?"

"Touché," said Rose.

"Point taken," conceded Alfred, pulling his smokes from a shirt pocket, unflappable.

But by now Angel had had enough. Maddy could see it coming. "All right, you've gone too far," her mother said. "All of you. I don't know why we can't have a nice, civil conversation. So I hereby disband today's discussion group. Maybe I need to tear a page from Loblaws's book and kick you all out for loitering."

"C'mon Rose. I'll walk you to your car," Maddy said, preparing her bare legs for the walk past Alfred. Good or bad, anticipation could be like this: skin rubbed with electricity, awaiting contact, a hair-raising jolt. What would he have to say?

Lighting up, Alfred said, "Ah. The era of chivalry is not yet dead, I see."

Russell to the rescue. "I seem to recall," he said, winking at Maddy, "some reference to female knights, in Denmark of course, the country of my forebears, where of course the same rules of conduct applied with respect to chivalry is what I'm saying."

Alfred waved a dismissive hand, the blackened match head falling to the floor. "Pish posh."

And Rose said, "Well, the era of chivalry might not be dead but I sure will be if I don't get home for supper. That's one thing Dad does get kind of bent out of shape over. Not to mention, I'm supposed to be the gravy-maker."

Maddy smiled as she opened the door. On an afternoon such as this, she could actually enjoy Alfred's luxuriant hatefulness. It had the smell of wet grass and cowshit in summer heat, a combination that set little swarms of houseflies abuzz inside her knees and elbows, certain, with their 360 degree vision, that life could only get better.

Reg and Loretta were in the basement. They'd carted two lawn chairs down where the air was cool and smelled of wet magazines even though there were none to be found. Loretta had looked—she despised that smell—but it was an empty sort of basement with nothing but shelves of preserved fruit and pickles and the furnace, empty beer bottles in cases of twenty-four, and cardboard boxes from Pond's IGA, and oh, she thought: boxes. Boxes would be the source of the paper smell, damp descendants of the tree. She'd get rid of them tomorrow.

Today, Loretta was in a better mood, almost playful. Getting away from the dealership and its books had been a good idea. And while everyone else was fed up with the heat and humidity, she enjoyed renewed energy. Plus, she and Reg hadn't spent time like this, alone, with no purpose, no television, no Jimmy Drake, no sad Cheryl, for as long as she could recall.

"I guess," Loretta said to Reg, "that was another sleepy, dusty delta day for Flax, Ontario." Like diners in a restaurant booth, they were sitting side by side, an overturned box supporting Reg's root beer and Loretta's gin.

"Delta, maybe. Not dusty." Reg crossed his arms to punctuate this mouthful-sized contradiction.

"Four words," said Loretta, covering her mouth in mock astonishment. "My goodness. You must have some to spare tonight."

"Yes," Reg sighed, deciding now to unbutton his shirt, "I think I can say I am officially getting tired of that game. When people start to take too much notice, I get tired."

Eyebrows raised, Loretta asked, "Who's taking too much notice?" On the issue of minding one's own business, she and Reg saw eye-to-eye.

"Everybody. Jimmy, Rocket, the whole town. As far as I can see it's become goddamn common knowledge.

So, I might just adopt a new system. Nothing whatsoever to do with talk. I'm not sure what," Reg said, pulling a wrinkled shirt-tail from his pants. "I can't be normal like I used to be, if you call what I used to be normal. That much I know. I know I can't go back to being totally normal. I have to have some pointless thing to keep track of, besides cars, that is, not that I think cars are pointless but you know what I mean. We'll see. Reginald Decker will think of something a little less public than word-counting. Anyway," putting an arm around Loretta, "I didn't see much dust today; too damn humid for dust. Dust would be a welcome relief."

The arm was nice. Loretta leaned into it. And although she would have preferred no system at all, Loretta wasn't about to complain; the death of the ridiculous word-counting program would mean new life for her. Reg and his reticence had been driving her batty, the reason she'd stopped doing the books, the reason she'd dreamed a half dozen times in the last year she was trapped in the showroom with a clerical error, adding and adding and adding again, always getting a different sum, the problem unmistakably hers to fix. The worst of it had been one night more than a month ago. Lying in bed, back to back, she'd been complaining, nagging, she supposed, wishing for the love of God Reg would just say something other than yes, no, or maybe.

"All right," Reg had said, "all right already. I've got twenty-one words left. What in Christ's name would you like me to say in that amount of talk?" She'd be sorry she'd insisted.

Flipping onto her other side so as to face Reg's naked back, Loretta had said, "Oh, I don't know Reg." Did every conversation have to be such a big production? A favour to her? "How about, why don't you say this? Why don't you say, 'Loretta, don't forget your mother died of cirrhosis?' Or, 'Loretta, if you didn't have all those bottles of gin in the house, maybe Richard would still be around.' Why don't you say that, Reg, and get it off your chest?" And then, "And are you *ever* going to get a haircut again or is that part of the program too?"

"Fine then," he had said, raising himself on one elbow to peer backwards at his wife. "Consider it said."

"Consider what said?" Loretta asked, the urge to shout, no, scream, like an aerosol in her throat, contents under pressure, keep away from open flame.

"That your mother died of cirrhosis," turning away, head returning to pillow with an unanswerable flop.

Loretta'd thrown back the covers in disgust, gone to the bathroom and sat on the toilet in a rage beyond words, seeing numbers, adding, subtracting, erasing, until she had herself a dirty and smudge-bordered hole, a messy window into the next clean page. Might as well take a ruler and tear it out, might as well throw away the entire ledger at that stage. Sitting there, she could not remember if she had ever hated Reg, or anyone, more than she did at that moment.

So this, today, sitting side by side in the damp basement, was progress; no more word counting. "Well," Loretta said.

"That's *all* you have to say?" asked Reg, a little ironic.

"Maybe I'm counting mine too," and she poked him in the ribs. "Just kidding."

They fell silent then. The furnace gave a metal thunk, a sound Loretta liked but why? She supposed it meant, despite the days and days of heat, things were still expanding. Such a strange September. While others continued to complain about the weather, Loretta took comfort. With temperatures in the eighties, even inanimate objects got the chance to grow and come to life a little.

Loretta had a thought. "You know what? I wanted to tell you something," she said. "Kind of a funny thing but also sad, I guess, what isn't these days, but it made me feel good for a minute or two. You want to hear it? It's about Richard."

"Sure." He ran a hand up the back of his neck. Freshly shaved, he'd been to the barber yesterday and as a consequence looked a little more optimistic than before and Loretta wished with a hard pang that she had something real to offer him, a story Richard had written, a Father's Day tribute she'd tucked away and forgotten until now.

"It's really nothing. I suppose it's this heat that started me thinking. Or maybe hallucinating is more like it. I was coming home from George's and nobody, I mean *nobody*, was outside. Nobody on the streets, no cars even." She lit a cigarette, inhaled and said, "I *am* going to quit Reg. I promise. Soon as, I don't know, soon as George Drury gives me a raise."

"Well, that'll be never," Reg offered.

"Now, now. Anyway, listen, you could hardly tell the place was a town, except for the buildings. Everybody was inside, I guess, more than inside, in their basements like we are. I didn't see a single soul, so I thought, I suddenly realized, this could be any day, any summer day." Why was she saying this now, to Reg? Talk like this was pointless and worse, almost cruel. Reg had been right to count his words because there were so few left in their one big dictionary, the Random House: appropriate, she thought. Apparently someone had broken in and, using very small scissors, clipped out all the definitions, leaving two covers, a collapsing spine, and a range of syllables with no fixed meaning. Blah blah blah. And look at Reg, look at him, smiling already as if Richard had just this afternoon called from Toronto. *Turns out it had all been a big misunderstanding.*

"So what I started thinking," Loretta went on, her mind's print vanishing to white, "what I told myself was," what did she tell herself? Oh yes, "this could be last summer, for all we know, or even two summers ago. I told myself, as long as you don't see anybody, not one person, it could, in actual fact, be last June. Remember how hot it was? So I played a little game with myself on the way home. As long as I didn't see anybody, it could be any day. It could be last June or the year before." Her voice rising to a girly squeak. Play with me, Reg. Play with me or I'll tell.

Reg stopped smiling, rubbed his forehead, and sighed. "You shouldn't play games like that. Remember what Reverend Rochon said about acceptance and all that stuff?"

"I know, I know, I know but this is different. This is fully conscious pretending." Or semi-conscious lying. Or desperately undead clawing at dirt. "Somewhere along the way Reg Decker, you have become too literal. The best part of the Decker in you has always been that you could play along and make things up. Remember how we used to pretend we were meeting again for the first time? We even went to that Rotary dance separately. Remember that, Reg? It was fun. It was made up." More squeakery.

"I know. I *was* more fun. There is no disputing that fact."

"Oh, don't start feeling bad now. Just listen. I'll do the pretending here; you just have to listen. So what I'm saying is, I told myself if I don't see anybody, it's a different year and month and when I get home, Richard will be in his room, asleep." There, she'd said it, revealed her crazy little pleasure, her sickly relationship with herself. "And I didn't see anyone, Reg, not one person. And for a few moments, I believed it. I didn't really, of course, but I thought I did, if you know what I mean."

Reg took a drink, shaking his head.

Now look. Dammit all. The urge to cry was opening a door in her stomach, shifting its weight against her throat. "So I got to that big oak tree on the Gees' lawn and I stopped there for a second or two and just thought that thought. It was so pleasant and real I could actually touch it, almost like it was in the humidity, and a very strange thing happened: I felt happy for a moment, Reg. Not like it might really happen but like maybe I *could* feel happy once in a while," and at this Loretta fell silent, laid her head on Reg's shoulder. "End of story," she said and the tears rolled down, wetting his shirt.

"Oh, Loretta," said Reg, pulling her close. "I spend a lot of time wishing too, probably too much time. It's funny how it can make you feel better for a minute, kind of like a pill. Then it's all dissolved and gone, pissed out of your bloodstream and you have to come up with some new angle, some way to trick your own brain. It's not that gullible though."

Loretta sniffed and pulled a tissue from the pocket of her dress. "Yeah," she said. "I mean, no," and blew her nose loudly. Upstairs, the screen door slammed shut. Cheryl was home.

May 12, 1971
Dear Alfred Beel,
I guess I was born with some kind of problem. I did smash my hand through a window when I was twelve and it wasn't really because Rose was calling me Adry Anne or because my Mother was dead. I had been wanting to for as long as I could remember, purely for the reason of smashing something that would shatter and crash and create a lot of commotion with one fell blow. There's not much available other than glass that has that potential, which is really more a problem with glass than Me, wouldn't you say? In case you had-

n't noticed, it, I mean glass, is everywhere, just barely holding itself together because it's made of sand you know, Mr. Beel. Did you know that? So as dramatic and juvenile delinquent as it sounds, smashing a window is actually not a lot different from jumping into a lake. Why, you ask? Because there aren't many alternatives for those desiring to express their dissatisfaction with world events by jumping into some type of unsolid space. Wells are out. Skydiving is expensive and unlikely to occur without the cooperation of a Pilot. This may be a poor analogy but what I am intending to say is, were it not for my window-smashing tendency, I would not be writing You this letter. Why, You ask? Because You, Alfred Beel, are like a large, not plate, just ordinary pane, glass window, forever reflecting the sun into my eyes. Maybe in fact you are slowly blinding Me to everything else, burning away my retinas and corneas like an unusual Eclipse that has lasted and lasted for months.

The problem now is, I hate You Mr. Beel and I'm sure You don't understand why, which is reasonable enough. My hatred is a simple matter of starting points. People talk about the Big Bang but even I who have an average mark of 40 in physics know there were events leading up to it. A bang, small or big, does not occur in a vacuum or an empty room with no electricity or no pictures hanging on the wall. According to Miss Eustace, prior to the Big Bang, what would become the Universe was nothing but a little knot of hydrogen atoms, maybe no bigger than a few inches. Slowly it has pushed apart into the Universe. No one knows what got it started but I have an idea. It would certainly not surprise Me to learn that the Big Bang was caused by one hydrogen atom blaming another for Everyone else's problems.

Many people say I was the Starting Point of our Flax and East Flax troubles because I didn't ask Cheryl to the Dance Hall Dance. And I did not, that is true. I asked Laura van Epp or she asked Me by making it clear she wanted to be asked by Me and that she would be going in her mother's Mercury Meteor. That was a mistake and I know it. If I had asked Cheryl things might be different but that is not my point. My point is and I know this to be true: Cheryl was already sad. My sister knows this and so does Graham Rochon, as does Mr. Greig, the Vice-Principal, or at least He has told Me in so many words.

So this is my main Point, Mr. Beel, my thesis statement. Cheryl was already sad but Maddy was not already Guilty. Do you see what I am saying? Not only was Maddy not Guilty, no one except the gym teacher and the basketball coach paid the slightest Attention to her until you came along with your expert Opinions on ladders and autopsies and times of death. For some reason or other, to You Maddy was a Window that had to be smashed mainly because You could smash it. Not that I hold you responsible for what happened to Maddy, the actual small bang, just events leading up to it, events some say I set in motion.

Perhaps You are tired of phone calls from Me and now this, Letters of Complaint. Well, there is something You can do to correct the situation. You can make a Public announcement. Here at Flax Composite High we hold monthly assemblies that are actually called Literary Meetings. It would be no problem at all for me to sign you up for five or ten minutes of time. With the entire student and teaching body watching, I would like you to explain, maybe even with an overhead projector, how you manipulated the story of

Maddy and the ladder and planted ideas in people's minds and by that I mean Jimmy Drake Senior's.

Adrian's pen moves to the margin of the foolscap and stays there. From the front of the history classroom, a voice in a suit: "How's it coming along there, Adrian?"

"I'm making some real headway here, thanks to this book you gave me, Mr. Rigg. You know, the salt industry really is pretty interesting. I'm kind of glad nobody signed up with me. This way I'll probably learn at least fifty per cent more than I would have with a partner." Adrian was smiling and confident. Mr. Rigg would not want to see his work because Mr. Rigg was not the type of teacher who moved among the desks.

"Well, it's four o'clock," says Mr. Rigg, gathering up some papers. "Are you going to stay? You can if you want but I think I'll head home."

"No, I'm going up to the typing room. Typing club is in there now but they should be done any minute. I want to type some letters so I can apply for summer jobs. Might as well do it right, right Mr. Rigg?"

"Good for you, Adrian." This is one of Mr. Rigg's controlled and finite bursts of enthusiasm. When you're a teacher, excitement and praise and zeal are precious metals, in limited supply. You don't want to run out. Then it's back to business. "If you need a reference, let me know."

"Oh, thanks Mr. Rigg, thanks." Adrian folds his letter in half, once, then twice and tucks it inside his binder. He'll have to burn it. His dad has a little wood stove in the garage, his shop he calls it. "See you, Mr. Rigg."

The typing room is up one flight of stairs in a bright corridor, lined on one side with windows that look out into a courtyard. This corridor is all about business practice and

girls and the typing teacher, Mrs. Cody, whom Adrian believes to be a figment. Mrs. Cody, the typing teacher, looks so
entirely the way she should it is possible the eyes of hundreds
of expectant typists have made her up, cast her image against
the front of the room by a process of group imagination. As
a result, Adrian loves to look at her. There she is now behind
her desk, tall and thin, white hair knotted in a bun, white
blouse, and long plain skirt like a Mennonite, cardigan
draped over her shoulders and dreamy, unearthly expression.
Adrian can tell what she is thinking. Mrs. Cody is singing to
herself the names of the home row keys. J, K, L, SEMI.
That's all she can say. That's her entire vocabulary. Last
year, when Adrian was famous and popular, he shared his
creationist theory of ghosts with one or two people and two
weeks later, everyone was calling Mrs. Cody by her nickname,
Casper.

The typing club has begun to leave, Casper Cody in their
midst, but Adrian waits for the room to empty. He stands opposite the typing room door, looking into the courtyard no one
uses. Snow in the corners, although the benches look warm
and polished in the afternoon sun. There are the two midget
street lamps that shine all night, every night. When the school
is open for evening performances or games, Adrian has seen
them on, beaming their feeble wattage into the squared off
dark. The courtyard is the exclusive landscape domain of
Jimmy Drake Senior, which adds to it a goblin theme. Adrian
has said before and he will say again, if he were ever to be
alone in the school after dark and happened to encounter
Mrs. Cody in the courtyard, he would pass out cold. He's surprised he hasn't already, simply from proximity to so many
spectral people and places.

Only one set of keys remains, clattering out sentences, dinging and whizzing as the carriage returns so Adrian peeks in. It's Laura Van Epp. What's she doing here? Adrian believes he should avoid her, has made some effort to do so but in the process has not been able to resist (reminding himself a little of Randy Farrell) compiling this brief and unhopeful list of everything they have done and said since the night of the dance hall dance. He has it memorized.

Late last November—

Laura: Maybe we should not say anything at all for a while, to each other, I mean.

Adrian: Fine by me.

Early in the new year—

Laura: You dropped this (handing Adrian a pencil in the library).

Adrian: Thanks.

End of April—

Laura: If you talk to Rose, tell her I'm thinking of going to U of T too.

Adrian: No response

Laura sees Adrian hovering in the door. "Are you coming in?" She is able to look away from the keyboard and ask a question while typing at a secretarial rate.

He might as well. "Yeah, that's my plan. Just waiting for the club to leave. I'm going to type a couple of letters for jobs I might apply for."

Hands suspended above keys, Laura smiles and asks, "Why don't I type them for you? I'm working on the business formats." She is wearing penny loafers and white knee socks and a short, white skirt. Her shirt is white too but her legs and arms are brown because at Easter, the Van Epps went

to Mexico. Looking at Laura, Adrian thinks, if a human opposite of Casper Cody were obliged to step forward, commanded to identify herself, that person would be Laura Van
Epp.

"No, that's okay," says Adrian. "I took the compulsory
typing course just like everybody. I guess that's what compulsory means. Nobody escapes the jaws of compulsory."

"Glad to see you're still the Adrian Drury of yore," says
Laura, repositioning a sheet of paper with several whacks of
the return arm.

To this, Adrian says nothing, although he notices a warming in his chest, specifically the heart, as if it had moved closer
to the sun than the rest of him.

"Where are you applying?" Laura asks, typing again.
Adrian can see she likes the overlapping of words and keys,
not to waste a second, not to be her ordinary self.

"The pool. Not sure where else. Maybe Pond's."

"The pool?" Laura stops typing, she is maybe even excited. Her eyes are wide and she is wearing pink lipstick, unordinary for her, maybe she has applied it specially for typing
club. "Me too. Maybe we could work there together," she says,
yanking the paper from the typewriter with a zippery sound,
opening a manila folder like someone years away from school.

"Yeah," says Adrian, picturing them both tanned and
swimsuited, attached to opposite ends of a white, nylon rope,
floating in the Flax pool. Why is that? He remembers. Then,
as if by being in this room he has fallen under a compulsory
spell, Adrian cannot seem to stop himself from saying, "You
know, I had this dream about you. It was like I was in outer
space and I could see the earth and I was drifting around
outside of my spaceship and I all of a sudden I realized I was-

n't attached to anything, I could just drift away into nothingness."

"That's scary."

Adrian can see Laura means what she says.

"It kind of was. So I was drifting in the atmosphere and I could see earth and suddenly I realized there was a white rope around me but it wasn't hooked onto the spaceship and that kind of puzzled me but it puzzled me like in dreams, which is not the same as life. So anyway, I pulled and pulled on it, like I was reeling something in and guess what? Guess what I was reeling in?" Not wanting to wait for her to guess, Adrian hastily adds, "You. You were on the other end of the rope. You came drifting in out of space from the other direction."

"Oh," says Laura, and "wow." And to Adrian's relief chooses not to add, I wonder what that means. Instead, she raises one eyebrow the way she does when he has seen her working on math, then fixes her gaze on the floor. Adrian follows suit. Focusing his eyes, his corneas and lenses, on the same spot as Laura, even when that spot is a beige, flecked, institutional tile, not-so-spotlessly maintained by Jimmy Drake Senior, gives Adrian some cause for hope.

Laura says, "I guess I'd better go. Anastasia's waiting for me. So," she stands up, holding her manila folder like someone playing the part of someone at a job interview, "I'll see you around and maybe at the pool, maybe."

Adrian nods, more sideways than up and down, watches her go before falling into the desk she's left warm. There is always paper in the typing room, Mrs. Cody having infinite resources, supplied by her heavenly father and his stationery store, and Adrian carefully threads a sheet into the carriage.

He is aware of liking typewriters more than typing, this is self-evident, what boy does not, and thus, he is aware he needs to stop and think. Resting his hands upon his lap, he remembers the phone booth, the thrill of those calls, the off-limits pleasure of being Loretta. Loretta, he says to himself. I am Loretta Decker. Then, from the stability of the home row, Adrian proceeds.

> *May 12, 1971*
> *My Dear Alfred,*
> *I have been meaning to write to You for some time.*

Every student was required to bring an egg to school and keep it warm and safe for three long days. The purpose being to warn against the consuming burden of parenthood, expose them all to constant vigilance. Babies are small, breakable, and full of slime: you'll wish you hadn't. Follow-up discussions were mandatory, segregated by sex and led by a nervous and tongue-tied gym teacher gripping a piece of sport equipment—a tennis racquet, a volleyball—for reassurance. No one had questions, not even comments. The end result was a jumble of impressions having to do with white knuckles, egg cartons, shame, school spirit, and fear.

"That was more or less the opposite of a valedictorian's speech, wouldn't you say?" Rose asked Anastasia, exiting the girls' talk.

"Ha!" Anastasia said. "That's funny. Can you picture Eleanor Gee getting up there on stage and saying, 'Uh, well, once the egg is fertilized that's it and uh, well, your life will never be the same again? In fact it will be over. Any questions? No? Good. Let's play ball."

Her own little scenarios filled Anastasia with glee, practically made the circuitry of her brain visible, oscillating strings of light behind that pale forehead. "Listen to me, Rose Drury. Eleanor Gee *will* be the valedictorian. Mark my words. I've heard she's already got the dress. I'm just saying this so you don't get your hopes too high up there. Like hopefully not as high as the hem of that skirt you're wearing, if you know what I mean. I'm being Miss Clevitt now, just so you know."

"Yeah, I know you're being Miss Clevitt. I've heard you be Miss Clevitt enough times to know the signs. And I don't really care that much about the valedictorian thing. I don't know what I can say to convince you of that."

"Nothing. You can't say anything because I'd know you're lying. It's a problem when *I* know you better than *you* know you."

No chance of losing Anastasia in the hall because they were both headed to their lockers, their adjacent lockers, Rose thought, the adjective suddenly unpleasant to her, in the same etymological grouping as serrated and entrails and most detestable of all words, vivisection. "But after listening to Miss Clevitt," Rose said, "the real Miss Clevitt, it's no wonder so many people missed the whole point. Half the people I know were getting all sentimental about their eggs by day two. And there were those guys Adrian told me who were playing firing squad against the back school wall. They say, ready, aim, fire and they throw their eggs at some victim but the point is to miss. Come close but miss. So there's all this yellow yolk and gooey protein drying out there in the sun. They're calling it the abortion wall."

"Ha," Anastasia said again, for probably the tenth time in this school day. "I wish I'd thought of that." Dialling combinations now, racing as usual. Summer air filled the hall from doors propped open and people were happy. How could they not be? Somehow, school had mistakenly wandered into this too-hot September and now was the time to escort it out. In similar weather last spring, Rose and Anastasia would have driven off in Mrs. Van Epp's beautiful Mercury Meteor, going nowhere, up and down the highway, the two of them and the car, kindred spirits. But this year was different. There was a strain, caused by Maddy, a strain of virus, Anastasia would have said.

"Beat you," said Anastasia, jerking open her lock and dumping her books onto the floor of her locker with a great clatter. "I call that avant disregard."

"Why avant?"

"Because I did it before you did, Drury."

"Yeah, well, I have homework so these guys are coming home with me," said Rose, grimacing at her textbooks. "But you know... you know you could think about the egg thing in another way, too," she went on, prepared for Anastasia's snort or Anastasia's laugh or her other favourite: *Frankly, Rose, I'm nonplussed by your attitude.* "It doesn't necessarily have to be about sex and birth control."

"What? Of course it has to be about sex and birth control." Anastasia was putting on her jacket. "It's about don't have sex if you don't want to have some little white thing made out of half-baked calcium you might squash."

"Yeah. But it could also be about something larger."

"Anything could be about something larger. Except for maybe Maddy Farrell." Slam. Her locker door was shut.

How could she be so quick? How could she predict the direction of every conversation? "Well," Rose began, "you could think about it as we're all one another's eggs," then paused to wonder, for one dizzy moment, if Anastasia might punch her in the teeth for that comment. Fist fights, Adrian had told her, usually erupted at one of the opponent's lockers.

Instead, a parody of sagacity, chin propped between thumb and fingers, Anastasia nodded and said, "Ah. Really? Maybe you should bring that up with Eleanor Gee. We are all one another's eggs. No matter what size, no matter what height. Even the six-foot variety. Even those in an orange hat. I'm serious. You should mention it to her. She's likely looking for an idea."

This was Anastasia at her worst, dis-disingenuous. Or something. "I'm going," she said and was gone.

Well, so? It was true. We *are* one another's eggs. And Maddy, specifically, was hers. Anastasia would just have to adapt. Maddy needed protection and care. The egg was Rose's own personal metaphor, one that had grown a soft, impermeable membrane around the two of them. Made of them a zygote, Rose thought, or one of those double-yolked eggs. How could she expect her old friends to understand? They were from a previous era, a time remembered for its improbability: polio, ice-boxes, a killing influenza. Sometimes now when Rose saw Anastasia in the hall or across the parking lot, she thought she might be watching a grainy documentary from the CBC.

Almost every day now, Rose drove Maddy home from school, even when there was basketball practice, like today. Maddy's dad would pick her up, no prob-lem, easy enough to make one more stop in his custo-dial rounds but if Maddy had a chum—that was the word he used, *chum*—willing to give her a ride, so much the better. Meaning Tuesdays and Wednesdays, Rose waited in the parking lot with the moms and the boyfriends for Maddy to appear. Sometimes she read or studied, other times she listened to the radio, aware that people knew she was waiting for Maddy and could make no sense of it. Tutoring, Rose said, again and again. So you have to wait for her? Yeah, she comes to my house and gets picked up there. These questions were the reason she kept the egg wrapped in tissue in the glove box of the Vega. Sometimes she'd take it out, hold it up to the setting sun, put it back, as if she thought there might be a chick inside.

Rose couldn't explain to people, especially Anas-tasia, that the situation with Maddy was simply a good arrangement. Along with the tutoring, Maddy had someone to talk to and—a little known fact—she liked to talk, and Rose wanted to help. And the wanting to help *was* a kind of pregnancy, Rose realized, building in her belly like a baby with more and more parts until one day, there it was, not actually born but too big to conceal. Hence, the waiting in the parking lot, the driving here and there, the dentistry.

"Dad can fix your teeth for you," Rose said one afternoon, day one of the egg assignment. She'd rehearsed the statement several times, wanting teeth to sound neutral, just a noun like car or bicycle chain, nothing to suggest human body parts in decline due to lack of care and a hopeless store in the middle of a swamp. So an appointment was made, an evening appointment the very next day after basketball practice, tutoring, and dinner. Maddy would stay for as long as necessary, lie on the couch while Rose brought ginger ale with a straw or painkillers in the palm of her hand. One of her father's patients routinely needed two days and nights to recover full use of her muscles; numbness was an idiosyncratic affair, said Dr. Drury. The appointment was confidential, Angel and Frog didn't need to know but if worse came to worst, Rose might have to call East Flax and tell Randy (cross your fingers he would answer the phone) this was a period of intensive tutoring and Maddy would be staying in town for the night. Adrian would have to cope.

In the double-barrelled light of Dr. Drury's lamp, Rose saw four blackened caps and a fifth turning grey, the colour of bread mould. "Might as well do them all, Dad," she said, besotted with her own capacity to halt the decay of Maddy Farrell, the thrill of looking inside that mouth. So much history. Rose now knew the many phases of Maddy's life, and this mouth had been with her through them all. The dirty period, the hungry period, the screaming period, giant sedimentary layers that settled and shifted while Rose Drury was a mere three miles west. So funny to think about. If Anastasia were now a documentary, Maddy was an archaeological site, something to examine and preserve and brush away the mud and wonder what was she doing the day Rose and her mother were right there in East Flax?

That might have been the dirty period. The dirty period was before she started school, Maddy said, when Angel must have been depressed or perhaps just a bad mother but that was more or less every period. Before they'd had the store, when they were living in a rented place out by Greta Leopold's. Everyone knew it was Mrs. Leopold who called the Children's Aid Society because Maddy was so dirty and her wrist was swollen. Rose loved hearing Maddy's half-remembered story of dirtiness so extreme the authorities had to be involved. She imagined Maddy as a creature from outer space or from a lagoon, a one-inch hide of cracked and mottled mud. Point a hose at her and melt it away; next time you turned around, there it was again.

How dirty do you think you were? Rose had asked two or three times. How dirty exactly? Maddy had no idea, only knew that Cora was not and Randy was expected to be, still in diapers as he was. There'd been no indoor plumbing at that house, only a sink with a pump and an outhouse but they'd had a big metal tub for bathing; Maddy could remember it. Maybe she'd missed her turn for a week or two—she could be like that, pig-headed her mother said and therefore pig-bodied—and Cora would probably have found a way to have extra turns to make Maddy look worse. She'd have come downstairs in the night, sat her six-year-old body naked in the sink, and pumped well-cold water over it if she had to. No cost too high for Cora Farrell.

Whatever went on, Maddy had been the cause of the call. And when the social worker arrived, the very sight of her had elicited that sharp intake of breath she remembered and wondered about still. Told Rose she wished she had a picture of herself from then. Was she just plain coated in mud? Or was it grime, that streaky look from filth pushed around with a damp cloth or hand? Or did her hair contain a house of spiders like those stories of girls with beehive hairdos supporting generations of insect life? Had it been so long between shampoos? If she had a picture, for sure she'd show it to Rose, but she didn't.

The social worker took Maddy to the hospital and gave her a bath and x-rayed her wrist. She could recall bits of the experience, driving in a blue interior followed by the white interior of the hospital. People's faces, worried, surprised, a little like Halloween when they looked at you close up for some sign, pretending not to know everything about you. They put her in different clothes from a bin. Clothes left behind by girls who had died maybe. A green dress with rickrack and underwear with pink dots, shoes, and a coat. Her things disappeared, went with the dead girls she supposed. Maddy thought the house would have changed by the time she arrived home but nothing looked different except for another car in the yard and her mother's face, which was white as the porcelain of the kitchen sink. The social worker was giving warnings, telling her mother off. Cora was nowhere in sight and her dad held the squirming Randy who wanted down, not understanding, thinking the visitor was a good excuse to run around and show off. The whole place, Maddy said out loud to Rose, felt the way she did when she peed her pants. "Nerves," Maddy said. "I had bad nerves until I was eight. You can kind of see why. Then I stopped all of a sudden."

While her dad was doing the work, Rose couldn't help glancing at Maddy's crotch once or twice—she had to be nervous after all—watching for a darkening of denim. Had anyone ever wet their pants in the chair? She'd decided to ask her dad later but never did.

To be honest, Rose had thought, handing her dad instruments, she would rather it was the poor period, the day she and her mother were in East Flax. Rose liked to think of Maddy in the store while she was standing on the bank of Minnow Lake, liked to imagine she had seen Maddy when they bought Popsicles. Maybe she'd been on that stool behind the till; Rose thought she remembered her, for sure it wasn't Cora.

The poor period started, Maddy told her, when they bought the store, the precise moment Minnow Lake entered its decline. Angel did not believe that the Blue Lake resort, ten miles west of Flax, would succeed; she was certain those Toronto types wouldn't last a season. So the Farrells spent all their credit on wieners and buns and hot dog relish and batteries, mosquito coils, fishing lures, and all the other stuff of picnics and Sundays and summer holidays. But the Blue Lake Resort took off like a graph you might see illustrating good business practices while the Farrells spent their last reserves of cash on another freezer. Angel slipped into bad motherhood once again and started screaming but Frog was determined to intervene: Did Angel want another visit from the government on top of everything else?

"They have to eat, Angel, they're growing," he said, reasonably, one evening on the cusp of poor and screaming. "You can't grow without eating."

"They are eating," Angel yelled, so loudly Maddy had looked up at the ceiling, expecting to see some damage, the light fixture loosening or paint peeling off in stained, curling sheets. "What do you call this?" Angel screamed, "a floral arrangement?" Holding Randy's plate with its untouched ice cream scoop of boiled cabbage and half slice of baloney—Randy never liked to mess up the symmetry of his servings—she went on. "For the time being, this is a meal. When things return to normal, so will the plates," Angel had concluded, suddenly quiet and rational, as if the china were the source of the problem.

A screaming, blonde mother. In Rose's imagination, the Farrells resembled a Blondie and Dagwood arrangement gone sideways. Angel was Blondie's bad sister married to Dagwood's country cousin, Frog. Cora could be Cookie, Randy was Alexander, and

Maddy, well, Rose didn't know. Maddy could be Cookie's egg in the glove box.

The Farrell kids had to take care of themselves. Cora, up in the attic, began setting her alarm clock for three a.m., waking Maddy on the way downstairs for cereal: Randy was too unpredictable and he never seemed that hungry anyway. They'd take a box of Alpha-Bits from the back of the shelf, to be served with or without milk and returned to the back of the shelf. Inventory was not Angel's strongest suit. Or they spread peanut butter on crackers; everything replaced and remembered for future use. Who was ever going to buy the stuff anyway? They'd sit on the floor behind the former meat cooler, its motor generating an oily heat, eat themselves silly, and go back to bed. Probably when the cavities began, Rose surmised. Going to bed with a coating of sugary cereal on your teeth couldn't be good. Peanut butter had sugar in it too, glued to your molars with all that oily crap.

Mr. Farrell started up his custodial service then and Angel pitched her supplies more to the surrounding farm wives, even started to offer specials, which were still more than the same item in town but some of the women were willing to give her their business. They had enough and that was no period at all. No division of time other than phone calls from Randy's teachers and Maddy winning races. Not until Cora was in ninth grade did the current period, the Alfred Beel period, begin, which extended to the present.

Dr. Drury had said, "You're an excellent patient, Maddy. You've no idea the fuss I put up with in this office. Grown men yowling about the pain and begging for gas. You, you're a trooper."

But she wasn't after all, nearly fainting as she stood up and Rose having to grab one arm and steer her to the couch. "You got up too fast, that's all. Anoxia," Rose said, loving the chance to use the word. "You'll have to lie down and let your body regain the proper balance of oxygen and carbon dioxide. You'll have to convalesce." That's what this couch was for, apparently, the same one her mother had convalesced upon, or failed to convalesce. The word did imply recovery, didn't it? "I'm convalescing, dear," she used to say. "Can you keep Adrian quiet? Take him outside?"

Sure Mom, sure. Her six-year-old body radiant with good works done.

Maddy would not have a temperature from four fillings so there had been no practical reason for touching her forehead, but never mind. At that moment, and ever since, Rose's hand held the power of an eraser, a pink gum capable of erasing all of Maddy's autobiography, making empty, lined space for another having to do with perfect teeth, fresh ironing, the interior of china cabinets, floor polish, and unrusty bathtubs. New clothing that came from a closet and not the luggage of dead girls.

Rose closed her locker, locked the lock. She had everything she needed. By now Anastasia would have left the parking lot, either alone or with Eleanor Gee. Rose could hear the girls practicing in the gym already and considered going to watch but no, she'd wait in the car with the egg. Completely silly, she knew, and if

Anastasia ever found out, she would, what would she do, she'd write a story for the yearbook about two girls named Faddy Marrell and Dose Rury who kept their birth control egg alive in a glove box. Or, more likely script a play on the same subject for a lit meeting. Or assemble one of her Barbie tableaux, inviting Rose and Maddy to the opening night gala. Rose turned and headed for the open door. She couldn't get too worried about it and what's more, she liked the name Dose Rury.

Alfred was in his recliner chair, listening to the radio and evaluating the neatness of the kitchen. No clutter was the rule. Alfred liked to have things in place. His vision of the perfect dwelling would have been a three- or four-storey structure modelled after a chest of drawers; at night, everything pulleyed in on waxed tracks, stored away from sight, leaving only a smooth wooden plane. He'd explained this to Maddy, along with everything else. Magazines in stacks, not fanned out; shoes in the closet, not the entrance; pens and pencils in the jar by the phone and that meant all of them, not one or two by the pad of paper to suggest messages recently received or imminent. There were no messages. Maddy grasped it all and even took it one step farther, the way she'd organized the contents of the stove drawer in nests, put the pot scrubber in that clay dish by the sink. Every so often she'd come up with something new, which was why he couldn't get rid of her, why he was stuck with this intolerable situation, among others. But never mind.

Today, September 22, 1970, Alfred Beel was fifty years old. Nothing to write home about. Were his parents still living, they would no doubt be disappointed in their son's lack of achievement and lineage. No profession. Too late for children. His sperm were snapping and crackling and popping. One thing he had learned spending day after day in that store: "on the shelf" was a most suitable phrase. With Cora gone, the three of them—the Maestro, Russell, and himself, with their can-shaped bodies and flattened rear ends—were brilliantly on the shelf. Stack them up and call them The Unmarriables. Then add Maddy to the display case, no, subtract Cora, then add Maddy and you had yourself an unrecognizable mash, indigestible even with the help of Eno, a flat and tasteless product with no icing and certainly no bride or groom atop the confection. Little three-inch figures of the Maestro, Maddy, and Russell, snapped free of the evolutionary chain, dangling outside any notion of conjugal life.

Not Alfred, though, count him out. On this day, as a gift to himself, Alfred was heaving his carcass off the shelf, he was changing his ways; he already had, having avoided the store for one entire afternoon. Of course, the Maestro'd driven round to check, expecting, no doubt, to find him sprawled out, face down, half dressed, the way the dead plaster-cast themselves into the hereafter.

And there was the place all locked up with the car in the driveway, heightening his alarm, Alfred knew for sure, pleased with the idea of the old Maestro's heart ticking like a metronome at *presto*. Well, was Alfred required to submit any changes in routine to a plebiscite before they took effect? At half past five, Angel finally got him on the phone. "Where have you been?" she asked, having heard from Cora he was in for tests, having now most likely got so used to the idea he was dead, she may have been a little disappointed. Alfred didn't hold it against her, though.

"I went for a walk," he said. "I am allowed, aren't I?"

"Naturally you're allowed but we thought you'd had an accident or something. The Maestro came around and pounded on the windows. We decided we'd break in if we hadn't heard from you by six, despite not having a quorum, by the way."

"Oh for heaven's sake. What a bunch of alarmists. I've just decided to improve my circulation. I want to be more like those men in Sweden, the ones in the Volvo ads who can run a mile at age sixty-five. I might start doing that race-walking, heel toe, heel toe, with the elbows going. If you'd been watching, since you're so interested, you would have seen me go past the store at around three, around through and out the ass end of East Flax, up Dance Hall Road and down the trail to the lake and onward until I came to the road allowance for Concession Fourteen. That's my street you know. The whole trip is a country block and I did it in less than two hours. Not a record, I know, but I stopped three times to look things over and finish off a pack of smokes. I may quit that as well now. So let the

Maestro and Russell know they're on their own now. I'll be in for provisions, naturally, in the morning, most likely, but won't be lingering to talk. Give my chair to someone else."

"I can't see it lasting," said Angel, by way of encouragement.

"Like I said, mornings for me. Brief, practical trips to the store. More emphasis on healthy food, less on opinionated hot air."

Maybe. Maybe in the early morning light that dungeon of a store, that cave with its intellectually slumbering inhabitants might appear for a moment a little less than painfully ugly, something other than the visual nerve gas it was in the afternoon. Although bathed in eastern light, with its forlorn dusty shelves and its five-year-old Campbell's soups, the place might actually look worse. Dear God. How old was that soup in dog years, he'd wondered more than once from the comfort of his dirt-brown armchair. Alfred figured the accumulated age of all the products in Angel Farrell's store could take you back to the recession of the glaciers. How *had* he sat for so many years in that museum of poisons? And, more importantly, why?

Because of Cora, needless to say. Cora could appear in the midst of cans bursting with botulism, Popsicles melted and refrozen into sack-shapes of radioactive dye, drinks long exhausted of their carbonation and still be the beauty she was. Unfixed to her environment. A seed that had blown in from someplace up by Manitoulin. The paradox being, with Cora gone, it was not as if the light had gone out but as if it had been turned up, as if some hand had replaced all the forty-watt bulbs with one hundreds. Shelves of the unnecessary in an unforgiving glare.

Well, that was not to be Alfred's fate, not this fifty-year-old Beel, he thought, in high beam, resolved with enough intensity to induce a stroke, had he not already possibly done so. In this precipitous change of routine, who could guess what might be cause and what effect? Were his arteries so hardened, the passage of an original idea might pop a couple of old, bloody corks? Easy enough to imagine them in there, ricocheting from mental pillar to post. Oh, let Angel Farrell worry about it. He wanted to enjoy the day, he was determined to enjoy the day and here was his request. Here it was. He reached for the dial and turned up the volume.

Every year, Alfred called the local radio station on his birthday and dedicated a song, to himself, from a friend in Toronto. This year he'd even thought of asking Maddy to make the call. He would have paid her twenty bucks; there was nothing wrong with her voice after all, she *sounded* like a girl. And the people at the station must be wondering, who is this old guy phoning in requests for some other old guy? But he had, thankfully, averted disaster and rejected that idea. What made him think he could trust Maddy to keep her mouth shut? She'd have told that Leopold girl and she would have told her mother and within days everyone in the area would have known. To have even contemplated such a plan! Such utter foolhardiness.

Here was the song now. Jim Reeves's "He'll Have To Go." Alfred's face pinkened. He lit up a smoke, reclined farther, into what he thought of as his frankly ugly brown chair's second gear. Funny how a song could adjust your mood, could work like a squadron of minnow-sized scuba divers in the mind, yanking out long-buried sentiments, raising a murky dust that cleared and there you were, forced to take a look. Close your eyes; make a wish. How about one night with Loretta Decker?

The mellifluous voice of the disc jockey interrupted Alfred's reverie. "That was a song going out to Alfred Beel in East Flax. And the dedication reads, Happy birthday, Alfred, from your old friend in Toronto."

Your friend. Your old friend, Loretta Decker. With Cora gone, Loretta had become an awakening, recurring pleasure, a miniature addiction. And all, really, truthfully now, because of one intoxicated comment in the Legion, one drunken observation. Were this an experiment, the evidence would suggest that the unmarried patrons of the East Flax store were so desperate for flattery they would give up smoking, take up exercise that might kill them, and consider bribing the household help all because of a passing comment. This was not normal, no, and neither was Alfred's temporary and birthday-induced satisfaction but, never mind, leave it be.

Loretta Decker. Here came the memory; there went the feeling. Alfred was of the opinion that certain memories insisted on being remembered. Against all odds, they worked their way upstream, against the circulation and into one specific chamber of the heart.

Loretta at the Legion was a case in point. Here it came again, warmer than blood.

Abruptly, Alfred sat up, the recliner chair's footrest vanishing with a wooden thud. The phone again? Who could this be now? Twice in one afternoon? Alfred stood and briefly admired his tidy living room with its shining maple floor. After Maddy'd been there, he often enjoyed a little slide, and so he did now, took a little run and skated in his socks to the telephone. It was Ila.

"Happy birthday to you and are you having a fine day?" she asked in her best society girl voice.

"Thank you and yes I am." Maybe it was true, didn't feel like a lie.

"I just heard your dedication on the radio. Very thoughtful of your friend in Toronto. Is this someone I know or have perhaps heard mention of in conversation?"

"Well, you know how it is. The old friends remember the birthdays, the ones from grade school. They stick in the mind forever."

"So the friend in Toronto is someone you went to school with."

"Yes, yes. A girl named Eileen Stack. A girl. Listen to me. She's the same age as I am."

"Well, that's very nice. I've never heard you mention her."

"Most likely because I'm not really the mentioning type now, am I?"

"I suppose you're not. But you could have mentioned it was your birthday. I had completely forgotten

I'm embarrassed to say but now, thanks to the miracle of radio waves, I'm up to speed."

Silence, and Alfred aware of a third ear, another phone, the sound of concentration. Those damnable daughters.

"So I've decided to make some changes, now that I'm fifty."

"Such as?"

"Such as walking every afternoon instead of sitting in that store. Quitting smoking. Getting out more."

"Finishing decks?"

"That too. Tell Peter I'll be out there next week."

"No great rush. I know you Virgos are the methodical types."

Oh, oh. The scuba divers had swum right up to his mouth, were about to say something he knew he would regret but when had that stopped him in the recent past. And this *was* his birthday. "I know this is ridiculous," Alfred began, "but would you tell me again what you told me about Loretta? That day early in the summer when I was starting the deck?"

"What I told you about Loretta? I don't know what you mean. Give me a bit of context, Mr. Beel."

"You know. What your cousin said Clive said about Reg and Loretta."

"Okay. What's going on here? Are you writing a society column for *The Reminder* now as well? Is this another of your midlife changes?"

"No, I'm just curious. That's all."

"You *know* I know that's a very thin explanation but anyway," Ila took an expository breath, "what

cousin Jean said was, she said Loretta's not happy with
Reg, that things haven't been the same since Richard
died, that she's likely going to leave Reg, she wouldn't
be at all surprised, once Cheryl's finished school." Ila
stopped here. "Just a minute," she said, then bellowed
"Anastasia, are you listening in on the other line?"

A faint tick, an insect falling from a ledge, landing
on its hard back.

"Sorry about that," said Ila. "I don't know what
they think they're going to hear. Anyway, I should go.
So what day next week? I know Peter will ask."

"Tell him early in the week."

"That won't be good enough."

"Tell him it's my birthday."

"All right. Happy rest of the day," and they said
their goodbyes.

Ila would be jealous now. She really did not want
him to like anyone else, wanted to keep him as a handy
eunuch, a deck-building, renovating, eunuch. A number of times she'd asked about Alfred's history with
women, an oblique effort to determine if he had the
equipment. What was he supposed to say? I had a couple of girls overseas. Who didn't? Then the accident,
then no one, then Eileen Stack. The entire tale could
be fit onto a Christmas card. He could do that, in fact.
Put everyone's worried mind at ease next December
with a mimeographed summary. Dear All. Season's
Greetings and by the way, I had sex a few times while
in the service and then there was Eileen Stack, the
Eaton's clerk I met at my old man's Christmas party.
Until she saw the chest. She'd been willing and inter-

ested and we had sex five times. I kept my undershirt on for each incident. Then she got too curious and pulled off the undershirt I liked to wear as if it were all a humorous striptease, and there it was, the red and bubbly sausage casing called skin. And how, I ask during this season of comfort and joy, do you keep a woman with that kind of vulnerability hanging on your front? Your heart practically visible through the mess, a little like the doughy fistula I saw once on a sheep at the Royal Winter Fair. So, Happy Holidays, one and all and that's not really Eileen Stack who calls in those birthday requests every September: it's me. Ho ho ho. Merry Christmas.

This too made him laugh. He was in a better mood than he thought and one's fiftieth birthday comes only once in a lifetime so why not give oneself a real birthday present? Why not? Loretta would be at the dentist's office, most likely. They stayed open until seven on Tuesdays. He could call and make an appointment, and at least talk to her. What possible harm was there in that and it was not by any standard of judgment irrational or impetuous to arrange for dental care. He'd call right now. He had no time to lose. When his father was this age, the seeds of dementia were already sending their white roots into his solid grey matter.

"Hello," came the voice. "Dr. Drury's office."

It was *her*. "Yes. Hello. I'd like to make an appointment."

"Certainly. It's Alfred Beel, isn't it?"

Aha, she knew his voice. Of course. Why shouldn't she? He was the handsomest man in the tri-county area. "Yes, yes it is."

"I'm afraid the earliest we can get you in is October the twelfth."

Get me in? "Nothing earlier? I'm rather anxious to... get in, to see Dr. Drury, that is." He couldn't resist: his problem in a nutshell.

"I'm sorry. We've been really busy. I don't know what's going on. Too much candy floss in the diet, maybe. All those fall fairs."

"That's good enough then. Sign me up for October twelfth. What time have you got for me?"

"Two-fifteen."

"Sounds positively..." he wanted to say prophylactic, thought better, "preventative. Sign me up."

"We'll see you then.'

Five minutes later, the phone rang again. It was Loretta. My God. Listen to him now. Heart hooked up to a loudspeaker. She was calling; she was leaving Reg today. "Alfred? We've had a cancellation. Can you come in this Friday morning? The twenty-fifth? Eleven o'clock? Not a lot of notice, I realize."

"Yes. Certainly."

"See you then."

"Yes you will."

She hung up and he held on, sniffing, realizing finally the phone smelled of soap and vinegar. Apparently, Maddy had given it a wash.

This was biology class, the topic was extinction and

Cheryl Decker had a question. "Do you think the last of the passenger pigeons knew it was the last?"

"I'm not quite sure what you're getting at." Not even noon and Mr. Busby had his jacket off to air the sweat moons in his armpits. If Adrian were here, he'd be whispering a comment; he'd be thinking Cheryl doesn't sweat much. But he wasn't in this class.

"I mean, you've just said part of the problem, evolution-wise for these pigeons is that they only had one egg at a time. So if they were going extinct, somewhere in nineteen-fourteen when the last one hatched, and there were no other passenger pigeons, what did it think? Did it just sit there in its nest and not bother to even fly anywhere?"

She knew it was a silly question but Laura van Epp would make note of it and maybe even mention it to Adrian who would then have no choice but to think about Cheryl.

"I don't think the survival of the species is much of a conscious process," said Mr. Busby, loosening his tie, "even for the higher order mammals much less the birds. So to answer your question, the last passenger pigeon thought next to nothing, just went about its business with maybe a vague sense of unfulfilled duty." No laughter; had another student asked the question, there would have been a few obedient titters.

"You don't think it suspected something was up?"

"No, I do not. Any other questions?" He was eager to change direction. And the class was worrying up the room a bit now, contributing another type of sweat. Cheryl could tell they were thinking that was a weird question. Now what is Cheryl Decker going to do? Faint? Cry? Ride her bicycle into Blue Lake and pedal herself into extinction? That's what they expected from a Decker. Though there'd been nothing dramatic since Richard's accident, apparently this family was still at cross-purposes with evolution, destined for quiet chromosomal collisions, plans unhinging and sliding the length of their helix into a plasma pool of bad car deals, nervous mothers, jilted daughters. Who could tell what might happen next? Cheryl, that's who.

Adrian Drury was leaving Cheryl Decker. She had divined this impending biological disaster from recent events, and now, from the absence of phone calls, so had her mother. Last night she had asked the inevitable question, girlish desperation sweetening her voice. "Will you be going to the dance with Adrian, honey?"

"Of course," Cheryl had answered. The last passenger pigeon had felt a duty to cheer up its parents, give them reason to hope, prevent the loss of any more emotional blood. Adrian was the dentist's son; for some reason his interest in Cheryl was a sort of fuel to Loretta's sputtering pigeon heart, revved it up, gave it a bit of horsepower. What would she do without Adrian, the future son-in-law?

Spellbound by Mr. Busby's armpit as he wrote on the board, Cheryl thought, we really should have got married in the first week of grade eleven. That would have sealed the deal. Oh yes, our son was killed in a tragic accident and then our daughter married at age fifteen. Those Decker kids, her mother would say, there's no telling what they might try next. No one's *ever* been married in grade eleven. Oh, they had to make a few allowances for them, Loretta would boast, proud to be the mother of Flax's youngest wife. They had to have a special desk, two desks bolted together, sort of a studious loveseat, I guess you could call it. And they were *required* to cordon off a married students' change area in the locker room. The school board said so. Imagine.

But, they didn't get married. And, as a result, the last night she went to Adrian's house, everything fell apart. Maybe she shouldn't have done that; maybe it had been a serious evolutionary mistake. A Decker should not have entered the Drury habitat for sexual purposes because the Drury habitat was perfectly outfitted for evolution. It had been naturally selected to cooperate. There, change occurred without effort, cells stepping calmly to the side, making way for death. Next stop, lesbians in East Flax. No matter what, each day bound up and recombined with the last to create a smooth and perfect skin surface over events other families might need prescriptions to withstand. The Deckers, for example.

She and Adrian had done it there, in his bed, Rose being out in East Flax, as usual, and the dentist being at his Rotary Club meeting with Reverend Rochon and every other decent man in Flax. That's when it happened; that's when Adrian left. Ten minutes after firing his DNA into a plastic sack, the phone rang and it was Laura. Adrian ran downstairs in his underwear to get it. Hi Laura, Cheryl heard him say, how are you?

And that is what you get for being in the wrong environment. If they have to, the forces of life will pull you by the ankles, through a watery divide to the other side of the arrangement. And glub, glub, glub, water up your nose and inside your windpipe.

Next day at school, Cheryl had become a difficult sight to see, as if in the company of Adrian one arm became significantly smaller than the other, or she had a water head like Morley Nickle; they hadn't drained it soon enough. And the day after, Adrian talking to her as if the skeleton inside his skin had turned around and was trying to go, with only his face making the effort and barely. *I'll call, I'll call.* Two lies, perfectly understood by the palms of Cheryl's hands and their fine layers of sweat.

She had already abandoned hope, which was the wise choice, Adrian not being the sort to come right out and say. And the result had not been entirely bad. She no longer felt as if she were filling with mud, for example. The opposite. If she sat and thought about it, paid attention to her limbs right here and now in biology, they were light, her body more like a soda cracker left in water, about to separate into puffy and structureless floats. Oh, oh. There was that feeling, like an unpolished marble sinking down the back of her throat and now she had to worry she might cry, realizing that was what Adrian would say, he would say floats, not her. Best to pry open the rings of her binder so as to free her pencil case and unzip it in her lap. There she could rattle pencil crayons against pens and breathe in the comforting smell of trapped wood and lead and colour. To cry would mean Mr. Busby asking her to stay after class, eyes fuzzing over with annoyed concern, more crying, her mother on the phone, Graham Rochon and all the soggy air in the town of Flax collecting in his office, blowing in just to listen.

There. She was going to be okay. The problem was, no one but Adrian Drury understood. He would have understood the pigeon question, for example. If he were in Mr. Busby's place, he would have said, "Of course the pigeon would have known it was the last living passenger pigeon. Animals know these things. They just do. Words aren't all they're cracked up to be. Like Skokie for instance, when we took her to the vet, she knew what was happening. We didn't have to sit down with her and say Now Skokie, we've got some bad news for you. She knew and she also knew it's just better that way. It's a kind of extra sensory perception but for animals it's not extra, it's compulsory, like remedial English is for me. So to answer Cheryl's question, the pigeon would have known because how could it not know? It's the last of its kind. It'd be like you or me being born and we're the last human baby. We somehow manage to make it to age four or five, maybe some wolves feed us and then we head out of the nest. How could you possibly not notice there were bears and cats and eagles but no people? Except I'm not sure you would go back to your nest all hopeless; it might have the opposite effect of permanent hopefulness. Just keep looking and looking, as if it's always Easter. There's gotta be another egg somewhere."

Ha ha. The class would laugh.

That's where Cheryl and I see eye-to-eye, Adrian would say. She doesn't believe you have to say a whole lot of things out loud either. She understands. She gets it that I'll be going to the dance with Laura and likely that's it for her and me but it would be almost against our code to say that out loud. She knows that. Cheryl knows more about me than I know about me, in actual fact. She's kind of like Skokie in that regard. That's what Adrian would say. And Cheryl zipped up her pencil case and returned to studying Mr. Busby's armpits.

It's Sunday evening, the middle of May, and Adrian is at the Flax pool. There's a lock on the gate but he knows the combination and, unlike Jimmy Drake Junior, has not broadcast it all over five counties. He realizes he should be working on the salt project, it's due tomorrow, but he can't be bothered, knowing he's already completed one such assignment. Re-doing an assignment that cannot be copied strikes Adrian as an event so perverse it could or should be capable of growing feathers and a hard yellow beak, two crazy eyeballs attached to a ball of string brain. He'll ask Rigg for an extension tomorrow and surely some day this week Farrell will start talking again because Montreal has won the Stanley Cup so his gumball designs have done the trick and proven that the future is under his control.

Adrian jumps in at the shallow end. Somebody's been doing maintenance and shovelled away the leaves and this gladdens his heart as it represents human certainty and thus absolute proof of an approaching summer with holidays, swimming lessons, and the sounds of kids. Kids. Adrian loves the way they walk along the pool deck with their blue knees bent, the way some of them can swim just like that and others it's like you have to teach each quadrant of their bodies separately.

Might as well lie right down on the cool concrete floor. That is one good thing about the pool versus Minnow Lake. You would never want to lie down on the floor of a mud hole known to contain water snakes and weeds capable of living in a mud hole. Also, due to the absence of lifeguards and swimming lessons in East Flax, someone, somewhere along the line has no doubt drowned in Minnow Lake, meaning a skeleton or two sunk in the mud, preparing to rise up. And also, here in Flax the occasional little kid might pee into the water but in East Flax, Adrian has heard, they flush their toilets right into the lake. Little kid pee is one thing but Russell Hansen pee is another thing altogether. Still, Adrian wonders what the lake is looking like today.

He stretches right out where no one is likely to see him. Above, there is still sunlight, slanted from the far west and the sky is that giving-up colour of blue. Adrian wishes his exhaled breath could emerge from his lungs in that particular colour, simply cloud the atmosphere around his head with the unmistakable shade of hopelessness but George Drury would never stand for such a show of self-pity. Oh for God's sake, Adrian, snap out oif it. It's not self-pity though, Adrian would say, it's worry. Adrian is worried, very worried in fact, someone might be drawing up a petition this very moment encouraging parents not to enroll their children in Adrian Drury's swimming class, and keep them away from the pool when he's guarding: drive to the pool at once and pick them up when his shift begins, sound an alarm from the firehall. Surely Laura Van Epp won't leave, she'll stay and swim a couple of consoling lengths. And Anastasia will make a point of appearing: Well, Drury, maybe you've got the bloodiest blood after all. Congratulations. This is going to make one helluva tableau. Yes, a tableau. Some l.d. Ken by a pool while hundreds of little Barbies and Midges with chopped-off legs run for cover and scramble into the Barbiemobile, a purse-lipped Cornelia Laine at the wheel. Maybe it'll win a prize at the fall fair. That's about as famous as you could get in Flax. Adrian guesses that is one good thing. He can move to Mesmer or Telluride and live in relative obscurity.

One half-good thing: Friday he got a letter from Terwilliger, meaning the plan is in progress. He's kept the letter with him, planning to rip it up here and leave it in the rusty drum outside the pool fence. It's always full of crap so Adrian can bury the evidence, or, preferably, submerge it. He tries not to think the verbs "bury" or "inter" but trying not to think certain words is like a shining gold invitation to the vocabulary portion of the brain: you are cordially requested to think all the words you don't want to think whenever a word-sized space makes itself available in this particular head. A phenomenon worse than paranormal. Ghost-words typed out by Casper Cody. B-u-r-y. I-n-t-e-r. His fingers want to touch the corresponding keys; might as well give in to it. He knows he's more or less at the same depth as Cheryl, although he is neither interred nor buried, but were he a human drill bit he could spin his way through the wall of this pool and be on his way. Through the basements of Flax, past and between astonished tree roots, under the highway and into the cemetery, dodging caskets until he found Cheryl's and drilled through the bottom, right next to her sleeping head. *Hi, Adrian,* she'd say. *I knew you'd come and get me.* And he'd drill them to Toronto where they'd stay with Rose.

Unfolding paper is weirdly soothing and helps prevent crying and in anticipation of this and similar moments Adrian has folded the letter from Terwilliger into a very small square, which he now unfolds, unfolds, unfolds again, and again. Something about creased paper and its minimal resistance.

Drury! Terwilliger begins. *How's life in Flax? Getting any action? If not, maybe you should try the town of Wheat. Or Barley or even Sorghum. I heard there are some hot chicks in Sorghum. Is that true?*

Hey, no wonder you're all developmentally delayed out there. The kind of project you're doing in grade eleven is like something I would of done in grade three. But just keep the dollar bills coming and I'll mail your clues for you. Maybe send a nickel for this stamp while you're at it.

What's on your horizon? I'm boning up for law school when I'm not boning up for other reasons. Think I'll do litigation. Don't like those bad guys.

Signed, Ter.

One good thing: Beel would have his first letter.

And Adrian sits up and realizes in a slow-motion, underwater way it's possible he won't even be hired at the pool this year. In that case, maybe he could work in East Flax. It was about time they got a lifeguard and some safety precautions out there. Nobody would hire him, of course, they wouldn't have a mud hole budget for Minnow Lake but he could volunteer, he could spend his summer sitting on the ski jump

watching things. Sooner or later Farrell would paddle out,
maybe with the salt project.

Angel's heart was flip-flopping in her chest, she
was that mad. It felt like a bird on its back in there, unable to right itself, stunned by the ridiculous impact of
a plate glass window or a car headlight. In a rage at its
own skull. If she could, she would take her head between her two hands and bang it against the wall sep-
arating her room from Randy's. But that would only
create a messy hole for six embarrassed eyes to look
through.

The conversation she had just overheard in
Randy's room began like this. "Maddy," Randy said,
so clear he might as well have been right there in
Angel's room, "Adrian's already getting those pictures
in his locker again."

"From Jimmy Junior?" Maddy asked.

"Yeah. They're gross. Just parts of people doing it
or whatever and then Jimmy makes it into a drawing.
So of course he makes what's supposed to be a picture
of Adrian and Cheryl."

"Did you see it?"

"Them. There were two already."

Two already? Angel used a glass tumbler to listen in
when they had the door shut, and she pressed it
against the wall now until the plaster gave a little. Was
it possible she was really hearing this? Or did eavesdropping in this way with just one ear scramble the

message? The brain was used to hearing with two ears after all; maybe the other ear was filling in the blanks all wrong. It was a guilty ear after all, attached to a guilty person.

No, the glass amplified better than a microphone. There was Maddy blowing her nose and Randy creaking the bed. He'd be lying on his back; she'd be sitting on the edge of his desk, legs stretched out in front, long as a playground slide.

Maddy: Well, what are they? Describe them.

Randy: They're gross.

Maddy: They're actual photographs?

Randy: Yeah. Of, you know, a dick and somebody's ass. I don't know. I'm too young to know about that. I don't want to know.

Maddy: Then he draws people attached to them?

Randy: People who are supposed to look like Adrian and Cheryl and then Adrian shows me and then he rips them up. Then he talks about how he's going to beat the shit out of that prick Jimmy Junior.

Angel pulled the glass from the wall with a damp sound, a little like Jimmy Senior slurping himself out of her body. Not really but she couldn't help thinking that, just like she couldn't help listening in on Randy and Maddy when she knew she shouldn't. Although clearly she should have listened more and sooner. The pictures were appearing *again*. Again? My God. What had she gotten herself into?

Angel made herself sit until her heart stopped flopping. Then for a moment, everything stopped; she went a strange kind of blind and deaf where she could see but nothing looked real and the little hairs inside her ears that moved the sound along got stuck like a needle in a scratched record. The only sounds they could shoulder along were " a dick and somebody's ass." That's apparently what they had heard, and they weren't about to be told anything else. "A dick and somebody's ass," they said again, and again, now to the tune of "Farmer in the Dell," "heigh-ho the dairy-o, a dick and somebody's ass."

Shut up, she had to say to her own inner ear. Shut up or I'll gouge you out with a pen. That seemed to do the trick.

Seven-thirty. Frog was at the till. They usually stayed open until nine at least. There was only one phone, on the kitchen wall, but she couldn't call Jimmy Senior now anyway; he'd still be at the high school polishing floors. She could make a quick trip into town and confront him but his perv of a son would most likely be there hanging pictures in lockers. Angel managed to stand up and close her bedroom door, noticing she'd gone a little cold now, the temperature of Minnow Lake, as if someone had hooked her up to an IV of mossy water in an effort to bring her around. Think. Jimmy wouldn't be home until ten at the earliest. Frog never went to bed before she did and you never knew when he might get up for a drink of water. The truth was she would be crazy to risk making a call to Jimmy with Frog in the house but what choice did she have? She'd wait until midnight, then make a move.

God damn that Jimmy Drake. He was more like a

skin problem than a man, some kind of fungus that made you want to scratch yourself right down to the underside, where the suede is. Or even beyond, like that group of plantar warts Angel once had with its rooty connections to the bloodstream so that you had no choice but to burn them off with dry ice. Repeated applications. That was what Jimmy Senior needed. Repeated applications of something but she wasn't sure what. Or maybe she was the one in need of the applications. Could there be a cream or salve that would even begin to reduce her irritation? Or a pill strong enough to sedate her rage? Examining her fingernails, Angel was surprised they didn't blacken and curl themselves from the tips of her fingers in disbelief. Along with her toenails. What was to be done? She went to the bathroom and washed her face.

Remarkably, the evening passed and Angel supposed she managed to resemble herself but the others, Frog, Maddy, and Randy, might as well have been from Outer Mongolia. They reminded her of customers she'd had once from Germany who'd wound up lost in East Flax looking for something not to be found in the store or on any map. Angel remembered how incomprehensible they'd been to one another; no matter how much noise passed between them, at whatever volume, they might as well have been dogs. Though you tended to think dogs divined some sense from one another, understood the basic bark but maybe not.

She took over at the till and watched the lifeless street beyond the thirsty geraniums in the store window. Why on earth had she gone back to Jimmy

Drake? She could have done without for a spell. But Jimmy, well, the thing about Jimmy was he could be dirty and at the same time, oddly devoted. He himself said there were only two people on this earth he truly cared about, besides Jimmy Junior, and they were Reg Decker and Angel Farrell.

Well, he certainly had a strange way of caring, not like most adults, and Angel realized Jimmy Senior was in many ways like a toddler with size eleven feet and prematurity of the penis. He delighted in making people mad, pushing and pushing with his warm and wienerish fingers until they snapped. Then he was sad; then he was sorry. Not even as advanced as a seven year old who could have seen the consequences coming or talked back. He was nothing but a big screw that came loose then tightened itself up when Reg or Angel let fly. A big screw. Ha. He'd like that.

"I'm going to close and go to bed," Angel said to Frog, knowing he would follow soon. And she was right. In bed, Angel turned on her side to watch the clock—9:35—and within two minutes, Frog was deep in his underground sleep, his nightly hibernation. Once asleep, Frog breathed so slowly Angel used to worry the brain mechanism responsible for inhaling was rusting over and soldering itself to a halt. No more. The gears were simply slow and ponderous and now Angel wondered when they might decide Frog Farrell had good reason to be suspicious of his wife.

Where the hell was midnight? Angel waited, held her breath, counted to one hundred, breathed in unison with Frog, counted to one hundred again. Oh, forget it. Ten o'clock was going to have to do. Jimmy might be home; he wasn't famous for attention to detail. He'd likely be out of his work duds by now, strolling around nude, his big sausage stuck to its balls. Ham and eggs, he'd be thinking; that was his pet name for his apparatus. She'd call and if he didn't answer, drive to Flax, ruin the countryside with her radioactive rage.

"Angel, my little cherub, what can I do for you?"

His voice was a mouthful of castor oil. "Jimmy, I need those pictures from you. I need them delivered to my mailbox tonight, in the dead of night. I'll be up waiting."

"You need the pictures? The pictures are safe with me, my cherub, you know that."

"No the pictures are not safe with you, as I suspected all along. The pictures are apparently making appearances in lockers at the Flax High School. The pictures are not and never have been safe with Jimmy Drake. In fact, nothing is safe with Jimmy Drake and as a consequence, Jimmy Drake is in a very vulnerable position right now because if those pictures don't show up in Angel's mailbox, Jimmy's house might inexplicably go up in flames. It's been a hot summer and we're heading into a hot fall and that's the kind of thing that happens when the conditions are hot. It's called spontaneous combustion." She was watching the stairs, listening for the slightest creak overhead.

"Angel, Angel, you're talking nonsense. The pictures are in a strongbox. You know that."

"No, Jimmy, they are not. You don't get it, do you?

They are in a very weak box. So weak that they are showing up in lockers, like I just said, high-school lockers, Jimmy. Isn't that strange? How could that possibly be? Never mind answering, Jimmy. I just want you to listen. I have friends, Jimmy, important friends and I have credibility. I am a Cobb. Do you know that?"

"Yes, Angel, of course I know that." Trying to soothe.

"And I might be a slut with bad judgment but my brother is a judge and my sister is a lawyer. All I have to do is let this slip. I'll find a way that does not incriminate me. Even if it does, I don't care. So you see where you've made your mistake, Jimmy? I don't care about reputations but you have to. I'll let it slip that you have dirty pictures; maybe you've got a camera set up in the girls' locker room or a peephole into the lavatory. I'm sure I have no idea what Mr. Green Eggs and Ham is capable of. But once Allan and Muriel Cobb know, and Philip Rochon knows, and Dorothy Limb knows—we were friends in school, you know—and Jerome finds out...well, people don't like pedophiles, Jimmy Drake, especially the school board. The school board has a real aversion to them."

"Yes, yes, fine Angel." Now he was nervous. "I don't want the things anyway."

"The things? Now you call them the things? And you don't want them? My. That was certainly a rapid change of heart." She could play with him a little but she was feeling faint; she was going to faint. No. It passed.

"You don't want me to want them, do you?" And

now he was earnest, and sad, of course, and sorry.

Angel sighed so hard her throat wanted to cry. "No, I guess I don't. But the mailbox is no good. Too public. You bring those pictures out to Dance Hall Road. There's a shed. Leave them there in an envelope. *Tonight*. No later than three. I'll be there at four to pick them up."

"It's done. Consider it done, Angel."

"It had better be."

A pause, a silence, did Frog have the tumbler to the bedroom floor?

"So does this mean we're not seeing each other any more?"

"Yes, Jimmy, that's what it means. In any language. German or dog or fucking tap dance. That's what it means." And Angel hung up so hard the phone gave an injured little yelp.

Jimmy Drake Senior was spooked before he'd even left the house. He knew he would be. Just like some nights at work, he would anticipate the spooking, the hall-length dreads before the sun went down. Then he would spend the night at school wondering what the whirr of the floor polisher concealed, imagining locker doors opening and closing behind his back, freeing students who'd gone missing and were now white and stretched and diapered for some reason, like New Year's babies from 1954. His mind liked to go to the worst case. That's when it helped to have Jimmy Junior around.

But now it was three in the morning. Jimmy hated the middle of the night so much he didn't even like the phrase, preferring to think the night did not have a middle, a place you could unzip it and inside, who knew what? All the arms of all the dead people hanging out, brushing their skinless fingers against him. Push them back inside to get the damn thing zipped up: a duffle bag full of rot.

All right. He had the envelope and the pictures *and* the negatives. Angel hadn't mentioned the negatives but once she had the pictures she'd think, wait a minute, and there'd be another call and another covert middle-of-the-night operation. This was the whole kit and caboodle. He'd gone through each one and matched it with its negative and there were indeed two missing. But unless Jimmy Junior had learned dark room techniques, this was it, the whole kit and caboodle. Jimmy liked saying that. Kit and caboodle was a comforting little thought, what you might say heading off to the beach or a picnic in the heat and liveliness of afternoon. Have we got the whole kit and caboodle? He'd say that five hundred times between here and East Flax if he had to, might help regulate the heartbeat to a pleasant clip-clop.

That wasn't working. Hadn't even left Flax and the shaking had begun. God damn it. Once he got started, there was no stopping. He'd be shaking and shivering and teeth-chattering all the way there and back, and to make matters worse, nobody in the entire town was up, nobody that is, except for him. Nothing but dark and shut down houses, lights out, blinds drawn. Jimmy hated that. At least when he had to work late—weekend nights when there was a dance in the gym—he could count on one or two people's being up, fans of the late-late show, or the occasional house party, even better, spilling its noise and drink onto the sidewalk. This, unfortunately, was Thursday and all those resentful street lights seemed to say, if it weren't for you, we wouldn't be on. And the blackened windows: Our people are in bed. They don't scurry around at night with dirty pictures.

And of course there was still the problem with the headlight. Once again, the left one had burned out because there was water in there. He'd told Reg the thing was damaged when he bought the car; there must have been a break in the glass, but Reg said no damn way, he didn't sell cars with defective headlights. Offered to sell him a replacement at cost, just charge labour for the installation: that's the best he could do. The best he could do—Reg Decker's personal mantra. Meanwhile, the whole electrical system could go because Reg Decker wouldn't admit he'd sold a car with a broken light. With friends like Reg...still, Jimmy wished now he'd got the thing replaced because outside of town, one feeble headlight was almost worse than no light. Low beam was like driving in a gravel whiteout with a flashlight, and high beam, there were all those branches reaching into the light, like they wanted something and had been waiting now for hours. At last you're here, Jimmy Senior.

Jimmy stayed with low beam. Having Reg to be

mad at soothed him a little and the shakes had now subsided. Maybe he could enjoy the drive. The countryside was less lonely than the town. Dusk-to-dawn yard lights illuminated the farm buildings, reminding him of drive-in movies, and here and there the trees came so close you could hear the breeze on their sharp, stiffening leaves. He could almost believe they were encouraging him along, whispering in a friendly type of language shared by the beech, maple, and elm.

Here were the swampy curves now. Jimmy couldn't say he was bothered by the swampy curves or the bog he knew lay behind them, not an actual lake but a Siamese twin to Minnow Lake, joined as they were by an underground tributary of quagmire. It was nothing but a sink hole full of absorbent plants that sat all bubbly on the surface of thick, murky water intent on tricking you. Come for a walk and then slurp, up to your armpits in warm mush, earth puke. Once, years and years ago, he and Reg went out there on their bikes, they were maybe ten, no more. They sloshed their way through the marsh until they found themselves standing on a rock shelf, in water to their knees. Reg took a giant step off the shelf and sank up to his chin, practically his nose, stood there in the brine, blinking, pretending he wasn't afraid. He couldn't swim, and add to that the number of underwater vines that came to life the minute they smelled human blood in the bog and, Jimmy could tell, Reg was pretty scared if not terrified. The funny thing was, he just stood there, balancing on his tiptoes in the blue muck, tiny ripples thickened with water life flickering all around him, catching the

sun, pulling even the light from shore. Jimmy could remember heat on the top of his head, like a hand, and
a smell of old water, stuff that had been around since
maybe the day after God created it.

Jimmy cranked the window down some more. Listen to those frogs! No doubt distant relatives of the
ones that jumped out of Reg and Jimmy's way those
many years ago. Anyway, what happened was Reg stood
there, scared to move for fear he might topple backwards and unwilling to ask for help until Jimmy
stretched out an arm and dragged him back to the
shelf. Dragged him back so Reg could live to inherit a
bunch of money from his old man and start up a three-
million-dollar car dealership while Jimmy went on to
become the high school janitor and father of one bastard son.

Then up the little rise, into the clearing and nothing but empty, lonesome, harvested fields and there it
was, Dance Hall Road. Jimmy hadn't been to the
dance hall for more than sixteen years, could probably
calculate this hiatus close to the day by subtracting
nine months back from Jimmy Junior's birthday. He
and Hazel Smart had spent some time in the woods
after a dance and bingo, she went off to a home, was
going to give up the baby but came back to Flax, after
all, with the baby named, to everyone's surprise, James
Paul Drake. Everybody said she was right off her rocker
for a while, hating Jimmy Drake but wanting him to
marry her. Well, he asked and she said no. And the
end result? People saw Hazel as a kind of hero, she'd
done the right thing, you had to give her credit, every-

one said, meaning, isn't Jimmy Drake a little sono-
fabitch?

Hazel lived with her parents, went back to high
school, and one summer day when little Jimmy was just
out of diapers, she dropped him off with Jimmy Senior. "Your turn," she said, and left, went off to university and took some courses in household sciences and
six years later, she's on the radio with a household advice show, tips on meringue and stain removal. "This
has been Kitchen Smart with Hazel Smart." Apparently it even got broadcast out west. And as if that were
not enough, rumour had it she was a dyke, rumour
Jimmy refused to believe because what would a dyke
be doing with a kitchen show? Seemed to him a dyke
would have a radio show on, he didn't know what,
motor oils perhaps. Diesels. What the rumour did was,
it went to show you how far the town and surrounding
countryside was willing to go to fuck with his mind.
Not only does his ex-girlfriend abandon their out-of-
wedlock baby, not only does she go on to become a famous radio star, *but* she is also rumoured to be a
lesbian. All for the benefit of Jimmy Drake. He was
surprised they didn't hand out brochures with the
Gideon's Bibles: How to fuck with the mind of Jimmy
Drake Senior.

Pulling into the parking lot was both better and
worse. He could get rid of these pictures and get the
show on the road. But outside the car, above the black
and sullen lake, surrounded by trees and quiet and nature's ESP, Jimmy thought: What if Frog Farrell is inside that shed? Who's to say Angel hadn't told him

everything? She said they had an open marriage. Jesus. Frog Farrell. There was something half-animal about the guy, more than just the name, his eyes were too far apart and his skin was too tight on his carcass, froggish for sure, and he didn't say much, just watched people as if they were flies he might decide to catch with his tongue. If he knew, he'd be waiting in the shed; that's what Jimmy would have done if anyone had tried this with his wife if he'd happened to have one.

For a moment, Jimmy thought he might cry, considering the inevitability of Frog inside the shed, sledgehammer or rifle poised for retaliation. He could cry and shake and dissolve into a puddle of piss and tears with only his hair floating on the surface, a receding patch of greying black fuzz, left to blow away like a dead dandelion when the puddle dried up.

No matter how lightly each foot was placed, sounds of parking-lot treachery rose, little crunchings of round and dusty bones, joints, ligaments grinding the way his would when the hammer met his jaw. Along the perimeter in the grass was no better, twigs having been dropped by vigilant trees and Jimmy remembered the possibility of traps. Frog Farrell had a trapline somewhere, why not here? This could very easily be a fox migratory route for all Jimmy knew and at the thought of a spring-loaded trap, metal serrated teeth clamping down on him with the fury of the school secretary, Mrs. Liebling, at the paper cutter, his mute and trusting ankles could have shed tears. Back to the gravel. He was a dead man. So be it.

The latch lifted easily and with zero effort the door

opened into the shed, creating a vacuum pull on all the fears housed in Jimmy's body, standing them next to him, smiling and leering and choking with relief. No one there. Nothing but an empty shed filled with the smell of tools and twine and ladders. Jimmy dropped the envelope onto the packed earth floor, closed the door, and ran to the car. Thank you, God. Down the hill and away from Dance Hall Road. But like a premature birth that had changed its mind, within minutes Jimmy's fear had climbed back inside him, down the dry tunnel of his throat, and now: if Frog Farrell had any brains at all, he'd hide out behind a tree and shoot him as he passed by. Of course. To kill him at the dance hall would be too obvious. A roadside shooting would be much harder to prove, especially if he got rid of the weapon in Minnow Lake or its sister the bog. He'd be sitting, waiting for the headlights right now, step out into the ditch and blam. Frog was a hunter; he shot deer bounding along at thirty miles an hour. How was that any different from Jimmy Drake in a Ford?

Jimmy turned off his headlight. Within seconds his eyes had adjusted to the few kilowatts of ivory moon and once more, he was calmed. The road was now a pale and welcoming pathway that seemed to indicate everything would surely be fine. The danger was past. As long as the headlight is off, you and your car are night creatures like the raccoon and the porcupine, and Frog Farrell did not, to Jimmy's knowledge, own a pack of hounds. He was safe. He sped up. He was, after all, a distant cousin of Sir Francis Drake. Euphoria settled inside him like new eyes, transplants that gathered up the faintest bits of light and shone like dollhouse lanterns in his skull. Eighty miles per hour. He'd be home in a couple minutes and soon it would be going on four and the morning on its way. Everybody up, he shouted to no one.

Out of nowhere, out of a side road, came lights you'd never expect, red and partyish. What the...? Oh, for Christ's sake. The cops. How could this be? What were they doing up and out at this hour? On this of all roads? He could see in the rear-view mirror it was Jerome Limb. Jerome Limp. Oh well. Jimmy would dream up some reason for driving with no lights. Wait a minute. Was driving with lights actually a legal requirement? And furthermore, what would Jerome Limb know on the subject? Jimmy would get him distracted, then maybe they could head into Lalonde's for a coffee. The night was, after all, still young.

Rose Drury wished there were a passport office at the entrance to East Flax, a rickety shed at the end of a worn dirt road housing an old man, Russell Hansen maybe or the Maestro, sifting through application forms and pencil-written pleas. Only the lucky few would actually find the place and fewer still be allowed in. "I'm afraid your documents aren't in order," he'd say to most, sliding shut the window to his checkpoint, an unfinished structure open on the nether side to lake, frog chorus, bog smell: the kindling of life. But to

Rose he'd always say, "Go right on ahead, miss. Go right on up to Dance Hall Road."

The town of Flax had most certainly not noticed but Rose had all but taken out citizenship in East Flax. The dance hall with its dishes and cutlery for two hundred and its private basketball court had more or less become an apartment for her and Maddy. Rose had arranged to leave home without having gone anywhere. A sleight of body, she thought, moving through the routine of school, home, and the dentist's office reception area, with the co-operation of just a few layers of skin, while beneath them the organs and blood and muscles were forming into plans with Maddy. She was living a type of lava lamp existence, visible only to herself, suffering the women of Flax, kindly declining offers of feminine support. "*The Nutcracker* would be lovely, I'm sure, but I'm afraid I won't be able to attend this year." "Shopping? No, I believe I have everything I need. My dad employs me and I have the use of a car, so as you can see..."

And her friends had stopped asking, except to communicate occasionally with Adrian via Laura Van Epp on behalf of Anastasia who would still like to know exactly what was going on. A legitimate question, Rose would concede, but unanswerable perhaps even by Graham Rochon were he to have all the pertinent details bulging from one of his green file cabinets, the force of its own mystery pushing the drawer open late at night. I don't know, she wanted to say to Anastasia. Honest. Honest as hell, as they used to say. Their own private expression, meaning Satan in a judge's robe would want to hear it all, would never flinch, on the contrary, would long to hear the worst.

You'd have thought she would miss her and the others but Maddy's teeth, Maddy's grades, Maddy's fashion sense, Maddy's basketball training required so much attention there was no time to spare. Some days Rose felt tired and harassed like a babysitter left in charge much longer than expected, awaiting errant parents while cooking macaroni and cheese amidst the soggy mess of the cereal bowls in the Farrell kitchen. Other times, Rose couldn't sleep for the excitement of unformed plans. Dropping off Maddy last week, she'd had the urge to turn right instead of home to Flax, keep going and drive all night. How odd for one so suffocated by her hometown that she'd never driven herself past Mesmer. What was stopping her from going east of East Flax, to Toronto, Montreal, the St. Lawrence River, and the ocean? She could become a missing person, like the poster Anastasia had taped to her locker one day, a shady photocopy of her last year's school photo beneath the two-inch stencilled message: *MISSING! Rose Anne Drury. Anyone with information leading to her whereabouts is asked to contact the Flax Police Department.*

Rose had left it up for a few days, just to confirm Anastasia's point, but began to realize, especially late at night in that moonlit countryside, that the identity of a missing person offered deep consolation, the sort of solace a sermon should. What if Reverend Rochon were to grant weekly disappearances? There might be a few takers.

Her dad thought she'd caught a bug, something long and drawn out like mononucleosis, her throat was a little on the red side. Take it easy and stop running around so much, was his advice. But she did not. Brought her books with her to the dance hall and planned to study, but there was always Maddy to watch. Maddy had to practice and Rose had to watch with, appropriately, an intensity she associated with cramming for exams.

Not that Rose didn't wonder from time to time how this East Flax lifestyle might appear to a third set of eyes. More than a little bewildering, undoubtedly. There was Rose on a folding chair, talking, reassuring. Every other day Maddy would ask: Do you really think they made Cheryl Decker captain because they felt sorry for her? *Absolutely. Compassionate reasons.* Are you sure? *Of course I'm sure.* This was not coaching. No interested observer would mistake this type of talk for coaching. And when Maddy took off her shirt, ran around in her ribcage and size A bra, Rose's face said nothing. It's a little like an art exhibit, she thought; modern art can be anything. Or a movie made by the CBC. You're not meant to understand but to keep on watching. Never reveal your bumpkinhood.

"What about the dance tonight?" Maddy asked. They were turning right in the Vega. Heading up the hill to the dance hall.

"The dance tonight?" Rose repeating the words as if they were a place name in Russia, too many consonants and unfamiliar vowels.

"Yes. The September dance. On the last Friday in

September. I think I'll go."

Rose's thoughts had huddled themselves into this possibility a few times, arcane as the Flax Composite High's football team, all backs and unnatural padding and secret strategy, indecipherable. What *if* she and Maddy were both at the dance?

"I thought you'd be working. Don't you clean Alfred Beel's house on Fridays?"

"Every other Friday. Last Friday for example."

Could it be that Maddy was challenging Rose to a public demonstration of her loyalty? It wasn't as if they didn't spend time together at school but there, Rose was always busy with Maddy, always moving, more accurately, from one place to the next with great purpose. A dance offered no purpose, no destination, and very little structure. Swarms of girls watched by swarms of boys in an atmosphere, Rose realized with a hard-as-eggshell swallow, much akin to their times alone in the dance hall. An atmosphere of great visual busyness, eyes watching with an appetite, eyes that hadn't been let out much.

"Well, if you're going then I will too." Still plenty of time for the car to die, tires to blow, spark plugs to require replacement, distributors, carburetors, radiators—as many reasons not to come as there were movable parts in a Vega.

They were at the dance hall now, parked.

"Let's practice dancing then," Maddy said. "My transistor's in the hall."

"But what if somebody looked in? People do walk by the place. That creepy Alfred Beel being one of them."

"Then let's go into the woods. I'll get the radio. Come on."

"But it looks like it might rain."

"So what? So what if it might rain?"

What was that rumour about Maddy's dad and traps? Eating skunk or coon? What sort of effect might one anticipate from the ingestion of such low-to-the-ground game? Why did the longer-legged animals seem more civilized fare? Although now that she thought of it, the lawyer woman in Rosedale had proudly shown off the rabbit marinating in her fridge. But rabbits hopped and dashed on powerful legs, were the subject of fairy tales, whereas the skunk and the coon were considered varmints. Which meant vermin.

They walked, Maddy leading the way, thumbing the dial on her pink radio, last year's Christmas gift from Angel Farrell. The dizzy whine of radio waves in fast and cluttered approach and then one clear signal, the disc jockey from London.

"This is far enough. No one will see us here, if you're so worried."

"I'm not worried, Maddy. I can't really recall the last time I worried. Rose Drury and worry are a kind of parallelogram. We're almost incapable of meeting." She was talking like Anastasia.

"Unless you were a parallelogram drawn by me."

"What's that supposed to mean?"

"It means I'm not good at geometry. Anyway, this is good. Jackson Five. Good beat. Easy to dance to. That's what they always say."

What was happening? They'd slipped through the looking glass or more likely the rear-view mirror of some hillbilly's truck. Maddy was altered. She looked as if she'd been given a drink of uranium or the heavy water manufactured at the Bruce nuclear power plant and it had pooled like clumsy weights in her hands and feet. Maddy was jumping and kicking and Rose now understood her purpose here: to teach Maddy to dance, to prevent shame on the dance floor for Maddy Farrell.

"Maddy, Maddy, Maddy. Not so wild. Like this. See? More in control and not hardly any movement of the feet. That's how Anastasia Van Epp will be dancing, I guarantee."

The instruction continued through "Ain't No Mountain High Enough" and then, coincidental with "Dance to the Music" with Sly and the Family Stone, Maddy threw off her shirt and said, "You should take yours off too. You never do."

Rose had larger breasts, better quality brassieres, and to be honest, she was a little tired of Maddy behaving as if she were in fact the captain of the basketball team. Warm for late September, so why not?

And just like that, as if Maddy had choreographed the situation or was manipulating the radio waves with the new fillings in her teeth, the transistor cackled out a slow song. James Taylor, "Fire and Rain."

"Will you just teach me one slow dance please? In the unlikely event a guy does ask me to dance?"

"I'm not an expert on slow dancing but okay, I'll try." She had done this at summer camp on Georgian

Bay, long ago when she was ten or possibly eleven, girls dancing with girls, the recreation director Pam insisting, almost ordering them not to be so uptight. Calling them middle-class princesses.

"Okay, like this," said Rose. Extending her arms like a boy did not particularly bother her. Then, Maddy placed her hand on Rose's back. Then, they began to dance. Rustling between the roots and leaves of the forest floor, the sun broke through, and, to be funny, "It's a spot dance," Rose said. Spot dances were only ever won by couples, she was thinking, when Maddy did a strange and delirious thing: undid the back of Rose's bra, pulled it off, and threw it into the trees. Then laughed and laughed. Laughed harder when it caught on a branch and failed to return, fell to her knees laughing. While Rose stood, in charge now at last, or so her breasts seemed to think with those two very hard nipples pursing themselves up in the September breeze. Nudists disported themselves in this manner and were healthy. A lack of vitamin D caused rickets.

"I'm sorry," Maddy said. "I just did a nutty thing. You know how sometimes you can't help yourself?"

There'd been mottoes at the summer camp on long silk and felt banners hanging from the cedar beams of the dining hall, concise meditations on wind, water, and pine. Were East Flax to have a motto drifting above the heads of its citizens it might be: You know how sometimes you can't help yourself?

"You're going to have to get my bra down."

"That's easy. There's a ladder at the dance hall I can get. I'll be right back." Then she crumpled into laughter again, lay in the leaves examining Rose from the angle of a squirrel, leapt up, found her shirt, and took off.

By the time Maddy returned, Rose had knotted together a modest garment with several long-stemmed leaves. "It's a deciduous bra-bib," she said, "a bracidu-ous bib."

Maddy ignored this, as she did most of Rose's attempts at cleverness. "We were right to avoid the dance hall," she said. "I ran into Alfred Beel on my way out of the tool shed."

Alfred Beel was brilliantly happy. Astronauts might just be commenting, he thought, peering from their space capsules at his reflection. What on earth? Literally. All of the earth's mirrored glass laid end to end on the bald prairie could not have matched the blinding radiance of Alfred Beel reborn. He now understood that time spent on Cora was nothing but an apprenticeship for Loretta. Even the ill-advised trip to London had yielded results: he now owned a fashionable suit, should there be a suitor's need for it. And, Alfred would always believe that, were a neurologist to do a thorough examination of Cora's head, hiding inside that medicine chest of information on makeup and medication, was a bottled memory of Alfred. She didn't have to empty that ashtray if she didn't want to; no one forced her to wear those tight jeans. However, he would confess to one or two flights of fancy. Not so with Loretta. This was going to be the genuine article. Alfred Beel's period of gestation had finally come to a close.

Alfred was Alfred no more. He was *Field and Stream*, he was *Rod and Gun*. As of today, Alfred was all of the images from all of the birthday cards for men. He was a fishing lure, a hammock, a stag, a stallion, a chainsaw, a lawn mower: everything mechanical. His heart had left off beating for a smooth and motorized hum. The Motorola, he called himself, the Chevy Impala. Names he thought Loretta might someday invent, imagined she secretly had but was too shy to say. Alfred knew if he could occupy the same room as Loretta for ten minutes, she would be his and damned if he hadn't been right. Let your testosterone do the walking in the dentist's waiting room. His only surprise being the lack of response from the other waiters. Had they been completely blind to the movement of hormones in the room, ridges of high pressure colliding with moist Atlantic fronts? Half-expected to see the pages of magazines lift in the cross breeze, Adele Pond and Nestor Limb to exchange encouraging glances. From the moment Alfred entered the room, Loretta was a uniformed radiance. Don't ask how he knew, but her eyes behind the desk were lights flashing green and brighter than the sun. A nova of consent. Astronomers worldwide must have wondered, dispatched researchers to the Flax vicinity in burn protection gear.

"How have you been, Alfred? Long time no see," Loretta said, leafing through his file.

"You know what they say: if it ain't broken, why fix it?"

"Yes, but, teeth are a lot like cars. Maintenance is everything. You wouldn't go two years without an oil change, would you? You know, I can put you on recall if you want."

"Recall? Isn't that for cars with mechanical flaws?"

"Yes. And for dental patients who neglect to make appointments. I call you every six months or once a year, whichever you want, to set up an appointment. No mechanical flaws necessary. Some of our best models are on recall."

"When you put it that way, might as well sign me up." But why now? Why not previous years? And which best models were on recall? Nestor Limb? He doubted it. He watched as she wrote something in his file, her white pen moving, white as her starched uniform and most likely, the white underwear beneath it. The hidden agenda. Alfred was of the belief that all women in uniform wanted sex, with the exception perhaps of those prison guards at St. Joe's. If only he could radio them now, advise them that in this very town there lived a most efficient and professional receptionist, also in the field of health care, who found Alfred Beel attractive. Not laughable, not contemptible, possibly even fashionable. Or at least more fashionable than that Reg Decker in his plaid pants. You might see Alfred in an old-fashioned suit, you might see him in galoshes, but you would never see him in plaid below the belt.

George Drury kept to the schedule. In less than ten minutes, there he was opening the door to his chair, summoning Alfred. There was nothing wrong with his teeth but Alfred made up a story about a molar sensitive to cold and sometimes hot. Time for an x-ray. "I've had so many of those, my head's going to start glowing in the dark one of these days, George."

"They say the effects aren't cumulative."

Dr. Drury disappeared to develop the picture and Alfred hatched his plan. Loretta needed a reason to call sooner. That was the message she was trying to convey. He'd have to leave something behind. When he paid, he'd set his wallet on her desk, behind the potted plant, not easily visible to anyone but sooner or later, she'd notice and have to call. *You forgot your wallet, Alfred. I'll drop it off for you.*

"Nothing's showing up here, Alfred," the dentist said. "Keep an eye on it. It if starts to get worse, come and see me."

"Guess I'll just have to stay off the ice cream."

Dr. Drury said nothing. He was at the door, five minutes early, calling for Nestor Limb. Just as well. Less time to think, just execute the plan, which he did, brilliantly, paid his bill and left the slim billfold wedged behind the clay plant pot and unlikely to be spotted until the next patient checked in. He left in a hurry, glad he'd parked around the corner and out of sight in case someone came running after him. Adele Pond saw everything, but not today. Alfred made his way home to sit by the phone. He had no qualms now, none at all; this was going to work. The office closed early on Fridays; Loretta would leave by four. She'd be straightening up her desk and what's this? Oh dear. Call immediately. Until then, he'd sit and watch the phone. Sooner or later that indifferent plastic animal would speak. And it was an animal, a turtle or an armadillo. This was the sort of thing nature photographers did: sat for days awaiting the appearance of a rare lizard or hundred-year-old boa constrictor. The Galapagos or Patagonia; that's where he should be with Loretta. It was never too late to become a nature photographer.

Alfred fried eggs, poured lye down the drain—a job Maddy should have done—tried to watch some daytime television but fell asleep. He dreamed a dream about Loretta. They were rowing together on Minnow Lake, Loretta with the oars and Alfred sitting, admiring, dipping his hand into the water and wondering why it was so warm, growing warmer by the minute until he had to wonder what was wrong. Was there a little volcanic leak in the floor of Minnow Lake? The ambivalent pleasure of the water was odd enough to wake him up, worried about Reg. Funny how consciousness could flood a simple dream with guilt, make you want to call the cops on your own imagination.

There was the phone. Almost three o'clock. It had taken her long enough.

"Alfred. Loretta here. Are you missing anything?"

What the hell was that supposed to mean? Why couldn't women just talk the way the language was set up to be talked? Questions were meant to be questions and statements were meant to be statements.

"We've got your wallet here. And, lucky for you, I've got some Avon to deliver out your way. So I can drop it off for you. You going to be in around four-thirty, five?"

He wasn't entirely awake. Avon? That was a little

worrying. Was this standard procedure for Loretta? Did she have access to a warehouse of props to cover all manner of tracks? No. She was careful, that was all. God knows you had to be careful in this small neck of the woods. Everyone knew your business and your car. "I'll be here. Thanks a lot. Getting forgetful in my dotage, I guess."

He'd have to call Maddy Farrell and cancel. Tonight was her night. Maybe she was already on her way. There was a chance she would show up with that Rose Drury chauffeuring her around as she now did. He couldn't decide which would be worse: Maddy Farrell face to face with Loretta in his driveway or Maddy arriving, being asked to leave, and departing minutes before Loretta's arrival, leftovers of her half-baked life ruining his appetite. Wait a minute. This wasn't her night anyway. She'd just been last Friday.

And so he passed the hour waiting, emptying his mind as if between the bone and the metal was nothing but sand, an hourglass dripping its contents into his barrel chest. The man of a million thoughts could barely think. How did a fifty-year-old man prepare himself for his first encounter with a woman in ten years? He wouldn't have minded a blood transfusion for starters. Draw out the time-worn stuff circulating for too long and replace it with fresh, unweary blood, preferably manufactured in a sterile plant somewhere, unused. "Used" made him think of Reg Decker and his cars. Although different had to be an improvement upon his own endlessly circulating, no doubt artery-hardening fluids.

Well, here's hoping that which needed to harden would do so if and when the moment came, which it surely would. Loretta Decker was not expecting tea. This much he knew. What did it matter if she was a tart with a trunkful of Avon? *Oh, Reg, by the way, I've got to deliver some lipstick to East Flax. Oh Reg, did I mention I'm dropping off some moisture cream in the greater Mesmer area? Reg, I'm afraid I have to get this hair remover cream to Angel Farrell pronto.* Surely not even Reg Decker would fall for the same story more than once.

He'd better make some coffee but there she was now, in the driveway. Four thirty-five. Hadn't wasted any time. Disconcerting to see from his window that she was not getting out of the car. Did she expect him to open the door? He stepped outside. "You might be needing this," she called from the driver's side, waving his wallet in the air. "Comes in handy." She was still in uniform; that said something. "I'm in a bit of a rush here. No rest for the wicked. These women and their beauty products. Emergencies, all of them."

Loretta was definitely not planning to get out of the car. For Alfred to open the car door now would be worse than the trip to London—this much he knew.

Make the best of it. "Thanks a lot, Loretta." He had to at least say her name.

"No problem. You're looking well, Alfred."

"Walking a lot."

"Now that it's cooled down, it's good weather for walking."

"Yes," said Alfred, "yes it is." Could he not think of something other than the weather to discuss? Apparently not. "Very seasonal now, I would say."

"I'd better run, Alfred. Nice to see you."

He watched the car out the long laneway, curlicues of exhaust reiterating these facts: You're looking well, Alfred. Nice to see you.

You're looking well, Alfred.

Nice to see you.

Alfred Beel did not disappoint easily. Off for his walk in the contented blue of late afternoon, he concluded he'd been on a date of sorts. A first date. He would not believe otherwise as up the road allowance he went, the back way to the dance hall. Today he'd come some distance. For the first time in ten years, he'd got far enough. Seemed he'd spent the past decade on his hands and knees crawling about in the attic of East Flax amidst raw, pink insulation, bats, and trapped heat, and had finally stumbled upon the staircase down to a better climate, the perfect climate. As if he alone had come across the necessary conditions for life, was genesis himself, the first little spore of existence lucky enough to land in the lap of earth.

Adrian is encouraged by his letter-writing talent; he thinks he might have a flair for persuasion and as a result, his colourless future is a little rosier. Apparently one does not need a high-school diploma to effectively convince the skeptical. Not that he is a huckster or a phony—he doesn't have those scary eyes like Billy Graham—and he is definitely better looking than any of the carnies who travel with the midway

with their skinny arms and wispy beards and switchblades. No, Adrian's authority and charm are more in league with the TV news anchorman. They'll see. Adrian Drury has a certain power and a certain glory, forever and ever, amen, and he smiles for the first time that day.

The second letter was a work of art and by now has reached its destination. Adrian had hit upon the idea of including a stamped, self-addressed postcard for Terwilliger to mail, simultaneous with Beel's letter. It was Adrian's job to collect the mail from the post office, so no need to worry about the dentist and his prying mind. Ha ha. Prying. And yesterday, two days ago, his postcard arrived, an old one he had lying around of Niagara Falls lit up at night. Above suspicion because who's ever going to check the postmark on anything about Niagara Falls? This really is proof he is smarter than most people and add to that the references made in his second letter, mention of Beel's brawny torso and his carpenter's apron. Adrian could not be sure but he was inclined to think, where consenting adults were concerned, in the talk department you pulled out most of the stops. With no evidence whatsoever, nothing more than the clear blue sky, Adrian is now certain he has the undivided attention of Alfred Beel, has that sour old fart's brain tuned to one signal–Radio Free Drury.

It's after school and Adrian has decided to do what he has not yet done–walk to the cemetery to take a look at Cheryl's grave. Enough time has passed, most of the snow is gone, and who knows, there might be some indicator; he has no idea what, but meanings and portents find their way to him. Perhaps that's what he'll do, have a TV show on the paranormal. Sit in a big leather chair with his legs crossed,

telling tales of the unbelievable and the mesmerizing. Yester-
day, for example, leaving Lalonde's, he passed Beel in the
street; their eyes met, of course, because Beel hates Adrian
and the feeling is more than mutual. Yes, audience, our eyes
met and that was a transcendental occasion, more than any
maharishi could manufacture and do you know why? Because
that much hatred at close range, volleyed between two heads,
that much energy made from nothing, from ions and elec-
trons, could convince anyone to believe in the power of some-
thing beyond what is seen before the eyes. A presence. A
presence that passeth all understanding, dear audience. Un-
crossing legs. Rustling papers. Fading to fireplace.

Adrian is alone. Anastasia and Laura offered him a
ride home but no thanks. That's his standard RSVP. So much
so that last night the dentist gave him a bit of a pep talk on
the subjects of moping and getting out more. Sign up for baseball or the dentist would do it for him. Grief was one thing
but wallowing in melancholy was another and served no purpose at all. And what, by the way, was he planning on doing
this summer?

"I've applied for a job at the pool."

"You have? When did you do that? You never told me."

"Why would I? I always apply for a job at the pool."

"Because I'm your father," said George Drury in his no-
torious half-bellow.

The dentist, too, was a presence but never did he passeth
understanding. He was too close for that, with too much mun-
dane attention paid to teeth and lunches and lawn mowers;
homework; semigloss paint; oil changes. All things opposite
the mysterious. Adrian liked empty houses and drained out
pools and dried out riverbeds, fossils, bird skeletons all in one

piece, and rabies. At no place did his interests overlap with his father's but there was little to be gained from contributing that observation to the pep conversation.

Yeah, yeah. I know.

Adrian decides to scoot along the side streets, avoiding people and their cars, hoping in vain they might not see him. Whose idea was it to build cemeteries always a little out of town? Although he supposed you couldn't have them mixed up with the water and sewer systems and, due to the incurable nature of death, acres of room were required for expansion. A cemetery in town would mean annexing and bulldozing houses. Oh, people would say, that's exactly where I used to have my train set. Now Bert Lalonde is buried there and one of these days his wife will be joining him. Adrian couldn't see how people—mostly wives—could do that, get their tombstones all set up with nothing but the date left empty, the one day out of infinity that was waiting for you with enough force to chip numbers into concrete.

Maybe he'd run now. He's beyond the streets and onto the highway where the ditches are full of leftover snow. Funny how old snow, as compared to new, was so unwelcome. Adrian didn't mind it, though. Old snow embalms things, he hopes, kicking at it to reveal nothing but older snow. His books must be left behind and he wedges them against a fence post, beneath the barbed wire. They'll be safe there. Falling-apart textbooks were not what most bandits were after.

Less than half a mile to the graveyard. He's going to stay on the right side of the road, like a slow moving vehicle on the shoulder; maybe he should have one of those reflective orange triangles tractors have. Although maybe not, since the sun is still up, high in the west; it's only 3:45. So as to improve

upon himself aerodynamically, Adrian zips up his black wind-
breaker, and then begins to jog. He should really try out for
track or at least pretend he's thinking of trying out for track
because a guy running in jeans and a jacket is not a normal
sight. If someone stops to offer him a lift or if Limb comes
along, suspecting something, that's what he'll say; he's trying
out for track.

The sun is warm; it's actually hot, at last. All over this
continent, this northern hemisphere, seeds and eggs, bears and
frogs, all forms of life hidden and caved and shelled, are getting the hint. Such is the penetrating power of the sun that
lakes and riverbeds erupt into life with the right angle, the
precise number of minutes. So it is reasonable to assume
Cheryl might be feeling better, possibly a little warmer. Like
that day at the pool last summer in that white bathing suit
with her shoulders peeling, pink and tattery skin turning to
brown. That was the day she told him his arms were all the
known colours of hen eggs. That was that day. This is this
day. Same sun, same highways and lakes, same blackboards
and leafy green vegetables except for one night a bleached out,
ropy arm not the colour of any egg pulled Cheryl Decker underneath it all. What can she see from down there? He hopes
it's like in the pool, looking up at the swimmers and the wavering sky, although the underwater sky Adrian always thinks
looks a little frail, like it could cry even on the sunniest day.

Cars are zooming by but no one stops. Adrian glances
back, hoping now Jerome Limb might come along in his
cruiser. Once Jerome drove him up to the jail in Telluride and
then they went to Dairy Queen. Adrian remembers being impressed that the jail had managed to arrange guilt and horror into the shape of small rooms. Step in; step out. Even

*without the walls he was pretty sure the atmosphere would
have held onto its cubed nightmares. Or maybe once in a
while when the inmate was innocent, the room ran away
from itself and drifted above the houses, looking for a guilty
party.*

*Adrian had planned to stop at the cemetery gate and
walk respectfully but being in training, he feels the need to
continue running along the soft roadway, spruce needles softening his tread. A good idea to make the place thick with
trees and shade, keep out the day and most of its weather,
maintain a separate climate, like a picnic shelter with pil-
lars and roof but no walls, a place where you could stand beside a downpour but not in it. Melancholy.*

*He knows where the Decker plot is and there it is already.
One large headstone of an angel, maybe eight or nine feet
tall, with wings and assorted other headstones, but Adrian is
in training and now is not the time to slow down. There is
Cheryl's grave, he can see it well enough. The sod has survived the winter but looks new still, a separate green. Put a
knob on it and pull and it might open like a trap door. And
the trees—one thing about the trees—yes, they are beneficial
but why do they need those giant roots? Absolutely nothing
moves a tree. They'd be better arranged on underground
tracks. Push a button and they reposition like clothes at the
dry cleaner. That way he could open up an alley for the sun
to stream through, Adrian thinks, running toward the gate,
feeling his face pinken as he turns away.*

Cheryl Decker was alone in the school. When the

3:20 bell signalled release into the sinking, yellow September light, she had stayed back, imagining all the students in lines and circles like a geometry lesson seen from above or those dancers on the Ed Sullivan show. Smokers would gather beneath the trees, bus riders snake their way onto buses, cars and motorcycles reverse and accelerate, all of them exhaling their plans and the imminence of departure. The laws of nature and the herd were understood in the language of the geese—just get into the V and go. Anyone resisting this pull must have a backward map in her mind, a magnetic hill of impulses.

For the initial flurry, Cheryl had managed to be busy at her locker, then moved to a downstairs washroom for the final lagging—the odd student wanting to talk to a teacher or lingering for reasons no doubt better than her own. But by 3:35, it was safe to emerge from this remote hideaway, relief building with each vanishing body. The hallways themselves seemed glad to have them gone with their debris of gum wrappers and three-ring paper and smell of rotting citrus fruit from somewhere, and in a warm shaft of sunlight between the home economics room and drama, Cheryl told herself it was now too late. Absolutely. Adrian Drury was not going to cancel his plans with Laura Van Epp, was not going to show up at her door having forgotten that he had forgotten to call. Was not expecting her to arrive at his house because this was now the casual nature of their relationship. Cheryl had conjured up a roster of reasons for Adrian's lack of communication, all of which now appeared transparent and inadequate, the way a magician's materials and methods must look in the full light of day after the show. That's *all* there was to it?

Adrian Drury was going with Laura Van Epp and this was common knowledge. Certain people had told Cheryl but she was not one to be convinced by the English language. No, her brain had split itself into two animal halves with opposing temperaments, one all tail wagging hope and devotion, the other froggishly digging itself into a muddy lake bottom of school work and winter, neither bothering to take out a helpful phrase book, pause to translate. Now it all made sense, unfortunately, the way animals likely figured things out after several guesses or a good hard kick.

With its closet-lined walls and boxes of mothbally clothing, the drama room offered the most protection. Perfect. Look at all this stuff. Hawaiian shirts, togas and pioneer clothes made by moms. Concealing lumberjack shirts and giant black coats from a Russian tragedy or something on Arctic exploration. Balaclavas galore from gangster scenes, and it occurred to Cheryl she could go to the dance under her own steam, cleverly disguised. Ride her bike in an old fur coat, balaclava, toque, and gumboots. Only the bike would give her away so she'd have to take Richard's ten speed. People would have no idea. They might think she was that pedophile they were looking for on the other side of Stratford or a hobo.

By five o'clock, dark storm clouds had rolled in from the west, the windows of the drama room were grey as February and the streetlights had come on, suggesting she should be at home. Premature dusk felt lonely and homesick in an empty classroom, like it was trying to get to the drive-in or at least a living room with the television on. She'd be crazy to turn on the overhead lights, that would bring the janitor for sure or worse yet, his son, so Cheryl put on her disguise and returned to the brightly lit hall. If someone chanced to see her in a smelly calf-length coat and toque, so what? People tolerated any and all forms of behaviour from the troubled Cheryl Decker, but even she would be advised to keep the balaclava pocketed for later.

Time to call her mother. This meant a trip upstairs to the pay phone outside the office door. Upstairs was altogether different, no lights but the clouds were parting, allowing a bit of orange onto the lockers and floor. They were spotless and scrubbed already, meaning Jimmy Drake Senior must be somewhere in the building. Loretta Decker would probably like to know what on earth he used on the floor to create such shine. Even with very little light, the hall was bright as eyes. Maybe hundreds of school spirits had been waxed into the tiles, everyone who'd died, Richard, and Noel the suicide, and the ones who would die soon. Adrian would like that idea. He would think that a building like this had the capacity to know certain mysterious facts; years of yearbooks could form a kind of brain able to predict who would and would not make it. If only she could call Adrian and tell him, Cheryl thought, dialling her own number in this place of left-behindness.

"Hi Mom. I'm at Adrian's. I'm going from there, I

mean here. Mitchell Flood's driving. No, I don't need to change. I'll just wear this. See you later. Yeah, yeah, everything's fine."

Adrian would be getting ready by now, applying his Brut aftershave, which she had to admit she liked: the smell of boys wanting girls. He would be thinking about Laura and his dick, wondering where they might get to tonight. Cheryl knew Adrian too well. She knew he had solved the problem of not hurting Cheryl's feelings through a series of mental stunts and tricks: I won't say anything to Cheryl and she won't notice there's a dance. She won't realize I'm going with Laura or wonder where I've been. In Adrian's view of the world, everyone operated in a dense fog of cause and effect, illuminated only by the headlights of his eyes. Cheryl would wake up Saturday morning and wonder vaguely why Adrian hadn't called but not to worry. She'd turn on the TV and in a couple weeks he'd tell her he'd fallen in love with Laura van Epp. It was out of his hands; the invisible forces knew best. No point arguing against them because, well, might as well argue against the Van Epps.

Sure, Cheryl would say. I know that.

Time to leave. No rain, after all, even the clouds were hurrying along and the place was starting to give her the creeps. So down the hill she went, on Marjory Street in her big coat and toque, walking slowly, limping, so as to be taken for one of the Coutts twins. They were always cold and overdressed and there was no reason why one of them wouldn't be out for a walk, except for the likelihood of rain. She'd put the balaclava on for the bike ride. Not necessary to give people a scare, though that might be unavoidable. If she saw herself in this getup, she'd be scared and that was from the outside. Seeing herself from the inside was worse, much worse. Despite the weight of the coat, she was feeling oddly light, like she'd lost her body then found it collapsed by her feet. Then she remembered, standing in the drama room there had been an inflatable Popeye, a punching bag with a sand bottom to keep it upright and yes, that was unmistakably how she felt. She'd become that Popeye. Another reason to call Adrian. He of all people would appreciate this phenomenon. She would tell him she felt as if she'd somehow grown a valve and got herself attached to the air pump at her dad's dealership. With enough air, she might even be able to bounce if she tried, despite the conflicting drag from the sand, and with some more air, Cheryl was pretty sure she could be airborne. Was there maybe even a rubber hose dragging from her back? Hooked on to her like a bloodsucker? Now that was an idea Adrian would find interesting.

She couldn't let her parents see her. They'd be inside watching the news, thankfully. They wouldn't recognize her anyway, dressed like this and floating. To be safe, she circled around the block and behind the lilacs into the garage. No one would find her and she'd stay until dark. But within minutes that was boring and the Trimbles were away so she'd spend a bit of time in their yard. This was a little risky because her mom always volunteered to keep an eye on the Trimbles' place when they were out of town. What if she looked out and saw a suspicious stranger in a red hat and long coat? Would she call Jerome Limb, the cop? Or would she just say, Reg, there's a prowler out there, bringing her dad to the back step to yell, "Hey jackass, get outta here." But she wouldn't, being stubborn, and he'd have to swagger out, take a swing, and knock her down. Then, "Jesus Christ, Loretta, it's Cheryl." She'd come to in Graham Rochon's office. Well, if that was the worst that could happen, so be it.

Here was the Trimbles' plastic swimming pool, inflatable just like Cheryl. Now she understood why she liked it so much. Perhaps it was her long-lost sister. Very funny. Adrian would like that too. She pushed the skin of the pool, slack from a summer of heat and cool nights, then pushed a finger on her own forearm. Less give but more or less the same species and this was a comfort. I have finally found my people, she thought.

The thing was full of brown and soggy chestnut leaves. Even the occasional chestnut had hit the pool and left its bloated, spiny shell, emerging all shiny and hard and beautiful. Conkers, that's what some people called them. Cheryl scooped out four and tried to think that Richard would by now be like this nut, a fresh soul popped out of its useless past. If only she could sink her hands into the soil and scoop him up like this, bring him back up to the surface. Why did he have to be buried, anyway, trapped in the mud and the dark? Why not adopt the conventions of the birds and squirrels and trees? Why not, she asked the pool.

Then Cheryl gathered up every last leaf from the standing water and arranged them in four poles around the pool: north, south, east, and west. If the weather held and no wind blew up, the Trimbles would find this configuration and interpret it as a miracle, part one of a building series of miracles culminating in Martha's recovery. Cheryl liked to think she could magic up a little hope for them. There was nothing wrong with that. Maybe people should scale back their definition of the miraculous; if you thought of them as inexplicable events, miracles happened daily. Richard's death, for instance. One day he was there in the house, moving his life around on the earth's surface like the rest of them and the next day he was not. Same with Adrian. One weekend there, pulling off her underpants in a garden shed, next weekend, not. Eyes unable to meet as lockers slammed a kind of abracadabra. All very supernatural. If the Trimbles did not notice the piles of leaves she would show them herself, ask, don't you think that's just a little out of the ordinary?

Time at last to don the balaclava and get going on Richard's bike. Once she was moving in disguise, she would be invincible. What intervention could be brought against a cyclist in a balaclava? It could be cold and face protection might be necessary and indeed the temperature had fallen a little. Even if the motorists guessed it was her, and some might, they wouldn't try anything. This was another form of miracle. Since Richard's death, no one had made a false move around her. Oh, it's Cheryl Decker, their faces said. Don't push. Stand back. She was a psychological celebrity; her emotional states were to be understood and anticipated and a path prepared for her. Hence, captain of the basketball team; hence, jilted girl riding frantically to the dance hall likely to elicit very little response. Had Graham Rochon sent them all form letters, summarizing her case? Involved the town in her treatment?

She was already at the town sign and quickly beyond. Bikes moved faster in the dark. Halfway there and no one had passed. Was she early or was she late? Did it matter? No. She was one of the clockless forms of life, clockless and noiseless like the birds this time of night. They must be there, on the branches overhead watching like an audience from their balcony seats, the road a beige screen for Cheryl to move across. They might rustle and perhaps shift but never comment once the lights were out. Politeness was key to the bird kingdom, that and attention. Cheryl had never understood Adrian's thinking that they were vicious.

At last came a car, slowed down to get a look, then took off. Then another, one elongated zoom. And a third, high beams on, then low, back to high, then low again. Slowing right down next to her then throwing gravel as they accelerated. It was the Van Epps' beautiful old car with Adrian and Laura in the back seat and Anastasia driving. They hadn't turned around to gawk because two things about Adrian: he embarrassed easily and he worried a lot. Chances are he surmised it was her and chances are everyone in the car knew too but no one would say a word. Don't mention it, radiowaving from the part in Adrian's hair, and no one would.

They were gone now and that was the worst that could happen so progress had been made. Even without a clock, you could plough through time, turning it up all warm and steamy on either side of you. Which made her think: another miracle. The way time was always behind you, could never see into itself or beyond with its own eyes to what might happen next time, even in the most extreme circumstances. In a better world, one where time might pull itself ahead and glance back, last time she and Adrian rode out here some muddy voice might have garbled from the ditch: before you know it you'll be on this road again, riding your bike to the September dance in an outfit stolen from the drama props. What do you think of that?

All in all, it would be better to know the future.

Now there were cars and cars passing her by. Rose Drury in her little Vega, Marty Pond and her friends from grade ten being driven by her mother, Mitchell Flood by himself. So what? Cheryl had grown a dance hall hide. She was on her way up the hill and only hoped to reach the crest during a lull in the headlights. This would give her time to conceal the bike, remove the layers, and slip inside unnoticed. Almost there and along came a car. No, that was bad timing. To avoid the possibility of goodwill or companionship, Cheryl crashed the bike into the brush and trees, a branch gouging her cheek as she went down but the feel of it was good. Must be the way a rhinoceros or elephant would enjoy the force of a scrape that could rip through the average human's baby skin.

From the trees and soggy ground cover, Cheryl could watch more cars arrive. From here they were bright-eyed animals moving on round paws in the

gravel. The little abrasions were almost vowels, someone trying to speak to her, drowned out by doors and
voices, and there they were, left behind like pets. There
were ways in which cars were preferable to their occu-
pants. Maybe that's why her dad got into the business.

At last a break in the parade of vehicles and
Cheryl walked, then ran, to behind the dance hall. Inside the walls she could feel and hear the purr of life.
How had that happened? She had missed the door,
much like in a dream where everyone but you has arrived at a place both brightly lit and elevated, smiling
down from a catwalk as if it all made sense and always
had. You had to agree.

There was a tool shed back there and Cheryl tried
the latch. In the moonlight she could see a lawnmower,
the ladder, cans of paint, and a ball of twine, which she
took, thinking, I know what, I'll walk into the woods to
that place I was with Adrian. Around the back of the
hall and along the trees into the woods was easy and
with the moon, bright enough. At first she'd thought
she could mark her way with the twine but now realized she'd brought it for security. People in danger of
floating should always carry twine, she said out loud, if
the need arises to secure themselves to a nearby tree or
boulder. Cheryl was sure that's what the guidebooks
said and even more sure Adrian would find this funny.
The ball of twine smelled nice and she held the loose
end and hurled it ahead like a yo-yo then wound it up
and did it again. She'd easily find her way back and besides it wasn't that far. From back at the dance hall she
could hear a group of boys outside, laughing in the

same language as the wheels on gravel.

This was the right way; this was it for sure.

From the base of a tree not far ahead flew a bird in crazy panic, tearing away like a catastrophe, an emergency on wings. Cheryl's heart switched on hard and fast as if there were a fan inside her or a blender or many of both, shelves of appliances that alternately calm and terrorize. Once the blender broke and her mother's hand smashed into the blade. Still, that was a normal tragedy. Not the sort that sends birds rocketing into the night or threads your chest with electrical wire.

Calm down, she told herself. Calm down. Birds are your friend. They are. She'd tried to tell Adrian this a hundred times. Climb this tree if you don't believe me, and she rolled up the twine, stuffed it beneath her shirt, and reached for the first branch. She was a basketball player after all and it was an easy stretch and she was light, being a blow-up clown. She was up, climbing past the lower limbs where the owls might sit although not tonight, thinking, you had to give Adrian credit, at least he hadn't been afraid to hurt her feelings. He hadn't worried that she'd go into a coma or stay in the girls' washroom until the janitor found her or anything dramatic. She was tired of everyone caring so much and watching her as if she were Martha Trimble.

Cheryl pulled the ball of twine from her shirt, had a thought, ravelled some out and wrapped it around her neck a couple of times. Now she was like Laura Van Epp. Laura had bought a necklace made of twine and beads from a hippy at a stand in Stratford. It was scratchy but that's what hippies wore, according to

Laura. The scratchier the garb, the more authentic the hippy. Laura wasn't a hippy but she was an authentic Laura. And now Cheryl was a copy of Laura, like a tracing on an onion skin and thinking this, she wrapped the twine around the branch above her twice, once for onion skin and once for inflatable dolls, either of which could blow away in a sudden gust. Cheryl felt strangely peaceful now, tied in place. Up on this branch was where she belonged. But there was so much string left over, an entire nest in her hand. What if she sat here long enough? Would a bird come and sit, lay an egg? No, it was September, not the reproductive season for birds or anything else. But having created a nest, she'd like to leave it, wished she had a knife but, oh well, she could put it in a safe spot so that in spring some thinking and resourceful bird could get a head start. Over there would be perfect and she leaned over to place it just to see, grabbing a little branch for balance and snap, what, how could it have made that frail and irreversible sound? How could she be so off balance? How could she be falling so fast? She's made of air, after all. It's the sandy bottom that's weighing her down. How could she be falling so fast?

Chop chop chop. Everyone heard the sound. By noon the next day, Reg Decker's brother was out with his helicopter and the search had begun. Chop chop chop. Confident sounds fading off in giant swoops. Some kids saw somebody on a bike last night; maybe she's on one of the back roads heading north or south. Who knows? All afternoon the helicopter scissored off into silence then returned with a military determination.

They were looking far and wide, too far and wide. Reports and rumours sent kids in cars down country roads all the way to the beach. But Frog Farrell was the one to find her. He'd been picking up bottles and cans—the kids were such pigs—and he'd found the bike where Cheryl left it, thought he'd take a look around in the trees, wasn't likely she'd be there but something told him to go this way, then that, he'd tell Angel later at least a half a dozen times. Something pulling on the back of his throat like a nervous feeling or a clothesline heavy with laundry. And there she was. At first he thought someone had hung a coat up or a suit—ridiculous thought—wanting to air it out but then the body had taken shape like a car accident about to happen or any inevitable terror.

First he'd run, thinking she might still be breathing because she was so close to the ground, less than six inches. Seemed insane. How could you hang above only six inches of space? He tried to hold her, lift her from behind because her face up close took away his muscles, turned them into lakebed mud.

Then he reminded himself not to tamper with a dead body, the authorities would need to be advised and he ran to the dance hall phone, got the operator and called for the ambulance, and within fifteen minutes everyone knew. All of Flax was calling itself, parallel lines of thought and talk and contagion while the helicopter readied itself to land, having cut the sky into a search map of ribbons.

Loretta had moved cautiously, for the past six days, from home to hospital, to home, to funeral parlour, to church to home again, her thoughts like tepid water in a tub, unable to move in any direction. Anything quick or sudden and she might fall, her balance lost to these interior and unwieldy sloshings. She and Reg had talked to the Reverend Rochon and yes, yes she would agree that this was certainly a Herculean test of faith; she appreciated his concern. And she was more than grateful for the abundance of medications. Dr. Gee had dropped off some Valium and Bill Laine had taken her aside during the visitation and given her some as well. Even George Drury had appeared at the screen door with some pain-killers. "Codeine kind of numbs you up," he said. He had tears in his eyes and Loretta wanted at that moment more than anything to go with him to his chair. "Thanks, George," she said. "Just leave it in the mailbox," as if she were talking to him on the phone. Then, "Sorry," opening the door to the disturbing beauty of the first October morning, warm air, reddening leaves and birds: correspondence from some place too good to be true.

At night, Reg sobbed. She held onto him and said, "I shouldn't have made her go to Rochon. He makes things worse." Or, "I should have made her go every day. I didn't take her seriously enough." She wanted to take the blame. And he said, "No, no, no, it wasn't anything you did." But it was talk that had the skin pulled off it, raw and crawling and wanting itself dead. Nothing to offer, it just stopped between them like some creature they wanted to comfort but couldn't lay a hand on.

So now was the time. She would leave the Valium for Reg but take George's codeine. She would pack a small bag but she would not leave a note. That was cruel but there was nothing to say. Reg was at the dealership. This was Friday morning and the funeral had been yesterday; everything was slowed down by the autopsy. People would see her backing out of the garage in her white car, the Mustang Reg gave her for her fortieth birthday. Everyone would see her and later they'd say: I saw Loretta in her car, she looked like always, tired but she had a cigarette, just like normal. I thought she was going to get groceries at Pond's. She always drives to get groceries. I never would have thought she'd take off like that. Thrilled though, the way people are thrilled when standing on the brink of catastrophe, watching and talking from a place of shelter.

Adrian stood on the shore of Minnow Lake, listening to Randy's fast, nervous, worried voice, the voice of a boy calliope, if such a toy were to exist. One week since Frog Farrell had found Cheryl Decker and by way of comparison, Randy was explaining, "If East Flax could be the inside of the store cooler, it would be as if some hands the size and shape of catcher's mitts had tried to change the display, knocked over the pop bottles, scattered them into one another's rows, and ruined the Velveeta pyramid. Then made it worse by trying to repair the damage, breaking a bottle or two of ginger ale, and mushing the mushy bricks of cheese into balls or hourglasses. Or did what you keep saying you want to do, Drury: take one of those cheese bricks and squeeze it so hard wings of cheese would sprout out between your fingers. Like you said, the people from Plasticine should go and talk to them and get some advice on softening chemicals. Can't you just see that? The Plasticine executives talking to the Velveeta guys in their lab coats, exchanging top-secret files. Remember when you said that, Adrian?"

"Yeah, I remember," Adrian said, rubbing his eyes. This desperate version of Randy was almost more than he could stomach. Adrian had seen it before but never this bad, almost like Randolph was a kind of medicine he wanted you to take, soothing on the way down your throat; he would be your milk of magnesia or, more likely, your fish oil.

"People would say they weren't," Randy went on, "but they were driving out to East Flax just to take a look. See, there goes a car now, crawling along with its windows up as if East Flax itself killed Cheryl Decker and might now kill them if they rolled their windows down. They won't admit it out loud but they've been driving up to the dance hall and walking to the tree with its police tape around it, as if Jerome Limb or Noah Jarvis would know what to do with a possible crime scene—probably neither one of them ever actually has seen a genuine scene of the crime. I've been up there now at least a dozen times and each time I swear the words on that fluttery tape are saying Frog Farrell found her, maybe Frog Farrell did it. A frog came out of his ass, after all."

"Oh for Christ's sake," Adrian said. "What have you got in that head of yours? An Old Faithful of worry? Every hour a new eruption? I'm the one who made her unhappy. I'm the one..." and here he broke off, unwilling to discuss the setting or the specific tree and his own geysers of worry.

"You know there was one point there at the funeral," Randy said, "you were just standing there and you looked like, you know, the way kids look when they play musical chairs, because that's how you looked, like you got left out with no place to sit. I had this big urge to tell them to start the music up again."

"Yeah, I didn't know where to sit or exactly what to do. The whole thing was like gradual strangulation. I don't think I've been to a funeral since my mom's and I don't remember it much. For Richard's, I had food poisoning. So it was all too sudden for me but not everybody else. Everybody else seemed like they could just walk in to the front, look in the casket, and sit down. I couldn't get over how prepared they all looked, like they'd all been to a course the night before or a rehearsal like they have at weddings. Just walk in, take a look, say a few words, and sit down. It's not that bad, I told myself, looking at Cheryl's killed body. It's not that bad getting thumpsful of dirt thrown onto your

casket and buried. It's not that bad. *You're* still breathing. *You'll* still be breathing tomorrow. Honest to God,
Randolph, that's what I was thinking, not even about
Cheryl but about me and breathing. I had to concentrate hard to keep it going—the respiration, I mean."

"Well, I don't think that's so bad because you can't
really think about Cheryl because she's not there. Do
you know what I mean? How do you think about something that's not there?"

Silence. The long drawn-out summer had finally
left and here was fall, smelling like water that knows it
has to freeze. Adrian shivered and stared at Minnow
Lake. Above it, the sky was perfectly blue and the sun
bounced and hardly knew what to do with itself on the
multitude of ripples, proof, Adrian concluded, the
earth and universe had no real idea of what went on.
And he said, "Yes I do, Randolph. I think I do know
what you mean."

"Let's stay on the land today, okay?" Adrian added.
They had planned to row out to the ski jump but Russell Hansen's boat was filled to the gunwales with water
and now Adrian just didn't have it in him: there was
enough of that sinking feeling in the environment without their adding to the problem. "The boat's too
flooded," he said, "although, you have to admit it's a bit
of a miracle boat. It's completely full of water but it still
won't sink. I guess it's so water-logged it thinks it's
water. It's a miracle of adaptation. Call Mr. Busby and
tell him we've discovered a new form of chameleonism.
It's like, if I have to be in the water, I'll become the
water. Just like, if I had to lie in the grass for a couple

hours green blades will start popping from my chest."
Adrian threw a stone and watched it skip twice, then
sink. "What do you think, Farrell? A new kind of
chameleonism, very fast little switcheroos, skin to bark
and then over to leaves. Seems possible." One good
thing—the first happy thought he'd had in a week.

"Maybe." Much as he wanted to cure what ailed
Adrian, Randy did not always embrace his good ideas.
Jealousy, Adrian was pretty sure.

"We can just follow the lakeshore to the bottom of
the cliff and scramble up the path to the dance hall if
you want," Randy offered.

"I'm not sure I want."

"But you haven't seen the crime scene or the road
allowance. People are coming to see it too. That's because Friday night Loretta Decker left town via the
road allowance. Rocket Lalonde was the last known
person to see her. He was fishing at the time and he
heard this godawful crashing through the branches and
the small trees, and there was Loretta in her Mustang,
looking like she'd never seen a human before and
wouldn't recognize one if it was standing right there
next to her, which was where Rocket was. She didn't
seem to notice him, he says, just drove on with the windows down but no radio or tapes playing."

"I know all that," Adrian said, watching the lake,
throwing another stone. A breeze now, more sun-
beams, more flashing, as if this were a happy lake, planning to go somewhere before it froze, fishing maybe,
with a bigger lake, a Great Lake.

"Needless to say," Randy said, "Rocket told everybody he saw that coming. He could have predicted that Loretta would be on her way. But Rocket Lalonde says that about everything—he could have predicted Richard Decker was going to kill himself in a car, and he could have told you the FLQ would kill somebody sooner or later. Well, what I want to know is if he can predict so much, why doesn't he stop a few things from happening? Why didn't he stop Cheryl Decker from getting killed?"

"Yeah," Adrian agreed. "You know what, Randolph? I'm just gonna head back to Flax. I almost feel like I might have food poisoning again, which would be pretty damn coincidental. So I think I'll maybe take a rain check on the crime scene. Okay?"

"Sure, Adrian, sure. If you've got food poisoning you should definitely go home and take something for it."

Between the accounts owing at her parents' store and the school secretary's disapproval, Maddy had long expected dire consequences in either a uniform or sweater set. And now here at last was Constable Jerome Limb, here was the cop car at the store, earlier than the sun, just to make a point. Leave the engine idling, keep the headlights on: this particular morning had better think twice about sleeping in.

"Just have to ask a few questions about this Decker situation," Maddy heard the constable say.

"Then ask away," said Angel. "Or did you want to

speak to Frog?"

"Your daughter, actually."

"Cora? Cora's in London. And what on earth would she know about anything?"

"No, I meant the other girl. Maddy."

"Maddy? What's the Decker girl got to do with Maddy?"

Then, barking like any average morning, "Maddy! Get out here. Limb needs to talk to you."

And there was Maddy, out from behind the bead curtain, bringing with her bacon smell and radio voices, in the orange hat again for reasons best known to herself, having to do with Rose Drury, bras, and an overblown euphoria that easily eclipsed any sadness over Cheryl Decker. The attention of Rose Drury was a licence with Maddy Farrell's name and picture: keep this with you and you can wear whatever you want including the orange hat. It was Anastasia who'd made all the comments anyway.

"Nothing but routine stuff," said Limb. "You went to school with her, played basketball with her. You might know something we don't. I can drop her off at school after," he offered.

"You will not," Angel snapped. "You'll bring her back here. The Farrells are not, as a rule, dropped off at school by the Ontario Provincial Police, thank you very much."

"I'll have her back in no time flat. I promise. I assure you it's routine stuff, nothing more."

Maddy didn't care, it was a relief really to exit East Flax in the back seat of this warm, plush car and enter the valley of the shadow of retribution and what you had coming to you so as to pass out the other end and start again. Maddy had some bills to pay—her undeserved spot in the academic stream, her boy's face, and now this: she'd kissed a girl. Maybe by cooperating with the authorities, even agreeing with them, she could atone for the family as well, rescue the store from its creditors and stop the big bank book in Angel's mind forever dripping its red ink on her nerves. Events would decide.

"Too cold for swimming today, huh?" said Jerome Limb. Not possible to be in East Flax without offering an obvious opinion on Minnow Lake. "Last time I was out here, must have been when I was in grade nine, that water in that lake was so warm it was like something that came from a can. A big can. You know what I mean? A soup can. You know what it made me think of? Chicken noodle soup. Partly because there was a water snake swimming around that day, a white albino water snake. Somebody said you could probably get a couple thousand bucks for an albino snake so I tried to kill it. Threw a lot of rocks but nothing kills a water snake. It just took off like a big old noodle. Ugh. Actually made me kind of sick. Then I thought, maybe they meant a live albino snake anyway. Ever seen one of those?"

"No. Only the regular black ones."

Maddy'd heard the story about the white one but didn't believe it. There were a lot of stories that came from someplace else and landed like flying saucers in East Flax. Like the albino water snake, the giant manta ray, the no-dick on Alfred Beel, Cora's dad was some guy from the Maritimes, and Mrs. Leopold had survived rabies but the sight of water still made her jump backwards. It was all made up. There were special landing pads in East Flax for made-up stories. Maybe you could only see them from the air.

"My sister tells me you're a pretty good basketball player."

"Sometimes. I could be more consistent."

Silence in the cruiser then and Maddy thought, Silence in the cruiser, Silence in the cruiser, like a judge issuing the order. Then wondered when she'd ever had a back seat all to her self. Not ever, came the reply and she knew she could ride alone in the back seat of a car, especially a cruiser, for several days. She wouldn't object to being driven to a penitentiary in this car: there was one in Kingston and a reform school in Orangeville. She'd be allowed to lie down and sleep, watch the blue sky, then somewhere along the way they'd stop for french fries. She'd like to lie down but Jerome Limb could find that degree of nonchalance alarming, might even think she was resisting arrest or at least planning to resist arrest. Was that an indictable offense? Maddy was unsure how much rope she had, here in the back seat. A lawyer would probably advise her to remain upright; he would not care that prone was best suited for recalling the kiss with Rose Drury, as if, when lying down, memories didn't have to climb any stairs, they rolled onto the linoleum like a jar full of marbles.

It had gone like this, she'd tell her lawyer. She'd

stolen some gin and three bottles of lemon-lime and set up a little bar for herself and Rose at a spot she knew, smooth as a tabletop, ideal for the china cups she'd borrowed from the dance hall. Anastasia joined them for the second round and even seemed to approve in her ironic way. *Oh, it's a lounge. Ladies and escorts, I see. I don't have an escort, so I hope that's okay. You have to have an escort, you know. I guess you know that, Rose.*

Maddy knew what Anastasia was getting at and she wouldn't say she didn't care but somewhere between the first and second drinks—and it was not the gin—she, Maddy, had decided to yield herself up to events. She turned a dial to "off." Like her very own house, she would say, where half the switches were defective and needed to be coaxed into connection, where the wires had had just about enough of carrying current, Maddy snapped every appliance and outlet off and abandoned the battle against her own wiring. And events weren't that bad. Since then, they'd taken on a late-night motion, not slow but essential, like the generators that hum away the night while everyone sleeps. The others had watched Rose and Maddy dance—no slow dances of course, only the fast ones—even Anastasia from the wall with a face that knew everything about Maddy's badly wired house and fluorescent meat cooler but this did not matter.

"We can have one more drink," Maddy said and they returned to the open-air bar. Midnight or a little past and the dance hall sat on its foundation like a container of very good weather a scientist had managed to trap. Rose and Maddy could see glimpses of it through the trees. They drank their drinks like lemonade and Maddy said: Let's throw the cups in the lake. They did, awaiting two splashes as the white meteorites entered the water. So, let's kiss now, said Maddy. I was hoping you might suggest that, said Rose, and Maddy stopped the motion and let the memory polish her insides. Then they kissed, Rose touching Maddy's front teeth with her tongue and Maddy grateful to have no cavities.

That was all that happened. They went inside and Rose stood by Anastasia and Maddy just stood, four or five arm lengths from Rose. Everyone would soon go home but Maddy would stay and help her dad clean up, sneaking back to the spot where they had kissed. Rose might reappear; you never could tell and if not, Maddy's previously frozen East Flax future was now a warmed up town of Flax, filled with classrooms and streets where Rose Drury was known to exist and would most certainly be seen.

Here they were in Flax already, outside the station, across from the hockey arena. Extremely unlikely that Rose would be anywhere in the vicinity—she'd be at home, getting ready for school—but Maddy looked up and down the quiet street anyway. Nothing but overhanging maples and leaves turning orange in the morning sun, the occasional car with its driver watching.

"Okay, if you'll just come inside with me, Miss Farrell."

"Sure thing."

There was Ruth Ann Phelps behind the counter.

She'd finished high school two years ago and now was the police receptionist, with the same long hair and split ends Maddy had once stared at, sitting behind her at an assembly on sportsmanship. This was what the four-year commercial stream led to, a seamless movement of hairdos from one Flax setting to the next.

"I'll be talking to Miss Farrell in my office."

Ruth Ann nodded as if this type of questioning were routine, as if she worked in a downtown police station alive with real and dangerous suspects, not girls she'd gone to school with, overgrown clowns in ridiculous hats.

Maddy decided to keep the coat and hat on. She'd been to church twice, not counting Cheryl's funeral, and knew that was what you did in the presence of a higher power, as if the higher power might decide to switch off the heat.

"All right, Miss Farrell, I'll get to the point here," Jerome said. "There's been a witness come forward who claims to have seen you entering the trees behind the dance hall with a ladder the afternoon of the twenty-fifth, which is, as you know, the day Cheryl Decker went missing. So I have no choice but to ask you some questions as you can appreciate, I'm sure."

"Yes. I can appreciate that."

"Now you do have the option of consulting with counsel before we proceed here. Do you know what I mean by counsel?"

"Yes, I know what you mean. You mean a lawyer. No thanks. So it was Alfred Beel who talked to you?"

"I'm not at liberty to say. Regardless, I need to have

you understand your rights here before we proceed with the questioning.

"Yes, I do," Maddy said, having an understanding of what was going on but not an appreciation, the way people will watch the first torrent of rain, thinking later, we had no idea it would develop into this: flood, devastation, furniture and bloated cows floating by. No idea. "And I can explain why I had the ladder," she said.

A grimace from Jerome who had realized with a sickening thud, like a sack of grain, a sack of hammers, he had to record this. Damn. "Just a minute. My apologies. We have to start again," and he was off to locate the tape recorder while Maddy sat, imagining her orange hat increasing in brilliance like a mood ring on her head. Now she had time to start to feel suspicious and ridiculous and fully illuminated, an embodiment of the Farrell house at night, lights on, blinds open, everything flickering in rhythm with the washing machine's agitation, the smell of electrical fire coming from someplace.

"Okay," Jerome said, plugging in the tape recorder, pressing *record*. "I'm going to assume this thing is working. To back track, you can explain your presence at the dance hall with the ladder, the night of September twenty-fifth?"

"Yes, I can," although Maddy was now unsure what to say, the tape catching her voice as it would, holding onto it like some cruel impersonator. And what about Rose? It was one thing for Maddy to be seen throwing around bras and kissing girls but another altogether for Rose. What should she say? Options fluttered back and forth with the speed of hummingbird wings, blurred until you slowed them down and picked one.

"Yes, I can explain why I had the ladder."

"Go ahead then."

"Well, I was up at the dance hall and I was practicing."

"Practicing?"

"Basketball. There's a hoop in the hall. And I decided to take a break and I went for a little walk in the woods, which I do quite often." Maddy was confident now again, the blurring had stopped. She leaned into the tape recorder. "So I was walking along and I saw this hawk up in a tree. So I stand there watching it. I clap. I throw a stick and it doesn't move, so I start to think it's injured. So I think maybe something bright will get it moving so I take off my hat, which you can see is orange, and I throw it. And the hawk takes off but my hat gets stuck in a branch. So I go get the ladder, encountering Alfred Beel on my way into the trees, get my hat down, and put the ladder away."

"And approximately what time was that?"

"That was approximately four-thirty or maybe five o'clock."

"You're not absolutely sure?"

"I don't have a watch as you can see," and Maddy displayed her naked white and freckled wrist. Exhibit A, she wanted to say but did not.

"And you were alone?"

"Yes, I was."

"And you were wearing the orange hat?"

"Well, not when I got the ladder because it was in the tree."

Silence. Maddy should say more but had no more to say. Like on written exams when all other pens scratched away and inside Maddy's mind was a kind of inflating balloon of emptiness

"All right. What about the dance? You were there?"

"Yes."

"What time did you arrive?"

"I was there before it started, helping my dad get things set up so maybe seven. Then I helped Rhymin' Ronald, the DJ, a bit. Then I just waited for people to show. Then I hung out with my friend Rose until about one and then I helped my dad tidy up." Maybe the kissing hadn't happened after all. In her memory now, the scene was lit from above as if they'd been caught in the light of a hovering spacecraft. Maddy'd begun to wonder if the whole thing wasn't an East Flax story made up by her.

"It's true that Cheryl Decker was the captain of the basketball team?" Jerome asked, proud of this new direction.

"Yes,"

"And you're on that same team?"

"Yes." Through the venetian blind, Maddy could see Ruth Ann's long ponytail, which looked more like a horse tail, expected it to maybe switch at a fly on Ida's shoulder.

"How did you feel about that? About Cheryl Decker being captain?"

"I felt okay. It doesn't make a big difference who's

captain."

Maddy'd had enough now. She didn't like the way this was going and couldn't help thinking the tape recording would fall into the hands of Anastasia Van Epp and be put to some unkind use by the drama club at the next school assembly.

"Did you ever think you should be made captain?"

"Maybe once in a while, but like I said, it doesn't make much difference. And I think I'd better get going now. I need to get to school. I've got a history test this morning I can't afford to miss."

"All right. Fine. No further questioning. You wanted to be dropped off at home, right?"

"Yes." Thunk. The tape recorder made a painful sound like a blow to the throat.

Out on the street, Rose was nowhere in sight but never mind; looking for her was its own reward. And Maddy returned to the welcoming back seat, a different person now, as far as she knew, the only student from Flax Composite ever to have been questioned by the police.

Adrian thought he might be going blind. Cheryl had told him this could happen in certain rare cases when there was simply too much for the eyes to manage, so many disastrous sights in a row the brain was forced to make a decision. Enough was enough. Though if asked by the optometrist in Mesmer to name the details surrounding him, he could have and with a 20/20 precision. That's a Rolo wrapper next to Anastasia's foot; that's a rock chip in the windshield; that's the "You Are Leaving Flax" sign. He'd have to say it was more as if the lights were dimmed, as if he were operating in a world lit by interior car lights or Anastasia's white-blond hair, crimp-permed and angling out from the crown of her head like a lampshade.

So it was ironic that Anastasia would insist on driving to East Flax because, as she said, there was more to this story than meets the eye. And if that were the case, Adrian would have to encourage his pupils to remain open a little longer and funnel the sights through like a lumpy, chunky sauce and try to determine: was it good or bad what Randy Farrell told him this morning? That Limb had picked up Maddy for questioning.

Picked up Maddy for questioning. Adrian didn't like the sound of this sentence. It reminded him of a creature that moved by crawling, each syllable shoving over to let the next one follow along: before you know it, it's at your door. At Adrian's door that is, not Anastasia's. Nothing was at Anastasia's door but trees turning red, freshly blacktopped highways and her mother's Mercury. You might have thought someone lifted a heavy, orange tarp off each new day and said, Voila, Anastasia. This is for you.

"What a luxury to be a cop," said Anastasia. "To be able to pick up someone for questioning. Anyone. Such a privilege is lost on a Limb, especially Jerome. To make questioning worthwhile, you need a speck or two of imagination. And anybody who leaves Flax, goes to police school, and returns to Flax has less imagination than this steering wheel I am holding here. Although I've heard they kind of pushed him through police school just so they'd have somebody here, somebody in a uniform. Like a meat grinder or a sausage machine, they squeezed him out through those holes and into a blue casing. Have you heard that Adrian?"

"Uh, no, I haven't heard that. But I live next door to the Limbs so they're not going to spread that kind of story around about themselves." Adrian blinked rapidly. "Did it suddenly just get darker there?"

"Well, yeah, the sun went behind a cloud."

"Are you sure?"

"Yes. You're not going blind, Drury. You might be going nuts but not blind. Not yet."

"Thanks."

Why why why had he ever thought he could or should go out with Laura Van Epp? It was a lot like thinking you could write an earnest letter to Mick Jagger and he would write back because this time it was you, a lot like the thinking of many in his remedial literacy class, himself included. Maybe these were the requirements for admission to Resource—a kind of dopey, Adam's apple bobbing optimism combined with a level of hillbilly gullibility. Think back. He'd entered Resource at the age of eight, the same year, he was pretty sure, Anastasia told him her intelligence could be attributed to her blood type, AB, the rarest, she said so Ha! Ha! And he'd accepted this as scientifically sound until today when, consulting the encyclopedia, he found no data, no studies, graphs, or charts linking blood type to intelligence. Just a picture of red blood cells clustered together like mushroom caps from Mars, a Jell-O kind of red no one ever saw, because combined with oxygen, blood browned a little. Which was blood's most interesting feature, Adrian had learned: it latched on to everything that got under your skin, hormones, penicillin, carbon monoxide, and vaccines. So maybe, who knows, the A and B combined soaked up more information than the lowly As and Bs and Os on their own. Let's hope so. Maybe the AB type soaked up radar and Morse code and bat conversations, the motives of Maddy Farrell and Jerome Limb and anyone else in Anastasia Van Epp's all-knowing line of sight. Let's hope she was right.

"Now you're worrying about Limb, aren't you?" Anastasia asked. There she was with her omniscient blood.

"I don't know."

"Oh for God's sake stop worrying. You had nothing to do with all this. Stop worrying. I hate being with worriers."

"I'll try." Just go with the flow, go with the AB. Resisting Anastasia was futile. Try and you might wind up in one of her scenes and if that were the case, bring on the blindness now and the deafness and the full paraplegia from the neck down.

Since ninth grade, Anastasia had been staging her theatre of Barbie and Ken. Not plays, just scenes, Depictions she called them, of Flax notables in unflattering situations, Constable Limb lifting a dead Barbie's purse at the scene of a traffic mishap, Reverend Philip and Mrs. Rochon passed out drunk on communion wine. Or kids from school. Last year she'd dressed up a Greta Leopold in a rabbit's fur coat, sawed chunks out of her legs and re-attached them at the stumps to achieve that troglodyte stature, as she said. Knit a brilliant orange hat for Maddy and had the two of them vacantly awaiting the bus. She'd invite important people like Rose for openings, lesser types like Adrian and Cheryl for subsequent viewings. The best one for sure was George Drury fitting a matronly Barbie with a set of false teeth. Remember? Anastasia was smart, she had AB blood and she was an opinion maker. If she thought there was more to Cheryl's death than met the eye, then, whether or not there was, there was. And this relieved Adrian's mind a little. As they drove, he felt the blood returning to the shallow spots in the backs of his eyes; little pools formed, dislodging a gathering of scabs.

"You saw the person on the bike, didn't you?" Anastasia asked.

"Oh yes. Yes I did. The person on the bike looked like Cheryl."

"But she or he was wearing a balaclava and riding a boy's bike so you really have no idea who it was. Isn't that right?"

"True enough."

"And she or he was wearing a bright toque. Red, most people are saying. So who does that make you think of?"

"I don't know," Adrian was tired, convinced he hadn't slept a wink of rapid eye movement sleep for days. "Nobody? Somebody? Somebody from the Montreal Canadiens?"

"No, no, no. Don't be stupid. The answer is Maddy Farrell. You know it was her. Who else would ride a boy's bike and wear a ridiculous hat on top of a balaclava?"

"But why would it be Richard Decker's bike?"

"Well? Don't you see?" Anastasia geared down as they turned onto Dance Hall Road. "She could have got that. Maddy's a basketball player. She thinks in strategy. See? She somehow strings up Cheryl because she's jealous, then hides out in Flax, rides Richard's bike in a ridiculous disguise so people will think it's Cheryl and there we have it."

"I guess it's possible," Adrian shrugged. "After all, as Mr. Busby says, anything's possible."

With a prehistoric roar, the Mercury climbed Dance Hall Road. Almost five and the late afternoon of early October was bright and warm but again Adrian must blink and blink, witnessing his mind go grey and cold as the interior of a fridge when the power failed and more than anything else, Adrian hated power failures. Everything you depend on switching off in one silent blink and what if the sun ever made the same mistake? What if? Our idea of cold wouldn't even make it into a dictionary of cold from that time and place. Adrian closed his eyes for the tumble into his sunset worry of Cheryl under ground. If only he could wrap her in a blanket but this was a backfiring wish, more like the opposite of Anastasia's tarp, a lifting off of a covering that revealed all the people buried, all the pets awaiting needles. Adrian standing by, unable to cry, unable to think, thoughts like animals left off in an unfamiliar place; they stopped and sniffed the air for some sign of where to go next but couldn't catch the scent.

"In the event that Frog Farrell might be in the hall cleaning or Maddy's inside there running up and down the floor, I'm gonna park here at the end of the lot," Anastasia said, turning off the engine. "Plus we can look at the lake from here, such as it is."

There was the ski jump, water lapping against it as if it were trying to lift it up, the way the team hoisted Cheryl onto their shoulders the night they won their first game. Later, Cheryl saying, "They just did that because of Richard."

"How come nobody ever hauls that thing to shore?" Adrian asked.

"Because this is East Flax. They don't have a town council or elected officials or a town manager. No one's in charge of ski jumps or other public monuments. They need volunteers. You'd think Randy Farrell would take care of that. He doesn't like things to be out of order. Although he probably thinks the place for the ski jump is right where it is and he might be right."

Anastasia leaned over to open the glove box, rooted through a pile of maps, and said, "I wish I had a cigarette. You haven't got any, have you?"

"No. Not on me."

Snapping the glove box shut, Anastasia asked, "Why the hell is Rose hanging around with Maddy anyway? I'd like to pick her up for questioning on that topic. Did you see them at the dance? They were dancing all night together. I thought they'd even start slow dancing. I was embarrassed for Rose. Then they went outside together. For what? To neck?" Anastasia was mad. All Adrian needed.

"I don't know. You know Rose. She's always trying to be unconventional." Why couldn't a poltergeist lift him away from here, if only to the ski jump where for sure the remnants of the last afternoon he spent with Randy might still be found like a lost and favourite comic book or last summer's faded bathing suit, something that had managed to go backwards across the international date line fifteen or sixteen times, showing up unscathed. Cause for hope.

"Well, I'd say she's succeeding. Anyway," Anastasia opened her door, "let's go look at this tree."

Adrian sat. What if it turned out to be *the* tree? Adrian knew which one it was, the curse of his superior spatial skills. This trip was turning out to be much, much worse than expected. He'd imagined the dance hall parking lot to be a horror movie, nothing more, with him watching, interested, unblinded by his guilt, but instead it was more like extreme nervousness, like being picked up for questioning and never put down again. Observing the jittery shadows of the red and yellow leaves clinging to their branches, Adrian decided, on the creepiness quotient, birds were nothing. He'd be happy for birds right now. Trees were the problem. The way the ones outside the car were rustling, he was pretty sure they had talked to other trees who had heard from somebody close to the scene of the crime that, yes, it was that tree; yes, the one that had already had some trouble earlier in the year with those kids and their sleeping bag. With each new gust of wind, they rustled like hundreds of pages from hundreds of newspapers, bigger and soggier than garbage bags blown in from the dump, stuck onto branches and messy and causing the sky to smell. He would rather not come back to East Flax ever again if he could possibly help it.

Adrian said, "I think I'll stay in the car."

Anastasia was fed up. "Fine. I can go by myself. Apparently there's a path, so many people have been out to take a look. And there's tape, of course. It is a possible crime scene. More than possible. Probable is what I heard on the news this morning."

"I know. I know. I just don't want to come. It's better for me to sit here by myself."

Anastasia slammed the door without a word, leaned in through the open window. She was like a tall yellow species from outer space, a blue-eyed Midwich Cuckoo. "I'll be back soon."

"Okay. That's all right." He had the ski jump to look at, the ski jump that at this particular moment might happen to be his best friend. Adrian could see why Jesus would want to walk on water because sitting on it was probably the best thing to do around here. And funny how sitting on water could be the best thing as compared to, or contrasted with, the second worst thing—going through the ice. And going through the ice would be the second worst thing because it could only be compared to one other experience and that would have to be the gallows. Having the support pulled out from beneath your feet, discovering that your body's mass moving through space had nothing to grab on to and that was an educational discovery. You would think a rope, a ladder, a hand or a branch, some instrument of escape would automatically appear. But nature was unhelpful. That's what he had learned and not from Resource and would like to tell Anastasia because even with her AB blood he doubted she had a clue.

Rose had to go to the library so might as well do that now. The past few days she'd had too much time on her hands and didn't know what to do with it, felt burdened and a little embarrassed by the hours as if they were a collection of dolls she'd once found lovable and now would like to stuff inside a sack. Maddy didn't seem to need as much intervention. The basketball season had been cut short out of respect for Cheryl, ending the need for practice. And Maddy'd started wearing that hat again, drifting back to her old habits and spending time with Greta. Rose had seen her sitting on the bus with her when it roared past, windows down, and Maddy's cheeks pink with the pleasure of being seen by Rose, pink as icing on a white cake. Bah. It was all too much, there had been too many ingredients in the past couple weeks, the days were coming out of the oven as big, puffed-up, overly risen, layered desserts pocked with raisins and currants and maraschino cherries. More than most people could do to look at them, let alone consider taking a bite.

And Adrian was a nervous wreck. Rose expected him to ride his bike through the plate glass window of Reg Decker's car dealership. She'd thought of calling Rocket Lalonde and asking him to keep an eye out for Adrian torpedoing toward the place but what could he do but interrupt his trajectory with a car or truck, a lever to send her brother higher and more mightily into lacerations? If Adrian were intent on self-destruction, he would find a way. She hoped her dad had the medication locked up, because one more death would send the entire town of Flax through a plate glass window, never to return.

As far as Rose could tell, Cheryl had killed herself because she was depressed; Rose had told Adrian this now a dozen times. The entire Decker family was depressed. You didn't need to be Graham Rochon to read that in the expressions on their faces. Rose had been observing this for some time. It was as if all the muscles responsible for the social arranging of their features had been numbed into indifference by Novocaine. Maybe Loretta had been stealing it from the office.

"That's not funny," Adrian said.

"I know. Sorry. But you know what I'm saying. All the action under the skin was stopped, like the muscles couldn't reach or the synapses got too big."

"Shut up about the synapses."

"Okay, okay."

That was yesterday, Rose's last attempt at counselling and now, by way of thanks, Adrian had driven off with Anastasia in her mother's Mercury, the one they had taken to the dance and not a healthy choice of conveyance, in Rose's opinion. If they had needed a ride somewhere, she could have offered the services of the Vega.

Well, so what? To hell with them all, everyone who'd driven off and ridden off and left her to walk alone to the library. And even Cheryl Decker. Cheryl Decker who had managed to kill herself on the one day of Rose's life when she'd danced half-naked in the trees and kissed a girl on the escarpment above Minnow Lake. If word of this had gotten out on an unremarkable Flax day, she might have earned a degree of infamy, maybe been exiled to East Flax like the Maestro. Now, relative to Cheryl Decker dying and Loretta Decker vanishing and Reg Decker bunkered into the Decker address, no one would ever notice. The CBC could air a documentary tonight on the abnormal behaviour of Rose Drury and draw an audience of two: Mrs. Liebling who might call in to say she'd known all along that Drury girl suffered from megalomania: even at a time of terrible municipal suffering, she expected to draw attention to her shenanigans. And perhaps the lawyer lady from Rosedale, Astrid What's-her-face: I had my suspicions about that girl the first time I met her.

Rose pulled violently on the library door, hoping to rattle its bored old hinges. And as for the rest of the viewing public, she supposed indulgent distraction was the best one could hope for. Isn't that George Drury's daughter on the television? Such a lovely girl. She's kissing another girl? Throwing clothes into trees? Must be one of those experimental dramas.

Here was the library with its peculiar air. Amazing how books, inanimate, beshelved, could radiate the smell of paper, almost as if they were always baking a little between their covers. At least the place was nearly empty and reverentially silent except for the churchly murmuring of Reverend Philip Rochon and the librarian, Veronica Greig, wife of Vice-Principal Greig. They were deep in discussion by the periodicals rack, possibly turning over the implications of the Decker debacle. Rose was sure she did not know. She had work to do anyway and a superb idea as well. She needed to write a paper on Alexander the Great and had decided on an interview format between her subject and a contemporary broadcast journalist. The history teacher, Mr. Rigg, would love it.

At the card catalogue Rose tried eavesdropping but Mrs. Greig turned her substantial back to her. Good. Maybe they were talking about Rose Drury, maybe she had in fact taken her place in the brief chronology of Flax scandals. Maybe in time she would be compared to Lesley Rochon. Possibly Philip was making that observation right now. He was like that, always able to admit to his own failings and those of his children, Lesley and Graham, impressing everybody with his white hair and his slow, deliberate walk, and his phony empathy.

The Lesley incident happened a long time ago, probably when Graham was sixteen or seventeen and Rose was six and in love with him. She could remember as if it were yesterday that sensation of a city of lights in the pit of her stomach every time she saw Graham. He practically owned the church and the Sunday school and the adolescent rights to making fun of Jesus of Nazareth. Philip had him read the scripture to the Sunday school congregation from, as Graham would say, St. Paul's letter to the Flaxians or St. Paul's epistle to the Mesmerites. Everyone would laugh, not least of all Rose in her crinoline and hat.

But there were ways in which Graham's older sister, Lesley, was even more transcendent. She had hair to her waist and bangs to her eyebrows before anyone even knew it was the style to come; she played the guitar and had recordings of black singers from the States. And, the night of the Christmas pageant of 1961, Lesley Rochon stayed behind to clean up the church with two boys from the youth group, one of them Rocket Lalonde, the other one of the Pethick boys, and had sex with both. The convivial Reverend found her straddling Rocket in the choir loft, while the other boy sat watching from a pew and, allegedly, sucking on a candy cane. After that incident, Lesley went to a Toronto girls' school and never came back, not even for Christmas or perhaps most especially.

But now, and here was a point to ponder, according to Rose's dad, Lesley was now a librarian. Maybe Veronica had news of her; perhaps they'd attended a conference together. Rose guessed back then and probably to this day, Lesley knew how it felt to have a circus act trapped inside the body of a minister's daughter. Just like Rose, who had the great misfortune to reside within the body of a dentist's daughter and part-time orphan. Maybe one day soon the trapeze artists would tear through her skin where it was most worn and begin balancing plates on sticks in the hallway, the former Rose Drury cast aside like Lesley Rochon's Christmas skirt, a narrow waist band atop a pool of satin lining and taffeta. Something had to happen before her destiny pulled her onto its own lap and held her.

Lesley Rochon was a librarian. All along she'd been sewn onto herself with much tighter seams than she could have ever undone, two hundred stitches to the inch, doubled over, French. Tear away at those with a seam ripper and all you'd get for your effort was sore thumbs.

The thing they needed, she and Lesley, Rose thought, heading for the history shelves, was a library of lives, or better yet, reputations, housed on shelves like books with exposed spines. How fitting. To adopt a reputation, check out the spine of its owner and through a simple yet radical medical procedure, baste the borrowed spine to your own. There you go, says the librarian; now you're Bonnie Lalonde for two weeks. Bonnie, the girl with the tipsy walk and the sideways, knowing smile. Anastasia said she had a birth defect, some form of palsy, but all the boys liked her, girls too. Why? Bonnie Lalonde was off-kilter. And she could act. She couldn't walk like she herself was intended to walk but could imitate Mr. Rigg's springy gait and read announcements over the p.a. system exactly like Mrs. Liebling, everything one and a half times but with differing inflection: Mr. Hodgetts, you have a call on line one; Mr. Hodgetts, line one.

For the duration of a book loan and one renewal, Rose could be as content as Bonnie Lalonde. Bonnie would not fuss over Alexander the Great or ask Anastasia to dress dolls in a pretend television studio and take a Polaroid for the cover of her Duo-Tang and make sure she got it to her by Sunday night. Bonnie would hand in an unillustrated essay on three-ring notepaper, probably pencil-written, with a title such as "Alexander the Great or Not-So-Great? Which?" She never liked to leave anything understood.

What's more, Bonnie Lalonde would not have become preoccupied with Maddy Farrell and danced all night with her and would not have kissed Maddy Farrell while another girl was hanging herself from a tree. But if she had, which she wouldn't have, but if she had, Bonnie Lalonde would not now feel that the events of that night were forever preserved in formaldehyde like the specimens in the science room—unforgettable little pigs saturated with a heavy poison. If she had, if Bonnie Lalonde had, which was the reason for her popularity *she wouldn't have*, but if she had, she would not now be thinking Rose's thoughts about Maddy and her semi-clean family, the bed-wetting, and Randy's arrangements. People said he went berserk if you knocked one over. Angel and the social workers: once you've been reported like that it hangs from you like loose skin on someone who once weighed three hundred pounds. Frog Farrell and his traps: who knew what they ate behind that store? Bonnie Lalonde wouldn't think those thoughts or suffer from an unpleasant memory travelling up her nose like formaldehyde. She would carry on into the next days as if they were a pressed and pleated back-to-school wardrobe.

Rose found the books she needed then moved to a table behind the stacks. Just in case Anastasia wouldn't cooperate, she'd need a couple of pictures. So, invisible to Veronica Greig and the Reverend, using Adrian's small, red-checkered, Purina products jackknife, Rose did some defacing, excising the two illustrations most suited to her assignment, a close up of Alexander's face with giant eyes like a velvet painting and hair like yarn, and a chunk of pottery with a broken bit of horse. This audacity would impress even Antastasia. *You cut pictures from library books with Mrs. Veronica Greig in the same room? Mere paces away? Mrs. Veronica Satan-hyphen-Greig? She who conspired to have her husband strap poor Mary Louise Pethick just for belching and creating a disrespectful scene at the card catalogues.* Yes, I did, Anastasia; I guess it's the sort of risk I'm willing to take.

Rose walked home in that slightly abandoned time zone of five-thirty when small town people are already making dinner and awaiting dinner, and if you're not why would that be? By the time Rose arrived, Adrian was there on the front lawn waiting to ask, "Did you hear they questioned Maddy Farrell about what happened to Cheryl?"

"What are you talking about? Who? Who's they?"

"Limb."

"The cop?"

"Yes of course Limb the cop. What other Limb would question Maddy? Mrs. Limb the mom?"

"That's hilarious," Rose said, setting her books in

the grass, "You're almost standing in the anthill, did you know?"

Adrian moved two paces to the left, staring into Rose's eyes like a religious fanatic, someone with very good news she didn't want.

"But why would he question Maddy?"

"Some witness."

Conversations like this confirmed her brother's suitability for Resource. "Witness to what?"

"Somebody saw her with a ladder."

"Somebody saw her with a ladder?" said Rose. "That's what you heard, Perry Mason. So what? What's incriminating about being seen with a ladder?"

"Up at the dance hall. The same day."

"Sooooo?"

"So Maddy killed her."

Rose's lungs came as close to gagging as they could, heaving forth a pocket of incredulous, tongueless noise. "What? What kind of garbage are you listening to? You know what this kind of thing is called? It's called an apocryphal tale. You know what that means? Of doubtful authenticity. I just learned that reading about Alexander the Great."

"There's nothing doubtful about it. There's a motive and now there's evidence."

"Motive?" Rose shouted. "Are you insane?" she asked, tapping her brother's forehead with an index finger.

"Yes. No. Because of the basketball team thing. She was jealous. And so I had nothing to do with it. Cheryl didn't kill herself because of me."

Rose shook her head, picked up the books. "No way. I was with Maddy when she had that ladder. It was the middle of the afternoon and we were getting something out of a tree."

"Oh good alibi. What? What were you getting out of the tree?"

"Nothing. A bra, that's what, and it's none of your business," said Rose, leaning into her brother's face so close their noses almost touched. "Cheryl killed herself because she was depressed and you had nothing to do with that. You didn't make her depressed. I've told you that a million times now."

Adrian stepped back a pace. Obvious he didn't believe her, standing there, shaking his head like a disappointed, disbelieving parent. What was wrong with him? Who the hell was he listening to? But now her own thoughts began to take off, to run like the basketball team in knots of offence and defence, sweaty and panicky predictions of what might happen next. This was too absurd and too unreal, though Jerome Limb was real enough. He occupied a uniform and an apartment in Mesmer.

Adrian shrugged and went inside.

Maybe she should call Jerome. No, she shouldn't call Jerome, that would be pointless; she'd go and see Jerome. He'd grown up right next door. She'd known him all her life. He was a Limb. She'd seen him taking a shit in the yard once with their dog, for God's sake. She could drop in on him whenever she wanted. It was a free country and cops had friends and neighbours just like everybody else.

Adrian hasn't been to Toronto since he and Farrell went to the CNE three years ago. They took the bus, the Ex Express, with a bunch of other smalltown losers, moms and throwing up kids, retired farmers in plaid shirts sitting with other retired farmers. Right away they went to look at the freaks, starting with Hugo Huge, the world's fattest man. He was wearing an undershirt the size of a sail and shorts that looked like two tablecloths sewn together so the audience could see his thighs. He said those exact words: I'm wearing these shorts so you can see my thighs. Rolls with crevices deep enough for small animals to set up house or a family or two of Anastasia's dolls to be suffocated in the name of art. Hugo said, in his quavering, lardy voice, that he'd been normal until the age of twelve when he'd had his tonsils removed and because of an allergy to the anesthetic he'd begun—uncontrollably—to gain weight. He was selling miniature Bibles for extra cash to send his son to college. No one had any questions; just gulping sounds.

And that almost became the end of the day because upon exiting Hugo's tent of thighs, Randy fell ill with the obsession that soon he would have tonsillitis and this inevitably would lead to an allergic reaction followed by weight gain and a tent at the Mesmer fall fair. Randy wanted to get on the bus and go home so Adrian could get a small quantity of anesthesia for Randy as a test—he'd never been to the dentist or the hospital – and thought with a little nip of freezing, he'd know. They could stick it in his hand and wait for it to fatten up like a catcher's glove, then he'd know. It's better to

know, he said to Adrian at least a dozen times. Then he'd
have to have an operation on his fat hand, the doctors would
think it was a tumour, and then after that, watch out. His
teeth were chattering so much as he pictured his future as a
freak-show fat man, Adrian knew it was hopeless and left
him in the sweltering, parked, Ex Express. Not even the promise of the world's smallest horse could lure Randy from his
vinyl seat of worry. It was only a quarter but he wouldn't
budge and even though the world's smallest horse turned out
to be the world's largest disappointment—just an ordinary
Shetland pony—Adrian told Randy it was smaller than a bea-
gle, which snapped him out of his tonsilitis and the bus. Although they had to go to first aid to get his throat looked at
and later Randy spent some midway money at the Better Living Centre on a tea towel he wrapped around his neck like a
gingham cast.

And that had been the difference between them then:
events couldn't get freakish enough for Adrian whereas Randy
saw one exceptionally fat man and was wrapping his neck in
a tourniquet, gasping for air. All the way home, Adrian lec-
tured Randy. What're you going to do for Christ's sake if
there's a nuclear war and once it's safe to go outside everything's growing extra large or on weird angles? You won't even
notice Hugo Huge. The world's smallest pony will be the size
of a swing set and Randy Farrell will be afraid to come out
of his house. By way of responding, Randy made frequent adjustments to his tea towel.

Now everything in the world is growing in weird angles
and Adrian is afraid of the next day. He is in Toronto and
he is visiting Rose in her co-ed dorm and he is realizing that
he is now the freak show; in some not-very-metaphorical way,

Adrian Drury is the fattest man in Flax. Just set him in the empty pool and watch him gradually fill it with his unstoppable self. He is the incredible big bang boy. People will picnic next to him, the eyes of little children bulging out on springs as they wonder where they can locate the antidote for that particular future.

Even Rose looks at Adrian from the other side of a roped-off area. Now she has a boyfriend named Paul who drops off a six-pack and disappears, after looking at Rose as if he might have carnal knowledge of her, which further frightens Adrian. He had been counting on Rose never doing anything worse than what she did with Rochon. And now that he thinks about it, Adrian observes the entire co-ed dormitory has an alien feel to it, a place where smart people meet smart people and have a smarter kind of sex that perhaps does not even require a penis and vagina, just two brains penetrating one another with beams of thought.

Rose is sitting on her bed while Adrian sits on the roommate Nancy's bed. Nancy has gone somewhere for the weekend and Adrian does not necessarily want to sleep in the bed of a Nancy but there is no other option. Maybe he has the same condition that flared up in Rose with the rabbit cooker. Maybe he has extreme apartheid. Apartness. That's what Mr. Greig said it meant. Adrian was in his own township and did not wish to share it with Nancy.

"Anastasia was right," Rose says. "You look like somebody taking heroin. You're not, are you? You're not getting into Dad's meds, are you?"

"No, of course not." Adrian finds this accusation a little nauseating, like frying sounds can be, like the sound of sputtering grease drained from the thighs of Hugo Huge. "Are you nuts? Why, what else did Anastasia have to say?"

"Here, read the letter," and Rose tosses Adrian a pink envelope containing pink stationery, Anastasia's unmistakable writing and a hand-drawn Barbie seeming to be dropping an egg from its mini-skirt.

Rosita! Did you know your brother looks like Keith Richards? What's up with him? Can't he get no satisfaction? Seriously, Ro, I know your dad has some soft-ish medicaments in his office that might just lead to harder medicaments if they fell into the wrong hands. Anywho, the big story here is they're saying Mr. Rigg got Miss Clevitt pregnant and she had to get an abortion. I'm pretty sure it's true because you know how I can hear a maxi pad rustling at about one hundred feet? Well, with Miss Clevitt it's more like half a mile because I guess she's wearing the industrial strength post-procedure type. I guess she didn't take very good care of her egg, did she? Or maybe she thinks we are all one another's eggs, like who was it who said that? Oh yes, Rose Nietzsche Drury the first. And we are, indeed. Sigh. And, a proposterous of that, M. Farrell has irrevocably and irreversibly quit school. They say she's not coming back next year even though she was supposed to get a basketball scholarship to Arkansas or one of the dull normal states. Unless her leg clears up, so it can haul her chromosomes maybe even past Cora's, which I very much doubt since a leg is a leg and a bone is a bone. Speaking of which, I did it with Stanley Russell. Never mind the details but the deed is done. I am no longer a flower. Could this be another case of avant disregard? Only Rosita can say for sure. And Connie Laine is now Constance because Connie is apparently insufficiently valedictorienne and she now believes she is it and not Eleanor Gee or Eleanor's dress, whatever the case may be. Since Eleanor cannot speak in a public forum I say just strap a tape recorder inside Eleanor's New York City gown and roll it onto the stage on a dress form and save us all the embarrassment. Seriously, if she steps onto the stage and develops that mutism goiter like she did when she was running for student council, the town of Flax will die, if it hasn't already. I'm sure one day soon they'll discover that Flax as an organism actually did die several decades ago and we've been living in a kind of municipal husk. That's what they'll find out, when they finally find out. AVE

"What does she mean about Flax being dead?"

"Nothing. She always talks like that. It's not a reference to any specific people or events. I want you to have a beer, at least two."

"Ah. A pusher, huh? I've heard they have them on university campuses."

"Ho ho."

Adrian wonders about the owner of Nancy's bed. He pictures her on the deck of the Flax pool as he is spilling over it like old stew in a body. She is thin and tanned and has never seen a freak and would like very much to lie down in her dormitory bed but...

"You're seriously not into Dad's stuff, are you?"

"No, I told you."

"Well, you look a little rough."

Adrian says nothing, guzzles one entire beer with drips dripping from his chin and opens a second. "I might have a touch of chronic food poisoning."

Rose rolls her eyes, lifts her beer, and says cheers.

"Anastasia writes a mean letter."

"I know. It's kind of good to have one hundred miles between us."

"Yeah." Adrian pictures himself slopping more and more over the edge of the pool, his skin lumpy with carrots and potatoes and hunks of meat and Nancy running. He wonders if there might be little banging sounds coming from his body, skin-popping craters. He might almost laugh. "Yeah," he says again, "I've been writing these letters."

"What do you mean?" Rose looks worried as if he's been sending mail to Cheryl or Skokie.

"Just letters...to people."

"Well, you mean Randy?"

"No, not Randy," and Adrian pours half the second beer down his throat.

"Where'd you learn to drink like that?"

"I take George's beers. He doesn't even notice. He gets a case of twenty-four and leaves it in the basement for months."

"I think he notices, Adrian, he just doesn't say anything."

"Oh right. Cuz of the hand through the window."

"No, not because of that. Because he knows you're sixteen and he'd probably rather have you drink his beer than some bootlegger's. He's not all bad, you know."

Adrian is silent. Then he asks, "Are there places to get U of T postcards?"

"The bookstore."

"Oh," and Adrian starts laughing like a drugged man, "because I was thinking of sending a card to Alfred Beel." He laughs more and harder; he is a roly-poly laughing skin of stews and Jell-O, a liquidy bag that has squeezed itself beneath the Flax pool fence and is spreading elsewhere, all shaky with laughter.

"What?" Rose is annoyed.

"Just a greetings from U of T. Nothing fancy. I should probably do something to make up for phoning him. I was making these crank calls because he's such a fucking asshole."

"I don't think a card's a good idea."

"But I should do something."

"No, no, I think nothing is best for now." Rose is examining Adrian as if he might have the makings of an electric chair beneath his shirt. "Let's drink this," she says, "and we'll get some pot from this guy Don I know who's got some good stuff and we can walk around campus and maybe you'll decide you want to come here."

"Yeah, in the Bachelor of Resource Room program."

"Adrian, please don't make every single moment negative."

"Okay, okay. Laura Van Epp says to tell you she wants to do early admission next year too."

"Oh," says Rose. "Hmmm."

Now that he has said Laura Van Epp's name out loud, Adrian says, "I'll just go to the bathroom," and there he sits and his forehead glistens like a sick person but nothing happens. Neither vomit nor diarrhea. He lifts his shirt to examine his ribs and knows he's thinner than he's ever been but that's no proof of anything.

Loretta had been gone now for almost two weeks. Everyone had their theories as to where she was, knew of a friend or relative in the Prairies or up North or down South: they all thought she was gone for good, had entered a yonder wild and blue. Not Alfred. He was of the opinion she hadn't gone far and furthermore, she would be back. The evidence was there in the way she'd held his hand at the funeral, the way she'd said Alfred and nothing more. As if in the tiny space between those two syllables was the route by which she would return.

Two days after she'd left, Reg was back in the helicopter, insisting he and Clive search as far away as Lake Huron and up the Bruce Peninsula. As if Loretta would be found running through a field of grain stubble or rowing her way to Michigan. As if surveillance, noise, and large, rotating blades would flush her out of the woods like a flock of quail. Whatever the plan, its execution appeared to include daily swoops, which Alfred had grown to expect with an invigorating hostility, over his land. Was it not enough that Reg had sold him a car inclined to rattle over sixty-five miles per hour? Apparently unfulfilled with this disturbance, Reg needed to shake the walls and windows of Alfred's home, his teeth, and worst of all his old nerves, raise a powdery dust from them like the plaster in his living room, let it settle in his veins, plug them up, and presumably kill him.

Even if Reg had been a tolerable husband before Cheryl's death, which he had not, he was now a reckless madman; it was all the talk. Twice he'd taken the helicopter out unaccompanied while Clive was at his constituency office. He had no pilot's licence but apparently there was nothing to flying a helicopter when you had years of experience with Ford products. He and

Clive had almost come to blows, Reg wanting to know: Do you think a cop's going to pull me over up there? Do you think this is "The Jetsons?" His unwashed hair matted into fuses leading to a nest of firecrackers. Clive's thinking was, best to back off for a while.

But as the days themselves began to slow down and slur as if the month of October had taken a dulling medication, Alfred couldn't help looking too. Though his was a different kind of looking, unfrantic and quiet and only after sunset so that Alfred reminded himself of a giant moth, following the headlights of his own car. He watched the coming events on television and made note of card parties and baby showers, thinking he might find her where women gathered, thinking she might be in a motel somewhere nearby. The other women would keep her whereabouts secret, being women and as tight as army intelligence when it came to classified information. So last week he'd driven off to Concession 13 and the home of Stan and Louise Darling where Louise was hosting a night of autumn crafts. Loretta could knit, he knew this and drew hope from it with an unfamiliar intensity, an intensity he worried might illuminate his face and hands and all other exposed skin as he parked at the end of the Darling laneway, exercising caution. Stan was always watching, for what Alfred did not know, but if he came charging out from the barn or the shed on sentry patrol to ask what's the problem here in his accusing and meddling way, Alfred would plead fuel shortage. Simple.

Stan must have been out on an errand because Alfred sat in the laneway with the emergency brake on and the headlights off for more than fifteen minutes, close in to this gathering of women. He loved the cars positioned neatly in the farmyard; there was something about cars recently driven and carefully parked by women that filled him with pleasure. Each car was evidence of future possibility, of a female mind powered by gas pedals and nylon covered calves. All of which would, sooner or later, add up to Loretta Decker.

Last night, Saturday night, he'd even tried the dress shop in Mesmer. He'd anticipated at least momentary discomfort entering the bright and feminine store but not at all. He'd been in the drama club in high school and after the war even joined a little theatre in Toronto but like most things, let it go. For Alfred Beel then, this entering of a womenswear store was nothing more than stage left. Indeed, they all seemed to have been cued to await him. Mrs. Belfour, the owner, had just been thinking about him, having had so many compliments on their rumpus room.

"What can I help you with?"

Wouldn't she just like to know? "Well, I have a niece in Toronto. Eighteenth birthday's coming up and I've been told this is important nowadays," said Alfred, confident with his script. "My brother's a lawyer there, makes more money in a week than I do in a year but is he happy?"

Mrs. Belfour thought not likely.

"Last I heard," Alfred was enjoying himself, "yes, in fact he was. Doesn't that stick in your craw? When they're both rich and happy?" Meryl Belfour laughed. Her eyebrows were grey but her hair black, dyed no doubt but that hadn't stopped her having a good flirt or two with Alfred while he built the rumpus room. She was the type of woman who wore high heels at home, at least she had with Alfred in her sights.

"We have plenty to choose from," Meryl said, as Alfred followed her tight-skirted walk to a rack of sweaters and blouses. She was a businesswoman doing women's business in a good quality lined skirt and Alfred found himself wishing he didn't know the difference between lined and unlined but thanks to Ila Van Epp, he did. And he honest to God wouldn't mind working here. Would it be completely ridiculous to fill out an application form? Of course. Even the Maestro would know better but he could certainly see Russell Hansen sashaying around the place, returning sweaters to shelves and bras to boxes. There was the difference between Russell and Alfred: Russell liked the trappings of women while Alfred liked their company, although he had to admit, if it meant the company of Meryl, he was not averse to the ringing in of brassieres.

Alfred selected a pale yellow blouse, asked for a box, he'd be mailing it. And Meryl said the town needed more men like him, most men wouldn't even come inside and if they did, stood in the doorway waiting. "They think they're going to lose their gonads if they come into contact with tulle or hooks and eyes. Honestly." Thrilled, Alfred could clearly see, with this forthright talk of balls.

At home, Alfred took out the yellow pages and made note of other dress shops in the area but this morning ripped up the list and hid the blouse in his closet. Was he perhaps going the way of the London trip? Dressed in a suit of ridiculous motives, cause for concern among dress shop owners for miles around? He made himself a coffee and thought a new thought. Maybe Reg wasn't so misguided; since Loretta had last been seen driving through the road allowance behind Alfred's place, maybe she was on his property. Why had he never considered this? There was a sugar shack among the maples with a wood stove and if that were too obvious, plenty of high and dry spots for pitching a tent. The evenings had only recently turned cold and still only a trace of frost in the early morning. You could survive easily with the right equipment, especially if you were the invincible Loretta.

So he left the house for the low sun of a Sunday morning thinking he might come across her sleeping on the forest floor. Maybe this was a fairy tale without trolls or candy houses, a fairy tale with a solitary builder of decks and rumpus rooms, a sad and unfaithful wife and an airborne husband fit to be tied. Bit parts for Russell Hansen and the Maestro, Alfred laughed to himself. Fairies aplenty for that cast.

A V of geese flew over the treetops, close enough to be looking for Loretta, and Alfred wished they were, wished Reg could send out trained geese instead of that infernal machine every single day. Then wondered, allowed the question to ooze between his ears like a gently burst eardrum, thick stuff collecting in a pool of slow-motion thought: did Reg Decker suspect something? Something between Alfred and Loretta, that is? It *was* possible. People saw things they had stored away for years until the right moment breathed meaning into it. Hundreds of fragments of hundreds of stories piled high as branches in a bonfire until—you know, I saw Loretta once driving out past East Flax, down Beel's concession. Never thought anything of it at the time, she delivered Avon, you know, and maybe he was getting himself one of those soaps on a rope but didn't something go on between them at the Legion one night? Oh, it was just talk. All talk.

Alfred knew how this part of the world worked, knew how events could collect themselves into eavestroughs, trickle into rain barrels and overflow on to the street as a moving current of rumour. Nothing explicit but, like water, coming to rest in the low spots, reproducing mosquitoes and algae. Everyone knew he had a dick for instance and yet, the story was there.

Loretta was not in the sugar shack and really, would she be living in a tent? Just because she could did not mean she would. Loretta wasn't a rucksack kind of a girl and Alfred had to wonder what was wrong with his thinking. His thinking was a growing cause for alarm. Strange ideas and impossibilities popped up in his mind like the small, misguided shoots beneath the layers of leaves thinking it might be spring. Pale green thoughts in an artificial cap of heat: one little breeze or the movement of a squirrel and it would all be over in one blast of cold autumn air.

Fucking Reg Decker. Alfred hated the guy and had every right to tell him to stop flying over his property. Didn't he know anything about the regulation of airspace? Guys like Reg Decker needed a stint in the military to set them straight. In fact, maybe now was a good time to drive into Flax and have a word or two with the son of a bitch. Everyone was being so damn solicitous—poor Reg, poor Reg. Your wife hated your guts, Reg, and I'm probably the only person west of the Atlantic to know that. She'd still be around if you weren't such a prick. And to think you have the up-side-down balls to fly your brother's ridiculous heli-copter over my property every day, strafe the place with your lunatic suspicions...Yes, he was going to go. This was not some wild geranium thought in need of tram-pling. He had the car keys in his pocket. Why not seize the moment? Speak now.

Alfred tore through East Flax in his Decker Mo-tors purchase. Past the store, past Angel Farrell at her till wondering what's got into Alfred now? Around the bends created by Minnow Lake and into the straight-away. Not another car in sight, so he pushed it up to ninety, then ninety-five while the car shimmied and shook. And why? Because most likely this vehicle had once been in a ten-car pile up, had once been pur-chased by some pawn shop owner at a police auction, had subsequently been rebuilt by a team of convicts in Florida before being shipped to Flax for sale at Decker Motors.

Alfred hit the pavement at the edge of town and slowed to twenty-five. Reg would likely be at home but he'd swing by the lot first. Nothing but rows of cars shining in the sun, attention to paint jobs being critical. The plastic pennants snapped in the October breeze but the place looked closed. Of course it was closed, this was Sunday. Good. Excellent. Here was the Decker house not more than a block away, festooned with grief and mayhem but Alfred was undeterred. He'd seen more death and marauding bad luck than Reg Decker could imagine. Reg Decker had not been to war, had not had his chest melted, his head sundered, or his dick rumoured to be blown away. Nor had he spent more than five minutes in the East Flax store.

Knock, knock, knock. The place emanated the walled-in horror of a jail or a sunken ship. Reg was likely passed out or gone searching but the door opened and there he was, drink of whiskey in hand, resembling a tabloid version of Dean Martin, all contempt and bad breath and booze. Alfred could see he was expecting a handout, a casserole or a berry pie.

"Reginald," began Alfred, "I recognize that this is a difficult time for you but I'd appreciate your flying your helicopter over someone else's property for a while. Surely there is a wide world of search options, which you seem to be overlooking. And my nerves, frayed at the best of times, in times of perfect peace and quiet, are in need of a sabbatical. Your wife would have no reason whatsoever to be on my property. You do know that, don't you?"

Reg swayed silently on the doorstep, turning down the corners of his mouth, lifting his shoulders in an infuriating and self-pitying shrug. A toast to poor Reg Decker.

"Shall I trust you to cease and desist with the strafing of my property, then?"

Identical downward smile and maudlin overdone

shrug of a mime. Not a word. And he had the audacity to close the door in Alfred's face. Asshole. He could stand there behind the door like a deaf mute as long as he wanted, he couldn't *not* have got the message to stay away from Alfred's and with this point having been made, Alfred had won the skirmish. Although as songs will, one had now tangled itself in his mind, Dean Martin crooning "Everybody Loves Somebody Sometime." Drink in hand, ice tinkling, handsomest man in the tri-county area. Alfred would take a different route home and watch for Loretta among the trees.

In the lamplight of his bedroom, Adrian reads. Dear Alfred, I understand you probably want to write to me but it is best for me to keep this address secret. Why you wonder aloud? Because I need Time. And also I do not trust the postmaster. Ben Horsburgh is a friend of Reg and will be on the lookout for any Vancouver postmark. It would not surprise me in the least if he were handing my precious mail intended for you to Reg, which is a risk I hope you are willing to take, my dear and handsome Alfred. I can only trust and hope that these epistles are reaching you.

And so I have an idea. Imagine me clapping my hands and jumping up and down with joy because that is what I am doing as I write this, not at this precise exact moment but You know what I mean, dear man.

I believe We must see each Other. We must. If it takes all of my account from the Royal Bank I will find a way to fly back if only for a night or two. As far as I am concerned it is not optional because it is compulsory.

I will write again soon.

Yours,

L.

Adrian has lost confidence in his ability to counterfeit Loretta's signature and the Ben Horsburgh anxiety is all his. Yesterday, while at the post office for the dentist's mail, Horsburgh looked at him through the glass with an expression not normally seen on the human face. Because, Adrian realized with a flash of insight, it was a paranormal look. And in a second flash he realized the proof of the paranormal was all around him in Flax in the form of telephone operators and postmasters, psychologists and reverends, pharmacists and cops. The paranormal was not so much something you can't see but something that can see you, all the time, through its transparent shield. They were watching. Maybe they always had been but with Randolph talking nonsense about craters and sea level and time dumps, Adrian hadn't noticed. Now he had no choice.

And further to that, now he has no bills, not a single dollar to bribe Harold Terwilliger because he is broke. This means stealing change from the dentist's dresser and facing the humiliation of changing change for a dollar. Got any dollars I can have for this change? He'd had to ask Bonnie Lalonde once before and now, this evening, he'd be doing it again. Not that she would mind. She had nothing much better to do at the restaurant this time of night and last time she'd seemed almost happy to see him, making fun of him, telling him his hair looked like it had been stirred with a stick and there was the evidence in the mirror behind the counter, beneath the shelf of upturned milkshake glasses, the embodiment of stirred and shaken and whirred. You'd think he might have been insulted but it was the opposite. Once he had his dollar, he wanted to stay, wanted to reincarnate into the smell of the place—smoke and coffee and gravy and old winter coats still being worn well into the first mess of spring. Then, using whatever method smells had evolved, microscopic claws or cellular paste, he'd attach himself to Bonnie's clean apron. She might not mind, she seemed to like him, offering him free desserts that he usually declined. There were girls who liked murderers and wrote to serial killers in prison, probably even girls who liked guys accused of starting chains of events culminating in a shootout or a fight to the death between an old fart and a high-school student in Resource. Fight to the death. That might have to be it. And Adrian thinks back to the five stages of death and dying they talked about in health class and how Beel might have to move through them pretty fast. Either him or Adrian. Although Adrian still wonders like he wondered when they had to read some condensed section of the book on death and dying why only the soon-to-be-dead were supposed to be experiencing the stages when everybody everywhere was dying all the time. He had even made up some diagrams with boxes showing the different groups. Babies—angry, always screaming because they never asked to be here. Likewise little kids, usually mad at being bossed around. High-school students in denial of algebra and Shakespeare. Dentists—eternal bargainers: if I buy the Torino I'll have to forego the rider lawn mower. Mothers with cancer—they were expected to be depressed because they were in fact dying and that made sense. Acceptance—flat out nobody. And back to the anger box: old farts, Resource-room flunkies, Van Epp girls with bloody blood, cops, teachers, principals,

Members of Parliament, and so on up the chain of command. Of everybody Adrian knew, Bonnie Lalonde was maybe the only one without an identifiable stage since she made fun of most things during the day at school and in the evening, gave away rice puddings.

Despite the certainty of humiliation, Adrian admits he is looking forward to seeing Bonnie. He does not jingle his change in his pocket because that is a George Drury trait, but holds it in his right palm and walks purposefully, as if to a bank, the bank of Bonnie. Less than three blocks and Lalonde's is still open, of course, not even eight o'clock, people come in for pie, coffee; people come in for nothing, just like Adrian. Inside is warm with the smell of winter coats absent at last and the china tinkling more like summer—funny how the weather changes sound—and Bonnie is behind the counter and Beel is in a booth. Maybe the fight to the death has been moved up in time by its handlers; maybe time is sick and tired of waiting. And Adrian sees the place spattered with blood, dishes broken, crying women, and two months later, Anastasia's tableau, two Kens, one Barbie, ketchup smears, Mrs. Van Epp saying "Anastasia that really is enough." Laura never recovering, maybe staying at home for ten years studying the migratory routes of birds.

Adrian slides onto a stool with his back to Beel and Bonnie says, "Hi, Adrian. I thought you might be in tonight."

"I'm here for the exchange program," Adrian says, handing Bonnie three quarters, two dimes and a nickel.

Bonnie hands over a bill, no questions asked and tells him his hair looks better, is he using a spray (she is ironic), maybe Sudden Beauty? And she says she won't let him leave until he eats a rice pudding that she prepares, shaking a can of Redi-Whip, spraying white, fatty wings onto the rice, plopping a maraschino cherry on top. "Red dye but so what?"

Beel is watching, jealously, Adrian is certain, since when was the last time Bonnie Lalonde or anyone under the age of seventy-five made a fuss over him? Adrian watches Bonnie ask, "Did you want more coffee, Alfred?"

"No thank you. I'm fine. Should push off."

Adrian imagines their two hatreds might be caught on camera with the right very sensitive film. Two mushroom clouds in a desert, armoured cars at the ready, code words sailing through the hot, wavering air.

Now Beel is at the till, two empty stools from Adrian and he is filled with glee, his mushroom cloud is billowing with ecstasy like Redi-Whip. Beel is getting out his wallet and he's thinking: Adrian can feel a pronouncement taking shape.

"You know what I've always thought, Bonnie," says Beel, "is the lowest form of life?" Knowing Bonnie is more on Adrian's side than his, Beel does not await a response. "I've always held that the anonymous phone caller was the lowest of the low. Right up there with people who send letters to the paper, unsigned, all full of opinions but too scared to claim them for their own. Though of course the phone caller from the public booth, now that's the purview of the truly troubled."

Bonnie is making change, delivering Adrian's quarters into the paw of Alfred Beel. Always diplomatic, she says, "Lots of axes to grind out there, aren't there?"

"Indeed," says Beel, glaring at Adrian's skull before leaving.

"Such an asshole," says Adrian after the door closes. "Why's he so mad all the time?"

"I don't know. Eat your pudding like a good boy," and
she twists the top from a salt shaker and fills it from a box.

Rose had a stomach complaint. Not an ache so
much as an uninterrupted warning from that pink bag
down there, similar to when she'd been to Toronto
with Muriel Cobb and Astrid the lawyer had wanted
her to eat that marinated rabbit, while all the phones
seemed disconnected and the air outside grew increasingly saturated with evaporated forms of life, sea-
weed and tentacles reduced to microbes.

It was all Adrian's fault. He was no longer himself,
walking to school, walking home, sitting in his room,
and pretending to do homework. He wouldn't ride his
bike. George Drury talked to him through Rose, as if
she were a nurse. How's Adrian doing? Do you think
we should be worried? Should I be calling Rochon?

"I don't know, Dad. I don't know."

With Loretta gone, Rose was doing double duty in
the office because George Drury was reluctant to hire
a receptionist: that would send the wrong message to
people, especially Reg.

Inside the house it was Adrian. Outside the house
it was Reg. They were like storms of radio waves you
couldn't quite tune in. What were they going to say?
What were they going to do? Made you want to twist
on your very own ears as if they were dials to gain some
clear reception.

Monday night and it was just as well Anastasia

wouldn't deliver the Polaroids. Rose welcomed any reason to get out of Flax, if only to the Van Epp farm on the edge of town. Peter and Ila didn't get so weighed down by events; Ila had beautification to think of and Peter could scare away most anxieties through plain, loud talk. And Rose missed their farm with its strings of yellow lights on all five cedar trees out front. Why lights only at Christmas? Ila asked aggressively when she strung them up in July. Why one season for decorations? She was writing a piece for *Chatelaine*, "A Season for All Times" she was planning to call it.

And Rose missed King-the-Devil-Dog. How long had it been since she had seen King? King with his round, woolly body and parapsychological powers? Drawn to the funeral parlour for visitations, attending the lawns of the doomed. He'd been seen at the Deckers' the morning of the day Richard died, been found in the backyard of the Rochons' the night before Mrs. Rochon had her stroke. And he'd shown up at the funeral parlour two nights running when old Mr. Coutts was on display. He used to give King giblets, which reminded Rose to bring along the moist brown turkey meat she'd set aside earlier, now sweating in a plastic bag.

Pulling out of the driveway, Rose glanced up at Adrian's window in the hope he might be looking back, waving or making a face but nothing appeared behind the empty panes. He was in there though. Even from here, the room telegraphed the single word "cage," a place where one human, teenaged life paced and panted and stewed in its own skin until it smelled like an old person with too-long, unwashed, old-person hair. Suddenly the mix of King's turkey with her pineapple scented car interior was nauseating, raising a fine steam on her forehead. She opened the window. There was something about turkeys, she and Anastasia agreed, that was a little unnatural. All that meat on a bird. Why?

Traffic, traffic, traffic. People returning to the city from their cottages on Lake Huron and up the Bruce Peninsula. Brake lights in the dusk, everything grey now with parallel strands of red, hypnotizing Rose's stomach a little, cooling her brow. Anastasia would be ready with the pictures and an observation, maybe two. She'd be mean, or maybe not—who could tell? Another whiff of turkey and pineapple and Rose pulled hard on the deodorizer and tossed it outside, then sniffed her fingers, rubbed them on the wheel, imagining Foster Limb and his sperm and the possibility of babies with pineapple heads. The car behind her honked and she heard the driver yell something—Farmer? Fuck you? She'd had to brake hard for the Van Epps' laneway and forgot to signal. Oh go to hell everybody.

There was King already, halfway down the lane and sniffing for existential news. He rowfed and rowfed after Rose and her Vega "King. King. It's me," she said from the window. Had he forgotten her already? "It's me." But when she stepped out of the car, he was wagging like he did, as if hinged in the middle of his spine. In two gulps, the turkey disappeared. "Remember me?"

"Of course he remembers you. That's King. Be more likely you'd forget him, you've been away so long." It was Peter, coming in from his barn, his chrome and glass milking operation. So clean, he could wear his suit to do the milking if he wanted and he did, the day it was installed. Then he and Ila went upstairs and had sex, Anastasia told Rose.

"You heard about my close call?" he asked, all stories and unguarded opinion, booming voice, crooked teeth, polar opposite of George Drury.

"No." Rose didn't hear as much these days.

"Day before yesterday, I'm driving back from Telluride just before noon. I realize I'm behind Reg Decker in his pickup and he's going forty-five, no more, so I decide to pass. This is not too far from the curve there by Pethicks'. So, I pull out to pass and the jackass speeds up. I think, he wants to race, so I'll race, can't see anything coming. Then he speeds up, I swear to God, he's going seventy-five all of a sudden. Now I can see there's a car coming so I slow down to fall back in and damned if he doesn't slow down too. I think I'm not going to make it here; this guy is trying to kill me. The ditch is starting to look mighty appealing and then he takes off like a bat. I get out of the way but just in time. Some tourist roars by with his horn blaring. What do you think of that?"

He didn't wait for an answer. "I called Jerome Limb," he said. "He should be charged for reckless driving. It's not just me he's pulled this stunt on. And that's not all. Tomorrow first thing I am calling *The Reminder* and see if I can take out an ad warning people. There's a jackass on the road. That's what my ad will say. I don't care if he is all messed up with grief. That's

no reason to go around killing people with your auto-
mobile. What do you think? Anyway, come in come
in. Anastasia will be glad to see you. Laura, I don't
know. She's been too quiet since that dance. What do
you think happened out there?" They were on the
porch now, in the light of the closest cedar. "You know
that Farrell girl. What do you think of her?"

"I don't really know her that well but I don't see
how she could have anything to do with anything. Just,
Cheryl was depressed. That's what I've heard."

"I suppose. Having that ass for a father and everything else that's gone on. The Farrell girl's a bit of an
oddball though. She might have her reasons—jealousy.
The Decker girl was a nice-looking girl. Anyway,
Laura's not herself. Just warning you."

They were inside the big hallway with the real oil
painting and the old clock from Holland. "Anastasia!
Rose is here," Peter boomed up the stairwell. And
there was Ila in a black dress and a turban, the best-
dressed mother in Flax. Rose had forgotten.

"A hug. We must have a hug. I haven't seen you
for so long," said Ila, wrapping Rose in warmth and
cedar smell; maybe she'd been out fussing with her
lights.

"I'm up here, Rose. Come on up," came the voice
of Anastasia.

"Just a minute while I..." Ila pulled Rose toward
the living room. "Laura, say hello to Rose."

Laura was a sullen back on an ottoman, watching
television. "Green Acres." "Hello to Rose," she said,
without turning around. A pig wearing sunglasses trot-

ted across the screen. In dismay, Ila poked out her lips, raised a hand to her turban. At least Laura came out of her room.

"That's okay. I'll just head upstairs."

As Rose had forecast, the Polaroids were ready, laid out on Anastasia's desk. "What do you think?" she asked, fanning a hand over them in the manner of the game show hostess. No greeting, of course, no acknowledgment of absence makes the heart grow some sort of condition.

Rose looked. Of course, they were very good. The modern-day broadcast journalist Midge had her hair chopped short and was in a green plaid suit and Ken was convincing as Alexander in his burlap dress and shoelace belt. "I didn't know if you wanted Alexander in the present or the CBC in the past, so I did both. See, this one has them at a little table and the other has a desert backdrop drawn by Laura with this stuffed camel as a prop."

"They're great Anastasia. Thanks."

"Yes, I know. Some of my better work. So," she didn't stand up, remained in her chair, shuffling the photographs, "where's your beanbox at these days, anyway?"

Rose shrugged. "I'm not sure. It's hard to know where to put your beanbox these days. Flax is the shits but I guess that's nothing new."

"Well," Anastasia said, peering up at Rose through the black frames she claimed to need for homework, "there's always *East* Flax. Anywho, that reminds me. I've got one other picture I wanted to show you. Just one second." Anastasia reached for a shoebox she'd covered in blue, ironic, Kleenex flowers. "Here. Look at this."

Anastasia handed Rose another image of the journalist and Alexander the Great, once again in the desert but this time with another figure, prone, on Laura's rendering of sand, a female doll in orange head-covering and what resembled a basketball uniform, number fourteen, Maddy's number, visible on the miniature jersey.

"What is this supposed to represent?" Rose asked.

"It's Maddy Farrell. She's just stumbled into the setting. She fell." A rueful smile from Anastasia.

"She fell? I don't seem to recall Maddy doing a lot of falling."

Anastasia gave an exasperated sigh. "You asked what it represented. It's not meant to be literal. It's, you know, representative of gauche. It's kind of funny, that's all. I thought you might want it."

"Yes, I think I do want it," Rose said. Aware again of her stomach and its complaint, she pocketed the picture, leaning over Anastasia's pyramid of hair to snatch the others from her hand. "Well, I'm off then," she said.

"You're off? So you've sunk to just using me for my art? You just got here. And besides, you haven't told me what's going on in that beanbox of yours. The secretorium, I'm calling it. Rose and her secretorium. Like for example, why didn't you tell me you got Maddy to trade places with Evelyn Jardine in physics? Why did I have to hear that from Evelyn Jardine? Why didn't you tell me? Why am I always the last to know?"

"I really don't know why I *would* tell you."

"And I really don't know why you wouldn't, because that's the kind of information stored in the secretorium."

Rose examined the Polaroids and said nothing.

"Did you know that Evelyn Jardine's mother used to play on a baseball team?"

"No, I didn't," Rose answered. "I did not know that Evelyn Jardine's mother used to play baseball." Sarcasm, but what other tool did she possess?

"Yes, and *she* thinks it's quite possible Maddy did it. She said there were two pitchers on her team and they hated each other like poison. She said those athletic girls can really be aggressive." Anastasia began to switch the desk lamp off and on, watching the bulb as if it were a new and inscrutable gadget.

Rose was suddenly and literally sick and very tired of Anastasia and her warm questions and her memory poison and her method of creating words and constructing word cages for everyone but herself. "Well, this assignment's due tomorrow so I really have to get going."

"Suit yourself," said Anastasia, returning the shoebox to its spot, opening her Latin text with exaggerated interest.

"Goodbye then," Rose said.

Anastasia snapped her desk lamp off then on, off then on.

Rose was at the bedroom door. "I'll see you tomorrow at school, I suppose."

Then Anastasia turned a page and in the singsong of declension, said "Voco, vocas, vocat, vocamus, vocatus, voCUNT."

"You're impossible," Rose said and left, sneaking out the front door to avoid a barrage of hospitality and interrogation from Ila and Peter. *Leaving so soon? Have something to drink at least. Why don't we see you any more?*

King-the-Devil-Dog was waiting by Rose's car, thinking he might get a lift into town. "You're really too nice a dog to be a devil but I suppose with Anastasia around, it rubs off. Anyway, you can't come with me." But as soon as the car door opened, he made a woolly, weak-kneed and yet unstoppable effort to get inside, settling in the passenger seat like a round old man in a matted black coat. "Oh all right. Let's go for a ride. I don't want to go home anyway."

Dark now, the sun was down. At the end of the lane, Rose stopped and said to King, "So Mrs. Jardine, and also probably her entire bridge club, thinks Maddy did it. And how many others? And Maddy probably didn't help matters at all when she talked to Jerome Limb. Do you have *any* idea what she might have said to him? I'm sure I have no idea and for me that is pretty strange." Because given the time and enough paper, Rose could have scripted conversational exchanges from most households, businesses and institutions in Flax. What Maddy Farrell might say to an officer of the law, however, was unchartable territory. She might have told the unedited truth or just as likely might have invented a story as cockamamie as her brother Randy; may even have been advised by him in this regard. It was as hard for Rose to imagine the inner workings of Maddy's mind as King-the-Devil-Dog's, although both she featured as wordless environments. An unkind comparison but Maddy's mind could easily resemble the underwater world of Minnow Lake, a landscape of unrescued debris, readying itself to pop to the surface as a result of monumentally slow and random untetherings.

"Let's go to Mesmer," Rose said to King. Jerome Limb lived in an apartment there. He might be home and there was no reason on this earth why a former neighbour should not drop in to see a former neighbour. If he wasn't there, she would wait until he showed up. If he was working the night shift, she'd stay until dawn, call her dad from a pay phone and say she was sleeping over at Anastasia's. Nothing in Flax was difficult.

Rose opened the window to let the cool air blast in. It seemed angry to have been kept out during her short stay at the Van Epps' and Rose was unwell and grateful for King's company. The occasional bug hit the windshield and this was unavoidable, Rose realized, although she had spent considerable time this summer wondering about the possibility of a cowcatcher-like attachment for car windshields, an aerodynamic accessory that would scoop and lift them to safety. She'd even asked Miss Eustace to go over Bernoulli's theorem a second time, thinking there might be some application.

Sighing, Rose reached for King's flat little head and gave him a pat. She really wished Maddy wouldn't sit there in physics with her left arm so close to Rose's right arm, her left arm which always seemed to radiate bewilderment, as if it belonged to an immigrant or an exchange student. *Can you explain that to me after class? Yes, yes, okay Maddy, sure.* If only Maddy would like Rose a little less, not be always looking at her so much and smiling. And then on the dark highway Rose saw a turtle and in swerving to miss, hit it with two shell crushing thumps and before she could stop herself, thought, oh no, reptilicide, and wanted to laugh. But it wasn't a joke, was it, it was sad and serious; she had just killed a turtle. And she couldn't really stop to scoop it off the road, and even if she did, what would be the point and what if Anastasia saw her crying now, then what? "Let's just get to Mesmer," Rose said to King, and, "I don't suppose you have a Kleenex do you?" Calm down, calm down, calm down and Rose closed the window to create silence and peace and regained her composure and realized, fully, that something had to be done.

Good luck. The cruiser was there; he was off duty. It was all meant to be. "You wait, King. Okay? Wait. Stay." King had no objections, shifting his bulk to the driver's seat as soon as Rose left it empty. On her way to the building, she looked back to see him watching over the steering wheel, a pointy-faced omen. Would the car's engine be dead by the time she returned?

The apartment building was two stories of eight units, single people or poor people without houses. People who won extra-large stuffed animals at the CNE and kept them forever, at least that's what showed in the windows of two apartments but not Jerome's, nothing in his but light and condensation. Maybe he was having a shower; maybe he wouldn't hear the knock but he opened the door to Rose with no delay as if he'd been standing on the other side waiting: police behaviour no doubt.

"Do you remember who I am?" Rose asked.

"Hmmmm." Eyes narrowed in pretend scrutiny, Jerome said, "You look vaguely familiar. Let me think. You wouldn't be Rose Drury, the girl who lived next door to me for several odd years? And I do mean odd."

"Okay, okay. Can I come in?"

"Certainly," said Jerome. But only as far as the welcome mat, apparently. Ducks in flight against a sky of hemp. "What can I do you for?"

"Well," Rose swallowed a gag reflex—she couldn't throw up on a cop's welcome mat—and wiped away a fresh spray of perspiration on her upper lip and forehead. "I'm sure there's a rule against discussing this sort of thing but I'm assuming it applies to you and not me and by this sort of thing, I mean Maddy Farrell."

"You're right there, missy. But just a minute. I have to turn down the spaghetti water." He disappeared, abandoning Rose to the hallway smells of starch and old boots. "All right. Continue," he said, now holding a gingham print oven mitt.

"I don't know what Maddy told you, but I hope she mentioned I was with her when she got the ladder. We were out in the woods. We were throwing our clothes up in the trees. No reason, just something to do. And something got stuck so she had to get the ladder. You might want to question me as well since I was there. You probably should if you're going to be thorough."

"Oh I should, should I? That's certainly very interesting Rose Drury," Jerome said, hanging the oven mitt from an index finger, twirling it this way, then that. "But Maddy told me she was alone and you have to wonder what Rose Drury would be doing in East Flax with Maddy Farrell?"

"She's my friend."

"Your friend?" He stopped twirling. "Well, your friend had a completely different story and I'm inclined to believe hers, unless she's a pathological liar which I'll know if she is or isn't once she's seen Graham Rochon for the assessment I've recommended."

"Assessment?"

Jerome slapped the oven mitt into the palm of his hand. "You heard it here first."

"You can *tell* someone to have an assessment?" Rose asked. Too much saliva now. What if she drooled? What if her complaint simply drained down the sides of her cheeks? She wanted Adrian to be there, to laugh about rabies and the Limbs.

"I can recommend it. It's part of the job. So you better watch out. I just might order one up for you."

"Very funny, Jerome," swallowing mouth-temperature froth. "When's that supposed to happen? The assessment, I mean."

"*That* is none of your business, Rose Drury. It's none of your business and," the mitt began to twirl again, "you can't do anything about it, which I'm sure you find deeply frustrating. So just go home and snoop around in your own backyard for a change. Just a minute." He disappeared into the kitchen again, returning without the dizzying mitt. One small mercy.

"You know, just because you're Rose Drury doesn't mean you can always get your way. And also, did you ever hear the saying what goes around comes around? Remember that time you ratted on me for taking a dump with the dog? It was a biiiig joke all over Flax. Ha ha ha. I asked you to tell people you had just made it up but you wouldn't, would you? Oh no. Not perfect little Rose Drury who never took a shit with a dog."

"Okay, okay, fine. I'm sorry," said Rose. Why could people not just forget things and move on?

"You sound *really* genuine. Anyway, the moral of the story is now I'm a cop and I could help you if I wanted to but I don't want to. And actually I wouldn't help you even if I did want to, if you know what I mean, because I feel it's important for you to learn that you can't rule the world."

"Oh. And because you're a cop, you can?"

"Small parts of it. That's what they pay me for."

"Fine. Well, my work here is done."

"I'm glad you think so."

"Then I guess I'm leaving."

"You're welcome to stay for spaghetti."

"No. Thank. You. I have a dog in the car."

"Got a replacement for Skokie?"

"No, it's King, the Van Epps' devil dog."

"Well, keep him off my lawn."

Rose sniffed, turned away, gagged ever so slightly and let herself out. From the street, she watched Jerome clear away a starchy cloud of condensation from his kitchen window. He waved. King barked and relinquished the driver's seat. "Maybe you should go sit on that patch of dead grass lawn for a minute, King." But Rose kept him in the car. The way things were going, best not to take any chances with an oracular dog. To her amazement, the car engine turned over with no problem. "Thanks for sparing the Vega, King."

At the Van Epps', Rose pulled over, leaning across King and his smell of old dog to open the passenger door. He fell out and stood for a moment, looking at nothing, then arched his old back and in one silent heave, threw up the turkey in a soup of bile and unidentifiable brown strands. Rose pulled the door shut and turned the car around expecting King to give chase, bark at the tires as was his habit, but this time he didn't. Rose presumed he'd caught her complaint.

Reg slept part of the afternoon and was up the rest of the time. The house seemed to want him up; it needed an audience. Late morning he watched the progress of the sun and the movement of the shadows across linoleum and chenille bedspreads. Even though the house has always been surrounded by trees, he had never noticed this activity before. The slightest breeze caused the shadows to break and converge and Reg was reminded of kids at play. He had time to make note of seasonal change, the diminishing number of ants appearing from the kitchen baseboards, and the building intensity of the sparrows' chatter around four, as if they were starting to discuss the winter's plans. Occasionally he could almost begin to feel as if the place were in good hands, as if he might have tumbled inside an insurance advertisement.

Without fail, Reg watched the eleven o'clock news. For all he understood, it could have been read in Russian or Japanese; it's the visit he wanted, from a familiar, unseeing face. Not that Reg was without visitors, or attempted visitors. He met them at the door, accepted their casseroles and pies but could not invite them in because that would represent a public and final admission: yes, this was indisputably the state of affairs, and in Reg's mind, room still remained for negotiation with misfortune.

After the news, Reg sat in the backyard listening. He'd always had good ears and would tell you he could actually hear the sound of a single leaf landing in Martha Trimble's pool. He wondered if the tree cared about hitting the pool, if it were like tossing cards into an overturned hat, if, ideally, the tree would like each and every leaf to land inside the pool's perimeter. He could hear the pennants in the wind at the dealership down the street. Like everybody, he wondered what would become of it. What was Reg going to do? He wondered about Reg as if Reg were somebody else and worried, then squinted and concentrated on bringing the two together. Maybe he needed a stronger pair of glasses.

Then he went inside and shaved. This was undeniably the strangest part of the night because, despite having covered the bathroom mirror in newsprint, he continued to shave in front of it. His one realistic wish: not to see his own image. He had covered Loretta's full-length mirror as well and, when turning on Cheryl's night light, needed to crawl along the floor to avoid the vanity mirror. He had no explanation for this other than seeing himself was like looking inside your car after it had been stolen. Hard to believe something so yours had been driven around and lived in by a stranger.

Every night, Reg turned the radio on and tried to find a song he liked and invariably could not and turned it off. Sometimes he made a sandwich but supplies were running low. Then he turned the radio on again. The television made an unmistakable glow he did not want seen from the sidewalk. Reg is up a lot, they would say; what will become of the dealership? Rocket Lalonde won't stay forever. He knew what they were saying because he himself would say it.

The best part of the night was morning. Martha Trimble woke up too early and, weather permitting, was brought outside to sit by the pool. Her bus didn't come until 8:15; Martha was the last pickup before it tore down the highway to Mesmer with its cargo of mis-matched bodies.

This morning was grey but already Martha was by her pool, admiring it. She liked to watch the leaves float on the surface, she liked the miniature ripples, or so it seemed. Reg let Pellett out and he ran to her as if she were the last remaining source of meat and gravy on this earth. Martha responded with her biggest twitch and smile and her way of saying Pellett, which was more like Pay-it. She had a deep voice, which came from below her throat, as if her rib cage had to squeeze the sound from lungs of bagpipe. Knowing Martha had caused Reg to think he should have been a doctor. He was an expert on cars; how different could people be? If only they had a hood you could look under, he bet he could figure out most problems. There was usually a wire in there, some problem with the electrical that had come loose. He imagined a little electrical tape, black and shiny adhesive, and Martha gets up, moves just like Cheryl, is 100 per cent ship-shape.

"Ready for school, I see," said Reg.

"Yes."

"Pool's going to be full of leaves soon."

"Yes."

Reg saw Rainie Trimble's face at the kitchen window. She waved and smiled but it was a different Rainie from a month ago. Now it was a smile that could be on five different faces, like the ones Cheryl used to make, keep the nose but change the eyes and mouth, keep the mouth and change the nose and eyes. The face was Rainie's but the features seemed to suggest Reg could not be trusted or predicted. Maybe even Rainie had taken to seeing him as an electric chair: Jimmy Senior had certainly blabbed that opinion to enough people.

Well, look away, Reg decided. Maybe that's why he liked Martha more these days. They were both objects of fascination. Truth be told, people would pay money to sit in an auditorium and stare for as long as it took.

And how long would that be? Days for some. Never mind; he and Martha could make a fortune.

"What do you do at school, exactly?" Reg asked, recognizing the word exactly was suspicious of the possibility Martha could really be doing anything. But then, it was an honest question.

Martha smiled and made a shrugging motion from her hips to her head.

"Do you read?"

Martha nodded.

Reg was a little disappointed. He had never thought of Martha reading at school. Martha's school should be something completely divorced from the conventions of learning, should involve exercises and pools to relax the muscles, walking lessons. Now he saw her in a desk with other students and most likely friends too. Martha Trimble had a separate and regular life she visited without Rainie and Bob, just herself, and this filled Reg with nostalgia. What on earth had happened here? He had begun living in a reversal of the rule of days and family and jobs and school. His life had learned how to leave him behind, like a jacket on the back of a chair.

Rainie emerged from the house. "Almost bus time, Martha," she said, grasping the chair handles and freeing the brake, as if the chair might take off on flat grass in a back yard in Flax. Did she think I might try to push her somewhere? Reg wondered. How was it that Rainie Trimble now had the capacity to render him a potential kidnapper of girls in wheelchairs?

"Hello Reg. How are you *anyway?*"

What do you do in school *exactly*, Reg thought. "I'm not really sure, Rainie. I'm neither here nor there, seems to me, if you know what I mean." He hoped she did because he certainly had no idea.

Rainie looked at him, mouth hard, eyes soft, but one face now, no longer the drawing at the window. "I think I have some idea, Reg," she said, as the giant chestnut dropped a leaf, yellow at the edges.

"Missed the pool," said Reg. "Almost landed in your hair." And he stared into the leafy distance, focusing, focusing to keep the tears away. Women shouldn't be nice. "Well," he continued, "Jimmy usually drops by with a coffee about now. Better head back inside and get the place tidied up."

"Come over sometime, why don't you? We've always got extra for supper," said Rainie, tipping Martha back in her chair, ready for the pivot that would spin them back to the house and all the living people who called it home.

"Sure thing," said Reg. "I might just take you up on that offer."

Nothing in Flax was difficult. Assume Maddy's appointment could not be before four on Tuesday: her parents wouldn't want her missing school, more to the point, wouldn't want to write a note excusing their daughter for purposes of psychological evaluation, wouldn't want her going, period, but would be too compliant or too dumb to defy a cop and his bogus claims to authority. Call the receptionist first thing in the morning and if there were no openings, mention that since Cheryl Decker's death you had entertained the occasional self-destructive thought, alluding to the lack of emotional support you had, unlike others with two living parents. Make it quite clear you couldn't come after four-thirty, that you didn't want to inconvenience anyone, but it was more or less urgent.

"I'll see what I can do, Rose," Mrs. Horsburgh said, calling back ten minutes later to say, yes, she had managed to rebook another client and Dr. Rochon could see her at two. School hours. Was that going to be a problem?

"No, no. Not at all. Thanks so much, Mrs. Horsburgh."

Two o'clock would be ideal. If indeed Maddy was being seen on Tuesday, best not to have back-to-back appointments and best not to be seen in the waiting room with her. Best not to be seen with her at all, if in fact she had told Limb she was alone with the ladder because now there was a detective coming from London. Although, Rose now believed it was entirely possible Maddy had got the ladder again, later, for another reason, after Rose had left. Maddy had no fear of heights. Maybe her dad had asked her to prune some limbs or knock down a wasps' nest. Once you really concentrated on a memory, Rose had noticed, it started to talk back, like an answer in a multiple-choice exam. The voice of what you thought you knew was argued into doubt by the voices of several other possibilities. The bra in the tree, for example. Rose knew it had happened but the memory was faded because it had been so dark beneath the trees. Perhaps the entire episode had been seen more by the rods than the cones, recorded as night vision, which would explain why she remembered it like a picture taken without the flash, unrecognizable shadowy and mud-coloured figures against a background of wasted photo finishing.

The same applied to the kissing scene: Rose had to wonder now if that had really taken place. She'd had those drinks, after all, and once when she and Anastasia drank a bottle of wine, she thought the next day she'd called Foster Limb, but she hadn't. She'd taken the will for the deed, Anastasia said. This might have been a similar case. The mind was a well-oiled machine, Graham Rochon said, slippery.

Only physics class to get through. Each day since the dance, Rose would confess, it had been more like biology, or maybe the biology of physics. As if the day were a large piece of tissue you could dissect and place upon a slide. Through a microscope—see, ah, there it is, physics class, a cluster of blood vessels as if there'd been a stroke, a constriction time couldn't pass and so detoured in two separate arteries.

Rose still wanted to help Maddy; she told her so last week. Maddy said, "I know," then closed her notebook. She picked at the coil, uncoiled it, so already it was more a spike, a ringlet gone flat. Maddy had the potential to make most things messy.

But today Rose said, "See you tomorrow. I'm leaving early. I've got an appointment with the dentist."

"What?"

"Seriously, Maddy. He asked if I could get out of school early. Just this once. The office is a mess without Loretta Decker."

The walk to the clinic was easy and direct, down the hill and cut across behind the curling rink and the telephone exchange. Would Graham Rochon be looking forward to seeing her? Not likely. Take a realistic look at the scene, as Anastasia would say. Rose was seventeen, he was eleven years older. No doubt he had that girlfriend still, the pale one with the red lips and the black dress he'd brought to church a couple years ago—Oona from Germany. Unimaginable to a Flax mind. What did they discuss? Sigmund Freud's secret habits? Clouds shaped like ink blots? Still, she might be able to make him laugh by reminding him of St. Paul's letters to the Mesmerites. She could make herself laugh and that would be flattering.

But look at yourself, Anastasia would say. You're wearing a kilt with a kilt pin and a white blouse, a cardigan, bare legs because it's still warm. Not even nylons. Look at yourself. Why didn't you think before you left home? And she wasn't that pretty, truth be told; Rose knew that about herself. A drunk man in Mesmer had told her, had swerved up to her and Anastasia one Saturday afternoon, smelling like beer spilled in a basement and said, "You're okay. You're not bad, but your friend here is a babe. Can you get me her phone number?" Phlegm stalactites laughing in his lungs.

So there it was. Indisputable evidence. Rose was okay; she was not bad. Could be worse. You'd have to wonder what Maddy Farrell found appealing. Rose would like to ask Rochon that. What did he think, really, made Maddy Farrell like Rose Drury? There must be something a little unusual about a girl another girl would want to kiss? Wasn't that what psychology was all about? The study of individual differences? So? Maddy wouldn't have kissed Anastasia Van Epp.

Rose quickened her pace. She loved opening the door to the clinic waiting room, loved seeing who might be there, just leaving or waiting because Rochon had gone overtime with a patient. Diseases of the mind weren't contagious but the smell was like vaccinations. This time the waiting room was empty, the door to the office open. There was Graham Rochon at his desk, writing notes in the dim and intimate lamp light. "You can go right in, Rose. Here, I'll get the door." Funny how Mrs. Horsburgh always spared you the choice of privacy, as if you might just want all of Flax to eavesdrop.

"I'll be one second here, Rose. Have a seat."

What was he writing? *Patient seems doomed. Hopeless from birth. I wonder what Oona is doing.*

"All right. There," he said, slapping shut a file. Now he would stand, walk around his desk and sit in the easy chair opposite Rose. Correct. "What's up?"

"Well, it's nothing like I told Mrs. Horsburgh," Rose said with a shrug. "I'm not contemplating suicide." She crossed her legs and clasped both hands over a bare knee.

"I'm relieved to hear that. What is it then?" And he honestly looked relieved, even concerned, but facial expressions were part of his job.

"I wanted to see you so I could intervene on behalf

of my friend. Maddy Farrell. I think she's supposed to see you someday soon."

"You want to intervene. Okay," and he smiled a patronizing smile, as if Rose were a precocious child. "I've had irate husbands intervene on behalf of wives they thought couldn't properly explain themselves. But I don't think that's the situation we have here."

"No, it's not." Although Rose couldn't help blanching momentarily at the analogy.

"Then you're going to have to enlighten me."

Enlighten, Rose thought. A word beloved by those in charge. And he was in charge, Rose would be the first to admit.

"It has to do with Jerome Limb, the cop. He seems to think that Maddy had something to do with Cheryl Decker's death because apparently a witness saw Maddy with a ladder. And of course, Maddy doesn't help the situation by telling Limb she was alone when in fact I was with her."

Rochon stared. His face lifted itself a little, as if responding to instruction from an old graduate professor.

"I think I'm missing some key information here," he said, his tone a little indulgent. "What's the significance of the ladder?"

"You're kidding, aren't you?" Rose widened her eyes. "You haven't heard about the ladder? Oh, I know. You have to pretend you don't know anything. Fine. I can go along with that. All right. The significance of the ladder is that Maddy and I used it to get something out of a tree the same day Cheryl died. Somebody saw

Maddy getting the ladder from the dance hall shed and like they do here in Flax, put two and two together to come up with the ridiculous conclusion that Maddy had something to do with Cheryl's death. That Maddy used the ladder to string Cheryl up because, presumably, Cheryl was the captain of the basketball team and Maddy should have been or Cheryl had more earrings than Maddy or Cheryl's dad has a car dealership and Maddy's has a broom. I'm sure I don't know."

"So there's a possible motive of jealousy."

"What? Pardon me?" As handsome as he was, Graham Rochon could be both obtuse and irritating. "Possible motive? No. I'm not talking about possible motives because there is no possible crime. There's nothing to be said about motives. I was being sarcastic. I was *with* Maddy when she got the ladder and put it back and it was the afternoon. Cheryl killed herself that night. Isn't there a coroner's report that narrows down the time of death? Is Flax so far from the civilized world we don't qualify for coroner's reports? Do they think we can't read out here? That the alphabet has not yet arrived?"

"It's on its way apparently. The coroner's report, that is, not the alphabet. Some delay. He went on vacation and then the secretary got sick. It's supposed to be here this week. Things happen." He looked at Rose, head cocked a little to the side, exactly like the drunk in Mesmer, as if making an appraisal, a comparison to Oona. You're okay. Not bad.

"Well, good. That's good news. And in the meantime, I'm prepared to tell you what happened as long as you can assure me it'll be kept confidential."

"I can't assure you of that because I might be sub-poenaed, if this does actually ... You know what sub-poenaed means?" He was leaning back now, hands behind his head.

"Yes. I've seen 'Perry Mason' too." Rose uncrossed and recrossed her legs.

He smiled a smile pulled up from the ears.

"And what are the chances of that?" Rose asked and noticed the smell again, of vaccinations, and felt a little ill. Shots. The smallpox one was the worst.

"I have no idea." The sentence stretched a little in the middle, as if it had yawned.

"Well, if they can't get a coroner's report up here, how will they ever manage a subpoena? Anyway, you'll think of something. Okay. This is what happened on the afternoon of the twenty-fifth of September, as they say. Maddy and I were up at the dance hall. She was practicing—basketball practicing—and I was watching. Out of the blue, we decided to do some dancing. I don't know why but we took her radio out into the woods and found some music and started dancing. Then we got feeling sexy or something. I can't explain that either but that's your job so write down what you think, you know, unhealthy sexual tendencies or ex-ploratory behaviour or what have you. So we took off our shirts and then our bras and Maddy threw mine into a tree. End of story. She had to get the ladder. I stayed by the tree, we got the bra, and replaced the lad-der. Maddy had nothing to do with Cheryl killing her-self. You have to write that down, write something about Maddy that makes that perfectly clear. She only lied to Limb because she didn't want him knowing about the bra part of the story. That seems logical, doesn't it?"

"You want me to write a kind of alibi for Maddy Farrell? That's not what Limb is asking for." He was a little annoyed. "I'm not a lawyer. And besides, you yourself admit she gave false information."

"No, no, no. You're not getting it. He doesn't need to know it was false information. The information is irrelevant. He just needs to know she's a good person. That's what you're doing isn't it? A personality assessment? A bunch of free association and ink blots? That's all pretty subjective isn't it? You can't tell me there's a right or wrong answer to an ink blot test."

"Don't tell me what I get and what I don't get. I've had seven years of training in the art of getting it." Now Graham was full-blown angry; his face was under its own control now, off the pay scale.

Silence. In the waiting room, the phone rang. Mrs. Horsburgh would answer with her soft and loving voice. And this brought tears to Rose's eyes. Rochon combed his fingers through his hair, impatient, like he had more than once the time he brought Oona to the church. He wanted to get this over with but now there were tears to address.

"Tell me," he said. "Why don't you just tell this to Limb and not me? I don't really understand what you're trying to achieve here with your intervention."

Rose sniffed. "I tried to tell Limb that but he wouldn't believe me. And since then I've thought it through and, in fact, it would look worse if people knew we were both there because, realistically, we *could* have killed Cheryl and made it look like a suicide. Somehow, I'm sure. I don't know how these things occur but logistically, two people could strangle a person and tie that person up in a tree. It's not beyond the realm of the forensically possible whereas Maddy Farrell acting alone as they say, I can't picture. Hand-to-hand combat with Cheryl Decker. It's all too crazy but you must get my drift here. Whoops. I mean, I know you get my drift here."

"I'm afraid I don't. But let's just say this thing comes to trial, which it likely won't, you'd be a credible witness. And who cares about the bra thing? Think of all the stuff people hear in court. Murder. Fraud. Assault. Compare that to a bra thrown into a tree."

"But that's where you're wrong," Rose could hear herself pleading. "I wouldn't be a credible witness because people wouldn't believe I was there. They'd make up some reason for why I was trying to protect Maddy because I've been tutoring her and trying to make her into a better person and they all think I'm such a lovely girl it makes me want to vomit and so they would build a story around the story, which ultimately would be worse for Maddy. You have to believe me. I know how Flax works. And besides, to be totally honest, I don't want everybody in Flax knowing I was throwing bras around with Maddy Farrell. That's the honest truth. So really, the best thing is for Limb to think Maddy told the truth and what's more, according to Graham Rochon, is *incapable* of anything like what is being implied. That she didn't care about being captain of the basketball team, which she did not. You can do all that with your tests and put it in a report. Easy as pie."

"Uh huh. Well, no, in fact it's not *easy* as *pie*. I can't just fabricate an assessment. There's a death involved here, an investigation, a possible trial, my licence to practice, and other issues you can't seem to appreciate. To be honest, I'm not at all comfortable with this conversation."

"Oh." Rose had anticipated some resistance but this was not now a problem; she'd got a second wind, the course was clear. Inside her person, Rose Drury carried a pocket-sized emotional guidebook to Flax the way other students carried a French-English dictionary. Without text though, pictures only. Whirring through the pages with the self-possession of the student who always wins the French language essay competition, she stopped at an image of Dr. Rochon standing near his bookshelf. Then, in a new voice, submissive and sad, "Maybe I'm out of line," Rose said. "I guess I'm just a little run down by all the tragedy in this town. Do you think it's worse than most places?"

"Not particularly, although there's been a run of bad luck for sure."

Rose played with a button on her blouse, glad she had shaved her legs last night. Slats of light from the venetian blinds fell on them. She thought she might resemble someone in a French movie.

"My brother's feeling bad about it all too. Although, overall, he's less confused about everything now than he once was. Maybe I'm the mixed up one these days. He's pretty certain about everything; so certain I have to buy his condoms for him. Quite the Lothario or so he says. Maybe he's full of it, though. You can never tell with guys. He likes to talk. He's full of advice, unsolicited, the worst kind."

"Oh yes. Like?" Graham Rochon seemed distracted.

"Like for example, he told me the one thing all men like more than anything."

That got his attention. "You and your brother have conversations like that?"

"Once in a while. We're more or less all we've got after all."

"And what is it your brother contends every man likes best? I'm always fascinated by the adolescent male mind."

Rose commanded her eyes to look at his. "He says they like fellatio."

"Oh he does, does he?" No readable response.

"That's not the term he uses of course. You can likely imagine. The adolescent male mouth and all."

"Mmm hmmm. Indeed."

"You wouldn't have any books I could borrow? On the topic of the sexually mixed-up female adolescent? Anything at all?"

"Ah yes. Bibliotherapy." He seemed relieved to stand up.

Success. And now he was moving to the bookshelf. His back to Rose, his backside and belt at eye level. Don't stop to think. She reached up and brushed her palm against the inside of his thigh. He was wearing jeans, he always did, with denim you could never be sure, was it your imagination or your own self rubbing against your own self? He kept his back to her though, seeming to be looking for that certain book. And she said, "Maybe I'm a little too interested in sex lately. If you know what I mean. There was that incident with Maddy, which who could explain? And now here I am talking about it with you. I guess I'm at that age." Rose moved her hand a notch higher, leaned closer to the jeans and belt like someone approaching a sewing project, seams to be ripped. Or an examination of the plastic sex organs passed around in biology. Any laughing and it's an automatic deduction of ten marks.

"I'm not at all comfortable with the direction this is taking," Graham Rochon said, turning around. He had not yet found the appropriate book, was skeptical of bibliotherapy anyway, and his mind was heating up too suddenly like an element on a stove, tightly wound coils cooking up forbidden plans, bubbles cratering up from thick white sauces. "I should..."

But when Rose's fingers touched the belt buckle, everything in Graham Rochon stopped, as if he had encountered a rare bird or wild horse in the backyard. Just stand perfectly still. Don't move a muscle. That's what all the nature books advise.

Graham Rochon's penis freed itself skilfully from its housing of denim and cotton, yearning toward Rose's mouth so hard she thought it might have something to say. The main thing is to use your lips, Adrian had said, and keep your teeth out of the way, and so Rose did, thinking about East Flax and Minnow Lake, certain now that by Christmas everything would have gone back to normal and she and Anastasia would be friends again and no one would blame Maddy.

Two sounds from Graham Rochon. "Uh. Uh." Was he wondering what to say next? And Rose's mouth flooded with a salty brine that she gulped down thinking it a little like force-feeding, or maybe more like bottle-feeding. Her mouth emptied then, the ridge on the head of the thing scraping at her teeth and his back to her, tucking in motions and the finished sound of zippering. Rochon went to the chair behind his desk and sat. Rose took a tissue from the desk and wiped her lips. The seconds seemed to be collecting in her ears like cotton.

"I hope you know enough to keep your mouth shut, Rose Drury. Oh God. Poor choice of words. Quiet, I mean."

"I don't want Maddy in any trouble and I don't want people finding out things about Maddy that would make her feel bad. Things that have nothing to do with Cheryl Decker."

"Yes. I know that. You can go now. The door's unlocked."

In the waiting room, Rose heard him say. "I'll be a couple of minutes here, Nora." A voice pitched too far above suspicion. But Graham Rochon did not need to worry about Rose saying anything to anyone. He didn't know this, but Rose could have told the editor of *The Reminder* she'd initiated and performed an indecent sex act with the town psychologist and he wouldn't have believed her, would have printed an entirely

different story. Local Teen Stressed by Recent Events:
East Flax Girl Up on Charges.

Adrian thanked the god of glass and screens and
warm fall days for his luck: the kitchen window was
open. From upstairs, he'd seen Jerome Limb enter the
yard to talk with the dentist and raced to the kitchen,
praying the window would be open and here it was.
Even the direction of the breeze was a spiritual gift,
like a medium almost, really, as if it had two voices.
When all this was over and done with, Adrian would
have a seance. Except, what if Cheryl showed up?

The dentist and Limb were deep in discussion of
the detective. The dentist wanted to know everything,
being driven to Canadian Club and ginger by Adrian's
gloominess: the boy wouldn't change his underwear,
wouldn't talk to anyone except his sister and Randy
Farrell. With the position of the two men, Adrian
could kneel with his elbows right in the windowsill and
they wouldn't notice. And with his negative decibel
hearing and Casper the friendly wind...

"Did you get a glimpse of the famous Detective
Urichuk?" Jerome wanted to know.

"No, I never did get to see the man."

"Well, he certainly looked the part, like he went to
a costume shop and got himself a trench coat and a lot
of gum, along with the attitude. And the Lincoln.
Don't forget the Lincoln. And then Ruth Ann Phelps
says, finally something *real* happens in Flax. Like as if

to say this town's police force and even the crimes committed by its citizens were not what you'd call authentic until this detective arrived in town."

The dentist nodded agreeably and took a sip of booze. Adrian reached for an apple from the counter, then thought better: he was a loud biter.

"So what did this detective do exactly?" asked the dentist.

"Went to the high school. Questioned kids who'd been at the dance. When did you arrive? When did you leave? Complex stuff like that, *way* beyond my scope. Came to the station to read the coroner's report, then the psychologist's, and pronounced the death a suicide."

"Oh dear," the dentist said, while Adrian's blood stampeded for an exit. Poke a hole anywhere and it would spurt out from the pressure of each corpuscle pushing the other out of the way. Let me out of this carcass, they were saying, this guy caused a girl to kill herself.

"Oh yeah," said Limb, "this guy's pretty sure of himself. There was no doubt in his mind the Decker girl's death was a suicide and not likely before seven that night. The cause of the death and the condition of the body were all consistent with a nine-foot fall from a branch. There was no sign of struggle and frankly—and this is where he gets sarcastic—the idea of one teenage girl wrestling another up a ladder, securing her to a branch, and executing her was so far-fetched as to be beyond the scope of his considerable experience and vivid imagination. There were dozens of witnesses who could confirm that our suspect, Maddy Farrell, was at the dance hall the entire time because she had made a spectacle of herself dancing with another girl. And finally, the useless psychologist's report described Maddy as a *simple* and *compassionate* girl with no history of animosity toward the deceased who, coincidentally, had recently been treated for depression. So there you have it."

"That's it then? That's his entire investigation? Can I make you a drink by the way, Jerome? Here I am, imbibing without offering the guest..."

"No no. I'm not officially on duty but with the uniform on, probably shouldn't. Just wanted to say hi to Mom, see what's cooking. Literally. Anyway, the detective is a busy man with two genuine homicide cases to investigate in London and this frankly was nothing but a colossal waste of his time. Something I would know, had I pursued any post-secondary education in the science of psychology, is that suicide is a leading cause of death among teenagers. As for the geezer who'd seen the girl with the ladder, by that I mean Alfred Beel, he couldn't be bothered. 'There is no case here and there never was,' he said, 'So, if you'll excuse me,' he says, 'I may be able to make it back to my office in time to get some work done.' And with that he was gone, poof."

The dentist shook his head in disbelief, the breeze wafting in his thoughts as well, something like *Christ, what's Adrian going to smash when he hears this? How many stitches? Does he need to go to a special school somewhere? A place with nurses instead of teachers?*

Adrian set the apple back on the counter where it rolled and fell with a pulpy thump, forcing him to duck below the window frame.

"What was that?" wondered the dentist aloud.

Limb said, "You know, I may not have a university degree in psychology but that doesn't mean I haven't successfully mediated my fair share of disputes. Remember I convinced Margaret and Henry Baptiste of the wisdom and financial logic of seeing Graham Rochon, better than bashing one another's cars with baseball bats. And I counselled Larry Mellon to stop calling Geraldine Pelkey, stop idling his car in front of her house, and got Martin Brim into AA last winter." He didn't appear to need a university degree to get the job done. "Police work, George, is largely a matter of instincts and memory, and I like to think I have decent instincts, coupled with the Limb intellect."

"Certainly," agreed the dentist. "Detective Urichuk might be a big fish in the, well, I suppose relatively big pond of London, but no one in Flax would ever underestimate the intelligence of a Limb. Didn't each and every one of you make it onto that 'Reach for the Top' game show? My two certainly didn't make the cut."

Adrian nodded in derisive agreement.

"You've got to know a lot to get onto that show," the dentist elaborated.

"Yessir, you've got to know that Jonas Salk invented the polio vaccine and that rhubarb is a herb," Jerome laughed. "Although seriously, that 'Reach for the Top' stuff is why I still to this day love the facts and nothing but the facts."

The tinkle of ice, like Christmas decorations in the wind, and the dentist had more to say. "Something just doesn't sit right with me about this whole business. And not just because Adrian's blaming himself."

I'm not blaming myself, you dumbo, Adrian complained to the wall.

"Well, George, neither my instincts nor my memory will allow a complete exoneration of that Maddy Farrell. In the world of police work, coincidences do not usually just happen. In fact, coincidences are the product of information and remembering. This goes with that because I remember this and any fool knows that. And a girl with a ladder in the vicinity of a girl hanging from a tree is a coincidence worthy of investigation."

Limb actually thought it might have *been* Maddy and there was solace in his analysis. Adrian took a deep breath, reached for the apple—not the top—and bit into the soft bruise by mistake.

"Hard to believe Urichuk wouldn't even take the time to question Alfred Beel," Limb went on. "I actually just now drove out there to thank the guy for his lead. He deserves that much, at least, all blown up as he is and no family, living out here at the end of the road where even the snowplough sometimes gives up, trying to do his civic duty nonetheless."

"Good for you." The dentist sounded as if he were talking to a puppy.

"I like to think I do my bit."

"We all need to. That's the problem with this younger generation..."

So Limb thought, maybe Maddy did do it, that co-incidences don't usually happen. Adrian went out the front door and stood with the sun on his hair. The sun. Maybe today it wouldn't shine straight through him onto his skeleton of guilt and Flax would be illuminated like any ordinary town, just nature, birds, dogs, cats, crickets, and people who thought nothing in particular about anybody. Adrian took one more bite of his apple, then wedged the remains behind a wheel of the dentist's car. When he backed out of the driveway, splat. Adrian had always enjoyed flattening things.

"Here in Canada," Alfred Beel was telling Jimmy Drake Senior, "we're lucky to have a civilized police force, cops who exercise a bit of restraint and haven't been brainwashed into thuggishness. If you'd travelled as much as I have, you'd know that wasn't the case in a lot of places. Take Germany for instance. How did Hitler get so far so fast? He had a trained corps of thugs at the ready. And who were they? The police. Likewise, France. It was as if the cops there had taken courses in collaboration. Most places you go, cops and robbers are just two faces of the same coin. I'm surprised there aren't more situations like Germany, where some dim light goes on and they think, hey, if we just got together we could rule the world."

They were at the Legion. Alfred liked to slip out there for a couple of drinks on Thursday night, but not with Jimmy Drake. If he had to sit with anyone, it was

Philip Rochon or Bill Laine; if not them, preferably no one. Tonight it would seem they were elsewhere and Jimmy Drake was on the prowl, looking for company. Mind if I join you?

"That's why I at least respect Limb. People say a lot of stupid things about him but at least he's not a thug. Whereas Jarvis, given the right conditions, I'm not so confident about. Jarvis has a smugness about him. That's why I specifically asked for Limb when I called. Jarvis, him I could see laughing. Saying, okay, I've got it. I'll write up a report. Girl seen with ladder. Anything else, Mr. Beel? Just a hint of sarcasm. If there's one thing I can't stomach, it's a hint of sarcasm. Not enough to really grab a hold of by the neck. Just enough to make your ears want to spit wax. At least Limb followed up and took the time to tell me he did."

"According to Ruth Ann Phelps, the detective made a bit of an ass of Limb," Jimmy said.

"Be that as it may," Alfred said. He was lecturing Jimmy and he knew that, and being a little pompous. *If you'd travelled like I had*, but he was in the mood for letting people know a thing or two. "He who laughs last laughs loudest and so on. Cases close and cases re-open. Remember that doctor up in Telluride who killed his wife? Another case of indisputable evidence until the second wife and then the housekeeper died. Then lo and behold it turns out there never was an autopsy on the first one who'd somehow been given a therapeutic dose of antifreeze. Doctors don't question other doctors and detectives don't listen to some old blown-up soldier's report. Nobody listens to the little guy."

"You've got my vote there."

"And, I'm telling you I saw that Farrell girl and she had a ladder and that's not all she had. She had a guilty look on her face. You know how you can have a guilty look on your face? It's not even on your face so much as around your face. Like an eclipse of the sun."

"Well, there's something around that girl's face, that's for sure. I'd call it butt ugliness. I've never liked the look of her. There's something wrong with a girl that looks half man. It's not just her though, it's the entire family. I've never liked her old man. If it weren't for him and his cut-rate service, I'd have the contract for the arena and the town hall. But that's free enterprise for you. Still, you've gotta feel sorry for the guy who's married to Angel Cobb."

Alfred drained his glass and set it to the side. Green terrycloth covered the table, green terrycloth with cigarette burns that at this precise moment he attributed to Jimmy Drake. Jimmy Drake smoked and Jimmy Drake was in here too damn often, so had ample opportunity to leave a tobaccoish trail of brown-edged holes in terrycloth. He was not a desirable person, Jimmy Drake; he was an undesirable. And there he was, Alfred could tell, planning, through the mention of Angel Cobb, to move the conversation in an undesirable direction. Alfred could tell. Jimmy had started to look guilty himself, guilty of pleasure found, not only in the wrong place but also in the most obscure place. Like the time Alfred had come across him in his back forty, with a rifle, staring at the ground. Alfred thought he'd shot something or even somebody,

so focussed was his gaze. But the object of his attention turned out to be a used condom.

"Somebody's been screwing in grandpa's woods,"
he'd said.

Grandpa. As if Alfred were any more than five
years older than Jimmy Drake. And no matter how old
Alfred Beel might be, he would never have the time or
inclination to stand staring at a used condom on the
forest floor.

"Better put an electric fence up around the place,"
was Jimmy's advice.

"Can you guarantee it would keep you out?" Alfred
had asked.

Jimmy was an ass and Alfred wanted to go home already but the waitress came by and Jimmy ordered another round. Fine, if he was planning to pay.

"So it really wasn't just because of the girl I made
my announcement; it was more the whole family,"
Drake said, apropos of what, Alfred had no idea.

"What announcement?" Alfred asked. "What are
you talking about?"

"At the school. They let me make announcements
from time to time. So, I thought why not weigh in on
the whole issue? Like you, I'm a little tired of everybody missing the point. Plus, the Farrells, like I said,
who needs them? So I said something to the effect of
some individual needs to take a good hard look at her
or himself and ask her or himself if she or he can live
another day without coming forward and that she or
he owes that much to the people of Flax and in particular the Decker family. And then I said, this isn't a

game of snakes and *ladders*. This is real life."

"You said that over the PA system? They let you say that?"

"Why not? I'm entitled to my opinion. You seem to agree and Reg needs somebody helping him out."

"Well, yes, but I wouldn't grab a bullhorn and shout it out in the streets of Flax. I restricted my comments—and in fact they were empirical observations, not opinions, to an officer of the law. So what did the principal say?"

"He sent me home. Told me he thought I needed some rest. That's what we've come to. You tell the truth—you need a rest. Like I said, that's what we've come to. At any rate, Reg'll be pretty happy when he finds out. At last somebody does something."

Adrian decided to go straight to Decker Motors after school. He was back on the bike. The vehicle of the genus bicycle no longer seemed haunted, although if you stood a bicycle on its kickstand and took a long hard look at it, what did it most resemble? A skeleton. That is correct. Something buried and dug up, or interred and exhumed as people in Flax said. Somebody thought Cheryl should be exhumed for another look—Adrian wasn't sure who—but if that were to happen a part of him would be relieved, knowing as he did that Cheryl might still be alive, just breathing slowly like a bear in hibernation or a person under anaesthetic. Cheryl would be dug up alive and everything would return to normal. A bike would be a bike; a tree, a tree. Only certain birds and diseases would remain on the to-be-avoided list.

And if Cheryl were irreversibly dead and even deteriorating with no hope for an Easter brand of miracle, then what? A quick ride on the bicycle to Minnow Lake, aiming for the channel, the only depth with sufficient water to drown a person on a bike. Though, knowing the lake bottom as he did, fifty feet from shore Adrian would find his wheels trapped in a foot of elemental muck—Mu on the periodic table, a new one—and tied up in the white stems of thousands of water lilies. Nice enough when they had flowers but with just the pad, more like a pudding skin or even a tomato soup skin on the surface of that lake. He would simply have to stay put. And if these were the days of the Roman myths or the Greek legends, Adrian Drury would become a mountain or constellation, but these were not those days, nor were they the days of 30 A.D. and the rolling away of the tombstone.

The new cars were arriving and the seventies were being parked on the outskirts, like so many bad memories you wish had engines and could simply drive themselves away. Adrian made a mental note to tell Randy the future clearly arrived in cars, in cars upon trucks, and well ahead of its time. Forget that dump, Farrell. Adrian sure would have liked one of those Cougars but the chances of the dentist buying a Cougar were as remote as the likelihood that Skokie, through a trillion nuclear fissions of scattered ash, would reassemble herself and amble down Huron Drive.

Adrian propped up the bike and went inside the dealership. Rocket Lalonde was a good manager and a failed football hero. And also, he never had a girl-friend, not since the Lesley Rochon story. Somebody said they still saw each other but it was a secret. He had a wrecked knee, which he thought nobody believed. He thought they thought he was making excuses for not going to the States on his scholarship. At least once a week, Rocket Lalonde had to say to somebody: you should see the x-rays. Looks like a squid growing out of my knee where there should be tendons. And all that was fine. Adrian was prepared to listen to any number of stories and excuses in exchange for recent informa-tion on (a) Reg and (b) Loretta. Maybe here's hoping Maddy had killed Cheryl but if the domino effects in-cluded Reg—everyone was waiting for him to fly that chopper into Minnow Lake—and Loretta—people were certain she'd driven her car and herself into Turtle Bay—then, well, Adrian would require a fate worse than suicide. Perhaps dissection in the biology lab of Flax Composite, vivisection Rose had said they called it when you were still alive.

The office smelled like burnt coffee. Looked like Rocket had let the pot singe itself into a brown, topo-graphical map of blistery residue amid knocked-over Styrofoam cups and plastic spoons stuck in hardened pools of Coffee-Mate paste. All proof Reg and Loretta were nowhere nearby. Rocket was in the showroom opening doors and closing them, presumably to create the sound of a car door slamming in an indoor show-room. An all's well kind of sound and therefore out of place in Flax but once in a while foreshadowing made an appearance in real life situations.

Noticing a petition on the bulletin board, Adrian called out, "Hey Rocket, what's this?"

"What? Who's there?" asked Rocket. "Oh, it's you," he said, implying, presumably, the girl-killer. "That? That's a petition as you can see. Cornelia Laine brought it in. She wants the town to cancel Halloween this year. She says we've had enough horror for the time being and we don't need to celebrate it. Out of respect for Reg. I say, I don't think Reg will notice if it's cancelled or not."

Adrian felt dizzy, then woozy, certain a packaged lump of blood the size of a candy kiss was heading for a narrow valve. He sat down. "How can you cancel a day? Isn't it there stuck on the calendar? It's not like a math question or a cheque, is it?"

"Well, as you can see," said Rocket, "there aren't a whole helluva of lot of signatures. Isadora and Evelyn Coutts and they should really just count as one." Rocket took the swivel chair behind Reg's desk. "They're in here every other day. I call them the enquirers except for not national, local, I guess, or municipal. They're trying to put together a 'psychic map' or some such BS to locate Loretta. I had no idea they were into that kind of thing. Did you?"

"I heard they were a bit spooky, that they see their dead dad walking around and sometimes he writes messages through one of them or at least through her hand."

Rocket opened the stapler, checked the supply

within, and snapped it shut.

"So what do they say about Loretta?" Adrian asked.

"Nothing. They just repeatedly ask me for details about stuff like the look on Loretta's face when I saw her. They come up with these pairs of words. Was she seeming to be serene or overcome? Baffled or certain? I don't know, I say to them. Isn't there a point where you're so overcome you're serene? Same with baffled and certain. I don't know."

"Well, what did you tell them?"

"I have nothing to tell them. I say, our eyes met for maybe ten seconds. Loretta had the windows up. There was no sound. It was a slow roll-by. Just the snapping of twigs under the tires. Last time they wanted to know if she was listening to music. I said 'I DON'T KNOW,' just like that, loud for emphasis, and they haven't been back." Rocket put his head in his hands.

"There's a cup out there on one of the cars. Do you want me to go get it?" Adrian offered.

"Sure."

Seconds later, "It's just cold coffee with white scum," Adrian observed.

"Dump it in the sink there where the coffee pot is. I know the place is a mess. I've got goddam Clive Decker on my case so it's hard to forget."

"Clive Decker?"

"Yes, yes. Him and his big meaty face, implying that I'm not watching the place closely enough. Notice the bits of paper and plastic bags in the lot, he asks. Dust on the cars? He has to count them, Reg probably tells him to. So count away. As if I would ever want another Ford product. Reg more or less commanded me to buy the one I'm driving now, the piece of junk with the recurring ignition problem."

"So Reg doesn't come around at all?"

"No he does not. I go around *there* and then people come around *here* asking how he is. Reverend Rochon swung by yesterday. And Jimmy Drake although at least he doesn't ask, he tells. He runs around town saying Reg reminds him of an electric chair, saying having Reg holed up in his house is like a human electric chair plugged into the centre of town. Do I agree, he wants to know?"

"And?"

"No I don't think he looks like a damn chair. I'll tell you what he does look like though. He looks like a person in the care of a dog. The roles have been reversed. Reg's dog, Pellett, seems to be the custodian, seems to be the one with the haircut, the one most recently bathed, and the one with better manners. Pellett comes to the door and wags me inside, although Reg is friendly enough once the ice has been broken. 'You can give away the seventies as far as I'm concerned,' he says. 'Give them to your friends. But don't tell Clive I said that.' Then he writes a cheque for almost twice my usual wage. Apart from his looks, Reg doesn't seem that bad."

Ila pulled in then, drew up close to the office window, with Anastasia in the front and Laura in the back, climbed out of the car in a rusty red suit and nothing on her head for a change, black hair tied in a knot. "What's this I hear," she wanted to know, swinging the door open, "about a petition to cancel Halloween?"

"Oh nothing," Rocket said. "It's all downright wearying, truth be told. Cornelia Laine..."

"Yes, I thought so. Cornelia Laine. Well, I have decorated for the event and I am not undecorating so the girls and I have written up an opposing petition which you are both invited to sign. How are you by the way, Adrian?" she asked, mussing his hair. "Sign right here beneath Laura's name." And he did, thrilled he would have to admit, by this unexpected brush with all that was Van Epp. Suddenly confident that no matter what, in Flax, Ontario, Halloween would arrive, driving a rusty orange car, smelling the opposite of new-car smell, smelling of abandoned gourd, wet stringy fibre turning to furry mould and caving in at the bottom. An occasion to look forward to nonetheless.

It would all blow over soon. If Maddy Farrell stood still long enough, this recent nimbus of events would blow away above her head like a time lapse of vicious thunderclouds in from the west, rolled up neatly by the geometry of pressure systems and dumped into the vast Atlantic, leaving nothing but high white clouds. Rows of thumbnails in the sky, which at sunset would appear to have been painted with Greta Leopold's *Pink Satin* by Helena Rubenstein. Greta kept a ready supply on the top shelf of her locker—first aid for any high school girl with a run in her nylon. She also had a pharmacy stocked with aspirin and pads and tampons, the currency of Greta P. Leopold. She might be short and stocky and from East Flax but she knew how to interrupt the flow of human need like a capitalist. She herself said that.

Not Maddy. She used to at least believe she could stand in the hallway of this institution and manage, tentatively and with great concentration, as if the long and shiny corridors were made of ice and only she was left in smooth-soled shoes. Not now. Now the ice had melted and she had fallen through and all around and above her head the others were buzzing with the octane of motorboats, girls in groups like precision water skiers in a pyramid, everyone in position.

No one had said anything out loud and this was a fact. If someone really thought something surely he or she would have said so and it would have by now got back to Greta. Maddy wanted to ask if she had heard anything—that's all she would have to say—but what if the answer turned out to be yes? Greta would tell the truth. Her square, hard head was not built for protecting others' feelings. She would say, "Frankly, yes there are those factions who believe you killed Cheryl Decker but they are in the minority. I wouldn't let it get me down."

"Oh no. Not me," Maddy would say.

Maddy had never approved of her own face but her body she had begun to admire, especially the back, which she examined with the help of a hand mirror, thinking it an error in evolution that the human animal could never see its own best feature up close. Not only was it a pleasure to look at, being covered with the longest and most flawless and hairless expanse of skin, not only did it show off the symmetry of its bones, but in the event of a wound or sore or infection, then what? How did one bandage the back? Watch your back, people said, and Maddy wished she could because now in the halls of Flax High she had the unpleasant sensation her back was showing.

When you were pregnant, you showed. Maybe when you were guilty or presumed guilty, you showed in other ways. Swelling, lumps, maybe one night in Cora's attic she had swallowed a small animal that was now trapped between her muscles and skin, its desperate scurrying visible beneath her shirt and along her neck line. Tense your muscles and maybe you could suffocate the little thing. Or wait long enough and it would be digested by your bloodstream, carried off by the white blood cells. There had to be some end in sight. The detective had been and gone and since then, nothing. The blowing over must have begun.

And there was physics class with Rose Drury. They no longer talked much; Maddy preferred not to ask for help, she wanted something else. In physics, Maddy wanted the frantic little animal to show its silhouette, crawl down her left arm, the one closer to Rose on her science room stool, and pull her hand onto Rose's. She was in love with her and physics was, after all, the class of unlikely possibility. Miss Eustace had done her best to inflame them with the splendour and parsimony of Einstein's theory. Fine. Time might be a dimension but Maddy preferred to think of it as furniture that could be moved around and then replaced. Sit upon it and conjure up a future arrangement, move it all back and behind the current day so that what you had done was in fact still a plan, kissing Rose Drury a fantasy yet to be acted upon.

No, Maddy no longer wanted help from Rose. She lay awake inventing questions she could ask Miss Eustace, questions that would ricochet off the lab table and astound Rose Drury. What, for example, if a fish could get moving the same speed as water, would it then cease to lose time? Would it travel inside the same moment for as long as it kept pace with the water, she wanted to ask Miss Eustace? And what if the fish and the water proceeded to freeze at the same rate and moved in tandem? Would the fish then be stuck in both time and ice? Perhaps if the fish were lucky, it would be suspended in a moment of pure happiness, but that seemed unlikely even in physics. Despite being arrested and frozen, the sensation of happiness would find a way to free itself from the fish's frail and narrow skull, ease its way through the ice and away. Not everything was subject to the law of E equals mc squared, was it Miss Eustace?

What would Rose think of that? What did Rose think period? Maddy did not know and did not ask. She adhered to a superstitious belief that the two of them weren't allowed to think until spring, at which time they would find themselves in a clear channel of movement, a spidery connection of tributaries drawing them out of Flax.

People eddied around her at school. In the morning, some girls usually said hi, Ella for example, and

Greta, naturally. Because today was Friday, the hall was full of that hot anticipation she seemed always to be beyond, as if they were in the furnace ducts and she had got trapped in the cold air return. But never mind. She had seen Rose pull into the parking lot in her little car and the memory of its interior smell had consumed her like a plan. Everyone had plans on Friday and Rose's car was like the memory of a plan that could pull ahead and meet her somewhere; it was not entirely impossible, just ask Miss Eustace.

And now she couldn't remember her combination. She knew sooner or later the numbers would pull themselves from the sleeve of her memory but in the meantime Maddy stood and enjoyed the moment. Not remembering did not cause her panic. Instead, she found pleasure in this dangling suspension between forgetting and certain remembering. It was like knowing you will receive what you want, knowing a little door of cells with pictures would open and there it would be, your Christmas gifts, Rose Drury diving from the ski jump. An old memory catches up with an invented memory, a fantasy, and the two clasp hands like best friends at a science table. Voila. There it was. 22-3-36.

Yank. The lock opened and so did her locker door and there before her eyes was a sight she could not at first see, the way Randy's arrangements must appear to people unfamiliar with him, only worse. That gave way then to perfect sense, crystal clear but sick-making like an exam question you know you cannot answer. There, hanging by a string from the hook in her locker was a Barbie doll dressed in a silky red shirt and white shorts, the school colours. Someone had taken the time to write fourteen on the front of the shirt, Maddy's jersey number. And the shorts... what was that yellow stain? Food colouring? Oh. Maddy had never known a moment quite like this, so hard and sudden it might actually burst your skin. Like Greta's brother and the frogs he liked to throw at the brick wall of their house. That was this moment, the wall approaching your damp frog skin.

Maddy stood. Next to her, to her right, was Greta Leopold who'd traded with someone for the locker next to Maddy's and to her left, no one, Carl Ippolito having been and gone. Greta was busy with her books, huffing and puffing with the effort of pulling them from her bag. She always did a lot of sighing, as if preparedness for the day were an exasperating nuisance, beneath her. Maddy's face would show something; she knew it would. She knew at the moment it likely looked the way it did to her Uncle Lloyd who liked to take her for drives, liked to brake and pull three-sixties and watch her face with a boxed up look of hunger. But the rest she could hide.

With Maddy's strength it was certainly no trouble at all to reach inside the locker and break the string, fold the doll in half, turn herself sideways and stuff it into the pocket of the jacket she still had on. Good thing the mornings were colder now. What would she have done without a pocket? Stood in the hall holding her Barbie like a six-foot five year old who'd maybe killed someone? No one had seen or at least apparently no one had seen but how could she know that? They could all be planning not to look; they could all have planned that last night.

Greta, now prepared for the morning, took notice of Maddy as she would and asked if something was wrong.

"No, I just felt a bit dizzy there for a minute."

"Are you due?"

"Am I what?"

"Due? Are you getting your period? Cuz if you need supplies, I'm the one who's got them."

Greta's voice sounded as if it were travelling through miles of flannel-lined tubing.

"No, that's not it. I'm fine."

"Are you sure? You look like you've seen a ghost. Tomorrow's Halloween you know, not today. "

"No, I'm fine. I'm fine."

"I'll see you in gym then," and Greta slammed her locker shut.

What would she do? She couldn't walk home and make a spectacle of herself—people would see and know why. Best, for today anyway, to pretend nothing had happened, just get through the day. Although the piles and piles of minutes and hours stacked before her seemed as impassable as the walls and lockers and doors and bodies everywhere she looked. But that was okay, that was okay. She could make it until bus time. For now, she would go to the bathroom until this strangeness had stopped, hope for not too many other girls' eyes turning to look, and find the last cubicle. Sit for a while and wonder: if your eyes froze open, could you see clear as a bell or would everything blur, like looking through ice cubes.

Adrian spends math class thinking about probability. He would like to ask his teacher, Miss Eccles, her opinion, although she is so dopey about any form of life outside of equations and logarithms she most likely—most probably—wouldn't even get what he was talking about. Suppose a guy, he wanted to say, sent four or five letters to another guy pretending to be a girl the other guy liked. And suppose the guy writing the letters had no idea how the girl he was impersonating talked or thought, and is a little on the learning disabled side but has used a dictionary and thesaurus to prevent spelling mistakes and repetitious use of words. What, then, is the probability the guy receiving the letters has figured out (a) it's not the girl writing them, and (b) it's Adrian Drury, the same guy who made the phone calls (pretending to be the same girl he's pretending to be in the letters)? If Adrian were to ask Miss Eccles, throwing in a few other unknowns such as how smart or not is Alfred Beel, but assuming he is at least as smart as most people, Miss Eccles would say, in the warm light of the math room, the probability is extremely high that he would be suspicious and very high that he would suspect Adrian Drury, having had a previous and similar experience involving the same variables, substituting telephone for mail.

And, since Alfred Beel called the police the last time, what is the probability that this time, when Adrian rides his bike to East Flax and back past the dance hall through the road allowance to Alfred's house to watch his disappointment as closely as he possibly can with the binoculars Rose gave him for Christmas, what are the chances Jerome Limb will be there in his pretend cop car and pretend uniform? What are the chances someone might go right off the rails like Jimmy Drake and shoot someone else? What are the chances of one more very ugly event?

Ditto, Miss Eccles would say. Math has a way of repeating itself; that's what makes it math.

Adrian stares hard at the outside world, which, for reasons unknown to math and science, always looks imaginary from inside school. The odds are against him but he doesn't care and maybe that is the definition of crazy. Graham Rochon would likely think so. He would certainly never concoct a story and drag it from his bedroom or expensive living room couch out past the window and into the streets where the doors are all shut and the snow is hanging on like glaciers in certain shady places. Might as well be the final days of the ice age out there.

But in this math room, today, life seems a little dreamy and better and why is that? Maybe because this is the one class Adrian is good at, consistently smart, or maybe it is the one class he shares with Laura Van Epp who is one row over and two desks up, sideways, with her legs crossed in the aisle, talking to Cassie Limb. Maybe because Randy Farrell is absent today.

Despite Miss Eccles's predictions, Adrian is going to pedal out to Alfred Beel's, hide behind a shrub, and wait for his eager, desperate, and lonely self to drag its hopeless hope for Loretta into the yard and look for her and wait for her. That's what Loretta wanted, that's what she said in her letter. Wait for me in the yard, my love. We have no time to waste. As if that made any sense. Wouldn't she come into the house? Wouldn't they throw their clothes off and do it on the kitchen table?

Adrian can only hope Alfred is blind to such unlikely details but, as Miss Eccles would likely say, most people aren't. So what? He's going right after school. By four o'clock he'll be watching a magnified Beel, savouring every facial tic of humiliation and pain. Ha ha. He might need to disguise his laughter but laugh he would. Maybe he'd try impersonating a gleeful crow or a slap-happy seagull, make the old guy feel like he's really cracking up, like he's hearing things. If only Adrian could throw his voice, or throw Loretta's voice, speak a few words into his hand and toss them into the tree above Beel's head. How great would that be? Hi Alfred. How's the handsomest man in the tri-county area? Is he looking forward to seeing me? With Adrian's throwing arm, he could aim his voice through an open window and into a cup Beel happened to be drinking from. "Hello, Alfred you sexy hunk of meat." Or even when he's in his car, driving by, "Alfred, I love the way the wind stirs up your Brylcreem-covered hair." According to the international rules of voice-throwing, the window would have to be open, Adrian thinks, watching Miss Eccles's lips move, recalling the day he learned the disappointing truth about ventriloquism. Rose lecturing: "It's just that guy talking without moving his lips."

"But his lips are moving."

"That's because he's not throwing his voice, you dummy."

"Oh."

Which was maybe another reason why he had to like Randy Farrell, for his epilepsy, for his ability to throw his own body, the next best thing to throwing your voice. Maybe that *was what he, Adrian Drury, was finally doing, throwing his body from Flax to East Flax, participating in the East Flax heave, a new sport, just added to the Paranormal Olympics. Ha ha. Adrian laughs out loud, transmigrating this error into a cough. At last he has found his vocation: superhuman acts of revenge. He'll say: I've come all this way to show you something, Beel. I have catapulted myself through three miles of space, over trees, swamp, and mysterious bog to tell you you can't blame this mess on me. You can blame it on your own, chest-damaged self. Look in the mirror, you old goat. Look in the mirror and listen to the loudspeaker because you'll hear it announce this year, the Paranormal Olympic gold in feats of record-straightening goes to... Adrian Drury of Flax, Canada.*

Reg had not bought groceries since the day Loretta vanished. People brought casseroles, usually in the late afternoon, knowing he was out mornings in the chopper. Women mostly. They stood on the front porch, wanting to have a look around at the domestic spectacle within. What did they expect to see? The thrill of the near miss, maybe, homely objects gone berserk, flatware like darts in the kitchen drywall. He left them standing, would not invite them in, closed the screen door on their warm, Pyrex curiosity. Other people ate strange concoctions of noodles and corn niblets and cheese. Only good thing was, sometimes he felt like a kid again, when other people's cooking tasted like bad habits.

Rainie came to the back door. She didn't expect in, which he appreciated. And she didn't bring a casserole but an entire meal on a plate under stretch wrap and a piece of pie in a wedge shape of Tupperware. He guessed she understood him more than most. If worse came to worst, she would pick things up for him from the grocery store. This business of food was a problem. The thought of entering Pond's IGA created an interior sensation Reg likened to an engine seizing; the inevitable solicitude and sorrowful glances from the housewives of Flax, not to mention the occasional senior citizen of his own sex, was more than Reg could endure. Add to that having to push a silver cart with a fold-down baby seat, and Reg felt the odometer on his heart turn to a row of zeros. Hadn't he made more adjustments in the past year than most men made in an entire lifespan? No, he was not going to the grocery store or the drug store or Lalonde's for a grilled cheese sandwich. Nor was he going to the dealership. Rocket had things under control and so what if sales were down a little? They were in the middle of a recession. And he could run the place from the kitchen as well as the front office; that's why God invented phones and assistant managers.

Speaking of God, he'd called the Reverend Philip Rochon twice now. First to ask: did the Reverend ever entertain the notion that God might be a member of the militia? A new recruit, perhaps, because his accuracy was nothing to write home about. Reg was pretty sure God had a gun with a galaxy-length scope and Reg Decker lined up in the crosshairs. He'd aimed two or three times now and missed, picking off his kids and maybe now his wife, all in a youthfully enthusiastic effort to destroy Reg. Next time he fired, he'd know to squeeze the trigger, not pull. Reg guessed one of the job risks God faced would be the absence of qualified advisors, and, he supposed, even if someone did have the balls to make a recommendation, chances were God wouldn't take it. Reg pictured God to be much like his brother Clive, a born know-it-all. In fact, if God were to take himself a Christian name, which why hadn't he by the way, Reg thought for sure it would be Clive. Jehovah Clive. "Has a nice ring, don't you think, Phil?"

The Reverend listened and was unflaggingly sympathetic but in the end, as Reg had predicted, suggested a visit to his son to sort out some of this anger and confusion.

Two days later, Reg called again to say no thank you, having thought it over, he'd maybe talk to Graham if things got worse, but he had a point he wanted to make. Didn't Philip find it a little ironic that as soon as any ordinary layman started taking God personally, started to think God might have an interest in his own life, albeit malicious, that layman was immediately under suspicion of lunacy? It was perfectly acceptable, once you'd undergone ordination, to stand at the front of a church and speak out loud to a deity no one had as yet seen with the human eye. But let Reg Decker attribute his own bad luck to a random, ornery marksman of a God and he'd be referred to the town shrink. Where exactly did the town of Flax draw the line between spiritual health and disease? "Anywhere it damn well wanted," Reg told Jimmy Drake later on. But Jimmy wasn't interested.

He'd shown up this evening, not his usual time, looking agitated, hair smeared to the wrong side and wearing slippers. He'd just called the vice-principal to tell him he might be a little late to work tomorrow, he had to take Jimmy Junior to see the asthma doctor in London, and the v-p said to him, funny thing you called, I was just going to call you.

Beneath his tight, white T-shirt, Jimmy's belly rose and fell: he was breathing like a very worried Pellett.

"Yeah? So?" asked Reg, enjoying the temporary absence of attention, the ever-wondering public concern.

"So he says why don't you take the day off? In fact, I might as well be honest with you, Jim. We're going to have to let you go."

Jimmy's eyes were perfect circles, coppery brown, polished with umbrage.

"Did you hear that Reg? He says, 'we're going to have to let you go. We just can't have announcements like the one you made and frankly, we've been looking at Farrell's rates for a while now.' He can start—guess when, Reg?—tomorrow. Of course, we'd give you your full two months' severance so you're not left in the lurch, says Greig." Jimmy fell into a chair, holding his face, staunching disbelief with the palms of his hands.

"I don't get it. What's he talking about announcements?"

"The announcement. Didn't I tell you? It was nothing. I just said over the PA system that the guilty party should come forward and this wasn't a game of snakes and ladders. Ladders because of Beel and the Farrell girl. Because I know she did it. I know she did. I'm just trying to reveal the truth and you should thank me for it, Reg. Everyone should but instead I get canned from my job. Well, I'm fighting it, that's for sure. No way is Frog Farrell..." and he stopped talking to concentrate on breathing. Pellett drew near, mistaking the tight inhalations of Jimmy's anguish for whistling.

"But Jimmy, you don't have any proof and besides you're the *custodian*. I can kind of see Greig's point. Not that there's anything wrong with being the custodian but it's just not done. I know you're talking about my daughter and I appreciate the concern but to be perfectly honest, I don't think anybody did it."

The circular eyes blinked. "You don't think anybody did it? What's that supposed to mean? Somebody did it. For every event that happens, there's a somebody doing it. And that's *more* than a theory, Reginald, that's a law of nature," said Jimmy, breathing more comfortably now, mopping sweat from his brow with an oily handkerchief.

"Not necessarily. With Richard and Cheryl, I blame God. I think God was behind it from the get-go. That's where I lay the blame and that's why I like being up in that chopper. I feel like any day now God and I might be able to have a little showdown up there. It only seems fair. I take my gun along just in case I see him. Don't tell Clive though, for God's sake. Or for something's sake, the devil's maybe, I don't know. It's a little bit of fun. God the rifleman versus Reg the pilot."

"What gun?" Jimmy wanted to know.

"You think I'm off my rocker, don't you?" asked Reg, carefully peeling the plastic wrap away from his dinner. "Well, anyway, to answer your question, my old twenty-two. I've actually thought of asking if I could borrow your three-oh-three. I feel a scope would improve my accuracy."

Jimmy had no response.

"Did I tell you I've heard from Loretta?" said Reg, dipping a green bean into mashed potato. "Not in so many words, but in a kind of telepathy, I guess. I picked it up last night, a weak but yet strong, if you know what I mean, signal from the west. She's on her way back. Should be here in the next week to ten days. I'll just keep listening—well, it's not really listening—tuning, I guess, attuning myself to the signal."

"Yeah," said Jimmy. "You should."

"Your eyes look kinda watery," Reg said. "I know the place smells. It's the garbage and especially the onions. I've been eating lots of onions when there's no casseroles. I have to get the place cleaned up before Loretta gets back. Sorry about the smell."

Jimmy rubbed his eyes. "The smell's not a big deal. I can give you a hand, if you want. I am a custodian, after all."

While factions of boys she barely knew crowded by, Rose waited in the shop wing, her back to the metal door of Randy's locker. Most of these boymen did not carry books because books were not an accessory to shop classes, and so Rose felt a little endangered as if she were in a jail or reform school. A cold breeze shouldered its way against the movement of students from the door at the end of the hall, propped open at this time of day to allow smokers access to a blacktopped corner of the parking lot. And this too seemed vaguely correctional. Wasn't the yard where people got knifed? Rose could see now why Adrian had traded with someone to have a locker in the academic wing.

On either side of Randy's locker, boys kicked doors shut with a fury Rose might have associated with attempted murder. If only one could take the energy in this hall and put it to some use. These boys were nothing more than packages of apathy wrapped in large new muscles.

Randy was late but at least he was not six feet tall; he was an agreeable height and weight and smiled and said, "If Maddy finds out I took that doll, she'll kill me and she'll have Mom helping her. They're both obsessed with it. But Mom said yesterday to put it away and leave it so I'm hoping they won't notice it's gone. Mom has it in a drawer with her tablecloths as if it's a family heirloom or something even though we've only had it for four or five days. Plus, they keep it in a lunch bag. Don't ask me why. I only live there."

Randy's locker was a spectacle of efficiency, his jacket and book bags hanging from two opposite hooks, his books lined up on the floor, spines exposed next to what seemed to be a chunk of car floor mat, presumably for winter boot storage. And on the top shelf where most people threw lunches, papers, notes to parents, was the arrangement of plastic farm animals.

"How do you keep them standing in a row like that?"

"Glue. They're glued in place."

"Don't these guys around you give you a hard time?"

"No. They don't care. But Jimmy Drake Senior'll likely care at the end of the year when he has to deal with all those little hooves stuck in white paste. Anyway, here's what the doll looks like." From the book bag he pulled a smaller bag, brown and wrinkled like a worried newborn, and out of it came the doll, jolting Rose's heart with a nauseated beat. The doll was in fact a Ken with a crown of Brillo pad taped to its head. And there was the uniform; French seams leaving no doubt Anastasia had been the tailor and the number four-teen, the same jersey that had debuted in the Polaroid. Rose straightened it, then bent it in half, observing the yellow stain, feeling sicker than any twentieth century combination of virus and infection, more like the plague, more like a rapid loss of bone density.

"Here," Rose said. "You can put it away."

"Kinda sick, huh? But that's Jimmy Drake Junior. He's an asshole."

Hadn't he noticed it was a Ken? Rose didn't want to ask.

"My dad and I are going up to the salt mines tonight," Randy said, shoving the doll into its paper bag housing. "They stay open later on Wednesdays. I told Adrian he could come. Did he tell you we're doing a project together? The story of salt in Huron County."

"He hasn't mentioned it," Rose said, a rhythmic slamming of locker doors from somewhere, like machine gun fire, then gales of laughter. "What's Maddy going to do?"

"I don't know. Right now she's working for Beel. Kind of a housekeeper, I guess."

The smell of ham and roast beef and oranges was nerve-wracking. A hall should not smell so demandingly of school lunches. Did these people ever go to the cafeteria? Apparently not.

"Well, do Maddy a favour and don't say anything to your friends about seeing the doll. Especially that Van Epp in particular."

"I won't. Don't worry. I only told Adrian to tell you to bring it because I just wanted to know for Maddy's sake. I can't explain it."

"That's okay. I can't explain my plastic farm animals."

No way would she say anything to Anastasia. To mention the doll would be to endure her knowing smile, watch it spread across her face in rows of white teeth enameled with all you could never hope to understand.

After lunch, Rose had English. One and a half hours of free time if she skipped. The time had come to speak to Maddy. Talk some sense into her. The drive was less than fifteen minutes and even if she couldn't find Maddy, she could see East Flax and Minnow Lake, maybe replace the thoughts of the Ken doll with the look of the red and orange trees on the escarpment. Rose liked the way they grew right to the shore like kids wanting to run downhill. Nice, innocent kids, no one evil and vindictive like Anastasia or Jimmy Drake.

But the Ken doll was sticky like nausea or weather and attached itself to everything, the steering wheel of Foster Limb's Vega and even the music on the radio. Canned Heat: the name alone was enough to turn your stomach. Rose found another channel with talk and pleasantries. Pleasantries can be swallowed like medicine. The sky, for example, the western sky is as blue as a very clear and helpful thought. And the trees are indeed red and orange just as they are in Flax, belonging to the same tribe as they do, the maple tribe and the elm. Rose will say this to Maddy. But perhaps the tribes out here are more peace-loving than those in town; she cannot imagine these tenuous leaves or saddened trunks capable of such mean-spiritedness as the Ken doll, which would have been Anastasia's idea; Jimmy Junior could not have come up with that. And what was beneath the uniform? What would Jimmy have drawn beneath those shorts, those food colouring shorts? Maddy would have looked the minute she was alone.

Rose had to stop the car, she needed some autumn air. She was in the curves now, the place she'd stopped her bike that first ride out, and stepping onto that cool, worn road, smooth as a forehead, she found the nausea gone. But not for Maddy it wouldn't be. For Maddy it would be a long influenza, a trail of foods gone bad.

Maddy, Maddy, Maddy, Rose would say. I can help

you. I know about your troubles. Speaking of tribes, I know of some others. Humiliation and shame, for example, fellow members. I may not have had a great deal of first-hand knowledge but through my brother, well, I know enough. I know what it's like. It's like breathing bad air, air that has travelled up and out of the sediment of your own self and past all your worst memories and fears, blub, blub, blub. Old gas you recognize as your own but, so what? Who cares? I've learned that much from Adrian. There's not much to say but just being there in the vicinity can help, spending time together in the shambles of the periodic table—that's what Adrian calls it—just me being around will help your worries lift and float away. You'll see.

She would say all of this to Maddy. Speak it like a declaration or a treaty, confident words that would wrap themselves around the nearest birch and later be found, miraculous and comforting in parchment, delivered to an archive. Life was good.

First, the store. Unrecognizable as a store to any outsider except for the Drink Pepsi crossbar on the door. What type of store was nameless? If Rose Drury were to run this store, it would have a name and flowers outside in pots and pails, damp stains on the sidewalk from early morning watering and chairs for the mollusc men. And a pop machine filled with ice water cold enough to hurt the customer's hand, not a meat cooler with thirty-year-old bacteria and a roaring engine. And lights.

No one was at the till. The place was empty and silent. Frog would be out and Angel, maybe upstairs on the bed resting her anger and resentment, two big earrings she'd forgotten to pull off and therefore deepening her discomfort at every toss and turn. Perhaps customers at the Farrells' store were expected to serve themselves, use the till on the honour system.

Rose checked her funds. She hadn't had lunch and was in the mood for an ice cream sandwich. Taking a deep breath so as not to have to endure the freezer smell of the ice cream locker, as Angel called it, Rose rooted through the products. The inside walls of the freezer were coated in so much frost, Rose thought of getting the ice scraper from her car, had to resist the urge in fact, of the certain pleasure of peeling away rime like loose skin. She made her selection and awaited service. What was that smell? The chairs, of course, the chairs smelled of old men, Brylcreem, and dandruff and fabric that no longer expected to be washed or vacuumed, home to an advanced civilization of dust mites. Under an electron microscope you might see them building pyramids out of Alfred Beel's parings.

"Hello?" Maybe Angel was in the attic changing Maddy's sheets. Or maybe she'd gone to Mrs. Leopold's to settle some old scores. Was it possible Angel had a gun? Yes, very. But the Gremlin was parked outside. Well. Rose walked around the counter and peeked through the beaded curtain. Nothing but the unmatched tableware of the Farrell family, promotional items for 7-Up and the individual serving boxes of cereal they sometimes ate, not bothering with bowls. Maybe she would just pay and leave. The till couldn't be that difficult, although up close and alone with it, Rose wondered if it might just come to life if left under water, on the bottom of the lake for example. Seemed capable of moving two or three inches per year through the slow depression of its keys.

The ice cream sandwich was twenty-five cents— Rose had a quarter, so simply push any key and the drawer should spring open. But despite the musical clang of metal workings, nothing happened. Now what? Total. Of course. Push total. And voila, the drawer expelled itself in one smooth, unhurried motion. This was an unurgent till, confident its operator had cash in hand. Rose dropped the quarter in with its brothers and closed the drawer. For that moment, she could have been a Farrell.

"What...are you doing?" The space dividing the question leaving room to suggest, Rose Drury, I should have known you'd try something like this. I did, in fact.

And Rose answering, smooth as the cash drawer, "I bought an ice cream sandwich. I thought, better to put the money in the till than leave it on the counter with a note."

"That's what you thought. Well, and I thought I had told you not to touch the till."

"Yes, yes you did. But I thought this was an exceptional circumstance."

Angel shook her head in dismay. "No one obeys anymore. The kids aren't afraid to disobey. When I was your age, well, maybe a little younger, I was afraid." With both hands, she pushed her hair back from her face, then sighed, "Oh, maybe I wasn't. I don't know.

I was asleep. What are you doing here anyway? No school today?"

"I have a spare. I thought I'd see what Maddy's doing."

"What Maddy's doing? Well, what do you suppose Maddy's doing?" Angel lit a cigarette. She was beautiful and mean and weary and her hair was not obeying either as she picked a fleck of tobacco from her tongue.

"I heard she's working for Beel more now, almost like a full-time housekeeper."

"You heard? News gets around. Who'd you hear from?"

"From Randy."

"A reliable source."

"Is it not true?"

"Oh, it's a little bit true. I wouldn't go so far as to call her an almost full-time housekeeper but she's helping him out more."

"Then Randy *is* a reliable source," said Rose.

"That's what I said. I mean what I say."

"So do I."

"Do you?"

Rose was trapped between the counter and the wall and Angel Farrell, wondering if Angel might go so far as to slap her, wondering if she might actually hope she would.

"Yes, in fact, I do mean what I say," Rose answered.

"*Yes, in fact, I do mean what I say.*" Angel imitated Rose with a vicious inflection. "Well, I think you may have said to Maddy in one way or another that she could rely on you and that has not been proven to be

the case, has it? Your little friend with her doll art—
that's the kind of stunt that can really ruin a person's
day."

"I had nothing to do with that."

Angel took a deep drag on her cigarette, exhaling
from the side of her mouth like a gangster. "I'd like to
believe that but there are forty years of life in this part
of the world piled up inside this skull of mine and each
one has a vote and they are unanimous in their skep-
ticism where Rose Drury is concerned. But regardless
of that, go see her. She's either at Beel's or the dance
hall. I'm sure no further harm can be done. No, on
second thought, I'm not sure of that at all. But never
mind."

Angel allowed Rose to pass and exit the store, the
fully wrapped ice cream sandwich softening in her
hand, a ridiculousness, like all things going soft, Graham Rochon's penis in her mouth for instance. She
dropped the thing in the garbage can. She would go to
Beel's but only past. He hated her for being the dentist's daughter, which was fair enough, and refreshing
as Angel's rage. She'd go past Beel's and up the road allowance and if Maddy wasn't at the dance hall, so be
it. There would be other opportunities. The place was
still beautiful and she still loved it. Here was the worst
of the flooded part where nobody swam, shallow with
stumps and lily pads and frogs sleeping with their eyes
closed against a comforter of warm mud. Here was the
cemetery with tilted headstones and caved-in caskets,
and now fields, also mud, in support of stubble, hard
stubble of corn and some ploughed under already,

roots uptorn and gasping like fish on shore. Trees.
That was a sugar bush, Maddy said, and nothing now
but road and fence and Reg Decker flying overhead.

Rose's hands were sweating. The steering wheel
was too warm. Foster Limb had gripped it too hard and
for too long and now look. Her armpits were sweaty
too. Anastasia condemned all armpit sweaters as nervous Nellies. Only volleyball caused a slight moistening
of hers, nothing else. Rose would never have had the
courage to enter the Beel homestead. From the road it
seemed as alien as Muriel Cobb's friend's house in
Rosedale with its one lone soul shuffling amongst the
days. Maddy, Maddy, Maddy, stay away from him. Stay
away and come back to school.

Rose wanted Maddy to be at the dance hall and it
was an uphill want that drained the blood from parts
of her even though she was in the Vega. Small
branches and trees broke beneath its tires and first gear
was hardly low enough. Rose needed a gear somewhere
between first and desperate, something grinding like a
jaw on cold leaves and slippery roots. She didn't know
where Loretta Decker had last been seen and neither
did she care. People said she was in the bog, her car
was in the bog, she and her car were in the bog and
were now rising. The roof of her car would break the
surface any day now, reflecting the sun's rays, perhaps
seen by Reg from the air and they'd have to get a crane
to pull her out, a crane and some special hooks and
cables. It would be a big mess, bigger than any previous
mess and involving many levels of authority, the police
and maybe the detective from London, the coroner,

the fire department. Graham Rochon would have to see a few people traumatized by horror, by the look of Loretta's hair and face. Only Adrian would rouse himself from depression for this real-life horror movie. And she and Maddy would quietly leave town.

The car made the journey to the parking lot and fell silent. Yes, Maddy Farrell was in. There was the sound of the basketball on wood. Maybe they could leave this very minute. What was wrong with it, after all, this precise moment, that is? Seemed rather unused by the present because the present was barely interested. All of Flax and East Flax was looking in another direction, awaiting the next moment while this one sat. Come on, Maddy. Let's go. Let's drive to Memphis or Quebec City. We'll go to school. I can help you study. No one will know about Cheryl Decker or the Ken doll. Let's go.

Rose's knuckles hurt against the solid dance hall door. Inside, the bouncing stopped, a metronome in mid-swing, and Rose said, "Maddy! It's me. Open the door."

No response. Rose turned the knob, found it locked. "Maddy! It's Rose. Open up the door. I want to talk to you."

This was Maddy at her pig-headed worst. The silence was charged with her thoughts. But aha. Rose had an idea. She'd put the ladder to a window. If Maddy could only see her, she would open the door. Rose had faith in her face and its influence. The ladder was in the shed and Rose hauled it out, grotesque as it was with old guilt and false accusations and leaned it against the dance hall. It wasn't an extension ladder, just a plain old construction, ten feet tall but enough to get to the low dance hall windows. And one was open, thank God. Rose climbed like a tradesman, a roofer, bouncing along the rungs and looked and there was Maddy at the far end, taking shots from the line. She was in her uniform.

"Maddy. I'm here. I'm here at the window."

Maddy turned, holding the ball.

"Let me in. I want to talk to you."

Maddy looked at the clock on the wall. "Shouldn't you be in English?"

"Yes but so what? So what? Let me in."

Turning her back to Rose, Maddy took a shot, hitting the rim.

"You're not going to unlock the door are you? I know a little bit about you and it's enough to know that." Rose was shouting.

Maddy jogged for the ball, returned to the line, and threw once more.

"You know," Rose said, "you're not the only person in the world who's ever been made fun of or accused. My brother lives and breathes that stuff." The humiliation speech was turning cold in her mind, seemed as unappetizing now as the ice cream sandwich in the garbage can, sticky liquid mingling with wax paper and cigarettes.

"Well, your brother is one person and you're another."

"Oh now that's profound, Maddy Farrell. I never thought of that before."

Maddy walked closer to the window. She was spinning the ball on the tip of a finger. "Did it ever occur to you, Rose Drury, that there's three miles between Flax and East Flax for a reason?"

She had been practicing this line, Rose could tell. "No it didn't. What reason would that be?"

Maddy turned her back and threw from the centre of the court. "You're not as smart as I originally thought." She made the basket, and then disappeared into the entranceway. She was going to open the door after all. Rose's knees gave a little curtsy of delight. But no, Maddy was back already and carrying a long stick, the type teachers used to pull down screens and prepare for the incongruous thrill and disappointment of movies in class. Maddy was threading the hook into the pull of the blind on Rose's window. She was pulling down the blind. And now she was reaching beneath the blind and closing the window with an authoritative thump.

Angel Cobb Farrell stood in the dance hall shed awaiting the sound of Jimmy's feet on the parking lot gravel. She'd insisted on his leaving his car at the entrance to Dance Hall Road, creating the impression he'd walked into Turtle Bay bog, as people did this time of year, to see the geese on their migratory route. Current events between Jimmy and Frog necessitated extreme caution and Jimmy had not required much convincing of that. "Don't you worry. I'll take whatever precautions are necessary. I got spooked the last time I was out there. And despite the fact your husband is no friend of mine, I'd rather not rub it in his face. He's nowhere as oblivious as you think. Nobody is. Even animals fight over mating. You don't have to be able to think in words to get the drift. Not that I'm implying Frog can't think in words."

"I know, I know," said Angel, reassuringly. He wasn't going to wriggle out of this. "I just want to patch things up with you. Maybe I was too harsh about the pictures. That wasn't your fault after all. But this time, just to be on the safe side, I'd rather meet someplace where there aren't likely to be any cameras."

"But what if somebody sees me walking up Dance Hall Road instead of into the trees towards the bog? It's not going to be that late. People are still up and about."

"C'mon, Jimmy. You think they've never seen me parking on the street and walking up your alley? It's your turn to take a risk or two here, Mr. Drake."

"All right, all right."

"Eleven o'clock at the dance hall. I'll wait for you in the shed. I'll tell Frog I'm playing bridge with Muriel. That's usually a Saturday night thing."

And she was pretty sure the voice hadn't given her away. Other people's untrained voices betrayed them daily, but Angel's had long ago been to obedience school and could easily purr or bark or ask for a cracker when the need arose. When the time came to leave,

she stuffed a can of lighter fluid in her purse and cheer-
ily said her farewells to Frog. He had looked up from
The Reminder long enough to say sure thing. The only
glitch being she'd had to leave at eight-thirty, park the
car in the road allowance, and entertain herself for an
eternity.

The place did not scare her but she could see how
it might if she weren't Angel Cobb. If she were Jimmy,
which, thank the Lord, she was not. You had to be very
careful with that man. Along with all his other failings,
he was too emotional; he let his imagination run wild
and that was the literal truth. His imagination was like
a herd of wild horses. Leave it alone, walk quietly
around it, and you would be fine. But go running into
its midst, waving your arms and frantic, and the herd
would have no choice but to run wild. Possibly flatten
you with its yellow hooves or at the very least, fail to
show up because he'd shit himself with fear.

Angel's imagination did not run wild. It moved in
a single line like a predator, a bobcat or maybe a panther, a creature more inclined to stalking and revenge,
not skittishness and hooves. And right now, waiting in
this shed, she would confess, once again, to being so
angry she could have stripped herself naked, stood on
the edge of what people called the escarpment, and
glowed red like a bit of sunrise from wherever the sun
might be, Fiji or Tahiti or Guam. The type of morning
that causes people and animals to wither back inside
because it's going to be another scorcher.

The doll in Maddy's locker was too much. No one
but Maddy knew Maddy's combination, so Jimmy

Drake Junior had to be involved and that made Jimmy Drake Senior an accessory. They had to be dealt with. They were two of a kind, the kind that liked to take a situation that was a little precarious and, not exactly give it a shove, but brush against it, watch it crash and clatter in a million bits of broken glass and plastic and bone and then ask, what happened here? Anything I can do to help? If Angel were to get rid of the two of them, the town would thank her sooner or later. Why, they'd probably give her a gift basket like the one her sister got for planting bulbs in small public spaces. Not unlike the growth of perennials, town beautification would be the end result of Jimmy's mysterious disappearance. Her only hope was that the basket be filled with lotions and hair products and not tinned meats and crackers. Muriel had thrown most of it out. But of course she couldn't get rid of Jimmy or his son; the panther needed to come up with a more realistic solution.

Angel pushed the door open for some air.

Now Maddy was saying she wanted to quit school and once Maddy got her mind set on something, there was little anyone could do to change it. The idea of Maddy quitting school, mooning from room to room, thumping up and down the dance hall with a basketball, was too much for Angel. This was the daughter she wanted moving on and moving out, taking her big body and appetite elsewhere. It could happen. Maddy was no genius but with her athletic skills, some school, someplace would want her so much they would pay to enlist her on the team. People from Windsor had already been to the school to watch her and there were scouts coming from Michigan next week. Next week, Angel had screamed at Maddy earlier today. Angel wanted Maddy to go to Michigan. My daughter's in Michigan, she wanted to say, on a scholarship. No, actually, I don't have any pictures of her.

It wasn't just the quitting school. Maddy might be homely and a teen-recluse but she had not done anything to harm Cheryl Decker and most people knew that. But the allegation, the combination of blame and shame stirred up the lively pool of quicksand that had long ago replaced Angel's stomach. She saw it as a place where accusations plopped with a sound like sex, slowly sank and were gradually drowned by her own muddy workings. She supposed her insides were much like a bog. Didn't bogs preserve those bog men found in Ireland or Iceland? Hundreds of years old and yet fingerprints intact. Now the Turtle Bay bog, that would scare her, were she forced to tent on its shores for the night. That's where they found the body of the doctor's wife from Telluride; that's where they supposed Loretta was.

She'd spent some time looking at the sky, even lay down in a rootless break between the trees right on the edge of the escarpment. She could hear the lake, draining through the flume and into the creek, sounding like a faucet. And all the stars. Were they really far-off suns or were they places filled with people like her, people in a rage, lighting up the night sky with their kilowatts of revenge? In the morning, she supposed they went inside, and so did she then, relocating to the musty shed.

What a gloomy little box. Not even Angel's anger was enough to shed any light in this interior, absolute pitch black and no place to sit and the smell, Angel realized after some concentration, was the smell of Frog Farrell—the odour of the implements of repair. That was Frog, Mr. Fix-it. A real fixer-upper. Which would explain why he had managed so resolutely to resist her efforts at fixing him up and making of him another man. She'd thought long ago she had the ingredients for someone a little bit more like Clive Decker, a little bit less like Jimmy Drake. Apparently not. The apple did not fall far from the tree. Look at his brother Lloyd with his yard of junked cars. Look at old man Farrell rotting away on his farm, insisting that Randy inherit the place someday, babbling on about primogeniture but unable to get his sheets from their hundred-year-old bed to the washing machine.

And his sister with her accounting "degree." That did not change the fact she was a bookkeeper and an unmarried Farrell with a mustache. Angel shuddered. All that malarkey about beauty being skin deep. Without beauty what did you have? What could you do? She gave it some serious thought and came up empty, thought instead of checking on the lighter fluid in her glovebox. Did she really put it there or just think about putting it there? She couldn't be fumbling in her purse when the moment came. Maybe she should check, but hold on. What was that? A branch? Somebody was out there; Jimmy was here, unless, of course, it was Frog. In this windowless hut how would a person ever know what or who was crawling around the dance hall yard.

God knows it *could* be Frog. He might be a Farrell and a fixer-upper but he had his friends and they kept their ears to the ground. And Jimmy had his enemies and not much else. A friend named Reg who hadn't left the house for more than three weeks. Good God. What if it was Frog? She needed a smoke badly. Well, what if it was? He'd never raised a hand and she'd think of something to say. She always did.

The door opened and there was Jimmy, shivering in the warm November night, teeth chattering so hard, Angel could hear them. He was like a cartoon, Tweety Bird in the clutches of Sylvester. "Jesus H. Christ. Thank God it's you. I cannot do this shed thing again, Angel. My nerves, I swear my nerves are rusting away. It's like an old car in there," he said, pointing to his head. "I'll have to ask Reg. Do nerves get rust or bad connections or what? They certainly get something. Christ almighty." The words came out wobbly from his white, glowing face.

"God, you look like a jack-o'-lantern, Jimmy. Jimmy Jack O' Lantern. Anyway, calm down, calm down. Let's get into my car. I parked it in the road allowance. Nobody but nobody is going to stroll through the road allowance at eleven o'clock on a Saturday night."

"You know," Jimmy said, allowing himself to be led by the hand, "between the bog and Cheryl Decker, this place is starting to feel a little haunted, if you don't mind me saying. I swear I saw someone in a balaclava take off into the woods while I was walking up the hill just now. Seems to me we're just waiting to locate the third point in the Bermuda triangle and I am really hoping it won't turn out to be that tool shed."

Picking their way around the dance hall and along the road allowance, they came to Angel's car. There sat the Gremlin, all windows and suddenly rather too un-locked and Angel remembered stories of women driv-ing for miles and discovering, on a lonely stretch of road, some bearded killer from the most wanted list crouching in the back seat. This was the effect Jimmy had on her. With the interior light on, she leaned over the seat into the dark space behind it. "Just checking," she said to Jimmy.

They needed some heat. The battery wasn't much good and the car's engine turned over with some re-luctance; what if the thing had decided now was the time to lose all charge. Then what? Dingle, dingle from the hall telephone—Frog, could you give me a boost? She was leaving the Gremlin on now for the duration.

"Jesus, Angel. I don't know. I'm so shrivelled up from the cold and the worry I don't think I'll be much good to you," said Jimmy, looking more than shriv-elled, looking small and passengerish in his seat.

"What? What are you saying?" Angel scoffed. "It's hardly cold. It's seasonal, warm even for November. The heater's on and it's a good heater despite the no-good battery. You'll be too warm in a minute," she said, placing a hand on the back of his neck.

"It's not so much the heat. It's this place. It gives me the creeps. And Frog right over there, a stone's throw. If we go look at the lake we'll be able to see the store."

"But we're not going to go look at the lake and thus we will be spared the sight of the store. So that is a wasted bit of conjecture. Frog could be five hundred feet away or five hundred miles. If he's not here, he's not here. If he doesn't know, he doesn't know. He thinks I'm at Muriel's playing bridge."

"What if he calls there?"

"Why would he?"

"I don't know. An emergency. A fire in the kitchen or one of your kids gets a fish hook in the eye."

"Muriel will cover for me. She knows to. She's good for some things. She's got her own secrets."

Incredible that she was going to this much trouble, waiting, worrying, consoling and now reassuring—more emotion than she had spent on any single person or issue since the last freezer repair bill—all for the come-uppance of Jimmy Drake. She smiled, felt his dick through the thin fabric of his pants. "C'mon Jimmy. You know no one is as good as you are. Let's not waste an opportunity that might not come again." Groped some more. "You don't feel that shrivelled to me."

She was kissing him now, a necessary evil, and shifting herself from behind the steering wheel. She'd got his pants undone and now struggled out of her own underwear, thinking the word "demure" as elastic snapped around her shoes. The dress had been an ex-pedient idea: I want it here and I want it now, said the whispering cotton print. Angel climbed on top, then off. "Take off your pants. Right off. And the boxers too. I don't want any of this adolescent pants around the ankles business. C'mon. C'mon."

Jimmy lifted his backside and eased out of his pants in one smooth move.

"Give them to me," Angel said. "You don't want them getting all dirty on the Gremlin floor. Here, I'll fold them up for you. See, I'm a little bit compulsive about these things. Now, where to put them?"

"Just throw them in the back, Angel. They're nothing special, believe me."

"Now just a minute. Wait a minute," and unrolling the passenger side window, she dropped the pile outside, let the clothing fall in an intact heap onto the forest floor. "They'll get a nice natural cedar scent," she said.

"Whatever you say, Angel. Let's get down to business," Jimmy said, pulling Angel so that she straddled him again, kissing her.

"Wait a minute, Jimmy. Hold on just one minute. I almost forgot. I have to show you this trick I learned a long time ago, at summer camp actually. I don't know why it just came back to me but it did and I have to show you cuz you'll like it. It's an optical illusion kind of thing. Really quite eerie but you have to be in a car at night. And you have to close your eyes."

"What? What are you talking about? Jeez Angel, I'm gonna lose my hard-on here."

"Oh, I have no doubt you'll find it again," Angel said. "Just close your eyes and relax. We're not in a rush, are we? You have to relax." Quietly opening the glove box, Angel reached for the lighter fluid. "Keep those eyes closed." Rolled down the window and shot a liberal quantity onto the little heap of clothing.

"Why do I smell lighter fluid?" Jimmy wanted to know.

"That's nothing. Just my lighter, which I overfilled tonight so it still smells. It has nothing to do with the illusion and now, voila, you can open your eyes."

"And what?"

"Oh right. Um, look into the rear-view mirror," Angel instructed, swivelling it into position. "Do you see what I'm talking about?"

Jimmy shook his head. "I see nothing, Angel. Just a very luscious lady with her lingerie off."

"Just look into the rear-view mirror and concentrate on nothing."

"That should be easy enough."

"Still don't see it? Okay. I need a match. I've got some wooden ones in my purse here. Let me light one. Sometimes you need a bit of illumination..." and Jimmy's face burst into pale definition, then darkened again. "Damn. Bad match. I seem to be getting a lot of those lately. Lemme try again."

This time she lit the match and with zero hesitation, dropped it out the window and onto the pants, which immediately exploded in flames.

"What the hell are you doing, Angel?" Jimmy shouted, as Angel threw back her head and laughed with such force she hit the windshield and laughed some more. Jimmy pushed her off and grabbed his shoes, leapt out and began stomping, a half-naked man with his fire. Angel took the opportunity to pull the door shut, lock it and all the others, and roll the window up, leaving only a crack for her final summary comments.

"Tell your son he needs to stop playing with dolls,

Jimmy. What is he? A faggot? And what kind of per-
vert are you, out here in the woods with no pants?
Looking for a tree with a nice knothole?"

"For the love of God, Angel," Jimmy said, pulling
on the door handle, "open the door for me. Haven't
you done enough damage now? Aren't you satisfied?
Aren't you ever satisfied?"

"No, I haven't done enough damage and no, I'm
not satisfied. I need to do a bit more damage. I need to
tell you, for example, that the only reason I ever, and I
mean ever, fucked you was that you disgust me. Strange
thing but for some reason, I get turned on by people
who disgust me," she screamed, steaming up the glass,
"and you're one of them. And," she said, putting on
her underwear, "I don't know if you've made this connection with all your camera work and so on but disgust and lust can be very closely related. They can
almost be cousins."

"No, Angel, I never did notice that but I guess..."
Jimmy paused and thought, "if you're married to a half-
wit, it's one of those things that's hard to ignore."

"A half-wit with a job," Angel said, arranging herself behind the wheel, thanking God she hadn't turned
the car off. She jammed the transmission into drive
and roared ahead, then back and around Jimmy, illuminating him, throwing his long dark shadow into the
trees as he poked through the remains of his smouldering pants.

❧

Daylight saving time so the sun will be up for a while, no risk of that sad sack early sunset you get in November, the calendar's most worst month. Adrian doesn't have much time to spare and wonders now about the wisdom of Loretta's plan to meet Beel at four o'clock. Six or seven would have given him time to re-think the entire plan, maybe even send a telegraph to Beel—Can't make it today stop for some reason or other stop are there any foxes on your property stop what about rabies stop. But four is the hour and four is the plan and why wait, why dilly-dally? Get out of this town and go and let the events rise up from the Tamarack Township dump and organize themselves into Brylcreem-coated bristles in the yard of an old fart.

Not many people around for this time of day and the weather is fine and Adrian has to wonder if one enormous municipal posse has already been formed, has taken up positions around Beel's land and is fully alert, with dogs and tear gas, rubber bullets and handcuffs. Limb will be in charge with Ben Horsburgh second in command, having opened all the mail, having provided all the evidence, having always wanted to be second in command and not a postmaster.

Adrian rides down the hill from Flax High Composite and begins to sweat. Indeed, the sidewalks are empty and the town has an evacuated feeling as if all of the people heard the siren moments before school let out, Cornelia Laine picking up the Coutts twins in her station wagon—c'mon, c'mon, c'mon you two—and Muriel Cobb in her Gremlin, probably with some fresh new documents out of Ottawa, on the need— in certain troublesome circumstances—to reinstate the death penalty.

Why did he start this? What was his thinking? He no

longer knew. Maybe simply as a reason to visit East Flax. That was what he missed; more than Randy or the ski jump he missed the geography of East Flax and possibly East Flax knew that, that is, the animal and bird life and suction cup mud around Turtle Bay Bog, not so much the citizens. The citizens themselves knew next to nothing as evidenced by Randolph Farrell and his lined up gumballs.

Adrian stops at Pond's IGA and leans his bike on its kick stand—he wants candy—steps inside and enters the grocery-store smell of old lettuce and dirty floors. No one here either. Carts lined up and looking lost despite their shine; maybe they were on his side, maybe the carts could be counted on to rattle their way out to East Flax in a cortege of shuddering metal. On their own at last. Why did they think they needed humans to push them around? With that kind of ruckus and the paranormal shivering of Adrian's legs, even the still-sleepy frogs at the bottom of Turtle Bay Bog and Minnow Lake would get the message; that's what animals did in times of trouble, they heard vibrations. They'd get themselves up all covered in mud and signal to other menacing wildlife, not the geese and simple-brained robins but the owls, those already awake and on guard, beaks filled with the crushed bones and leftover fluff of mice, and wolves, water snakes, and catfish like the Land-Rover Beel encountered, maybe even the mythical manta: it could be real.

Adrian looks at candy, then his watch. He has to get moving. Oh Henry or Rolo? Or gumdrops? Juicy Fruit?

There would be worms too, plenty of worms and their millipede and centipede friends from every bit of bark and rotting wood, pouring out in streams like sap, filling entire pails and rolling down the sides, rushing on their legless or

*leggy bodies to help Adrian Drury, rushing with the metal
carts and that would be an eerie sight but not eerie enough.
All those legs and feet and rubber wheels and backboneless
bodies will set up an earthquake of vibrating messages to
species farther afield, off-course species like the eels just returning to this longitude after a pointless transatlantic trip
and they will signal to others, puffins, seals, walruses. By the
time the posse arrives, they will have surrounded Adrian in
a fortress of skin and metal and eyes and language-less brains
understood only by the spas-lexic and dead people. And they'll
say, they'll signal, just lie down and put your ear to the mud.
Things will be better. You're not as lonely as you think.*

*Adrian selects three black licorice pipes and advances to
the till. "Did you want a little bag for those, Adrian?" asks
Mrs. Pond. Is that a walkie-talkie beneath her big blue apron?
In his peripheral vision he sees the nesting carts, more lined
and arranged than a Randy job.*

"Yeah, a bag would be just great, Mrs. Pond."

Jimmy Senior wasn't angry, not at all. He walked to
his car, unspooked and unashamed, to find Angel's
underpants pinned beneath a wiper blade, "4U2 wear"
lipsticked onto the windshield, but he'd simply tossed
them into the ditch. He didn't need them. His boxers
were completely shot but the trousers had actually been
improved upon, as if a cannonball had blown through
both thighs and calves. Must have been the way they'd
been folded and the lie of the lighter fluid. Not at all
bad. Swashbuckling accents, he thought, in Hazel

Smart's approving voice. Suitable for the deck or crow's nest, plundering, a life of fresh air and muskets, the wide-open sea.

Strange. When Angel took off, he thought he'd be mad, blue-hot screaming mad, but he wasn't. He was angry like he usually was and this was a familiar feeling, Jimmy's anger being like a comet on a short little orbit, circling away and returning, daily, no, more like weekly, its tail blazing with more and more intensity until this, today, when maybe it had run its course, blown itself out at last, or more accurately, blown itself in. And realizing this, Jimmy's vision went clearer than microscopic and his ears, apparently they had been switched with some other species famous for its alertness, even during sleep, even during moments of furious calm.

It was wet now, rainy, and the tires hissed like water snakes on the run and Jimmy laughed a little to himself. Water snakes on the run, getting out of East Flax and who wouldn't? The Farrells, that's who. Because the Farrells were nothing but hillbillies, butt-ugly hillbillies living in a hillbilly store and Angel was nothing more than a whore who'd happened to be born a Cobb and as a result of that genetic accident believed that she and her frog-swallowing husband and her school queen daughter and her soon-to-be on a goddamn basketball scholarship daughter and her crazy-in-the-head son who'd likely win the goddamn Irish Sweepstakes were all better than Jimmy Drake Senior and Junior. Imagine that. Angel-ass-in-the-air-fuck-me-hard Farrell not only thought she was superior, she was disgusted, disgusted by Jimmy Drake. Strange way of showing disgust, Angel, very strange indeed, prancing your hot little pussy over to Jimmy Drake Senior's whenever it needed fucking. Seems the frog-swallower with a job wasn't up to the task. Well, Angel. Well fucking well. And everything began to go quiet in Jimmy's head as if he were already shushing the evidence, which he had no intention of doing, as if his head were stuffing and stuffing itself with cotton, like Reg that time he had to go into the hospital to get those polyps removed from inside his nose and they packed his sinuses with so much cotton you wouldn't have believed your eyes. Reg had to keep the cotton and show him, actually had to wrap it up as a joke Christmas gift. Look what they pulled out of my head, Jimmy, look at this pile of hard, blood-soaked rags bigger than the average skull, all balled up in a bag. Merry Christmas. Reg knew he'd find it funny or at least interesting and he wasn't going to give everybody hockey sticks, just his *best* friends, Bill and Augie. And Jimmy had gone a little faint at the time, his whole skin surface wondering, why? Because Bill Laine turned out to be a pharmacist and dealt with bandages and blood and sinuses on a daily basis now and Augie Pond owned the grocery store, also a purveyor of blood and guts, ribs, chops, shanks, and tongue. Any blood-soaked part the shopper might need. Don't even ask, Jimmy, don't ask, oh go ahead. What the hell did he have to do to get Reg Decker to treat him like an equal, stop with that slightly patronizing tone and the Rotary he was never invited to join? And at the memory of the injustice of it all, the fact that he worked in the

cleaning trade, as far from scabs and guts and bandages as you could vocationally run, the mushed up,
blood-filled rags inside his head gave a jellied shake of
laughter. Ha fucking ha. Well, Reg would see who his
friends were and who his friends weren't. And now
when Jimmy Drake opened his car window it was like
something got snagged, a hook maybe, a fish hook cor-
nering its way up his nose and snagging an unfrayed
bit of stuffing, mummy wrap unfurling and unravelling out the window like old, blood-hardened stream-
ers, a great loss of pressure spilling into the wet fall
night so that at last Jimmy could see the night was
clearer than he had ever thought possible, as if behind
the dark were a vast illumination, crowding to break
through, the tail of his own simmering comet, a giant
flashbulb taking one last picture.

Jimmy was home. Maybe it was three, maybe later.
It was officially November eighth, which was a good
thing, the seventh was over and so was Angel. Jimmy
Junior was asleep and could be counted on to sleep
past noon, which was convenient because Jimmy Senior was clear and single-minded now. Thoughts moved
unimpeded without the thickening and delaying bulge
of old bandages. He set up the tripod and screwed on
the camera, aiming it at the bed. He sat on the edge,
then propped up a pillow to simulate himself, then focussed. Got rid of the pillow and double checked.
Good. Everything was good. Depressed the red self-
timer button and sat. Jimmy crossed his legs and
smiled. And in the flash of the camera, in the flash of
illumination, Jimmy understood and saw that Reg was

not the electric chair, he was. He was the soon-to-be-unforgettable ex-custodian, Jimmy Drake. Everyone needed to know this. He could develop the picture right now and seal it in an envelope with the caption: by the time you receive this, I will no longer be the person you see. He could mail it to *The Reminder* on his way to East Flax.

Seemed every time Maddy was out walking, either to or from Alfred's house, the helicopter flew over arousing in her a ridiculous panic, the so-called flight response. Were she to flee, though, from higher altitudes she'd be mistaken for Loretta and from lower down, be recognized as herself, eluding the Deckers and therefore guilty as charged. So today, as usual, she maintained a steady pace in the flight path of the approaching wings, shadowless as they were, the morning being overcast and low as a basement. She wondered how she looked from that height, if the orange hat resembled a target, a bull's eye and if Reg Decker thought of shooting her. Maybe he would shoot her. Each and every time, resist as she might, Maddy's neck and backbone became an x-ray of fear. Then pop, pop, pop he was swinging away, the dying report of the blades a signal for Maddy's flesh to clasp itself back on to her shootable bones and all that remained was her, one moving figure between the crowds of black trees fenced back from the pale, old road. Last night's wind had ripped the few remaining leaves from their branches and now there was a dusty layer of snow, as if the fields had taken out a compact during the night and applied some face powder, to no avail.

Everything was grey and white, the colours of gravel. The landscape reminded her of a very dull card celebrating the arrival of fall. Greetings from East Flax, it would say, and inside: You might want to get as far away from here as possible. Or: Planning a vacation? Make East Flax your departure point. Or: Visit East Flax for the annual helicopter hunt. Look for lost wives. Shoot guilty people from the air. Relax later at the East Flax general store. Browse the shelves for pre-war soups. Talk to a man with metal in his head. They could charge admission; Alfred might co-operate, he was always looking for new ways to make money. And he had a sense of humour, didn't he? No, when Maddy thought about it, she had to admit he did not. Everything about Alfred and his house was of equal weight. Were the pens in the pen container? Was the raincoat hanging from its raincoat peg? Spices in alphabetical order? Maddy imagined Alfred's mind to be a military march of questions all identical in size and dress. A joke would lead to imprecision and disorder.

No, he had no sense of humour and in order to live in East Flax, a person needed some capacity to laugh. He wasn't from here and it showed. Alfred Beel was likely one of those life forms that crawls into a truck or attaches itself to a rail car and gets deposited in an alien environment but manages nonetheless to adapt. A crocodile that discovers the ability to grow an extra layer of fat then sits at the edge of the frozen lake all winter knowing there's been a terrible mistake. Maddy laughed to herself but made no sound. All she could hear was the wind and the crunching of her feet on cold gravel.

But what if she turned out to be like Alfred Beel? Unable to adapt? They had some common traits, even though they hated one another. They liked grilled cheese sandwiches and washing windows. They liked solitude and neatness. They didn't like new clothes. All of which was cause for alarm because Maddy was now planning to leave East Flax and what assurance was there she wouldn't become an Alfred Beel, at the end of a pointless road with a weird girl coming to her house to cook and clean for her?

Well, first things first. She *was* going to leave East Flax. It couldn't be that difficult. Here was the road heading both north and south, connecting with other roads heading both east and west. Why had she waited this long? She supposed she had Cheryl Decker to thank for this acceleration of plans. Prior to Cheryl Decker, Maddy would admit, her thinking had been the thinking of a plant with a burlap ball of roots, much like her very own head of hair, reaching down to the bedrock and searching along its surface. This was all you could expect: an immovable burden of earth resting upon a shelf of rock, her own sleeping self measuring the length of the days with her green and buried eyes.

Cheryl Decker had pulled Maddy's head of hair right up out of the earth; Cheryl had caused for Maddy the opposite of hanging, had applied some force upon her body away from the earth's gravitational pull. Maddy'd been given a good yank and pictured herself from time to time hanging upside down, hair dangling with dirt: she was out, she had some sight, and not only could Maddy Farrell see more clearly, she could be seen. Maddy Farrell who'd never thought of herself filling enough space to occupy a thought in someone else's mind had insinuated herself into many people's thoughts like quack grass or mildew, forms of life always around but preferably not right here.

Maddy shifted the bag of groceries in her arms. Alfred always called now before she left and ordered a few items; saved him the trip. And sometimes she threw in something for herself like a bag of chips and then another for him because she was uncomfortable eating without him. He never refused the offer, either, to her surprise. He was like a kid in some ways, she thought now, always wondering, soon as she arrived, what extras were in the bag. Once she'd brought two bags of Licorice Allsorts and he'd said, ah, a girl after my own heart, and not even looked embarrassed so she'd felt embarrassed for him.

This was Maddy's plan. Continue to work for her dad and Alfred, save every penny, and by spring she'd have more than enough for a bus ticket to London and to survive long enough to find a job and a place to live. Cora would let her stay with her a while. She was getting a place in the spring with some friends, moving out of the dormitory. Maddy hadn't asked yet but Cora wasn't heartless. She wouldn't turn her sister away, especially if she could make it clear to her through hand

signals or pig Latin that the bed-wetting was now behind her. A problem of the past. Cora certainly would-
n't want a smelly sleeping bag bunched up in a corner,
a plaid flannel, pee-hardened nest for the nursing
friends to step around.

Maybe she should send a letter to lay the ground-
work. She'd called Cora a few times, thinking she
might broach the topic but Cora always seemed so distracted, Can't you see I'm on the phone? her voice
seemed to suggest. I'm on the phone and you should
be somebody else. Not fair to spring such an announcement that way, anyway, better to send a letter
and give Cora time to understand. And she would.

Of course, Maddy would leave notes for everyone.
This was the benefit of leaving. One for Randy filled
with instructions and reassurance—you're smarter than
you think you are. Try to talk Mom into buying you
one of those madras shirts. You can have both my jobs:
you and Alfred Beel might hit it off with your pen-
chants for arranging. Stay in school. The list lengthened daily so that by the time Maddy left she would
be leaving behind enough paper to form a hovercraft,
a ream of lift between Randy and the thawing topsoil.

To her parents, nothing but the facts: I'm gone.
Living in London with Cora. Will call soon.

But it was the letter to Rose she wrote and revised
daily, thinking in ink as she walked the long way to Alfred's. Past the worst features of East Flax, the cemetery and the shallow, dammed up, swampy end of the
lake, the portion of the lake that was no more than an
industrial byproduct, its makeshift qualities evident

even in winter—roots, boards, and strangled bulrushes. The frozen surface of perpetual flooding; all that was trashy about East Flax. There was no other route to take; although to cut through the woods behind the dance hall was quicker, she hadn't been up there since September. That seemed a bad luck bit of geography.

Maddy'd probably written at least a dozen letters to Rose. Sometimes, like today, she would simply wonder, where was Rose now? Was she in physics class? She knew for certain she was, unless the schedule had been changed and schedules never were. She wondered if her stool was empty or if someone had moved to it for extra tuition, as Miss Eustace said. She'd like right now to go to Flax and stand outside the physics window and look in at Rose alone at her desk in the cubic room where she no longer sat. Maddy would be out in the startlingly white day, visible only to Rose, bright as a photograph. They would look at each other and that would be enough, words being only so much waterlogged debris when held against the weightless efficiency of the human eye. Miss Eustace would agree. Sound was a clumsy oaf; compared to light, sound was the Bigfoot.

Other times, she thought a card would suffice, from the East Flax Hallmark line, voicing one or two regrets. I wish I hadn't told you about the social worker, the dirty period or the hungry one. Those are secrets I hope you have not shared with Anastasia. The thought of Anastasia knowing what you know makes me feel like dirt on my own teeth.

Or she would call Rose a snob. Say, thanks so

much for coming to see me at the dance hall, taking the time to climb that ladder. Sorry I was so ungracious. I called to say sorry but Anastasia picked up the phone and my voice box froze. She has that effect, as if your entire throat is lined with freezer frost. Did she know it was me? Not likely, I didn't say a word. If it weren't for Anastasia, maybe we'd still be friends. Anastasia is not necessarily the best offence but she is the best defence. If she stands in the way, I can't even imagine a way to get around her. Seems like she has a dial and can move my thoughts up and down like a radio, leaving them at the very bottom, around 550 where there is nothing. And as for you, Rose, you could have called or driven out here one more time. A friend wouldn't give up that easily. The roads are fine; it's not as if they're snow-covered and impassable, not yet.

The roads. Give the weather another month and this gravel road would be a frozen strip, like very rough sandpaper and painful to look at. And why was that? Maddy wondered. Oh, she knew. Once these bits of stone were embedded in hard-packed snow, you couldn't help but be reminded of skin scraped off. Fall from your bike and that was what you had for yourself—three or four inches of rough road on your own exterior, small stones lodged in flesh. That was the road to East Flax in winter. The road Maddy expected Rose to drive just one more time; the road she turned to check each time she heard a car's engine, thinking this might be her at last. Maybe the schedule has been changed; maybe she has a double spare.

Dear Rose, Maddy wanted to say today. If only this

could be summer. I would take the money I've earned and buy us two air mattresses, the best quality with push-in valves. We could drift into Minnow Lake and into the channel, lie ourselves down in its unfreezable warm current until we passed through the mossy air of the culvert, into the deep end and Turtle Bay. Air mattress our way over stones and leeches and crayfish, into the Saugeen River and the speed of water, the speed of one Great Lake pulling on its rivers, sipping us up as if it wanted to hold us in its mouth.

Maybe Alfred didn't have it in him to love or hate. Look at the way he went after women who couldn't be had, women like Cora Farrell who would be sure to humiliate him or Loretta Decker who would be certain to be unfaithful. Or Maddy Farrell who would eventually be found unworthy of his or any passion. He'd tried to stoke his hatred for her because hatred was better than nothing. In the absence of woodworking projects or baleful conversations in the East Flax store, hatred, like the lancing of a boil or the unbandaging of a white and dented chest opened its own soggy valves of pleasure. For a while he'd taken to sitting in his chair watching her every move, making note of causes for complaint—this was going to be fun—such as, Insufficient wringing out of dishcloth. Then, through no real conscious process he could recall, began jotting down ways of killing her. Strangle Maddy, he wrote beneath, Failed to sweep in vestibule. Of course, he had no real intention of following through but the macaroni mess of unused emotion in his chest needed some destination so why not murder?

Drown in kitchen sink, he penned. She could flail her long arms around as much as she wanted, sooner or later they'd flop out of motion like those albino water snakes he'd heard about, dead ones, that is. Hit with sledgehammer. Stab with fish cleaning knife. Suffocate with pillow. Options wafted pleasingly through his mind like items on a menu. He knew it was wicked, evil thinking, thinking that might be thought by a convict on death row but it was, after all, only thinking. No different from a book or a movie and if the people who dreamed up books and movies could think such thoughts, why couldn't he? It wasn't as if you had to buy a licence or a typewriter or rolls of sixteen-millimeter film.

"What are you writing there, Alfred?" Maddy had asked.

"Nothing but a list."

"Well, if it's a grocery list, I could take care of it for you." And that was the beginning of the undoing of his delightful loathing. Maddy had made herself far too useful.

Next time, she arrived at nine and was still there at noon and since she'd raised the subject of groceries, Alfred asked if she wouldn't mind staying for lunch and frying him up a grilled cheese sandwich. Of course she wouldn't mind, cutting up a few carrots for some fibre and vitamins. Angel was on a health food kick and was thinking of stocking soy flour and going into supplements in a big way.

The sandwich had been black on one side and too greasy on the other but never mind. Maddy had been so right to put the pot cleaner into that little clay dish. And he had never in his life considered pulling out the fridge to vacuum the coils on the back—it was running better already—or splashing the sink with a bit of bleach to kill the bacteria. If you can't love or hate for more than a month, you're not cut out for any enduring institution. Not marriage or employment or the church or even the army. He was living proof of all of these.

Now here it was three weeks after Thanksgiving and Alfred had a kind of date with Maddy: come out as usual on Sunday and eat a kind of pre-American Thanksgiving brunch with him. He'd make the stuffing and put the turkey in the oven first thing in the morning. He'd *pay* for her time, he said, which gave him a frisson of power: Maddy was his *paid* companion, an arrangement both disgusting and genteel. She'd arrived after ten and helped cook the vegetables, then sat down with him at eleven. They should have some wine, he said, and pulled a bottle from the lazy Susan in his cupboard. He asked about the store, the Maestro, Russell, and her parents. And she told him she might go back to school next year, she certainly wasn't planning to stay in East Flax forever.

He said, "You know, about that ladder business, I never actually thought you had anything to do with that Decker girl's death. Now, in retrospect, I lay the blame at the feet of that Drury boy. A gentleman would never treat a lady like that. But at the time, though, you understand, I thought it was my duty to report what I'd seen to Limb. I'm an old soldier, you know, duty bound and so on."

"No harm done. It was kind of interesting being questioned."

He didn't add that he'd hoped the ladder would at the very least be considered evidence, some excuse for a trial, a reason for him to testify, a reason to bring Loretta back as quickly as possible, some possibility for heroics. He'd pictured himself in the witness box more often than he would ever admit even to himself.

"So, what about dating?" Was she dating now, he wanted to know.

Not really. How about him?

"Har har," he said. "Thanks for ruining my turkey."

"Oh, sorry."

And there'd been two or three minutes of serving, cutting, and chewing.

"Cora called last night."

"Did she now? How's nursing school?"

"It's hard work. She watched an autopsy. Two girls fainted and one guy, the only one in her class."

"A male nurse," Alfred said, thinking the words *queer as a three-dollar bill*. That phrase would describe a male nurse and Maddy Farrell and possibly himself or perhaps this entire situation. Look at him: a fraud. A kind of Thanksgiving john. Someone who had to order up from the Sears catalogue of unhinged persons a companion for a festive meal. And where was Loretta anyway? He'd had just about enough of this waiting.

How could one person be so unsentimental? Was her heart made of metal? Was it a granite rock extracted from the Canadian shield? He'd never seen the likes of it but then he hadn't seen much, sentimental or otherwise, he had to admit. He was an emotional prairie, a grassy surface scarred by one land mine but little else.

Back to the dating topic. Was there someone she liked, then, even though she wasn't dating?

Yes, she said, there was.

Well? He was a woman really when it came to gossip. If his chest hadn't been blown off he'd be one of those men with breasts, downturned pouches of fat.

"Well, someone I've kissed." She couldn't resist sharing this news, which had been baking away inside her now for more than a month, giving off an odour on her skin she was sure, turning it the colour of home made rolls. She'd had two glasses of wine.

"You've kissed? Well, here's to you, then," and Alfred raised his glass to conceal his annoyance at the injustice of it all, the promise of intimacy opening up for this boy-girl while it was slamming its door shut on Alfred Beel.

"Tell me more," he said. "You can confide in me. Who is he? Is he from the area? Is it a happy story?" He was a little drunk himself, mimicking "Front Page Challenge." "Does he have a name beginning or ending with the letter A?"

"A?" She didn't get the joke. "No. And I won't tell you any more."

Fine. He wouldn't tell her any more either, but he was good-natured enough about it. Then remembered the yellow blouse and thought why not give it to Maddy, insisted she try it on so he could determine the size of her breasts, she was always in so many layers of cloth. And they were small! Certainly smaller than Loretta's or Cora's so this alleged suitor had very little to look forward to, literally. But he managed a compliment.

"Lovely," he said. "It suits you. The colour and so on."

Maddy smiled and thanked Alfred. She had to get going but nevertheless, at that moment, some mutual change occurred, a loosening of the belts of hatred. They both began clearing away the dishes and from outside came the familiar sound of a helicopter. Or was it just a car engine? Who the hell was driving around now, snooping around where he had no business?

"Surely that can't be Reg Decker again," Alfred said. "He's already strafed the place once this morning."

"I know. He flew over when I was on my way here." And Maddy stepped outside to look around, as if this were her place.

The Story of Salt in Huron County was overdue. With help from Rose, Adrian had completed the written section covering the discovery and development of the salt mine on the shore of Lake Huron. Randy was to assemble the visuals and had insisted on getting to the salt mine for brochures and samples with the result being, Friday afternoon there were still no brochures and samples. Another extension. Frog Farrell was most definitely driving Randy to the mine first thing Saturday morning and they had until noon Sunday to deliver the completed project to Mr. Rigg's house in Mesmer. Meaning Rose would have to drive Adrian to East Flax first thing Sunday morning to fetch Randy's bristol board representation as he called it. Adrian had his licence now but did not want to drive to East Flax alone. He hadn't been there since the trip with Anastasia if you didn't count his dream life, which almost nightly dropped him into the trees behind the hall or cycled him along the gravel road in a sweat with a faceless girl in a balaclava. Everyone in his dreams travelling stupidly toward dread, eventually waking him in the perfect stillness of his room. Cheryl could haunt him forever and part of him wished she would because then at least he would know she continued to exist. And Cheryl as a ghost was easier to take than he himself haunted, which was a distinct possibility. Something in him was aging prematurely. If the doctors opened him up, they'd find a turnip like the one left in the fridge since Thanksgiving, sunken, wrinkled but uninclined to rot. They'd put him on a white table and say: this is the section of Adrian Drury that will be reincarnated.

Plus, he could tell Rose didn't want him to drive there on his own; she didn't seem to trust him to his own devices. He had smashed his hand through the garage window a couple years ago and then made the mistake of telling her recently the idea of his whole body smashing through a windshield held some appeal. Suicide's a contagious disease, she said to him. Now she watched him as if he was covered in open sores.

"I got a birthday present for Maddy," she said as they slammed the car doors shut.

"How come?"

"I don't know. It's not even her birthday till the end of November. I felt like buying her something. Her clothes are so bad. So I got her a white shirt."

"You mean like dad wears?"

"No. It's a woman's shirt. You think I would get her a man's shirt?"

"I don't know. It's too early to be up on a Sunday."

The temperature was in the hoar frost range and the Vega unenthusiastic, but compliant.

"What are you getting Dad for Christmas?" Rose asked. They were on the road, they were leaving the town limits, they were out of the hairnet known as Flax.

"Christmas? It's only November eighth. I'm not ready to think about Christmas. Maybe it should be cancelled like Mrs. Laine wanted to cancel Halloween. The idea of joy to the world for some reason feels like a tidal wave on my head, which maybe wouldn't be that bad. Who knows where the undertow might take you."

"Well, I think you should think about Christmas. It's better than thinking about undertows. It's a good subject for distraction. Think about what you want to get Dad. Do it or I won't drive you."

"All right," he sighed a weary sigh. "Maybe a bottle

of something from the liquor store. Do you think you could get into the liquor store?"

"Are you kidding? If I could get into the liquor store I'd be getting into the liquor store. It wouldn't be a conditional tense kind of thing. Anastasia's mom can buy something for you. She doesn't mind bootlegging if it's for a noble cause."

"Yeah. Or maybe I'll ask Mrs. Limb."

"Sure. One's as good as the other."

Why did Rose have to bring up the name Van Epp? And it *was* a little like bringing up, as far as Adrian was concerned; his stomach had a permanent little pool of bile that was associated with that name and it couldn't seem to flow away. Speaking of tidal waves, what were those little pools called that got stuck somewhere, between rocks, dropped off by a wave and eventually filling up with algae and worms? Tidal pools. Oh yes. Tidal pools and tidal waves. But impossible to avoid the Van Epp name or the Van Epps. How could you ever hope to do that in Flax, Ontario? Anastasia was always driving around in that Mercury and Laura was everywhere at school, coming to his locker, standing there like an electric eel or a hydro line lying in a pool of water, a tidal pool. Were he to touch her, there'd be instant and internal frying of human flesh, his or Laura's or both. They might manage to look the same but inside was that melted plastic smell, that smell of invisible trouble on its way. Smells like a fire. Smells like plastic burning. Can you smell that? Face it. There wasn't a single name or place in or around Flax that wasn't in some way tied up next to Cheryl: that was a town. Streets and houses

in rows but the place itself scrunched up like intestines—
stretch them out and yes, they would cover a distance of
so many miles but you never did stretch them out. Why
would you? You left them rubbing and digesting in and
around and on top of one another.

"I thought I'd get him a sweater," said Rose.

"A sweater. Now that's an original gift. Who ever
heard of giving a guy a sweater at Christmas?"

"Okay. Fine." But at least he'd laughed. "Here's a
question. Would there be Christmas without
sweaters?" Rose asked. "That's a question for Reverend
Rochon to address in his sermon."

"Yeah. Why didn't the three wise men bring the
baby Jesus sweaters? That would have made more sense
than spices or whatever it was they brought."

"Another question for the Reverend."

"Or maybe his son," Adrian said, looking at her
for a reaction.

"Maybe, if I'm ever alone with him again."

"You're not going to be, are you?"

"I don't know." She had told Adrian about the incident with Graham Rochon, told him, he knew, so he
would feel better about Cheryl and the shrivelling
turnip inside him. She wanted him to think she was
the bad one, the bad seed, but Rose's badness was innocent; she didn't know that. Her badness, it seemed
to Adrian, was like a girl wanting to climb up a ladder
with no underwear on, like a girl who wanted people to
look at her and be shocked but nothing more. Silly ac-
tions with no repercussions. Not failings that caused
people to ride bikes to dance halls and hang themselves.

They entered the shadowy bends lined with tall cedars and scrubby spruce. Not so picturesque but still could in fact be a cold day in summer, except for the skiff of snow in the dried up ditch. Here comes Dance Hall Road. There was the green sign – partyish in all seasons and circumstances. Adrian thought someone might have chopped it down or sealed off the road with four or five big boulders so that sooner or later everyone could forget there was a road with a hall at the end of it. The dance hall could become Aztec ruins and Cheryl dug up like those girls that were sacrificed because they wanted to be sacrificed. It was a great honour to have your head cracked open on top of a mountain. Adrian wished he could stop thinking such thoughts but the thoughts were in charge, they had their own engines. He was nothing but a racetrack for them, the Indianapolis 500.

He sure hoped Randy had the goddamn salt props. If he had to come back again, another day, he didn't think he could. Although, Randy wasn't so bad; he was a good friend in weird ways. Adrian would never have thought this possible, but he and the Farrells were now in the same unmentionable boat: the Cheryl Decker. Because of Maddy and the allegations. All made up but what wasn't?

Here was the store already, weather-beaten and certainly bereft of shoppers. "How can you have a store without any customers?" Adrian asked, as if it were a riddle.

"They must have some, otherwise they'd close. Anyway, let's go. Let's get this salt project licked."

"I don't want to go in there. I don't know what it

is. East Flax is giving me a bad feeling. When you tried to make a joke there just now, a joke in East Flax, I suddenly felt like a condemned guy on the way to the gallows, like I'm trudging along, trudge, trudge, trudge, and somebody says here, thought you might want to take a look at this before you go. It's called a laugh." And he started to cry, strangled barking sounds that got the car going again.

"We'll just drive a little farther," Rose said.

Adrian hadn't let Rose see him cry for years, not since he'd failed the maroon level of Red Cross swimming lessons, emerging from the locker room with a propped up smile that collapsed when he reached Rose and their dad. "I didn't pass," he said. "I'm the only one who didn't pass." Forcing upon them the weightless weight of nothing to be done. How do you even get a hold on it? Like missing the bar in gymnastics, trying for some tricky move and sailing off with nothing but bad news in your empty hands.

Rose steered the car past the half-frozen lake, ducks resting on open bits and flotsam. They pulled over at the cemetery.

"You have to stop thinking this way," Rose said. "You have to stop thinking you killed Cheryl Decker because I know that's what you're thinking. Just stop thinking it."

"I can't," Adrian said, leaning into the window, wishing his head would melt through it onto jagged splinters.

"Well, if you can't stop thinking it, start thinking it less and less. Think Cheryl Decker killed herself because she did and you couldn't stop her from thinking she wanted to do that just like I can't stop you from thinking it's your fault. You can't put your fingers inside another person's brain and switch things around like fuses. Some other girl would have just said, that Adrian Drury's being a jerk or she would have said, good riddance or she would've got back at you somehow. But not Cheryl Decker. That's how she was."

"Yes, but I should have known that."

"Well, you didn't. Just like I should've known to tell everyone I was with Maddy Farrell when she got the ladder but I didn't for some reason. Things just happen. Events, they're all lined up waiting to happen before you're even born. Like Mom with her cancer— it was probably started up before she even met Dad. You get born and you get shoved into a skin and then you're just an event too."

"No that's not true, Rose. You know that's not true." But the crying was coming to a stop.

"Due to circumstances beyond our control. That's what the voice on television says every time there's a problem. So then you just sit and stare at the test pattern because there's nothing anybody can do."

"Yeah. I know what you mean. I know what you mean."

Adrian thought Rose might want to hug him but that sort of contact with a brother in a car seemed to cross a romantic line and they didn't hug each other at the best of times, just let the air between them collapse and scurry away.

"Should we go back to the store?" Rose asked.

"I have to get that stuff from Randy."

"Right," Rose said, turning the car around, rolling down the window for some therapeutic air. "I wish it would be summer again already instead of just starting into winter. There's no sound out here in the cold. What is it with this place that it's so quiet? Once again, there's nothing making noise. Absolutely nothing."

A minute and they were there. "All right. Let's go in," Adrian said.

The hour was much too early for the Maestro or Russell but Randy had his bristol board propped up on the arms of Alfred's big chair. Glued upon it were at least twenty sample-sized silos of salt representing guardrails on the Trail of Salt.

"Do you get it?" Randy asked. "They put salt on the roads and as you can see, it's a road leading to the mine and then spokes to the different products salt is used for—glass, soap, plastics, etcetera. This hole in the middle is the mine entrance and when you get to Mr. Rigg's, then just paper clip this old saltbox to the hole with these flaps and you have the mineshaft. Those are the three dimensions, the guardrails and the mine and the products here, the bullet is for explosives, also a salt product little known to man. And here are the brochures."

"Wow. That's impressive, Randy. Mr. Rigg is going to be really impressed."

"I know."

Angel was at the till, smoking. "And how are you, Miss Drury?"

"I'm fine, thank you. Is Maddy here? I brought

something for her."

"No. Maddy's up at Alfred's. She cleans house for him Sunday and Tuesday mornings. She's thinking of starting up her own cleaning business now, which she'd damn well better be if she's not going back to school I say."

"Oh. Well, then. Will you see that she gets this—it's an early birthday present—and tell her I'll give her a call."

"Yes ma'am, I'll do that." Apparently Angel had forgiven Rose.

"Maybe I'll have a cream soda while I'm here. What about you Adrian?"

"Coke."

"It's on the house," Angel said, exhaling the offer in smoke.

Rose sat in the Maestro's chair and Adrian in Russell's while Randy watched them drink and talked about salt. He wondered if Adrian would go on the tour of the mine with him in the summer, or what Adrian would think of working in the salt mines. Randy had always more or less thought that salt was just for salt, not other things, so this project had been a real eye-opener for him. Some places didn't salt the road, which was a debatable subject because of the issue of rust. "Like I bet your Vega wishes they didn't salt the roads here by the look of it."

"Yeah. If a Vega could only talk, what would it say?" Adrian wondered.

"It would say, let me change my name. I'm not a crater on the moon."

You had to hand it to Randy—he knew and loved

the facts.

"Or it might be, if some of these rust spots get any bigger, I might be a crater after all." This was the kind of talk Adrian liked with Randy.

"Yeah," Randy said. "It's getting reincarnated into a crater. Hey do you get it? Rein*car*nated. That's funny."

"It's a little bit funny, Randy," Rose said.

"We've gotta go, Rose. It's after eleven already."

"I know, I know. I'm finishing this. It's only twenty after. I thought maybe Maddy might get back." Angel had said mornings and the morning was nearly over. Something to do with the surrounding canned goods probably but now inside this store, Rose wanted Maddy to appear with a want as hard and thick as Dr. Rochon's erection, a want that could have stretched it-self right through her winter coat.

"No, really Rose. By the time I get this in the car and organized with my papers...Mr. Rigg doesn't kid about eleven fifty-nine."

"All right already," and she drained the bottle, dropped it into the wooden crate of empties.

"But wait," said Randy. "Here," and he handed them each a licorice pipe. "Smoke these on the way back to Flax."

Good thing Jimmy Drake had made listening to Reg a lifelong habit. As a result, he knew Maddy Farrell was at Beel's Sunday morning, until past noon usually, that's what Reg said, sometimes later. He could take Dance Hall Road to the now-famous road allowance and park the car with his sights on Beel's doorway. The minute the Farrell girl exited, well—and Jimmy waited for his stomach to punch him like a nervous fist, his muscles to tighten into shaking, trembling frightened little smiles beneath the skin—but nothing; he wasn't scared. And who did he hate now? No one. Not Angel, not even Frog. Let him have the job and the PA system, give him the custodial page in the year book with its patronizing and insincere message of fake gratitude, blurry black and white images of some catfish-looking guy in the furnace room, some bottom feeder as Hazel Smart, mother of Jimmy Junior, would say. Was there a man anywhere more suited to basements and buckets, to mud, to plunging out Kotex-plugged toilets? No there was not. Frog Farrell was their man.

Even the Farrell girl, Jimmy doesn't really hate. She is simply there in a spot where many lines intersect, creating on paper a smudge, in life, a target. Or perhaps she was merely standing in the spot where the alarm was set to go off. Jimmy knew because Jimmy had become the clock, the only clock reliably set for miles around. He could tell you what would happen at 12:15 or maybe a little later and after that and after that. He had the future right there behind his face.

Time to wash the lipstick off the windshield and get the shotgun and box of shells because now already was the hour. He didn't want too little time and he didn't want too much. Better be going. Odd then. Odd for a clock to know it was a clock. Maybe he was a clock on television because now the surroundings seemed to have some inkling, like on the screen, the way everything goes still, no movement from the trees, no birds, nobody on the road except those Drury brats heading into town with candy hanging from their mouths; that summed up their experience of life. Nobody else though, nothing but puddles and one crushed porcupine. And at the dance hall, only windows in a row, reflecting what they saw, sunlight and emptiness, unable to pass judgment. And even more strange, through the brush and small trees, not even the crackling of a branch or the sound of leaves against truck, just that eerie silence from one person getting ready without knowing why. And why is that? Because the alarm has been set by someone else.

Close enough to Beel's now. Stop. Get out of the car. Everything dripped from the morning's snowy rain. Jimmy looked up to see rickety spruce trees closing in above his head, creaking and nodding in agreement. But he was going to have to find a lower branch for a gun rest because he couldn't hold this thing steady and he was not what you would call a marksman. Plowed his way into a cedar and picked at the bark; sniffed his fingers. Possibly the one good attribute of East Flax, the cedar tree.

Beel's door opened and there she was. The alarm was going off already, sounding too soon. He hadn't recalled setting it for now, so soon, he wasn't ready but the trigger squeezed and blam. Amazing. Bull's eye, well, no, bull's leg. There was Beel already, the sound still ringing in his kitchen, coating the appliances with unforgettability. He was trying to lift her up, help her up, and she was screaming and thrashing and Alfred saw Jimmy but said nothing because by then the trees had fallen quiet, they were playing dead.

It was over and the only problem was the car was like a horse, unsure if it wanted to participate, smelling blood and thinking its own language of shoulds and should nots and with no knowledge of all the time spread out backwards behind it. Christ. That was blood for you; blood spoke every possible language you could imagine, even Ford, everything but clock. The smell of blood was strong enough to make a steering wheel turn to rubber and tires to go their own way. But she was on now and turning around, barrelling through the underbrush. This vehicle would simply need to gird up its loins.

The drive home was nothing but scenic, like a post-card, everything stopping still before you and you coming out the other side, as if the landscape were paper-thin. Jimmy's eyes felt heavy with the burden of so much beauty as if some small insects were nibbling the connections away between them and his brain, like wires in a barn and that was fine with him. Let the bulbs go out. Let the clock stop. Let the chair blow a circuit. At home, Jimmy Junior was still asleep. He'd find out soon enough. Then what? Hazel Goddamn Smart could step up to the plate. He'd be taken care of. So now, Jimmy needed to call the cop shop and ask for Jerome Limb. He would never in a million years guess who was calling.

Adrian breathes hard and is aware of some relief. What in the hell was he thinking about carts on the move and sympathetic catfish? He needs to give his head a shake. This dry road, the sun on his neck, they are both trying to bring a better season, trying to suggest Cheryl isn't actually dead, there is an afterlife, ghosts have been seen on certain rare occasions. Once the earth is warmed up and the lake is melted and glittery, the ski jump baked like an old plywood bun, Adrian will see Cheryl somewhere, glimpses only because that is the arrangement, that's what they're told in the afterlife. You can't just walk right up to people and talk but you can watch from behind a tree, you can vanish at the exact moment your friends wake up, you can leave a trace but nothing more, a sign. These are the rules. That's what Cheryl's been doing, she's been in the required courses: how to be a spirit, how to let them know you're still around. She's in a class with her brother or maybe he's tutoring her, being so smart like he was, and here Adrian stops and balances on his bike for as long as possible, moving the front wheel in steadying jerks, suspended between his own divided halves of brain, wordless loss and wordless hope. Cut him open in biology and what would they find? Two parts. Over here, a wet sod door opening in to nothing; over there, a lit-up lake at sunset, reflections arranged in rows you can't believe are accidental. What kind of guts are these, the doctors would ask? Sew him up. There's not much we can do.

Adrian has more than enough strength to ride up the hill and crash into the road allowance with its bog smell and heavy shade like burnt-out lamps. He likes this dark green and quiet place because it is mossy and exhausted and tired of people and he would like to tell these surrounding and gloomy lives maybe now he will be the last one to pass by here, the last of the watchers and talkers. Maybe now things will finally be settled. And there is Beel's house and one good thing: no sign of Limb's car. Though it could be hidden in the garage or back around behind the house but when did a cop ever go to the trouble of hiding his cop car? Display of the cruiser was 99 per cent of the point of cophood.

Now suddenly Adrian can truthfully hardly believe what he is doing because it is the kind of behaviour most people would not accept. Not accept? They would condemn outright like everything else Adrian has done in the past nine months. You mean the little son of a bitch sent letters in Loretta's name then rode his bike right up on Beel's property, laid himself down behind some low cedars, trained his binoculars on the front door and waited for Beel to step outside. To watch him crumble. No more than a hundred feet from the house. What was the little bastard thinking?

Nothing, is Adrian's reply. He is thinking nothing now other than will he be caught? Are Limb and Beel circling way out behind him, bits of rope in a lasso of enraged human hearts? Adrian partly hopes so; he likes the idea of being ambushed by his two rivals, the ensuing battle of right versus wrong, of man against man where one innocent is clubbed to death like a harp seal by two others, especially knowing it won't happen.

His watch says 3:55. Zero sign of life at the Beel house. There is the door, shut tight, the door in the doorway where Maddy was shot at and her leg mangled up. Anger doesn't

have a skin but it seems to leave an empty one behind and it's
not a smell but it travels up your nose nevertheless. At least
the blind isn't drawn and inside Adrian can see what looks
like a chair, light in colour, possibly fake leather, and plastic.
Nobody in it. The birds are everywhere, watching and diving,
even ducks, mallards aiming for Minnow Lake and Turtle
Bay, wondering, why the ice? It's May or whatever word they
use for this month, maybe an Indian word meaning ice at
the wrong time, ice that made a serious mistake.

Where the hell is Beel? Surely to God he at least has some
room in his melted, scarred heart for a beat of optimism. If
he is out with Limb and a posse, one thing they're not going
to find is Adrian's bike. He hid it right over there in a stand
of long grass and easily accessible as a getaway vehicle. You'd
need a helicopter to see it and he's hoping to God they had-
n't gone that far. They wouldn't have, would they? Maybe.
Even his old man had been unusually quiet this morning as
if perhaps he knew something Adrian didn't. His very own
old man signing himself up for a search party. Adrian could
see it. The dentist thought he needed help or therapy or possibly just reform, reform school. The reformatory. And Adrian
laughs, picturing them all, hundreds of Flax's finest closing in
on him, their shoes and boots clomping and occasionally
mushing into the semi-frozen, duck-confusing earth. Fans of
people, on the land, in boats and overhead. Mrs. Pond with
her walkie-talkie and...

But wait a minute. Wait—a—minute. The door is opening. Beel was there all along. There he is. Jesus Christ. There
he is. Adrian aims the binoculars, locating Beel's face, bringing the old guy almost too close, focusing in on a creepy
amount of detail, eyebrows, egg yolk or some kind of stain on

his shirt collar. *Strange to think Beel couldn't see him, but that was the essence of surveillance.*

Beel opens the door and stands, breathing, looking straight ahead as if he knows Adrian is there, as if Limb– from a treetop, where else–has signalled his coordinates. Then he steps forward into the driveway and walks, step, step, step– Adrian's binoculars bouncing in pursuit–to where he can see the road. *So he's hoping Loretta will show up. He hasn't called Limb. He's hoping Loretta will show up. What a sad, pathetic ass.*

God. Look at him. His face is heavy, it's a hangdog face, and not a single muscle seems to be making an effort to combat the pull of gravity. Maybe that's because gravity is a distant cousin to disappointment, although he is trying not to show it. 4:05 and Loretta is not here and he's wishing he'd called Limb. But wait, no, he has not yet given up. The brown eyes are looking this way and that, as if Loretta might pop out from behind a tree or fall from the roof. She isn't coming, you dumb bastard, Adrian wants to yell as he lowers the binoculars. She's not showing up and she never will. Can't you add two and two together? Can't you see the similarities between the phone calls and the letters? He raises the binoculars again but finds the magnification actually causes queasiness. *Enough close up. Too much close up can probably cause food poisoning or worse. And also, better to be able to see the entire picture.* What if Beel makes a run for over here? What if his paranormal sources have tipped him off? The guy could easily kill; he's a veteran after all. But he turns and goes inside like an old shadow that got lost from its person and Adrian realizes he is stuck here until dark now because Beel will undoubtedly continue to watch from a window. Who wouldn't? Maybe he even has a gun, some army relic, a machine gun or rocket launcher and the minute he sees movement, rat-a-tat-tat. Shreds of Adrian Drury like red and gristly tinsel on the trees.

He's going to have to wait for a while. The dentist will wonder where he is but so what? He's probably a group leader for the posse, a scout. Adrian lies down in some cedar and roots. He hasn't been outside like this since the day with Cheryl, the last most recent time he'd seen a face up close, Cheryl half-asleep in the shade, her worried, sad face, paranormally knowing too much about Laura Van Epp and Adrian Drury. This was the problem with binoculars and close-ups: the nearer you are to a human face, the more likely you'll see what it's thinking, hear the mini-amplitudes of the muscles in the eyes. She's not going to show up, they like to say; or, he's already gone.

He'll lie here for as long as it takes because he is in no hurry to ride home to his condor's nest of a room, overlooking the empty town. Loretta Decker on the west coast now, for good, living with some relative. J.P. Drake sitting in jail. Reg Decker selling the dealership and moving to Telluride. And Adrian Drury awaiting the next chapter of revenge or justice, Molotov cocktails through the living room window, the entire town, arm-in-arm, closing in on the Drury house like some Dr. Seuss-inspired horror movie. Or maybe nothing at all. And he crawls a bit, like a worm or a water snake or a marine-in-training and s back at his bike and nothing has happened and back up the oad allowance he goes, away from Beel's back door and to the hadow of the dance hall. Adrian hasn't been there since the rip with Anastasia and he is worried and also hopeful Cheryl ill be present like a heavy new element from the periodic table, a low-lying fog that can't be inhaled, clogs the throat, wants to speak for itself and maybe it will.

Adrian is nervous but he's stopping by the hall and there is the lake. The sun, now low in the sky, looks old and faded this evening but the light seems newer than usual. Maybe there's been a storm up there or some unusual blending of gases, different octanes. Randy Farrell would know, possibly also Rocket Lalonde. The shadows are black and stretching toward night as though they thought it was home and why did daylight come and go come and go? There are the trees and one fence post where someone, possibly Jimmy Drake Junior, has draped a dead groundhog and Adrian thinks: nothing paranormal ever happens. The most paranormal it ever gets is Randy and his arrangements and Adrian remembers the licorice pipes in his pocket and decides he might as well go to the store. Randolph could never turn down a licorice pipe and tall, weird Maddy could have the other one. One more look before he sails down the washboard hill. From here beside the dance hall, he can see most of Minnow Lake, which right there and then, melting, softening up, reminds him of a sunken heart in the landscape, reconsidering events, admitting spring might be necessary after all.